FOUR *of a* KIND

FOUR *of a* KIND

Valerie Frankel

a novel

BALLANTINE BOOKS TRADE PAPERBACKS
NEW YORK

Four of a Kind is a work of fiction. Names, characters, places, and incidents are the products of the author's imagination or are used fictitiously. Any resemblance to actual events, locales, or persons, living or dead, is entirely coincidental.

Published in the United States by Ballantine Books, an imprint of The Random House Publishing Group, a division of Random House, Inc., New York.

BALLANTINE and colophon are registered trademarks of Random House, Inc.

LIBRARY OF CONGRESS CATALOGING-IN-PUBLICATION DATA
Frankel, Valerie.
Four of a kind : a novel / Valerie Frankel.
p. cm.
ISBN 978-0-345-52540-6 (pbk.)—ISBN 978-0-345-52541-3 (eBook)
1. Female friendship--Fiction. 2. Mothers—Fiction. 3. New York (N.Y.)—Fiction. I. Title.
PS3556.R3358F68 2012
813'.54—dc23   2011039023

Printed in the United States of America

www.ballantinebooks.com

2 4 6 8 9 7 5 3 1

First Edition

Book design by Karin Batten

*Dedicated to
Dana Isaacson,
my hero*

ANTE

1

Alicia

Alicia Fandine, thirty-five, walked as quickly as her sensible pumps would carry her from the subway toward the home of Bess Steeple, a blonde of the sparkle-eyed variety, for tonight's meeting of the Diversity Committee, a group of Brownstone Institute parents (mothers) from different backgrounds who shared a common goal: to ensure their kids grew up free of religious, racial, and sexual prejudices. Like organizer Bess Steeple, Alicia was as Caucasian as glue, and as "diverse," she thought, as a potato. It was an odd invitation, although Alicia had her suspicions about why she'd been recruited.

While she knew it was ridiculous, totally unfair, Alicia had an aversion to gorgeous blondes. When introduced to one, she instinctively recoiled. Over the course of her life, Alicia had known plenty of kind, caring, yellow-haired individuals, both male and female. And yet, when she met a new one, in particular, a vibrant, winsome, outgoing type like Bess Steeple, Alicia felt a kind of xenophobia, as if blondes were alien or cyborg. Run-of-the-mill brunettes, as Alicia saw herself, were all too human.

The irony was only too tart for Alicia. She'd been asked to fight prejudice by a member of the one group she had a bias against—namely, women more attractive, wealthy, and sunny than herself. Nearly every mother at Brooklyn Height's Brownstone Institute seemed to fall into this category. Alicia made snap decisions about them. The school year was just a week old, and she'd been able to observe her peers for only the few minutes at drop-off in the morning before rushing to Manhattan to work. Her general impression of the fourth-grade moms: they gleamed. In Dansko clogs, they glided. They carried an effortless, casual contentedness in their bones. Of course, the glistening patina could be a façade. Alicia prayed nightly that some of them—two or three, *please*—felt just as overwhelmed and inadequate as she did. Otherwise, she'd never make friends. Although Alicia could strike up an easy conversation with nearly anyone who had something to complain about, she didn't see how she could possibly break the ice with women who were so perfect and pretty and happy all the freaking time.

But if making friends would help Joe, her son, Alicia would try. He was the new kid: shy, small and awkward, clinging to her side at drop-off. After she left him in the commons and spied him through the door's peephole window, her heart broke to see her nine-year-old son standing by himself while other kids laughed and played in groups around him.

Like Joe, Alicia had been shy and small for her age. As a five-foot-two adult, she still felt built to hide. Joe's social dismay brought back all of her old anguish, redoubled. She had empathetic pain for her son—thinking about his loneliness could make her gasp for breath—plus, she had her own anxiety about fitting in with the moms.

Tonight, she'd be okay, she hoped. Alicia always did better in small groups. The smaller the better. One-on-one, Alicia was capable of genuine charm. Her mantra for the evening: *Be nice.*

The air had cooled considerably. Mid-September, and it was already coat weather. Alicia pulled her brown Banana Republic suit jacket tight and walked faster, low heels clicking on the sidewalk, trouser hem shushing against her ankles. On Joralemon Street, she passed glorious Victorian townhouses, meticulously maintained. Brooklyn Heights's pre–(Civil) war architecture, clean streets, and flowerboxes were certainly a switch from the deserted hinterland of Red Hook where Alicia lived now, or the shopping mecca of the Upper West Side, her neighborhood as of two months ago. In its antiseptic perfection, Brooklyn Heights was a Disney version of "city." Like a poodle was a "dog." Technically true, but lacking in gritty verisimilitude.

Alicia reached the address on Clinton Street. First clue that Bess Steeple was queenly rich: the buzzer panel had just one button. The family occupied the entire building. Having spent much of last year poring over Brooklyn real estate, Alicia estimated that the four stories, pointed façade, painted cornice, prime-Heights, prime-block townhouse would be in the $4,000,000 range— *post*-bubble. If the inside looked as good as the outside, that number would jump. Alicia suddenly felt (even more) inadequate in her economical suit, as well as intimidated and jealous—a potent insecurity cocktail. From a protective crouch, bracing for New Blonde contact, Alicia pushed the buzzer.

Beautiful Bess appeared in the vestibule. Like a beacon, Bess's luminosity was hard to miss at drop-off. Alicia had noticed her, but the two women had never spoken. Framed by the door's beveled-glass window, the host shimmered in the chandelier light, her smile white and welcoming. Alicia smiled back, she couldn't help it. Some people had that power to put you at ease in an instant. Along with her obvious other gifts, Bess had that ability. If she was smart, too, Alicia might have to spill something.

"Hello!" sang the host, welcoming Alicia through the doors and into the foyer. "I'm so glad you could make it."

"Alicia Fandine," she said, holding out her hand, which Bess clasped in a two-fister. Her host wore jeans and a cute red silk chiffon top. She could have worn a garbage bag and looked crisp and classy.

"Joe's mom, I know," said Bess. "What a sweet boy."

Alicia mentally groped for Bess's kid's name, and came up empty. Sensing her discomfort, Bess said, "I'm sure Joe and Charlie will be great friends."

Charlie? Which one of the boys was Charlie? A slideshow of kids' faces snapped through her mind, but Alicia couldn't put names on the faces. "Charlie is a sweet kid, too," she said.

Bess laughed at that. "R-iiiight," said she. "Come on in. Everyone else is upstairs in the living room."

Alicia followed Bess through the shell-pink-painted foyer, up a carpeted stairway lined with art that looked real to Alicia's untrained eye, to the next floor, an open space of some 1,000 square feet with two period chandeliers of colored-glass globes, a detailed parquet floor, Persian rugs, modern Swedish furniture, built-in custom book-cases that housed, among other electronic doozies, a 50-inch flat screen TV. Alicia gasped when she saw the space. Couldn't help it. This was *Architectural Digest*. Alicia wondered what Bess's husband did for a living.

Two other women were seated on plush comfortable couches. An enamel pot sat over a blue flame on the coffee table in front of them, with a basket of bread chunks beside it.

"I hope you like fondue," said Bess. "I impulsively bought the set at the cookware shop around the corner. Thought I'd use it all the time. Naturally, it's been sitting in a box for six months."

"Hot cheese, yum," said Alicia. Was fondue a *diverse* food, she wondered? To the other women, she gave a self-conscious little wave and said, "Hey."

The black woman in a creamy caftan nodded curtly. The caftan might count as ethnic, although it appeared to be straight off the rack of Ann Taylor. Alicia recognized this woman from drop-off, too.

Hard not to. She was among the handful of black moms, a dahlia in the field of lilies. Alicia introduced herself and held out her hand. The woman took it firmly.

"Carla Morgan," she said. "Zeke's mom."

The fourth in the group, a skeletally thin woman with a huge head of curly red hair, in a peasant skirt and gauzy top, smiled at Alicia and said, "Robin Stern. Stephanie's mom." Alicia hadn't noticed her at drop-off. She was relieved that, of the three other women, only Bess sent off waves of pure joy. Carla and Robin seemed as confused about their presence at Bess's house as she was.

"It's funny how we introduce ourselves by our kids' names," said Alicia. "Like we don't have identities of our own."

The three women blinked at her. Clearly, they didn't think this was funny—ha-ha or weird. Alicia tried to smile (passing for friendly) and she sat down next to Robin the redhead.

Bess took a seat next to Carla, who readjusted her caftan as if she was cold in the warm room. No one spoke. Four fondue forks and four little plates neatly arranged on the table lay untouched. The pot of molten cheese bubbled away. Finally, Bess leaned forward, took a chunk of bread from the basket, impaled it on a fork, and plunged it into the pot. When she lifted the fork again, the bread had disappeared.

"Oops," she said.

The other women instinctively leaned forward and peered into the pot. "Sunk," said Alicia. Like this evening?

"The cheese is awfully thick," said skinny Robin. "Did you cut it with wine?"

"I should have used more," said Bess.

"So there's wine left over somewhere?" asked Robin.

"Oh, God. So sorry. We need drinks, of course," said Bess. "There's a bar downstairs."

"I was hoping to get a look around," said Robin, standing. "This house is incredible."

Bess asked the other two women, "Would you like a tour?"

Alicia said, "Yes, please," slurping back her anticipatory drool. In Brooklyn, real estate was porn.

Caftan Carla, who Alicia had already characterized as intense and quiet, said, "Why not?"

"Okay," said Bess, slapping her thighs and standing up. "Is the fondue experiment officially a failure?"

Carla said simply, "I ate a big dinner."

"Communal dipping?" said Alicia. "Bit of a fon-don't."

To her surprise, the women laughed. Alicia thought, *Okay, then. Sense of humor detected.*

Robin said, "Cheese isn't kind to me," and patted her iron-flat stomach. *Anorexic?* thought Alicia. *Bulimic? Lactose intolerant?*

Bess smiled good-naturedly and called out, "Kids! You're up."

On cue, three boys burst into the room from a side door at the other end of the floor. They clamored to the coffee table, grabbed the long fondue forks and fistfuls of bread chunks. Alicia recognized the smallest kid, from Joe's class. Charlie was spearing bread with demonic zeal. Bess said, "Eric, you're in charge." The oldest of her sons nodded and chewed.

"You have three boys?" asked Alicia.

"And one girl," said Bess. "Amy is my oldest. She's sixteen. Upstairs sulking in her room, which is her favorite hobby."

"Where's your husband?" asked Robin.

Bess grinned. "He's at work."

Alicia couldn't help asking, "Where's that?"

"Merrill Lynch," said Bess. " 'Lynch' being the operative word. Borden is one of the few people left in his department."

"Which is?"

"Foreign currency futures," said Bess. "But lately he's been doing a little bit of everything."

"Four kids at Brownstone," said redhead Robin, whistling low. "That's a hundred thousand dollars a year in tuition. Why didn't I pursue a career in foreign currency futures? Whatever that is."

Alicia felt a mite squirmy about Robin's overt nosiness, but Bess took it in stride. She was obviously well trained at deflecting questions about her wealth. Bess probably grew up surrounded by money, great green piles of it. That said, Bess seemed relatively normal for a loaded person, thought Alicia.

Bess took them down two flights, to the garden level. "This is my husband's lair," said Bess.

Alicia's eyes took in the sights. A glass wall in the back showed the private garden, equipped with a built-in gas grill the size of a short bus. Some trees for privacy, flowering plants showing off the last bloom of the season. Alicia had desperately wanted to find an apartment with outdoor space, but even a Juliet balcony was out of their reach. Alicia was awed by the home-theater setup and the surround built-in speakers. She counted eight.

"Here we are," said Robin, spotting the mahogany bar, fully stocked with two mirrored shelves of booze. She went behind it, and started mixing herself a cocktail. Alicia would never help herself like that in another person's home.

"I'll have the same," said Bess as she watched Robin make a vodka tonic. "And for you two?"

Caftan Carla frowned. Was she a wet blanket? A lot of black moms in Brooklyn were churchgoing teetotalers. *Please don't let her be a Bible thumper,* thought Alicia. Although that would be diverse.

"White wine, please," said Alicia.

Carla said, "Wine would be great."

"How many kids do you have, Carla?" asked Alicia.

"Two," said Carla. "Boys. You?"

"Just one," said Alicia.

Robin said, "My Stephanie is an only child, too."

"We're a boy-heavy bunch," said Bess. "Six boys and only two girls among us."

The drinks poured, the women leaned around the bar, clinked glasses, and drank.

And stared blankly at each other. And smiled awkwardly. *So much for alcohol as a social lubricant,* thought Alicia. She drank up. Perhaps things would improve by the tenth glass.

Bess said, "I really appreciate you all coming. It's a lot to jump right in and talk about committee goals and an agenda. I thought that tonight we could just get to know each other a bit."

They began talking about (what else?) their kids. How old, how much of a handful, bedtimes, soccer league, art class, snack preferences, the fourth-grade curriculum at Brownstone. Alicia's mind wandered, and fixated on the paradox. How was it that discussing the most important people in your life sounded so banal? Women could blab about their kids from sunrise to sunset without exchanging a single heartfelt emotion. Even the intimate, profound experience of giving birth was usually reduced to a funny, scary, oozy story to swap like trading cards.

At work, all day, every day, she was surrounded by men who delved no deeper than last night's Mets scores. Except for Finn Clarke, her office mate. He could make a chat about the weather seem profound. Alicia smiled to herself, flashing back to the workday, beautiful Finn standing close behind her chair, the two of them looking at the latest Paris Hilton commando paparazzi photo on her computer. "Twat is her middle name," he said, speaking softly, making Alicia's own twitch.

"What's that you were saying, Alicia?" asked Robin, "about mothers having identities apart from their kids?"

Alicia forced her mind back to the women. She'd lost the last five minutes of their conversation, so she just said, "Exactly."

Bess said, "When men meet each other, their first question is, 'What do you do for a living?' "

"As if that defines who you are," said Robin.

"Yeah," said Alicia. "So. What *do* you do for a living?"

They laughed, even Carla, who then said, "I really need to sit. I'm on my feet all day long."

Bess said, "Oh, God. Worst host ever. Table and chairs that way." The blond host pointed at the unlit part of the floor. She turned on a lamp to reveal an alcove separated from the bar/home theater area by demi-walls. In the center of the room was a round table and six chairs. The tabletop was made of green felt. The chairs were hard-backed with cushioned seats.

Robin said, "What is that?"

"It's Borden's," said Bess, flicking on a couple more lamps. "Remember how poker became huge a few years ago? Celebrity poker, the poker channel. Extreme poker tournaments. Poker cage matches. Borden decided he wanted to get into it. So he moved the pool table out and the poker table in."

"What happened to the pool table?" asked Robin. "That's my game. You can't believe how many drinks I've won over the years thanks to my killer cue."

"We moved it upstairs," said Bess. "But I don't think you want to hang out in the boys' room."

"Your house is big enough for a poker room *and* a pool room?" Alicia asked. "I feel sick."

Carla asked, "What's wrong?" Her tone was professional, concerned.

"Just intense jealousy. It'll pass," said Alicia. "Actually, it won't."

Bess invited them to sit. They each plunked their drinks into the table's built-in cup holders, and smoothed their hands across the pill-free green felt. "The pathetic thing is that Borden had maybe two poker nights with his friends," said Bess. "And that was it. I'm waiting for him to replace this with a Ping-Pong table. Or a foosball table."

"The kids must like it," said Alicia, reaching for the tray of red, white, and blue round plastic chips. She grabbed a stack and put it in front of her. "Chips? Chips are irresistible. Fun to hold. You can't *not* play with them."

Bess said, "You realize since we're sitting down, we now have to deal a hand. That's the rule. Does everyone know Texas Hold 'Em?"

"You do?" asked Alicia.

"I watched Borden play a few times," said the host. "He made me practice with him."

Carla said, "I've never played."

"I can teach you," said Bess. "It's not too tough."

Robin said, "We have to make it interesting. Dollar a hand."

Alicia cringed inwardly—and, she feared, outwardly. Losing even ten bucks tonight would mean no lunch money tomorrow. They were on that tight a budget.

Carla to the rescue. "I'm philosophically opposed to gambling."

Bess nodded. "I agree. I don't want to take your money."

Robin smiled and said, "Oh, you're assuming you're going to win?"

The host blushed prettily. "You have experience?" she asked Robin.

Robin nodded. "You have no idea."

Alicia said, "What if we play for something else?"

"Peanuts?" asked Robin.

"Secrets," said Alicia, amazed to hear herself say it. Her subconscious had spoken for her, and wisely. Trading secrets was a shortcut to friendship, wasn't it?

The three other woman stared at her, their mouths partly open. Alicia felt her gut clench. She'd said the wrong thing. "I'll reel that one back in," she said.

"Secrets?" asked Bess, intrigued.

"Secrets *are* a woman's currency," said Robin.

"I have no secrets," said Carla stridently.

Alicia watched a ripple move behind Carla's dark eyes. This woman had secrets aplenty, she thought. "Forget it," she said. "Stupid idea."

Bess said, "No, I like it. Maybe not secrets per se. But something personal about ourselves. Children are the fallback conversation. You really can hide behind your kids. Especially me. I'm the only one here who doesn't have a career. Focusing on the kids has become my default setting. If I'm not dealing with them, I'm talking about them, or listening to other women talk about theirs. And it's just more of the same. Same classes, activities, playgroup, haircuts, expressions, comments, opinions."

Robin said, "And you're looking for something different—or should I say *diverse*?"

Bess laughed. "Okay, I'll ante up. Here's a secret. I'm not all that gung-ho about scheduling a calendar of multicultural events and lectures."

Robin gasped dramatically. "You're *not*? Then I'm *out of here*."

Bess laughed. "The real reason I invited the three of you over tonight is that you're nothing like me."

"You mean a WASPy, blond, rich housewife," said Robin bluntly and, Alicia thought, rudely.

Bess took it at face value. "Frankly, yes. Most of my friendships are like talking into a mirror."

Robin said, "So you took a look around at drop-off, and handpicked a black woman, a frizzy-haired Jew, and a scholarship mom to be your new best friends?"

Carla hooted. The biggest reaction from her all night, and the first show of her smile, which completely transformed her face from serious to sweet. She had a rich, deep, baritone laugh that made the table vibrate. "Now that's calling a spade a spade. Oh, I like *you*," she said to Robin, making Alicia feel a little jealous.

Bess shrugged. "I wasn't thinking 'new best friends,' but, yes, something like that."

On principle, Alicia, the "scholarship mom," wasn't terribly offended. She'd suspected her middle-class status had been her claim to diversity. If she was selected by the establishment for that reason, it was the first time her relative poverty had opened a door. Actually, it was the second time. Their income threshold helped get Joe into Brownstone. Although he had trouble socially, Joe tested well. Astonishingly well. His test scores zoomed him to the top of Brownstone's academic scholarship list, and he'd won a full, free ride. So Joe could get a top-shelf private school education in Brooklyn. Alicia and her husband, Tim, thirty-six, had turned their lives upside down, uprooting from their Manhattan apartment of ten years. Alicia had no regrets, only insecurities about the bumpy transition to the outer borough. All of them were still getting used to the change—including Tim.

"I'm cool with it," said Alicia. "It's not like the other scholarship moms were having a party and I had to make a choice."

"If the other black moms were getting together," said Carla, obviously relieved to have the black elephant in the room acknowledged, "they didn't invite me."

"I'd be in a club of one," said Robin. "Of all the Jewish families at Brownstone—and there aren't as many as you might think—I'm the only single parent. Then again, I can—and do—party by myself and always enjoy the company."

"So, then," said Bess, her blue eyes flashing. "Shall I shuffle? How about we play it like this: We go around the table. Whoever deals the cards shares a little something about herself. After a showdown, the winner of the hand gets to ask a follow-up question."

"Showdown?" asked Carla.

"When we show our cards," said Bess.

The deck well shuffled, Bess started dealing cards. Two facedown to each player. She said, "Each player gets two cards down—the 'pocket' or 'hole' cards. Then I deal five cards faceup in the middle. The first three are called 'the flop.' The fourth is called 'the turn.' The last card is 'the river.' I didn't make up these terms. They make no sense, and aren't terribly exciting. But it is what it is."

"Seven cards total," said Alicia.

"Right," continued Bess, dealing the faceup cards to the middle. "The objective is to make the best five-card hand out of the seven cards available to you. You're supposed to bet, call, raise, or fold before 'the flop,' again before 'the turn,' again before 'the river,' and once after. I remember Borden saying something about 'burn and turn.' Not sure how that comes into it."

"Who cares?" said Robin. "We can play by our own rules."

"Brooklyn Hold 'Em," said Alicia. "I've never been to Texas anyway."

Bess said, "Not missing much."

"I'd sooner go to Damascus that Dallas," said Robin, peeking at the two cards Bess had dealt her facedown. "Remind me. What beats what?"

Bess groped around under the table for a hidden pocket, "We have a laminated card somewhere. Here. Okay, it's royal flush, straight flush, four of a kind . . ."

Carla said, "Slow down! I'm never going to remember that!"

"Meanwhile," said Alicia, "what exactly is a straight flush?"

Robin asked, "Is it anything like a mercy flush?"

"That's lovely," said Bess.

Carla said, "Okay, I know which five cards I'm using. What now?"

"I dealt, so I'll talk," said Bess. "When I'm done, we showdown."

Alicia looked at her cards. Even with Bess's explanation, it was all pretty confusing. "Can I see that?" she asked, and Bess passed her the laminated what-beats-what guide.

"My mother," said the host, "is Simone Gertrude."

"I'd heard that," said Robin, sipping her drink. "Grapevine."

"The feminist?" asked Carla, impressed. "Burned a giant pile of pantyhose on the steps of the Capitol in the seventies, right?"

Alicia said, "I thought it was a giant pile of aprons."

"She burned both," said Bess. "If she hadn't been an activist, she would've made an excellent arsonist."

"Wow," said Alicia, suddenly realizing she had a flush.

"Are you saying 'wow' about your hand, or because I have a famous mother?" asked Bess.

Alicia said, "My poker face isn't fully functional yet."

Bess said, "Ready to show?"

Her guests nodded.

Using a combination of the community cards and her "pocket cards," Carla had two pair—deuces and tens. Alicia's heart beat a little faster. So far, she was winning. Robin had three of a kind—eights. Not a threat. Alicia put down her flush: clubs. Bess whistled low, and showed her pair of deuces.

"I win!" said Alicia, an instant convert, madly in love with poker. "I beat all of you! With my winningest hand. Oh, yeah!"

Robin sipped her drink. "And you play it cool, too."

Turning to Bess, Alicia said, "Now I get to ask a question." The host nodded. "What does your feminist icon mother think of the fact that you're a housewife?"

Carla whooped. "Hey, that was my question."

Robin nodded in agreement. "Good one."

Bess pursed her lips. "Exactly what you'd assume. Simone thinks I'm a bad role model for Amy. That I'm squandering my potential. That I'm throwing my life away." Bess shared this recrimination without much emotion. Being called a waste of skin by your own mother would be devastating, she thought. Alicia's mother had been a stay-at-homer, and she expressed nothing but pride in her daughter's career in advertising, such as it was.

"I hope you told her to fuck off," said Alicia. Seeing Carla flinch at her language, she added, "Sorry. I work with a bunch of guys."

Robin asked, "What *do* you say to defend yourself?"

"Only one question per showdown," said Bess. "If you want more of the story, you'll have to beat me."

Alicia took a second (third) close look at her beautiful, rich host. One shouldn't judge a blonde by her highlights. Bess might look like a pampered conservative, but she'd been raised by a risk-loving radical.

"Gimme those cards," said Robin, gathering them up and starting to shuffle. She paused to finish her drink, check her watch (for the second time, Alicia noticed), and tip her empty glass to Bess.

The host jumped to replenish Robin's glass, and top off the rest of their drinks. A lightweight, Alicia would be hammered if she finished a second drink. The others didn't seem to feel the alcohol.

Robin started dealing. "Eleven years ago," she said as the cards landed on the felt, "I weighed three hundred and forty-two pounds."

"No," said Bess. "You're a toothpick."

"Oh, yes," said Robin. "I was enormous. I looked like the women on *The Biggest Loser,* only fatter."

Alicia calculated the timing. The fourth-graders at Brownstone were nine-going-on-ten. Robin said "eleven years ago." Was she heavy when her daughter was conceived? Alicia knew Robin was single. Scenarios sprang to mind. Turkey-baster? Chubby-chaser boyfriend? Chubby-chaser husband, who left when she dropped the weight? How had she shed over two hundred pounds?

"About fifteen questions are running through my head," said Bess, echoing Alicia's thoughts. "I'd better win this hand."

Carla twirled the ice in her glass with her finger. Her face appeared completely calm. Maybe the twirl was her "tell"—the nonverbal giveaway that betrayed her good hand. In *Casino Royale*, the villain stroked a throbbing vein on his temple. Alicia made a mental note to notice whenever Carla twirled her ice.

Alicia examined her pocket cards, and then glanced at the five communal cards faceup on the felt.

She gasped when she saw she had three queens as well as a pair of sixes. Glancing at the cheat sheet, she realized she had a full house! One of the best possible hands. She couldn't help smiling.

Robin said, "Don't look now. Poker Face over there thinks she's got another winner." Alicia grinned. Bess smiled serenely. Carla twirled her ice.

"What happens if the dealer wins?" Robin asked. "Do I ask myself a question?"

Bess said, "Hmm. You get to ask any of us a question."

Robin nodded. "Let's show."

The women lay down their hands in turn.

Bess said, "Pair of nines."

Robin said, "Pair of jacks."

Alicia beamed and turned over her queens. "Full freaking house. Yeah, bay-bay!"

Carla, her finger by now numb from ice twirling, arranging her five cards of choice in a row. She took the two sixes, and a king from the communal cards. And then turned over a pair of kings. "Higher full house," she said. "My kings beat your queens."

"Shit!" said Alicia. "Why do kings beat queens? If we're making our own rules for Brooklyn Hold 'Em, queens are hereby better than kings."

Robin said, "I'll drink to that."

Carla nodded. "Fine, but I still win this hand. So my question, Robin: How on earth did you lose that much weight?" Carla herself was a plus-sized woman, probably a size eighteen. *Fluffy*, Alicia believed, was the latest euphemism.

Robin said, "Pregnancy. My ob-gyn said if I didn't lose weight, with my blood pressure, I was at risk for preeclampsia. I could have a stroke, lose the baby. Nothing like the fear of sudden death for diet motivation. I'm the only person I know who *lost* fifty pounds while pregnant."

"Incredible," said Alicia.

"And then you just kept on dieting?" asked Carla.

Robin started to answer, but Bess stopped her. "Only one question per win," reminded the host.

"But I want the whole story," said Carla.

"This one question rule is a tease," agreed Alicia. "It's like foreplay."

"Yes, but think how delicious it'll be to get the full story after your curiosity has had a chance to build, get taut and coiled, and then—*finally*—shatter with relief and satisfaction?" asked Bess.

The four women paused for a second. Robin said, "I need a cigarette."

Carla said, "I never thought of curiosity in those terms before."

"Who deals?" asked Alicia, eager to get back to playing.

"I'll go," said Carla, sweeping up the cards with her broad hands, shuffling them expertly, making a bridge, cutting the deck with one hand. "I don't let my boys watch TV during the week, so we end up playing a lot of gin," she explained.

"That better not be your secret," said Robin.

Carla laughed, that great booming thunder. "I'm getting there," she said, starting to flick two facedown cards to each player. "Today," she said, turning over the community cards, "I saved the life of a six-year-old girl."

"I'd heard you're a pediatrician," said Robin. "Grapevine."

"At Long Island College Hospital, right?" asked Bess. "Right around the corner from here. I love living so close to a hospital. Makes me feel safe."

"I'm not answering any questions," said Carla imperiously, "until I see a winning hand."

After a hasty bit of peeking and consulting the cheat sheet (Alicia noticed Carla hadn't twirled her ice for this hand), they showed their combinations.

Robin said, "Nothing. Pair of twos."

Alicia said, "Beat that. Two pair." Aces and threes.

Bess said, "Sorry, sweetheart. Jack high flush." All diamonds.

"Shit!" said Alicia.

Carla said, "Nothing. King high card."

The host and winner of the hand turned to Carla. "I'll have to ask the obvious. What happened?"

"I run the walk-in pediatric clinic," Carla started, adjusting her caftan as she talked. "A mom brought in her daughter. Low fever, abdominal pain, and nausea. Her mama thought it was a stomach bug, and kept saying she shouldn't have bothered taking off from work to bring the girl in. I insisted on a sonogram—and my hunch was right. Her appendix was an hour from bursting. If I'd sent them home, they might not have made it back to the hospital in time."

The three women listened, awed by Carla's story. She added, "Just another day. Feels strange—good strange—to talk about it. I don't discuss work with my family. It's home policy, like no TV. My husband, Claude—he sells medical supplies—he's too tired at the end of the day to listen. The boys are too young for stories about sick kids. I'd tell them about the happy endings, like today. But that's just presenting one side. You have to talk about life *and* death. It's both, or neither."

"You can talk to us about both," said Bess, smiling generously.

Carla nodded and shrugged noncommittally. She would say no more about either tonight.

A moment of stiff silence followed, until Alicia gathered the cards, shuffled, and dealt. The woman peeked at their pocket cards. Robin sipped her drink and glanced at her watch. Bess tapped the table.

Alicia, meanwhile, mentally scrambled for something to say. She was comfortable with the other women revealing themselves, but—even though it'd been her idea—she was reluctant to open up herself. Alicia had a big bag of personal issues: She was raising a socially stunted child. Her salary would never be enough to support her family. She was pissed off at her husband's chronic unemployment and apparent lack of ambition. She was halfway in love with Finn, even though he treated her like a frat bro. She could confess her deep, bedrock belief that most people were capital-L Living—having fun, making memories, adoring and being adored—while she was merely existing. Alicia glanced up, and realized the other women were waiting for her to speak.

Robin said, "Don't think, Alicia. Just blurt. Thinking is way overrated."

Alicia nodded, opened her mouth. No words came out.

Bess said, "Just a little something. Where you grew up. Start easy."

"My husband, Tim, and I haven't had sex in two years," Alicia said, and then clasped her hand over her mouth.

"Now that's what I call a blurt!" said Robin.

A male voice drifted down the stairs, "Honey?"

"It's Borden," said Bess.

Weirdly, Alicia had the impulse to hide, like she was in high school, about to be busted for smoking pot in the basement. All the women got edgy at the sound of a man's intrusion. And what a man he turned out to be. Borden Steeple appeared on the stairs, first his shoes, long legs in creased gray trousers, then his slim-fitting suit jacket across a broad chest, the red tie. Alicia couldn't help gasping slightly when she saw his face. He was a stunner. The most handsome man Alicia'd ever seen in person. Dark eyes and thick, nearly black hair. As he walked closer to the table, she saw the crow's feet, which made his chiseled face just imperfect enough to be truly gorgeous. He gave Bess a kiss on the lips, left a hand on her shoulder, and then smiled around the table.

Borden said, "I seem to have interrupted an interesting conversation."

The three other women immediately looked to Alicia, and started laughing. Alicia must have blushed fire-engine red, because Borden said, "Are you all right? Can I get you a glass of water?"

"I'm fine," croaked Alicia.

Borden said, "How long have you been down here? It's nearly ten."

Alicia was shocked to hear it. She'd arrived around seven. Three hours had gone by? Was it possible? Bess said, "Oops. I'd better put the kids to bed."

"I'll do it," said Borden good-naturedly. "Carry on."

And then he gave the players a rear view that nearly sucked the breath from Alicia's lungs. If she got into bed with a man like that every night, she'd die of happiness. The thought alone of rubbing up against a specimen like Borden flooded Alicia's panties. How sad was her sex life, that two minutes in the presence of a sexy man sent her reeling?

Carla coughed. "Your husband, Bess. He's . . ."

"I know," said the host, nodding. "We have a severe attractiveness discrepancy. You should see the reaction when we walk into parties. People can't believe he's with me."

"That's bull," said Robin. "He's a ten, you're a nine and a half."

Alicia considered herself a six. She was a shrimp, small-breasted, light brown hair, hazel eyes, nothing special about her face except she had a cute nose. Tim, too thin, starting to lose his hair, an angular nose, but deep blue eyes that she once took long, leisurely swims in, was a seven.

Robin said, "We should call it a night."

Bess asked, "Can we do it again? And next time, we can talk committee business, too."

Robin said, "We have to meet again." Looking at Alicia, she added, "And we're picking up where we left off. I, for one, would much rather talk about Alicia's non-sex life than scheduling lectures."

Alicia grimaced, and wished she hadn't blurted the shameful truth. Why had she done it? She didn't know these women! And now they knew the one thing about her she wouldn't have told her best friend, if she had one.

"Next week? Same time?" asked Bess, all too eager to make firm plans. "Same place, or should we alternate hosting duties?"

Carla was a woman of a firm mind, and schedule. "Let's make it two weeks. At my house."

Once that was settled, the women pulled back their chairs and carried their glasses to the bar sink.

"My car is parked in the hospital lot," said Carla. "Does anyone need a ride?"

Alicia accepted, once they'd established that her apartment in Red Hook wasn't too far out of the way to Carla's house in Windsor Terrace, a Brooklyn neighborhood near Prospect Park. The idea of getting on a bus after a glass of wine made Alicia preemptively nauseated, and she didn't want to spring for a taxi. Robin lived only a couple of blocks away. Brooklyn Heights was completely safe at ten o'clock for a woman walking alone, but Robin accepted Carla and Alicia's offer to escort her to her building on Hicks Street.

Once they said their good-byes to Bess on her stoop, the three departing players headed for Robin's building.

Robin lit a cigarette, and dished, "Bess's ten percent cheerleader—which is about nine percent more than I'm usually willing to stand. But I like her."

Carla kept a tight lip. The doc was not a gossip, which Alicia liked. On the other hand, Robin's brash honesty was alluring. "I like her, too," said Alicia. "Considering her house, her money, *her husband*, I'm shocked I don't hate her."

They arrived at Robin's building quickly. "Here I am," she said.

"You live across the street from a fire station," observed Alicia.

"Yup, hot firemen 'round the clock," said Robin. "See you at drop-off."

The two remaining women walked to the hospital parking lot a few blocks away. Not much talking. The silence was a bit strained. Alicia wondered if making a personal connection with Carla was only possible when they had cards in their hands. One part of the brain distracted by the game, the conscious mind relaxed its inhibitions. No cards in hand, the restrictions were back in place. They automatically reverted to Topics A and B—kids and jobs.

Carla asked, "You haven't said what you do for work."

"I'm a copywriter at a small ad agency," said Alicia. They entered the fluorescent-lit lot.

"Anything I'd know?" asked Carla. "I don't want much TV."

Alicia *wished* her clients had TV ad money. Too embarrassed to explain that her days were mainly spent producing small-type copy for insurance company print ads, she said, "Nothing splashy. No beer ads or car commercials."

"This is me," said Carla, pushing a button on her fob, and unlocking the doors of her Ford wagon in a Physicians Only reserved spot.

Buckled up, Carla steered the car out of the lot, and drove down Hicks Street to Atlantic Avenue to make a left and head into Red Hook.

"Is that Robin?" said Carla, pointing at a figure on the street.

Alicia peered through the windshield at the slim figure of a red-headed woman, dressed in a flowing skirt, as she ducked into Chip Shop, a pub on Atlantic Avenue. Through the storefront window, Alicia thought she saw Robin greet a man at the bar before the car pulled too far away. Could Robin have pretended to go up to her apartment, and then turned around to go back out? To meet a man at ten o'clock on a school night? Was he a friend? Or (thrilling to imagine) a friend with benefits? Did single moms make booty calls? The very thought was exciting and terrifying to Alicia. So she dismissed it.

Nah, she thought. *Had to be someone else.*

2

Robin

Robin Stern, thirty-seven, twirled her dessert fork on the tablecloth. That would be all the action the fork got from her tonight. Stan, her date, had eaten only a few bites of the cheesecake he'd ordered. He'd acted suspicious when she said she didn't want any. "I thought women loved to share dessert," he said.

"I'm not like most women," Robin explained.

Stan excused himself to the bathroom and the waiter brought the bill. It sat on the table, in a leather fold, waiting to be paid . . . by whom? Would Stan spring for the first date like a gentleman, or would he expect her to split it with him like a cheap bastard?

The problem with Internet dating, thought Robin, for perhaps the thousandth time, was that you never knew what to expect. You could exchange emails with a guy for months, have a dozen phone conversations, but nothing—*nothing*—was as telling as meeting a man in person for a meal. How he treated waiters, how and what he ordered, his table manners, eye contact, use of salt, chewing with his mouth closed, ability to listen, and whether or not he disappeared into the bathroom moments before the arrival of the check. Her late-night drinks date a couple of weeks ago with that loser at Chip Shop tore it. Recession or not, unemployed or not, the guy had to pay for the first date.

Stan had passed most of Robin's tests (although he ate too slowly, which annoyed her). Since she was lukewarm on him, she'd leave the bill where it lay, untouched. If he had the balls to ask her for money, she'd excuse herself to the ladies, and sneak out of the restaurant.

"Great smile," Stan said, reclaiming his seat opposite her at the Heights Cafe, an upscale restaurant on Montague Street. "What were you thinking about just then?"

Robin shrugged. "Thanks for coming to Brooklyn."

"No problem," he said, reaching for the leather fold, opening it and examining the check before he put his card inside it. "Brooklyn is the new Manhattan. I like what I've seen of it so far."

Of course, he was looking right at Robin. He was Trying Too Hard. She wanted to like him more, to find his fifteen extra pounds, comb-over, and prison pallor attractive. Life would be so much easier if she could fall in love with one of these shlubs.

The waiter took the card and brought back the slip. Stan signed it with a flourish. "I've always wanted to see the Brooklyn Heights Promenade. Would you show me? Take an after-dinner stroll?"

Robin would rather not. It was a school night, and she was tired. If she went home now, she could get in a solid hour of HBO before she put herself to sleep. She pictured her beautiful daughter, Stephanie, nestled under her pink bedspread. The image gave Robin a visceral tug to go home.

"I've got to relieve the babysitter," said Robin.

Stan checked his watch. "It's only nine o'clock."

"I had a long day on the phones," she said.

"What was the question today?" he asked.

" 'Do you feel like our country is moving in the right direction?' " she said, pushing her chair back, letting Stan guide her by her bony elbow out of the café.

"And?" he asked. "Did they?"

"Most respondents describe the nation as 'stuck.' Not moving at all."

"Do people hang up on you a lot?"

Whenever Robin told people she was a professional pollster for Zogby, their first question was always Stan's, or, in other words, "Exactly how much rudeness do you have to swallow on a daily basis?" Next, if Stan was predictable, he'd ask, "Have you ever made a personal connection with someone you called to poll?"

Robin said, "People hang up. People tell me to fuck off. But usually, people apologize and say they don't have time, or they just answer the question. Hardly anyone ever challenges the fundamental flaw of Yes/No/Not Sure answering. How often is a feeling—and that's what I'm asking about—so cut and dry? Promenade this way," she said, surprising herself by walking in the opposite direction of her apartment. "Feelings, thoughts, and opinions—mine, anyway—are never 'yes' or 'no.' Rarely, even, are they 'not sure.' It's always more complicated than that."

If Robin asked herself, "Do you feel like your life is moving in the right direction?" what answer would she give? As goes the nation, her life wasn't moving, like wheels in muck. Had been for a while. Her stagnation began long before the recession, and she had the nagging fear it was going to continue long after the economy recovered.

"You should rephrase the question," said Stan. " 'Do you *think* our nation is moving in the right direction?' "

"Pollsters like to ask about feelings. Everyone has feelings." In this way, pollsters weren't gathering opinions per se, but were taking the emotional temperature of a population sample. Therefore, emotional detachment in a pollster was an absolute necessity. Robin was excellent at detachment. Almost born to it. She was a natural at keeping her voice monotonous, her tone vague. Otherwise, she might unduly influence a response, invalidating it.

Right now, she feared she was transmitting an attraction to Stan— by taking an after-dinner stroll and by answering his questions. He was picking up on the message, and sending his own, that he liked her and hoped she liked him. If she wanted to keep him interested, she would speak to Stan in the neutral tone she'd perfected for work. When you were a blank page, people were only too happy to write their own ideas all over you.

He said, "Maybe ten in a hundred people are informed. And only one in a hundred can intelligently process information."

"But ninety-nine in a hundred think they can." Robin had placed two hundred calls today, conducted sixty-three full interviews (forty registered Democrats, twenty-one Republicans, and two Independents), ranging in duration from three to five minutes, most of that time spent explaining who she was and what she wanted. She asked the question, and dutifully logged the responses into the Zogby database online. There were thousands of pollsters all across the country conducting the same scripted interviews. The data would be culled, tabulated, and fed to the media in time for the evening news. The poll's methodology was hardly unassailable, despite the plus and minus three percent swing. And yet the numbers would be interpreted and analyzed by experts as it they were the word of God.

Stan said, "So do you feel like this date is moving in the right direction?"

"Feel, or *think*?" Robin asked.

"I'll take your evasion as a 'not sure,' " said Stan, bemused. Why wasn't he afraid of rejection? Was he that rational? "Mind if I ask a personal question?"

Did I ever hook up with someone I called to poll? she assumed. "Go ahead."

"I noticed you barely touched your pasta, and refused to eat dessert. You are very thin. I wondered if you have an eating disorder. Or maybe I just kill your appetite."

Whoosh, that *was* personal. Robin was impressed he'd be so direct on a first date. Impressed, but offended, too. Weight and body issues were Robin's core insecurities, had been since she was put on her first diet at age eight. She could talk casually about sex and money all day long. But when the subject of weight came up, Robin was instantly on guard.

She said (neutral tone), "You killed my appetite."

Small red circles formed on Stan's cheeks. He was embarrassed. Too bad, she thought. He'd asked for it.

"Where did the Twin Towers used to be?" he next asked, gesturing toward the lower Manhattan skyline, in full view on the Promenade.

They leaned on the railing and Robin pointed to a blank black space in the sky. She'd been pushing Stephanie in her baby stroller to a pediatrician's visit soon after the planes hit the towers. The doctor gave Stephanie a cursory once-over, and then said he was closing the office and walking across the Brooklyn Bridge to see if he could help the injured. By the time Robin and Stephanie were back outside, the debris blizzard of dust, crushed mortar, and (probably) organic matter had swept across the East River. It was almost too thick to walk through. She was sure they inhaled some of it. Once home, Robin got into the tub with Stephanie. Then she put the baby down for a nap, and opened the first of several bottles of wine. She watched CNN. Although, as it turned out, Robin didn't know anyone who died that day, she felt the sadness and misery as if she'd known them all. She was alone on 9/11, alone now. Just like Ground Zero—which, after all these years remained an empty hole; talk about a shovel-ready infrastructure project—Robin hadn't started rebuilding either. She looked at Stan—a forty-five-year-old, divorced marketing exec from Murray Hill—and wanted to feel a glimmer of attraction or hope. But she felt nothing.

Stan said, "Most people take at least one solid bite when they go out to dinner."

"Are you the food police?" she asked.

"If you weren't hungry, why order anything?"

She should have split the bill. Clearly, he was put out to have paid for a bowl of pasta that she hadn't eaten. If he was going to push it, then she'd tell him the truth.

"I had gastric bypass surgery nine years ago," she said. "I can't eat more than an ounce or two at a sitting."

"Oh," he said, genuinely surprised, as most people were when they heard the news. Surprised—and disgusted. "But you're so thin. I can't believe you were ever big."

The next question was on the tip of his tongue, she knew. Wait for it . . . five, four, three, two . . .

"So how fat were you?" he asked.

That was when Robin knew she'd never see or hear from Stan again. Fat terrified men, no matter how long gone it was. The fact that Robin had once been obese would turn him off forever. Her current size was irrelevant. Robin's defenses kicked in.

"I was *so fat*," she said, "I couldn't fit in an airplane seat or a movie seat. I had to order custom-made shoes to fit around my fat feet. I had skin ulcerations, under my boobs and between my belly rolls, that never healed, no matter how much cream I put on them, not that I did such a good job of it, since I couldn't see what I was doing under all that blubber." When she finished, Robin heard her short breath, realized she must've sounded a little bit hysterical.

Stan said, "The ulcers have since healed, I assume."

"All better now," she agreed, impatient for him to leave already.

He didn't, though. Stan stared at the illuminated skyline. They were silent for a minute. Robin's impatience grew. Then Stan said, "It's kind of insulting, how you assume I'll react like an asshole. If you don't feel—*think*—things are going well between us, just say so."

Robin sighed. Why did Stan have to be the one in a hundred who could intelligently process information? "I'm sorry. I didn't mean to insult you."

"But you did intend to get rid of me."

"Okay, yes. I gave you an out," she said. The date beyond blown now, she reached into her purse for a cigarette. "I thought we might have a connection from our emails. But when we met tonight, I didn't feel it. You're a complete stranger, and I have no interest in getting to know you better. That said," she added, "if you don't mind my not giving a shit about you, we could probably have decent sex once or twice. Up to you."

"Does your daughter know you smoke?" he asked.

"That's none of your fucking business, Stan."

"Okay, then," he said, pushing away from the Promenade railing. "Think I'll pass on the sex."

At this point, Robin was ignoring him completely. Why was he still there?

He watched her smoke. Robin wanted to flick her cigarette at him. "It's too bad, is all," he said, and then *finally* took off.

Robin looked down at the East River below, and at Lower Manhattan across. Another dating disappointment. Another cringe-inducing parting. She'd hurt his feelings, and that was too bad, as he said. She'd been on scores of dates in the last five years. Although she'd slept with some of the men, she hadn't registered a ripple of attraction—emotional—for any. It hardly seemed possible to be numb for so long. Yet, every day and date, Robin's cool streak continued. She loved her daughter, of course. But loving a child, however intensely, just wasn't enough.

Tomorrow night, she was going to Windsor Terrace, to Carla Morgan's house, for a Diversity Committee meeting. Each of the other members had husbands. Alicia and Carla had office jobs. Bess was president of the school Parents Association, as well as organizer of a few different committees, and spent a few hours each day in the

PA's basement office at Brownstone. They all got out of their houses, had daily face-to-face interactions with other people. If Robin didn't have a date, weeks could go by without her having to talk to anyone for longer than three minutes, besides Stephanie, her ten-year-old daughter.

Was Robin looking forward to surrounding herself with women who had fuller lives than she did? Short answer: not sure. The whole diversity agenda seems like dewy idealism, but she'd gone along simply to do something (anything) with other adult females. Robin had enjoyed playing cards last time at Bess's house. She couldn't say she felt bonded (would she even know what that felt like?), despite their swapping stories. She wondered what those three women thought of her, if they pitied her single motherhood, or were fooled by her jovial cynicism. She'd have to pretend again, but it was just more of the same, like she did every day on the phone, in emails when trolling for dates, at school drop-off when gossiping and chatting with Brownstone parents.

Robin stepped on her cigarette butt and suddenly felt exhausted. Time to go home, treat herself to a nightcap. She noticed Alicia had been counting drinks at the last committee meeting, but Robin hadn't felt harshly judged. She'd had decades of experience being harshly judged, on sight, by just about every person she met. Being obese had honed her paranoia or perception, depending on the setting. In this neighborhood, feeling judged was a near constant. Single moms might be plentiful in Bushwick. In Brooklyn Heights? Not so much. At Brownstone, she was a rare and dangerous species. Overcompensating, she flaunted her freedom, referring obliquely to cigarettes and cocktails, her many hot dates. Robin could gauge the happiness of the other mothers' marriages by how interested they were in Robin's social life. The women who avoided her like Ebola, or cornered her in the playground to get their vicarious thrills, had problems. The moms who seemed polite but indifferent—the majority—chalked her up as (1) a freak, (2) a pity case, and (3) not a candidate for double dates.

Thus far, Robin hadn't felt reviled, pitied, or envied by Alicia, Carla, and Bess. Nor has she formed solid opinions (or taken the emotional temperature) of the other three women—yet. At this point, she was most intrigued by Carla, if for no other reason than that she was black. Robin had no black friends: not much opportunity, no gravitational pull toward any particular black woman, and the fact that her limited social energies were focused on men. Exclusively white men at that (although not necessarily Jewish). Habitually, she clicked the "Caucasian" box in her online searches to find a racially compatible potential stepfather for Stephanie. The idea of dating a black man intimidated her a little. Robin had a white girl's fear of black masculine power. She couldn't help picture a huge black penis slapping against powerful black thighs. Robin would probably meet Carla's husband tomorrow night. She'd be sure to check out his package. Bess's husband Borden's trouser basket had been a bit disappointing.

Walking the five blocks home, Robin forced her thoughts away from penises of many colors. She fluffed her hair in the breeze, hoping to get out the smoke smell. To answer Stan's question, Stephanie had no idea Robin smoked, or had nightcaps, or slept with men she barely knew and didn't care about. Of course, Robin preached to Stephanie about the dangers of cigarettes, alcohol, and casual sex. The hypocrisy of modern parenting in a nutshell.

●━━━●

"Sorry we're late," said Bess. Her teenage daughter, Amy, stood behind Bess in the hallway outside Robin's apartment.

"Welcome," said Robin, inviting them in. "Stephanie can't wait to meet you, Amy. And thanks again for pinch-sitting."

Amy nodded. Robin smiled at the sullen girl whose eyes were hidden behind a drape of dirty blond hair. Bess was, as always, preppy perfection, her shimmering yellow hair tucked behind her ears, falling silk across her shoulders. It'd be hard to have a beautiful mom, thought Robin, although this Amy had potential in the looks depart-ment. She was tall, and had decent bone structure (from what Robin could see of it), her skin was relatively clear. Most important, Amy was skinny. Skinny was the ultimate genetic prize. Everything else could be fixed with makeup and gel.

"Stephanie is straight down the hall, first door on the right," said Robin, pointing Amy down the long hallway of her two-bedroom apartment toward her daughter's room.

The teenager skulked away. Bess said, "She hates me. She has no respect for me. She told me tonight that I don't deserve to consume 'everyone else's oxygen.' "

At sixteen, Robin had said far, far worse things to her mother. "It's a stage," said Robin. "What started the fight?"

"I asked if she'd written thank you notes for her sweet-sixteen party, and she just went off on me. 'Sweet sixteen' is an oxymoron," said Bess.

When Robin had been a sour sixteen, she'd refused a party, of-fered unenthusiastically by her kiss-kiss-slap-slap mother. What kind of celebration would it have been? Robin had three friends. Her mom would have forced Robin to invite the scores of girls who hated her and wouldn't have come to her party if they'd been paid.

"Did Amy cry?" asked Robin, thinking of her own teenage sob-fests.

Bess laughed. "We both did. Can't you tell?"

Robin searched Bess's creamy skin for puffiness, blotches, or smeared mascara, and found none. "It's good to cry," said Robin. "Like eating fiber, I make a regular and concerted effort to do so."

From the other side of the apartment, Stephanie burst out of her bedroom, dragging Amy along to show off her DVD collection in the living room.

Robin leaned close to Bess and said softly, "If all goes well, we can make Amy's babysitting a regular thing."

Bess said, "Keep her off the mean streets of Brooklyn Heights?"

Robin laughed. "Couldn't hurt."

"Can I use your bathroom before we leave?" asked Bess. They were to drive in Bess's BMW to Carla's house in Windsor Terrace.

"That way," said Robin, pointing Bess toward the powder room. Then she stepped into the living room doorway. Stephanie was excitedly cataloging her DVDs for Amy, trying to impress the older girl.

Amy glanced at Robin and then quickly away. Robin moved a step closer. Again, the teenager shot her a look, cautious, a warning. "Don't get too close," said the teen's body language. Robin could practically hear the grinding ax in Amy's teenage head.

"Did we agree on a fee?" asked Robin. "How about five bucks an hour?"

Amy said, "How about ten?"

Evidence of pluck, thought Robin, liking it. "Ten bucks an hour," said Robin. "That's a lot of money."

"I'm worth it," said Amy, pushing away her hair to make direct eye contact for the first time.

"I'll bet you are," said Robin, seeing the glint of steel in Amy's brown eyes. Robin doubted that the girl would be half as brazen if her mom were in the room. Robin took advantage of Bess's absence to ask, "Big plans for the money?"

Amy blinked like a rabbit at a fox, and instantly retreated behind her veil of hair. The girl was about to lie her ass off, thought Robin.

"Just clothes," said Amy. "Shoes."

"Shoes," said Robin, checking out Amy's tattered Vans. Obviously, the girl had other plans for her income. In time-honored teenage tradition, Amy would probably spend her babysitting money on pot, beer, music, taxis, and concert tickets.

Quickly, while Bess was still out of sight and Stephanie was distracted, Robin whispered to Amy, "Okay, I'll pay you ten. But there's no drinking or smoking *anything* in my house. No boyfriends or girlfriends. If you show up stoned or drunk, I'll know in a heartbeat. And if you break anything, you buy it."

"I hear and obey," said Amy.

Bess came into the living room. Now that they'd reached an understanding, Robin and Amy were all smiles. Bess seemed puzzled by the sight of her laconic daughter and new friend grinning mechanically at her.

Bess said, "I'm double-parked out front. We should go." The women left the girls with the TV on.

●—◦

Bess had to circle only once to find a spot close to Carla's house, a real house, not a townhouse. The three-story white Victorian, if dilapidated, had blue trim, gingerbread detailing, and a scalloped, shingled roof that made Robin's heart fly. This was mansion Brooklyn, as opposed to brownstone Brooklyn, where you could imagine the expansive spread into the borough of nineteenth-century families, eight or nine kids in petticoats and short pants, running around the yard playing with hoops and sticks, a horse and carriage parked in the mud out front. Each house on the block had a lawn, and a patch of earth behind. Plenty of room, but Windsor Terrace was an hour commute to Manhattan. The classic trade-off of city living: you could have location or space, or both if you were one of the five people left in America with insane wealth, like Bess.

Robin had a decent-sized cushion. She wasn't fantastically wealthy like the Steeples, but she had, as New Yorkers understood it, "money." She'd been left a sizable inheritance by her father, who died of lung cancer when she was twelve. Her mom followed Dad ten years later, netting Robin the remainder of the Stern accumulation of jewelry, property, and investments.

Free of parental intervention and supremely well off at twenty-two, only-child Robin indulged excessively during her early orphan years. A lot of extravagant restaurant meals. Travel was a bit difficult because of her size, but she took a series of lengthy cruises. She bought jewelry, if not clothes (shopping was a depressing trial). She lavished gifts on a string of opportunistic men. And then, as quickly as it started, the wild spending stopped. Throwing money around hadn't made her happy, alas. She purchased her apartment—the Hicks Street two-bedroom where she still lived; modest, but in a luxury building in a great 'hood—and scaled back to a frugal, hermetic life. She got pregnant, and was instantly grateful for having spent only a portion of her inheritance. She'd lost a lot less than most since the market downturn, thanks to having put the bulk of her nest egg in insured, triple tax-free bonds. Their interest was enough to support her life completely and indefinitely.

Nowadays, if people wondered how Robin, a single mom with a low-salary job, could afford private school tuition, expensive clothes (even Boho chic could be pricey), they didn't ask or were satisfied by her claim to have purchased 10,000 shares of Microsoft in 1987. As for why Robin worked at all: she felt compelled to keep herself tethered to the world somehow, even if by only a thread.

Carla greeted Bess and Robin at the front door of her house. The host wore a green caftan tonight, and seemed to be a bit on edge. Her lips were tight as she waved them into the parlor level great room with a vaulted ceiling. A mahogany banister gleamed along the stairs, which the women were not invited to climb. Robin bit her lip instead of asking for a tour of the house. She got the instant impression that the committee members were going to stay on the first floor all night long.

Which was fine. Robin would happily admire the teardrop molding, the marble fireplace (filled with philodendron in pots), the wainscoting and striped wallpaper. The furniture wasn't period friendly. Not by a long shot. In the dining room, where the women were brought, a chunky thickly lacquered black table loomed, along with chairs and tie-on cushions. The walls' built-in shelving held glass and ceramic figurines, the kind of stuff one saw at a flea market or Grandma's; dusty and precious, and not Robin's taste.

Carla said, "Have a seat."

Robin and Bess sat. They heard a rattling flush, and Alicia banged out of a powder room, having to force the door open. "Sorry," Alicia said, a bit flustered.

"Don't apologize," said Carla. "The person who should apologize for not fixing the door isn't here to do it."

"Your husband is working late?" asked Bess with I-can-relate geniality.

"The one night I asked him to be here," complained Carla, and then, the moment of candor was gone. She willfully relaxed the tension in her face, said, "I have food. Be right back."

Carla's marital boil had only sent up the one bubble. But the evening was young. Alicia looked rumpled and somewhat mousy—*the same,* thought Robin. Gray suit, straight from work at, what was it, an ad agency? Carla's three guests waited at the heavy table, and awkwardly smiled at each other. Early signs of discomfort. Perhaps the fun of that night at Bess's house had been a fluke. Thus far, the women had nothing to say to each other.

Robin needed a drink. And a smoke. She assumed that was not going to happen indoors. When Carla returned with a supermarket-bought platter of Italian antipasti, Robin's banded stomach lurched at the sight of the oily, spicy, and acidic food. No way could she eat that.

"Any Chianti to wash it down?" she asked hopefully.

"I've got soft drinks," said Carla. "We don't allow drinking alcohol in the house."

Bess said, "Don't want your boys to dip into it?"

"They wouldn't dare," said Carla in a tone that almost made Robin quake. "It's family policy that the boys never see Claude and me drink. It sets a poor example."

Moment of silence from the white girls. Alicia said, "Tim and I hardly ever drink, so we don't have alcohol in the house either."

But probably not as a house rule, thought Robin.

Bess, she of the fully stocked bar in the basement, said, "I think it's an excellent policy. Good for you, Carla."

"Yes, goodie for all of us," groused Robin, pining for a glass of something. "I applaud our diverse house rules."

Carla shook her head. Robin instantly regretted complaining, and felt a pang of shame. "I would *love* a Diet Coke," she said to Carla, who went through the kitchen's swinging door to get it.

The refreshment business concluded, Bess said, "I have some input about the Diversity Committee calendar. A few Parents Association members brought up the idea of having a multicultural food festival or bake sale. We can raise funds and use the money to draw a great lecturer, or a whole panel of experts on Islam or the Middle East . . ."

Robin groaned. "Can we put the agenda on hold for one more meeting? I think I can speak for Alicia and Carla when I say that we're still in the getting-to-know-each-other stage, and not ready to start banging out ideas just yet."

Alicia nodded. "I concur. Although I really do want to work on it at some point."

Carla nodded. "Me, too." She then dropped a cellophane-wrapped deck of cards in the center of the table. "Brand new pack," she said.

Bess said, "Wait, one more thing before we start. I have presents!" She reached into her oversized leather tote and handed out small wrapped boxes to each woman. Tearing away the red wrapping paper, Robin felt excited, giddy. A present! How unexpected.

Alicia said, "A computer game?"

They all had the same gift. A small box. The cover photo: a man's hand, deftly revealing the top corner of the king of hearts and king of clubs, a pile of chips on a field of green felt. The title: *World Class Poker with T. J. Cloutier.* T.J.'s stamp-sized photo appeared on the lower right corner of the box—the poker-faced, aviator-glasses-wearing "champion" didn't look too happy about it.

Bess said, "I thought we could learn how to play Texas Hold 'Em for real. Real rules, strategy. Make it competitive."

"But I like our relaxed version," said Alicia.

"I just thought that, if we're going to do this, let's do it right," said Bess. "Learning poker as an essential skill, like playing piano or speaking a second language."

Carla said, "I don't have a lot of spare time to play games."

Robin watched Bess's face fall so low it nearly hit the floor. It was horrible to watch. Shot down again, plus a fight with her daughter tonight, too. Robin hated to see disappointment on anyone's face. She'd seen enough of it on her mother's. "At some point, we should *absolutely* learn to play the right way," Robin intoned. "And thanks ever so much, Bess, for buying the CDs." Honestly, if playing by the rules made Bess happy, Robin was fine with following suit, not to belabor the card metaphor, even in her head.

Alicia took the cards and unwrapped the cellophane. She put the jokers aside and started shuffling the stiff cards. "So we're betting with chips now?" she asked. "No more playing for dirt?"

"She can't wait to talk about her sex life," said Robin.

Alicia kept her head down, focused on shuffling. She was embarrassed, but pretended not to be. This revealed to Robin that Alicia possessed the skill of Taking It. Robin wondered where Alicia got her stiff-lip training. The hard way? Or was she born with it?

The petite brunette dealt the cards. Each woman had two facedown cards. Alicia slapped down the five communal cards.

Checking her blinds, Robin smiled to see a pair of sevens. "Start talking anytime," she said to Alicia.

"Remember how I said my husband Tim and I haven't had sex in two years?" asked Alicia. "That's not entirely true. It's been two years, one month, two weeks—"

A sound from upstairs. A curious boy, Carla's older son—Manuel, was it?—appeared at the top of the steps. Fourth-grader Zeke lurked behind his taller brother.

Manuel said, "Ma, we finished the book."

"Good," said Carla. "Take showers, and then go to bed."

It was just after eight o'clock. Bedtime was on the early side in Carla's house of rules.

Manuel said, "Because we've been quiet, as a reward, I thought we could watch a half hour of—"

"Do not say another word," said Carla, in a terminal tone. The boys ran away from the landing and disappeared into their rooms. Carla lifted her hand to look at her cards, and said, "As you were saying, Alicia?"

The sexless brunette blinked at Carla in amazement. "Can I just say that if Joe asked me to watch TV and I told him no, he'd throw a fit."

Carla wasn't in the mood for tales of inferior mothering. She waited, as they all did, for Alicia to get on with it.

"Okay, here goes," Alicia said. "It's hard to say exactly why Tim and I stopped doing it. Sex got weird when we had trouble getting pregnant with Joe. Neither one of us expected it. We were in our early twenties, always the youngest couple at the fertility doctor's office. We tried for three years. The cycles of expectation and disappointment weren't exactly sexy. I think maybe Tim started to associate sex with failure, or uselessness. When we finally got pregnant, we pretty much stopped having sex. Fear of dislodging the baby—ridiculous, I know, but you make all kinds of bargains. Any of you had infertility issues?"

None had. Alicia continued, "No sex was a bit of a relief after the mechanical sex we'd been having. I thought we'd start doing it again after Joe was born. And we did. But it was never the same."

Bess asked, "How did you meet?"

"We both worked in the marketing department at Macy's," said Alicia. "I left for an ad job. Tim stayed at Macy's. He did really well there. He went all the way up, to president of marketing. He ran a staff of twenty, made a great salary. Benefits, discounts, lunches, dinners. Those were the days, let me tell you."

"Downsized?" asked Bess.

"He was let go during the first round of layoffs two years ago."

"You mean, around the time you stopped having sex," said Robin. Alicia's eyes got wide. She put her hand to her cheek, as if in shock. "Gee, I never made that connection before," she said, dripping sarcasm.

Robin said, "I'm just saying."

"Even before that, the sex was dwindling," said Alicia. "Everything was a mood killer. We had problems adjusting to parenthood. Working full time wrung us out. Joe had his share of problems that needed a lot of time and attention. Adjustment issues at his previous schools. Sex became less and less important. And then—yes, coinciding with the layoff—we just stopped doing it. For a while, Tim used his unemployment, feeling bad for himself, as an excuse. But then he stopped making excuses, too." Alicia shrugged. "It sounds bad. But Tim and I get along great. We love each other. We're in a happy marriage except for this one thing."

"That's a pretty big thing," said Bess.

Hmmm, thought Robin. Maybe Borden had a decent cock after all. Good for Bess. Alicia's home life, meanwhile, sounded awful. A sexless partnership wasn't a marriage. It was a friendship. Eventually one of them would look for romance elsewhere.

"I'm dying to ask a question," said Bess.

Carla said, "You have to win first."

Bess said, "Oh, God. I was so engrossed in the story, I forgot we had cards."

The women examined their cards, and figured out their best combinations.

Carla said, "Nothing."

Alicia threw her cards down. "Me, too."

Bess said, "I've got two pair."

Robin smiled broadly, and showed her cards. "Three sevens. Sorry, Bess." Turning to Alicia, she asked. "Do you cheat on Tim?"

Bess said, "That was my question."

"I've sure thought about it," replied Alicia, the celibate. "There's a guy in my office. Finn. He's the star of my sexual fantasies. But he's thirty, kind of a lothario. He doesn't seem to realize I'm a woman. And I'd never pursue it anyway."

"So you jerk off a lot?" asked Robin.

Carla bristled across the table. "That's too personal," she said.

Alicia's cheeks were red as cherries. "You'll have to win another hand to get that answer."

"What's the big deal? Everyone does it," said Robin.

"Talk about winning hands," said Bess.

Carla said, "I don't."

"You should," said Robin. "And you should have a drink once in while, too. It won't kill you."

"Speaking as a health care professional?" asked Carla, her dark eyes focused on Robin, a sly smile on her lips.

She likes me, thought Robin, *especially when I bait her.* "A blind woman could see that you need to loosen up, Carla. Starting now. Tell those kids they can watch a little TV."

Carla shook her head and said, "My deal."

The other women passed their cards over to her. Carla shuffled expertly while talking. "Even though I had a bad day, I'm not going to take the easy route and turn on the TV. I'm *not* going to give in to temptation by drinking in the house. When you feel weak, you have to be extra vigilant. Otherwise, TV and alcohol become the things you rely on, instead of inner strength." Carla drew in a breath, dealt the cards quickly while talking. "I've been seeing a patient for about a month now, a one-year-old boy who kept having respiratory problems. His parents didn't want me to, but I insisted on giving him a sweat test for cystic fibrosis. It came back negative. I gave the results to the parents in my office today, assuming they'd be happy with the result. Instead, they were angry because they'd have to cover twenty percent of an expensive test. They've complained to the hospital and are refusing to pay."

Bess said, "That's unfortunate."

"You don't even know," said Carla. "The hospital keeps track of complaints and unpaid bills. I've been given a warning by the board. They already think of me as a troublemaker. Sometimes I wonder why I bother." She glanced at her hand. "I've got nothing, by the way." Carla turned over her cards, showing a deuce and a five.

The rest turned over their cards. Alicia won the hand, with two pair. To Carla, she asked, "Why are you so pissed off at your husband for working late tonight?"

Excellent question, thought Robin. She'd been itching to ask the same one. That seemed to be happening a lot. Like minds? Or were they all clueing in to the same signals, grabbing from the air the one question that begged to be asked? Carla had said, "Why bother?" about her hospital job, but was her frustration only about work or about her home life, too?

Carla sighed. "I asked Claude to be here to take Manny and Zeke out to a movie so we could have privacy. I called to remind him to come home early. He said he forgot. Couldn't make it. The boys were disappointed. I'm angry. And Claude does it all the time. He makes promises but nothing happens—like fixing the bathroom door—and then I'm a nag for complaining about it."

"Textbook passive-aggressive behavior," said Robin. "He's making you angry on purpose, Carla, so he can blame you for starting a fight. He *forgot* to be here. *Forgot* to fix the door. Maybe he's forgotten a few other things, too?"

Carla stared at Robin for a few seconds, mentally spinning through a list of other things Claude hadn't done. "You just hit the nail on the pinhead," said the host.

Bess had gathered the cards and was shuffling the deck. "Since we're on a husband theme," said the blonde, "I have a complaint about Borden."

Alicia said, "I just realized. You're Bess and Borden. And," turning toward Carla, "you're Carla and Claude."

"Cute, ain't it?" said Carla.

Turning toward Robin, Alicia said, "And you're . . ."

"Just glad to be here," said Robin, smiling.

Alicia blushed. For a second, she'd forgotten that Robin was husband-free. *Maybe that's a good thing,* thought Robin. She was usually self-conscious about being single.

Bess finished shuffling and dealt the cards. "I'm sorry if this sounds strange, considering Alicia's situation," said Bess, "but Borden wants too much sex."

Robin looked at her pocket cards. "So gorgeous Borden is wildly attracted to you after many years of marriage," she said. "I can see how hard that must be for you."

Bess said, "I think he's got a compulsion, seriously. I get sore!"

"Tragic," said Robin.

"The thing is, I think he wants another baby," said Bess. "I'm forty years old. Four kids is more than enough. I can't bear another pregnancy." She paused, looking around the table at their unsympathetic faces. "This is a real problem. We fight about it!"

Carla turned over her cards and said, "Four of a kind. I assume I win?" The others checked and nodded. Looking at Bess, she said, "By the age of forty, you must have heard of a little thing we folk in the medical profession call *birth control*?"

Robin snorted. "How about what we folk at the singles table call a *blow job*? Or a hand job? Or anal sex?"

Alicia said, *"Eww."*

"Don't knock it if you haven't tried it," said Robin.

"I have a diaphragm," countered Bess. "If I went on the pill, I'd be withholding vital information from my husband. It'd be a little lie, every day. Don't you think that's wrong?"

Crickets.

"Go on the pill until menopause, and then you're done," said Robin. "So what if it's a deception? It's your body. Pregnancy is your decision. I'm sure your feminist mom would agree."

At the mention of Bess's mother, the formidable Simone Gertrude, Bess's blue eyes got two shades darker. Robin sensed that she'd stepped on a toe; she quickly gathered up the cards, and started shuffling loudly.

"My turn to deal, and talk," Robin announced while flipping out cards to each woman. "Since we're on the husband theme tonight, and since I don't happen to have one, I'm going to tell the true story of how I got pregnant with Stephanie."

The three other women ignored their cards, and leaned forward in their chairs, their full attention on Robin, their anticipation palpable.

Robin said, "I see you've been curious."

Alicia said, "Only a lot."

"I usually tell people one of two stories," said Robin, placing five cards faceup in the middle of the table. "Story one is from an old *New York* magazine article about a single woman going into a sperm bank, the name of her doctor, the money, the hormone shots. You give people a few specific details, they'll believe a total fiction. The other story is that I went on vacation to Quebec and had a fling with a French Canadian named Jacques. I never knew his last name. I had no way of contacting him. I didn't even know I was pregnant until I'd been back in the city for two months. Again, the lie had just enough truth to be believable. I had been to Quebec, and could mention my hotel name, the park where Jacques and I met, where we had a romantic dinner. There was no Jacques. I described the concierge at the hotel, if need be."

Robin checked the women's reaction thus far. Carla seemed appalled. Alicia was expectant. Bess appeared frankly fascinated. It occurred to Robin that this wasn't really a diversity meeting. Or a card game. It was grown-up storytime. Women needed stories. More than food and sex, maybe.

"Okay," continued Robin. "The *true* story, which I haven't told anyone, except my therapist, starts on New Year's Eve, 1999. The eve of the millennium. I was single, of course. A three hundred and forty pound woman who rarely left her apartment? Who was I going to meet? I'd been making Zogby calls all day—even on New Year's Eve.

That year, the big night was on a Friday, and most people were too busy to talk. I must've placed a hundred calls, but did only a dozen interviews. The question of the day was timely. Something like, 'Do you feel you'll be better off in the New Year?' I called one number and the woman who answered the phone asked, 'Don't you have somewhere to *be*?' and then hung up on me. I stared at the dead phone in my hand in horror. I had nowhere to *be*. No one to *be* with. I said to myself, 'Screw her! I'm going out.' The only place to *be* in New York on New Year's Eve when you don't already have plans, where a fat girl would be anonymous, alone in a crowd . . ."

"You went to Times Square," said Alicia.

Robin touched the tip of her nose. "It was a mad scene, total mayhem. Half a million drunk people cordoned off into five square blocks, cops on horseback, flashing lights, bright like the middle of the day. In the mass of humanity, no one paid any attention to me except to complain if I was in the way. I was sweating like crazy, even though it was freezing. I felt claustrophobic and hassled. I regretted going uptown from the second I got there. But I was determined to stick it out until midnight. A few minutes before the ball dropped—I was counting every interminable second—a guy started talking to me. He was also alone, had come to see 'what all the fuss was about.' We made fun of the drunk idiots around us. He was nice. Sort of cute, but too earnest for my taste. I assumed he was from out of town or a geek. When the ball *finally* dropped, he kissed me. He invited me to his place in Chelsea. I went. Maybe Carla can help with the next part . . ."

"And forty weeks later, a child came into the world," said the doctor.

"During Stephanie's newborn months, I barely left the house. I was entertained by the 2000 presidential election that went on forever. Which was exactly how I felt about her infancy," said Robin. "So, showdown?"

The women remembered they had a hand, and fumbled to check their pocket cards.

Alicia said, "Three of a kind."

Bess said, "Ha! Full house."

Carla said, "Pair of fives."

Robin said, "Nothing."

"I get to ask what we're all wondering," said Bess, glancing quickly at Carla and Alicia. "Did you ever see him again? Does he know he's a father? How was the sex?"

"That's three questions," said Robin. "You only get one."

"And you will answer all of them," said Carla, in her take-no-prisoner's tone.

"Yes, ma'am," said Robin. "The sex? It was *eh*. I was always suspicious of men who were attracted to me back then, that they had a fat fetish. I didn't get that vibe from him, though. We were both alone on a big night, found each other, and tried to make the best of it. We did it in the dark. I never got a good look at his apartment, but I wasn't impressed by what I saw. After he fell asleep, I took a cab home at three in the morning. No point in exchanging numbers. Of course, I didn't know I was pregnant until weeks later. The idea of tracking him down for a 'knocked up' conversation was too hideous to consider. Can you imagine the shock, him coming home from work, tired and stressed, and then seeing a huge—and I mean *huge*—lapse in judgment waiting outside his building with baby news?"

"You chickened out," said Carla.

"Oh, big time," said Robin. "It was just easier to go my own way. I didn't need money from him or to be talked into an abortion. Keeping the baby was a selfish decision. I had nothing else in my life. No husband, no meaningful career. I had means and time, and then I had Stephanie."

Carla asked, "And which story have you told her about her father?"

That sounded a tad judge-y. Robin said, "The artificial insemination story. And it was artificial, in a way. When I look back on that night, I don't think about the guy as much as I think about that woman on the phone. The one who said, 'Don't you have somewhere to *be?*' At the time, I despised her. But now, if I could, I'd thank her."

"Oh. My. God," said Alicia, her eyes popping.

"What?" asked Robin.

"I am that woman," said Alicia. "I remember taking a call from a pollster that night and being kind of rude."

Robin's jaw unhinged. "Are you fucking serious?"

Alicia grinned and said, "Nah."

Carla burst out laughing, an explosion that shook the room. It was infectious, and suddenly all four women were howling.

Robin was still breathing heavily from the release of tension. She made eye contact with Alicia across the table, and said, "Good one, Alicia. You must kill at your ad agency."

"I wish," said the tiny brunette.

Carla, meanwhile, had walked around the table to the bookshelf built into the wall. She gently opened the glass door, moved a few of her figurines aside, and knocked gently on the wood panel behind them. A hidden door unlatched.

Bess said, "Look at that. I *love* old houses."

Carla reached into the secret compartment, and pulled out a full bottle of Jack Daniel's.

Robin shook her head. "Bloody hypocrite."

"I said I don't allow drinking *in the house*," sniffed Carla. "Alicia, grab a few Dixie cups on the kitchen sink."

The ladies retired to the front porch with Jack, taking seats on wicker chairs or on the railing. Alicia passed out the paper cups, and Carla poured a finger of the lethal liquid into each. They toasted and sipped. Robin lit a cigarette, never loving the taste so much.

Alicia said, "We are TMI-ing all over the place tonight."

"With a surprising lack of sentimentality," said Bess. To Robin, she said, "You talk about major life events as if they didn't happen to you."

Robin nodded. She knew she came off sometimes as detached.

Was that why she was so good at her job? "When I was telling the story just now," she said, "it felt like I was talking about a made-up person. I'm a character in my own life." It occurred to Robin, at that second, that for much of her existence, she'd watched herself as if through a scrim, a transparent wall of gauze, like at the ballet. She'd been a witness to her own history, keeping a few steps of emotional distance from experiences and people, including, she was ashamed to realize, her own daughter. She'd lied to Stephanie about her conception, and that was wrong. The sudden insight wet her eyes, and she noticed that her hand shook slightly as she lifted the Dixie cup to her lips.

"What made you break out the booze?" Robin asked Carla.

"I figured you needed a drink," said Carla.

"You figured right," said Robin.

"You're going to have to contact this man one of these days. You need his family health history," said Carla. "And Stephanie deserves to know the truth."

"What's his name? Do you remember?" asked Bess.

"Tim Fandine," said Robin.

Hearing her husband's name, Alicia laughed. "Funny," she said.

"It's Harvey Wilson," said Robin.

A sedan pulled up across the street. Parked. The motor and lights switched off, and a man stepped out. Robin vaguely recognized tall and broad Claude Morgan from having seen him at Brownstone. He took long, but tentative strides toward his house, surprised to see three white women drinking out of paper cups on his porch.

When he got close enough, he said, "Evening."

The women said hello.

Carla introduced him and then said, "Did you remember to pick up milk? I asked you to get some on the way home."

Claude frowned. "You did. Sorry, Carla. I completely forgot."

The four women tittered into their cups, Carla the loudest.

3

Bess

"What do we have here?" asked Borden. He stood in the master bedroom, holding the box. The kids had been put to bed hours ago.

Sitting on the edge of their king-sized bed, Bess rubbed moisturizer into her elbows and said, "I bought those today."

The pair of black high-heeled, knee-high patent leather boots had thrilled her to tears when she tried them on at Tango, a boutique on Montague Street. They were totally impractical and cost way too much. But Bess felt exhilarated by the teetering height, the close fit around her calf, the shine of the leather as she strutted around the store. She felt like Wonder Woman, formidable and bulletproof.

They would be her armor, she thought, at lunch with her mother tomorrow.

"I'd love to see how they look on," said Borden, grin widening, his penis visibly hard in his boxers. He sat next to her on the bed, and nibbled her neck, pulled the strap of her nightgown off her shoulder.

Bess groaned. Not again. "What do you eat? Dried bull testicles?" she asked.

He chuckled into her shoulder. "I'm a healthy American male. And you're my beautiful wife, and I adore you."

"As I adore you," said Bess, "But I already put out this morning."

Borden woke her at six by grinding his erection into her thigh. She'd pretended to be asleep for a few minutes, but when he started slicking her anus with lubricant (at the ready in his night table drawer), she knew she'd have to speak up, or get a predawn ass fucking. He tried that move when he dared, going for her not-favorite activity when he thought she'd be too tired to argue.

"Just a quickie," he said.

"I'm exhausted," she replied. When wasn't Bess exhausted? Four kids, only part-time babysitting/housekeeping help. Bess had to address and satisfy the daily needs and desires of five people—counting Borden, but not herself. It was a tremendous responsibility, no margin for error, that required Herculean diplomacy, strength, and organization. Bess was convinced no man could do it for a day. Bess had been doing it for years.

Borden continued to kiss her nape. "Okay, I'll leave you alone. But try on the boots anyway. Give me something to think about."

Bess agreed, and zipped on the boots. She stood up, letting her nightgown fall to the floor in a silken puddle. She was bare beneath it, naked now, except for the knee-high boots.

"You are incredible," said Borden, standing to embrace her, his hands on her upper arms, stroking her skin and bending to kiss her.

Much as Bess appreciated Borden's unrelenting attraction for her, she often wondered what was *wrong* with him. His libido was off the charts. It wasn't normal. They'd just passed their eighteenth wedding anniversary. She might be well preserved, but Bess was not the fresh-faced, perky-breasted undergrad she'd been when they met. Why wasn't Borden taking his sky-high sex drive elsewhere? Why wasn't he having an affair with some junior trader?

If he did, and she found out, Bess would have to kill him.

The problem with having too much sex: Bess never got to miss it. Sexual tension wasn't allowed to build. The lack of anticipation made it hard for Bess—who needed *some* sizzle before the steak—to appreciate Borden's stroking, despite his skill and beauty. Bess knew she was blessed that he wanted her so badly. But two times a day was simply too much of a good thing! She resented it that Alicia, Carla, and Robin laughed at her complaint, and she felt a little guilty to have made up the bit about Borden wanting to impregnate her. But beefing up her grievance hadn't won their pity. She shouldn't have said anything. Fatigue and a weary vagina hardly compared to Alicia's celibacy and Robin's loneliness. Carla hadn't talked about her sex life at all. Probably never would.

Right now, Borden's hands exploring, Bess pushed him away and said, "Give my pussy a rest!"

Borden said, "Say that again."

"Pussy."

His cock jumped, and he groaned. Honestly, men were ridiculously predictable.

After twenty years as a couple—eighteen of them married—Bess was still amazed that she felt any guilt when she rejected him sexually. Once, Bess had made the tiniest reference of that guilt during a rare confessional conversation with Mother Simone. That crumb was all Simone needed to make a meal of the sexual enslavement of housewives. No matter how vociferously Bess defended herself—she wasn't Borden's sex slave; she was his wife, she loved him, and she wanted to make him happy—Simone dug in, and insisted that Bess was in deep denial about her marriage.

Simone, meanwhile, barely knew Borden, hardly spent any time with Bess and her husband together. Bess hated it, that her mother spoke in generalities at all, and especially when Bess, her own daughter, was thrown into a heap with the rest of the unenlightened masses of brainwashed American wives.

Bess wasn't brainwashed or a sex slave or fooling herself. She was blessed by a loving, handsome husband who couldn't get enough of her. She lifted his head away to look him in the eye, and said, "I love you."

"But you're too tired?" he said, nodding, backing away.

"I'm naked except for black patent leather fuck-me boots. I'd have to be dead not to be turned on."

And that was all the encouragement he needed. Borden playfully spun her around to face the bed. He guided her upper body down, so her elbows and forearms rested on the duvet, her legs straight, ass high in the air.

"Spread your legs. A little more," he said excitedly. Her heels made her legs too long for him to reach her. When she was at the right angle, he slipped in.

Borden was nothing if not gentle, loving, and polite. Good breeding led to good breeding, Bess thought. He gripped her hips with his hands, and ground into her, deeply, all the way to the cervix. He loved that, burying himself as far inside as he could go, and then holding her there, locked against him.

Often, he'd go down on her before, in the "she comes first" gentleman's tradition. Or he'd rub her clitoris doing intercourse, which worked depending on how turned on she was. Lately, though, sleep was what Bess fantasized about.

For the first few years of their relationship, Bess wanted him as much as he wanted her. Their nights were a sweaty wrestling match into morning. Her orgasm was the focus of both of their worlds. Bess's first pregnancy (with Amy) inflamed Borden's desire. Her boobs and ass got huge, and he liked having a changed body to play with. By the ten-year anniversary, they had four kids. Exhaustion squashed Bess's desire. She came less often. Borden tried to please her, but his ministrations weren't guaranteed to get her there, as they once had. She urged him to enjoy himself, that she was satisfied enough to see him happy. Bess's body had been through the wars. Her vagina was jaded. It had seen too much. Nothing could impress it anymore.

Borden, at present, was doing his best to make something happen for her. He leaned over her back to stroke her breasts. He bit her shoulder and breathed in her ear, "I love the boots. I love you." Her attention was drawn to her lower legs. She pictured the two of them in her head, her naked body bent over, the shiny black boots gleaming as he moved against her. Bess felt a flutter of real excitement. Oh, goodie! She might come this time. Bess moaned and tilted her hips upward. The new angle must have been good for Borden. Too good. He came quickly.

"Sorry about that," he said after, both of them collapsed on the bed. He hugged her against his chest. "I felt you change inside, and it put me over the edge."

"It's okay," she said, a little disappointed.

He brushed a strand of hair off her forehead. "It's not okay," he said. "Let me take care of you." He leaned up on his elbow, easing her shoulders down on the bed, and then started kissing her belly, his head moving slowly south.

Just then, they heard a door open, and footsteps in the hallway one flight down. One of the boys, up to use the bathroom. Frozen, as if caught, they listened for the sound of the flush. Then the faucet running briefly. Footsteps back down the hallway and a door closing.

Two minutes. Enough time for Bess's spark of excitement to flicker out. She sat upright, moving Borden off her, and said, "I'm fine. I'm great, really. I'm just too tired to come."

If he was insulted, Borden hid it well. He pulled his boxers back up, and leapt into bed. Bess unzipped her boots, placed them back in the box. She crawled into bed, blind tired. But sleep didn't come, either.

◦———◦

The biannual Saturday lunch was a tradition going back years. Bess and Amy—the boys were not invited—would go to Manhattan and meet Simone at a restaurant of her choosing. Today, they were eating at Michael's in midtown off Fifth Avenue. It was the kind of place Bess considered stodgy and old-fashioned. Then again, rejecting her mom's choices was reflexive. Amy, on the other hand, was easily impressed by the snap of attentive waiters and the flutter of maître d's when Simone made an entrance. A bona fide celebrity, Simone radiated importance with each step. She flaunted her iconic status for all it was worth—in this case, a good table and sycophantically fast service.

Bess and Amy arrived by cab. They were ten minutes early. Simone was sure to be late. Punctuality wasn't a priority for her, even though she became enraged when kept waiting. Amy seemed eager to get inside the restaurant. The girl was probably freezing, thought Bess, having insisted on her uniform of skinny jeans, a tank top, and ballet flats—in October. Bess didn't understand how her daughter could stand to have her shoulders and tops of her feet exposed. Then again, lately, Bess didn't understand anything about Amy.

Watching her daughter's scrawny arm muscle flex as she opened the restaurant door, Bess suppressed a pang of anxiety. Just once, Bess would like Amy to be on her side at this lunch instead of ganging up with Simone to criticize her. Bess used to seek the approval of her mother, and now she sought the approval of her daughter. Meanwhile, neither of them seemed to care at all about Bess's opinion.

They walked in and the maître d' warmly smiled. He brought them to a table where, much to Bess's surprise, Simone was already seated. When she saw Bess and Amy coming toward her, a smile lightened Simone's leonine face. *She's laughing at me,* thought Bess. She felt instantly self-conscious in her Wonder Woman boots— although they might set off a classic Simone screed on the politics of high heels. Bess could recite it from memory. She welcomed a lecture. Amy got bored out of her mind when Simone proselytized.

Amy sat next to Simone, and gave her grandmother a juicy hug.

Jealous, Bess had to sit opposite the two of them, watching their cozy display.

"You look wonderful," said Simone to Bess, glancing quickly at Amy. "And you, lucky girl, are the image of your grandfather."

Simone's husband, Bess's dad, Fred, who Amy absolutely resembled, had been dead for twenty-five years—fluke car accident. He had no life insurance, and left the family with a mountain of debt, a twice-mortgaged house on the brink of foreclosure, and zero savings. His death, and the family's sudden impoverishment, inspired Simone to find her calling. Simone's social status suffered a cataclysmic downgrading practically overnight. Her friends dumped her. She felt taken advantage of by (all male) bankers and lawyers who descended on them to take their house. Simone had no work experience (outside the home) to fall back on. Outraged by her situation, she started small, writing op-eds for neighborhood newspapers about the stigma of single motherhood, the perils of being financially dependent on a man, the belief that all women should be self-reliant. Simone expanded these ideas into a memoir called *Hung by the Apron Strings,* which became a bestseller and second-wave feminism movement starter.

Bess and her two brothers, Fred Jr. and Simon, watched Simone turn the story of her widowed poverty and isolation into fantastic wealth and fame. Simone's career took over her life. She made herself the living embodiment of her message. When people asked Simone who was caring for her three children while she was on the road promoting her book and doing lectures, she accused them of political baiting, trying to suggest a successful woman couldn't also be a good parent. Bess believed a woman could be both. But Simone *was* a horrible mother. From the age of fifteen, Bess had to be self-sufficient. She fed herself, did her own laundry, organized her activities, kept her own hours. Her friends envied her freedom, but Bess did little with it. She would have gladly traded independence for the way things used to be. She lost both parents the day of Fred's accident, as well as the comfort and security of family life. No wonder Bess had chosen family over career for herself—the life Simone called a "death trap." Bess's choice was an affront to Simone personally and professionally. Resentment cut both women both ways.

And then there was Amy. Whose footsteps would the girl follow? The feminist or the "freeloader" (Simone's term)? Bess's hope for Amy was that her daughter would pursue her passions, whatever they might be, and find love and happiness. Kind of vague. Simone, on the other hand, had definitive plans for Amy. A job was waiting for Amy at Women's Independence Nation (WIN), Simone's influential foundation, as soon as she graduated college. Simone was eager to start grooming Amy now for her future life of activism, asking Amy to accompany her on speaking engagements and book tours. Amy always wanted to go, but Bess wouldn't allow it—there was homework to do, responsibilities at home. As Amy got older, Bess knew it'd be harder to maintain control. Especially when Simone pressed the point that Bess coddled her kids too much. Amy was starting to spout the key words "self-reliance," "independence," and "freedom," and it scared Bess. Fear made her tighten her grip on Amy. In response, Amy fought harder to break away. Bess knew exactly what was happening, but she was helpless to stop it.

The waiter came and took their orders. After he left, Simone smiled at Bess and asked, "How are the boys?"

Bess said, "They're great. Eric is in the school play. Thomas is on a traveling soccer team. Charlie was put in a special reading group at school, and he's really improved after just a couple of weeks . . ."

Simone said, "Wonderful!" thereby ending the update. Simone didn't really care about her grandsons. She had eyes only for Amy.

"Now, Amy, tell me everything," said Simone. "What's going on? How's school?"

Put on the spot, Amy said, "The semester just started. It's been, like, a month. So far, so good. I'm getting the grades."

"Wonderful," said Simone, smiling warmly at her granddaughter.

"Are you in New York for a while?" Bess asked.

"Only a few days," said Simone. "I'm going to London for a conference on women's rights in the Arab world. I'll be meeting with representatives from twenty countries. It's simply ghastly, how women are treated in the Middle East. I'll never forget my trip last year to Dubai. Those poor women—little more than walking wombs. Breaks my heart. I have to speak up for their rights. Their eyes, they haunt me, always." Simone waited for Bess to nod along with her, and then added, "It would make an old woman happy if Amy came with me to London. It's only for a long weekend. If we take the red-eye Thursday night, she'd only miss one day of school."

"Yes!" shouted Amy.

"You're not giving me much notice," said Bess.

"Come on, Mom!" pleaded Amy. "I'm dying to go to London."

Bess said, "You're supposed to babysit Stephanie Stern on Thursday night."

"Robin can find someone else," said Amy. "Please, Mom."

"You made a promise," said Bess. "What does it say about your professionalism if you cancel?"

Simone said, "I'm offering to take her to *London*. Doesn't that weigh more heavily than a babysitting job?"

"It's only so Mom can play poker with her friends, anyway," said Amy.

Bess cringed. She hadn't wanted her mother to know about the card game. "It's a Diversity Committee meeting," Bess corrected. Amy rolled her eyes as only an obnoxious sixteen-year-old could.

Simone usually discounted any of Bess's pursuits as meaningless hobbies. A card game would be ridiculed as an excuse for a bunch of hens to swap casserole recipes, brag about the kids, and gossip. For Bess, it was an opportunity to immerse herself in other women's lives. Something Simone, for all her wisdom and insight, rarely, if ever, did. Simone might speak to a crowd of thousands about the plight of millions. But how often did she sit down with three strangers—no, friends, fast friends—and reveal herself, uncheck her feelings, and allow herself to be vulnerable? When was the last time Simone expressed a weakness or doubt? The rest of the world took comfort in admitting to their insecurities, in allowing themselves a respite from maintaining a façade of strength.

And the Diversity Committee didn't swap recipes. Not yet anyway.

Simone said simply, "Cards?"

Bess said, "Along with planning our committee agenda."

"Poker?" asked Simone with a condescending lilt.

"You better believe it," said Bess with a rush of unexpected pride.

Amy said, "Mom spends hours playing Texas Hold 'Em on her laptop."

"Really? Do you and the *ladies*," said Simone, using that derisive word, "play for pennies or chocolate chips?"

If she told Simone about sharing secrets and histories, it would taint the entire experience. "We play for fun," said Bess, fearing that sounded frivolous and lame.

"My parents had a card night," said Simone. "Do you remember, Bess? Mom and Dad would set up the folding table. The Colberts from next door would come over."

Bess smiled. Yes, she remembered. When Simone left Bess at her grandparents' for overnights, she watched some marathon gin or bridge games. She was the helper, emptying ashtrays, fetching bottles of wine, replenishing the snacks. "Grandma always let Grandpa win," said Bess fondly.

"That's right," said Simone. "She let him win. If he didn't, he'd abuse her about everything, how she looked, what she said, her cooking and cleaning. Of course, that was a different time, when women had few options. Women nowadays don't have to stay in loveless marriages to abusive men who deny them the smallest victories."

Simone remembered her mother as a victim; Bess remembered her grandmother as a saint. Obviously, Simone knew her parents' marriage better than Bess did. Bess was nine when they passed away within a year of each other. How would Amy remember Bess and Borden's marriage? Would she think of Bess as a needy sponge who lived off her husband and clung selfishly to her children? Or as a confident woman who played to win?

"You know, Bess," said Simone. "You remind me a lot of my mother. Around the eyes."

"I'm so sososo sorry again about Amy," said Bess to Robin several nights later. "But this trip to London was a once-in-a-lifetime opportunity. I had to let her go."

"No big deal," said Robin. "But if you apologize again, I might start to think it is."

Bess wanted to tell her friend that it *was* a big deal—a very big deal—that Simone had snatched her daughter from her clutches, and spirited her off to a glamorous adventure in a foreign land. What did Bess have to offer Amy that could compare? Packing nutritious lunches for over a decade didn't impress a teenager like giving a keynote speech at an international conference on women's rights. Amy was at that age when changing the world seemed possible. And Bess? At forty, "the future" wasn't what it used to be.

Robin found someone else to babysit Stephanie, and hadn't seemed to care that Amy bailed, which irritated Bess. The two of them climbed out of Bess's BMW, parked at the Red Hook Fairway. Alicia's apartment was in one of the lofts above the supermarket.

Robin, whose red hair frizzled spectacularly tonight, said, "Can you imagine the mad convenience?"

Bess shrugged. Living over a supermarket would be convenient, but what about the traffic? The crowds? The vermin?

They had to walk around to the side of the building. The East River lapped at the pier not ten feet from where they stood. "River views," said Robin.

And river smells, thought Bess. What was with her attitude tonight? she thought. She hated everything.

The building door buzzed, and the women took an elevator up four floors, to Alicia, Tim, and Joe's apartment. Alicia, wearing an oversized sweatshirt that made her look like a ten-year-old, greeted them at the door and invited them in. Bess glanced around the space and tried not to judge. The large main room was an all-in-one cooking/eating/living space, and felt claustrophobic with just the four women. Carla was seated on a ratty couch. A chenille throw was draped over one arm, partially hiding a rip in the fabric. A round rag rug under the pockmarked coffee table was faded. Books and CDs were stacked precariously against the walls, begging the question, "Haven't they heard of shelving?" Crates and boxes were piled in corners. The room was what Bess thought of as cookie-cutter architecture. A large cube, smaller annexed cubes, and you've got a two-bedroom apartment. No detail, no charm, except what the resident put into it with design. Apparently, design wasn't a priority for Alicia.

The host apologized. "We're still in the process of moving in," she said, taking Bess's and Robin's jackets.

Bess said, "It's charming, Alicia. Look at the view!" The view of New Jersey from large westward windows was impressive: several bridges, the Statue of Liberty, Staten Island, the dark river at night. That was the apartment's selling point. Looking outside the space was the best thing about it.

From the rear of the apartment, happy sounds. Laughter and singing. Bess could see down the short hallway from her spot on the couch. A door opened, and the lower half of a man appeared. His head and shoulders were tucked into the room, saying a final good night to Joe, Bess assumed. When Tim's upper half appeared in the dim light of the hallway, Bess sized him up as neat and slim. In fitted trousers and a crisp blue shirt, Tim was elegant. His brown hair was cut short to obscure its thinning. He waved at the women, and then ducked into another room off the hallway. A bathroom? Their bedroom? Bess itched suddenly with discomfort. She knew way too much about this man. His flagging sex drive. His stalled professional life. The picture of a sexless slacker that Alicia had painted didn't resemble the natty man in pressed pants and a close shave.

Robin, next to her on the couch, pinched Bess's leg. When Bess turned to her, Robin mouthed, "Gay."

It would explain a lot. But Bess wasn't convinced on affect alone. Male menopause—it existed, Bess had read an article—was defined by a late 30s, early 40s man's sudden emotional confusion, depression, and plummeting sex drive. Considering his chronic unemployment, Tim had to be depressed and confused. She already knew about his flagging libido. No, Tim Fandine wasn't gay, Bess decided. He was menopausal. Borden, forty-two, had managed to avoid a midlife meltdown—so far. It might hit him later.

Carla got up to help the host in the kitchen area. She asked, "Alicia, have you ever thought your husband might be gay?"

Robin cocked an eyebrow at Bess.

Alicia said, "Of course! I'd welcome that. Then I wouldn't blame myself for his rejection. It's awful to think you've lost it, whatever *it* is, as if I ever had any of *it* to begin with, in small amounts. I swear, if a guy humped my leg on the subway, I'd be flattered."

Bess had always relied on her looks, sexual allure, whatever "it" was called. She wasn't overtly provocative, like Robin, or appealingly confident like Carla. She was soft and fair with what Borden once described as "an intoxicating air of vulnerability." The sheen of helplessness was catnip for a certain kind of man, the type who wanted to see himself as a hero (and what man didn't?). Despite what her "air" might suggest, Bess was not helpless. Vulnerable? She just wanted everyone to like her.

Carla said, "He seems gay."

"I got a hint of that, too," said Robin.

"I've given him every opportunity to explore his sexuality," said Alicia. "I once offered to have a threesome with another man. Tim was insulted. Not for suggesting I bring another man into the picture. For suggesting we bring another *person* into it. I know he's thin and well dressed. This is one sad instance of a stereotype not holding up."

On cue, the door in the hallway opened. Tim emerged and walked into the main room. He'd changed into (ironed) cargo pants and a (spotless) T-shirt. After introducing himself, he pulled a fresh deck of cards from his pocket, plopped down on the couch next to Robin, and said, "Shall I deal?"

Bess said, "Just straight into cards? Didn't we promise to talk about the committee agenda tonight first?" Since seeing her mother, Bess felt extra guilt about ignoring a larger purpose at this gathering.

Robin said, "How about we discuss diversity while we play? Like our diverse opinion of the cocktails."

"Honey," said Alicia to Tim, "the meeting is women only. No offense."

"Correct me if I'm wrong: The only way to make sure you don't talk about me is if I'm in the room," said Tim affably.

Robin said, "Not necessarily."

Alicia brought over a couple of baskets of chips. Carla helped with a pitcher of what appeared to be margaritas. Sitting on the other couch, opposite her husband, Alicia asked him, "Do you even know how to play?"

"I played in a poker game for years," he said. Seeing his wife's questioning expression, he said, "In college. Before we met."

Carla said, "So you have the advantage."

Shuffling neatly, Tim said, "Who has the advantage? You all have been playing together for a while already. I'm guessing you know a lot more about me than I know about you."

Alicia said, "Your name hasn't come up, actually, at our games."

Tim said, "Now you're insulting me."

Robin said, "I'm okay with it. Let's see how a man stands up against four ruthless women."

Ruthless? Bess had been looking forward to a peaceful evening, after the bloody battle she'd waged all week with Amy.

Tim distributed two cards to each player, and said, "No ante, I take it? So any pre-flop bets?"

"We don't bet," said Alicia. "I told you, we have our own system."

"Then it's not poker," said Tim.

"What's the flop again?" asked Carla.

"You haven't spent any quality time with T. J. Cloutier, have you?" asked Bess.

"Who?"

"The poker champ," said Bess. "From the computer game I gave you."

Robin said, "I love T.J.! I've lost about $100,000 of virtual money so far. But I'm getting better. I think."

Was it Bess's imagination, or was Robin smiling at Tim when she spoke? Bess bristled. She liked Robin, had found her funny and gutsy. But put a man in the room, and Robin lost interest in women. Even another woman's husband. Even a man of ambiguous orientation.

Alicia said, "We usually deal all five communal cards at once, and then showdown."

"What's the fun in that?" asked Tim. "The best part of the game is round after round of betting. The pressure mounts. The tension builds."

If Simone were here, she'd say how typical it was for a man to muscle his way in and then insist on getting his way.

Carla would not back down. "We don't bet."

Tim asked, "Come on. How about pennies or chocolate chips?"

An uncomfortable echo of her mother's comment at lunch, thought Bess.

Alicia tried to make light. "Honey, we *need* our pennies," she said. "How else will we get the laundry done?"

"It's just a few dollars," he said. "And we might win."

"That's not the point, *sweetheart*," said Alicia. "We have a system that we're used to. It works for us. And then you march into the room and completely take over. None of the other husbands invited themselves into the game."

"Maybe the other husbands don't *have* game," said Tim.

"Or they don't have as much to *prove*," said Alicia.

The husband and wife smiled maniacally at each other.

Robin said, "I'd say the tension and pressure is building just fine."

Carla to the rescue. "I'm philosophically opposed to gambling. If you all want to bet, I'll just finish my drink and drive home. I had an impossibly long day anyway." For emphasis, she yawned big and violent, her shoulders shaking and eyes closed tight.

Going home sounded like a decent idea to Bess. Robin was irritating her. Carla was dragging herself through this. Alicia and Tim clearly had hours of bickering to do before they went to sleep with their backs to each other and pajamas on. She felt claustrophobic in this cube with the grungy furniture, stained rug, and piles against the walls. She'd come to talk. To unload. It'd been a lousy week. She'd been aching to purge her feeling of powerlessness and inadequacy. And, truth be told, she wanted to play poker. To enjoy the simple pleasure of holding sturdy cards, the breezy zip of shuffling, and focusing on the hand she was dealt.

Apparently, none of that was going to happen. The magic of the two previous meetings was lost. Where had it gone? She wasn't even sure if she liked these women. Robin was man-crazy and crass. Alicia was defensive and neurotic. Carla seemed disinterested and condescending. What was Bess doing here in Red Hook? Why wasn't she at home, putting her sons to bed, and then putting herself to bed with Borden? He'd kiss her and hold her, make Bess feel valuable and treasured.

"I have to go," said Bess suddenly, standing up.

Alicia said, "No, Bess, stay. I'll lock Tim in the bathroom with an iPod and a six-pack. He won't bother us again. We'll play our game. Plus," she turned to her chagrined husband, "we can feel free to talk about Tim all we want." That made Robin and Carla—even Tim—laugh.

Tim said, "Message received." He stood. "I just remembered there's an episode of *Law and Order* on TNT I haven't seen four times yet. You'll have to excuse me."

He walked purposefully out of the main area, disappearing again into the bedroom cube. Bess stood awkwardly by the couch, the eyes of the other three women on her. Bess felt woozy suddenly, self-conscious and embarrassingly impulsive. "I'm sorry, Alicia," she said, putting her hand on her forehead.

"Are you sick?" asked Carla, revitalized by a mission. "Let me see." The pediatrician beckoned Bess over to her. Carla put her cool, large palm against Bess's forehead. The contact was instantly soothing.

"No fever," said Carla, her cool fingers now taking Bess's pulse. "But your heart is beating too fast."

Robin said to Carla, "She's upset." To Bess: "I know what this is about. I used to need a week to recover from dinner with my mom."

Alicia asked Bess, "You had dinner with your mother?"

"Brunch," said Bess. "Last Saturday. Five days ago."

"Two more days before you feel normal," said Robin.

Carla said, "You'll live. You probably had a mini pre-panic attack."

Bess leaned back on the couch. "Amy's in London, an ocean away. I can't stop thinking about subway bombings."

"She's with your mother, though," said Robin. "Nothing but taxis and limos."

"Which bugs me, too." Bess said, "I wish there was a way to un-push all my buttons."

"In my biz, we talk about the 'takeaway' of an ad," said Alicia. "The one piece of information that's supposed to stay with you. Like in a Mercedes ad, the takeaway is superior engineering," said Alicia. "So what was the takeaway at your brunch?"

Bess said, "Basically, that I'm a worthless, sorry, sad excuse for a woman."

"Wait a minute," said Robin. "Did you have brunch with *my* mother? Has she come back from the dead? Please say no."

Carla said, "I'm surprised you let her get to you. You seem strong."

"I am strong. Just not with her," said Bess, feeling better by the second.

"Talking about mothers is giving *me* a mini pre-panic attack," said Robin. "Is there anywhere I can smoke?"

"Those open," said Alicia, pointing her toward the large windows.

Watching Robin fish a pack of cigarettes out of her purse, Bess said, "I'll have one of those."

"You will *not*," said Carla. "If there's one sure way to destroy your health, it's smoking." To Robin, Carla added, "If you quit, you'd add ten years to your life."

"But will they be *fun* years? Or would I spend them miserably craving a cigarette?" asked Robin. "And, for your information, *Doctor*, I smoke American Spirit Organics. No pesticides or additives. These are healthy cigarettes. They're *good* for you."

Alicia said, "If it's going to be smoking night . . ."

"You all disgust me," said Carla.

The three white women huddled by the open window and lit up, blowing smoke into the evening air. It was Bess's first cigarette since high school. She inhaled like she remembered. The smoke tasted harsh and foul, yet strangely satisfying.

"Prepare yourselves for an amazing fact," said Bess, a memory rising like smoke. "I was once a checkout girl at the Rye Brook Stop and Shop."

"I thought I recognized you," said Alicia.

"It was before my mom got rich and famous, during our year of abject poverty. I was sixteen—Amy's age now. The store manager, a married, heavyset, bald man, pulled me aside one night during my break and told me about the attrition estimate, the amount they expected to lose to shoplifters each month. He said they always beat the estimate, so he would look the other way, let me steal whatever I wanted, shampoo, toothpaste, if I let him jerk off on my boobs."

"That's disgusting," said Robin.

"I told my mom what happened and Simone went crazy. She stormed the corporate offices, wrote letters to newspapers, called the manager's wife. Basically destroyed the guy."

"Good," said Alicia.

"He had it coming," agreed Bess. "But it was the way Simone went after him. It was systematic annihilation—absolutely terrifying to watch. By the end, I felt sorry for him."

Robin finished her butt and squashed it out on the windowsill. "Sounds like Simone had an ax to grind, and she sharpened the blade on your back."

Alicia said, "I believe the word is 'cut*throat*.' If your mom hadn't become an author, she would have gone far in advertising."

Fanning away invisible cigarette smoke, coughing and wheezing, Carla said, "Don't expect me to kiss any of you."

Robin collected the three butts, doused them with water in the kitchen sink, and put them in Alicia's trash. They reclaimed their spots on the couches. Robin was the last to sit. "Okay, my worst mom moment?" she said.

Alicia said, "Are you doing worst mom moments?"

"Preferable to diversity planning?" asked Robin, collecting nods from the others. "All right, then. We go back in time, to the mideighties, the Bloomingdale's juniors' department communal dressing room. The year of the side pony, parachute pants, suspenders, and off-the-shoulder tops. I despise cropped tops, especially sweaters. A sweater shouldn't reveal a belly button. It's just stupid. Makes me hate all sweaters.

"So there we are, Mom and me and about ten other people in the dressing room," continued Robin. "All the other girls were scrawny pencils with no boobs. I was a butterball turkey in a training bra. At ten. I hated undressing in public. Humiliating. Mom had a huge pile of clothes for me to try on. Zipper pants, asymmetrical tops, spandex leggings, worst fashion ever, the entire year of 1983 should be erased from the collective memory. Nothing fit. Nothing came close to fitting, and it was all the largest juniors' size. Mom was determined to make something fit. I guess she couldn't stand the idea of her kid outgrowing juniors at the age of ten. She tugged and yanked, worked up a real sweat trying to force me into too-small stuff. All the other shoppers watching. The pity, the disgust, can you feel it? When Mom left in search of more clothes for me to try on, she insisted I wait right there. She left me undressed and alone in the dressing room for twenty minutes. Dozens of people came and went. Some acknowledged me, but none asked, 'Where's your mother?' or 'Are you lost?' or even, 'Are you *cold*?' No one cared about the fat kid in the corner in her training bra and stretched-out panties. Here's my kicker: We didn't buy a single thing that day. And now," said Robin. "I need another cigarette."

Alicia said, "I hate to buck the trend, but I love my mom. My dad died of cancer when I was five, so it was just the two of us against the world, and she was, still is, my biggest fan. She never made me feel guilt or shame. A bit smothered maybe, but I needed the extra protection. I was paralytically shy."

"Sounds like a lovely relationship," said Carla. To Bess and Robin, she said, "It's disrespectful to talk about your mothers with contempt. How would you like it if your daughters, twenty years from now, swapped 'worst mom moments' about you?"

Robin said, "I'm sure Stephanie will. I hope she does! It's healthy to air out your grievances." To Alicia, she added, "Instead of pretending they don't exist." To Carla, "Or emotionally stifling yourself with an overblown sense of loyalty, duty, or privacy."

Bess said, "I'm sure Amy is trashing me *right now*. And Simone is egging her on." She started to feel upset all over again.

"I just realized. Are we all fatherless?" asked Robin. "Carla?"

Slowly, Carla nodded. "Might as well be."

"Care to elaborate?" asked Robin.

"Nope," replied Carla.

Alicia asked, "What do you think that means?"

Bess said, "That I, as Diversity Committee organizer, somehow recognized a similar emptiness in our souls when I called us together?"

Robin said, "Yeah, something like that. You recognized it, understood it. You thought you were attracted to what makes us different, but actually, you zeroed in on what makes us the same."

Carla said, "I'm not buying it."

"I'm totally right," insisted Robin.

Bess thought about it, grappled with the idea. "I don't think I operate on that level," she said.

"You don't have to *think* you do," said Robin. "Everyone does, whether they realize it or not."

Alicia agreed. "I can see it. A subliminal attraction."

"If it is true, what does it mean?" asked Carla. "Besides that we have something in common?"

Robin said, "*Something?* We're not talking about a favorite ice-cream flavor here."

The creak of a door down the hallway. Tim tiptoed out of his bedroom, and said, "Off to the general's room." *They don't have a private bath in their bedroom?* thought Bess. Now, *that* was sad.

To Alicia, Bess said, "Ask Tim to come play poker with us."

"You practically ran out when he wanted to play before."

"I was . . . I don't know why I did that. I take it back." Bess couldn't control what happened in this room, or in London. She couldn't steer her relationship with Amy in the right direction. But she had found solace and comfort in Robin's idea that she had an intuitive sense of people, subconscious antennae that pointed her toward these women, as well as the motivation to create a circle of understanding and support. And why shouldn't that include whoever wanted to be part of it?

Alicia said, "If you're sure." When Tim came out of the bathroom, his wife called out to him. "Honey, change of heart. If you want to join us . . ."

In a flash, Tim was back on the couch, the deck of cards in his hands, grinning, shuffling. "Ladies," he said, his gray eyes shining, "Poker, like life itself . . ."

Groans from the women.

". . . is a game of luck and skill, flying blind, flips, flops, unexpected twists and turns. Put on your poker faces. Here we go."

4

Carla

The table was full. Seven players, including some nasty-looking gangsters and scary tattooed hags. A regal woman in a purple silk blouse, tight black jeans, and stiletto pumps settled into her chair, stacking $4,000 in chips on the green felt. She'd come to play, and to win. The other players sensed her gravity, her confidence.

A young Asian man dealt the pocket cards. An old woman to her right in pink sunglasses and a green visor asked, "Got a name?"

She peeked at her two facedown cards. Pair of aces. Her heart started pounding. Trying to keep her expression neutral she said, "Call me the Black Queen."

Players all around the table folded, except the Asian dealer, a young guy with a frozen stare, and an older white man, baseball cap pulled low over his eyes. The call was $200. The Black Queen was in.

The flop cards made her pulse beat faster: another ace, three of hearts, four of spades. Junk cards, rags, except that ace. Baseball Cap bet $500.

Maybe he had the fourth ace in the pocket? The Black Queen wanted to draw them in, lull them into her trap, so she called the $500. No raise. Not yet. She wanted to bide her time. Get as much of their money as she could. The Asian dude called, too.

The turn: three of diamonds. The Black Queen had a full house. Aces over threes. She couldn't lose, unless . . . stealing a glance at the other players, she tried to guess. Were either of them holding a pair of threes in the pocket? That was the only way they could beat her.

The Black Queen was willing to pay to find out. She called Asian's $1,000 bet. Baseball Cap folded. Asian dealt the river card, a three of clubs.

Damn, she thought. Triple on board. A measly pocket three could beat her now, and from the look on Asian's face, he might have it. Might. If he did, he'd bet big, and then she'd know. But the bet was to her. She could check, and see if he put money on the table. Or she could bet big, scare him into folding. The pot was a few thousand already.

"Five hundred," she said lazily, casually.

Asian said, "Reraise, all in."

The Black Queen called. She went in all the way, her whole $4,000. Win or lose. Put up or go home.

Time for the showdown. She went first, revealing her full house, aces and threes. Asian turned over his blinds.

No three, no three, whispered the Black Queen.

Five of hearts. And four of spades. Full house, threes and fours.

"Yes!" she couldn't help shouting. "Come to Mama!" The pile of chips clicked and tumbled as she gathered her winnings. The victory hoot might've been a little too loud.

The hag to her right said, "Take it easy."

"You take it easy," she said. "I'll just take it."

●━━●

KNOCK.

The intent rapping on Carla's office door broke the spell. She closed her laptop, regretfully leaving her winnings in cyberspace.

"Yes?" she asked.

Her R.N., a twenty-five-year-old woman named Tina Sanchez, opened the door and said, "What are you doing in here? I heard you shouting."

Oh, no, thought Carla. The Black Queen had better learn to control her mouth. "Nothing. Just reading the *Times* online."

Tina squinted at her. "Must be a fascinating article. Three exam rooms are full," she said, not buying Carla's story.

"I still have another five minutes," said Carla, who would not be rushed through her one and only break of the day, forty-five minutes for lunch.

Tina clicked her tongue, and said, "Check your watch, Mommy. You're ten minutes late."

Ten minutes late? That would destroy her schedule. She had patients scheduled from now until six o'clock tonight at fifteen-minute intervals, and there were *always* walk-ins.

Carla said, "Okay, I'm coming." Tina stood with her arms folded, not leaving until Carla made a move. Why a five-foot-tall, hundred-pound twenty-five-year-old intimated large-and-in-charge Carla was beyond her comprehension. Maybe it was the way Tina called her "Mommy," constantly reminding her of her responsibilities. Then again, Tina called all women "Mommy," and all men "Poppy."

Carla would not get the ten seconds of privacy she needed to quit and hide her World Class Poker CD, the disc that had become her second husband and new best friend in the last couple of weeks. From the first game—which she'd started playing reluctantly, only because she promised Bess she would at least try it—Carla was hooked. The money wasn't real. The other players weren't real, just impressive 3-D animations. If she won a big hand, netting thousands from an opponent, Carla felt sweet and visceral victory, not the guilty conscience of taking an actual person's rent money. The game was pretend, and yet the thrill of winning was real.

At forty-two, Carla learned something new about herself: She liked to win. She *loved* to win.

The game was her secret. How could she explain to Claude or Tina the excitement of being a calculating, ballsy, ruthless mercenary? She was the Black Queen, a tower of confidence who made other players quake in her presence. In real life, she was an overworked, unappreciated mother and wife.

Change your name, change your personality. At age twenty-six, when she became *Dr.* Carla Smith, a new seriousness came with the suffix. When she'd become Dr. Carla *Morgan,* a wife, she transformed again, halving herself to be one with her husband. Then came Manuel and Ezekiel (aka Manny and Zeke), and Carla became Mommy, a champion worrier and humorless taskmaster. The Black Queen, the name she gave her cyberself, was young(er), wise, tough, smart, selfish, and greedy. She didn't care about hanging arm fat, dire financial straits, raising boys in a complicated world, a Mexican stand-off marriage, three patients in exam rooms, a tongue-clicking R.N. The Black Queen was Carla's best—and worst—self.

Taking the charts from Tina, Carla exited her office, careful to close the door firmly behind her. Her pediatric clinic was located on the ground floor of Long Island College Hospital on Atlantic Avenue, serving the medical needs of downtown Brooklyn for half a century. Many of the clinic's patients were uninsured, coming in for health crises only. It pained Carla that her walk-in patients were nearly always black and Latino from neighborhoods that were miles and light-years away from the hospital's Brooklyn Heights location.

In exam room one, Carla smiled as she entered. A little boy was in a striped shirt of faded colors, filthy sneakers with new white laces. He smiled back. He sat on the examining room table, legs dangling. His mother, in the room's one chair, wore work clothes, a poly-blend cobalt skirt suit. She'd had to leave work early to be here today, probably exasperated for the disruption. Tina followed her into the room and closed the door.

"Hello, Jamal. How are you feeling today?" Carla asked, while skimming his chart. Six years old. Average height, weight. Sketchy medical history. Fewer than annual checkups, immunization schedule incomplete.

"Itchy," he said, scratching his head.

The mother said, "I've been washing his hair with dandruff shampoo."

Tina clicked her tongue. "Did you examine his scalp, Mommy?"

"Yes, I did," said the woman, sounding offended to be asked.

Carla put on some gloves and tried to appear calm. Despite years of experience dealing with blood, plasma, excrement, vomit, boils, broken bones, open wounds, she was still grossed out by lice.

Carla said, "Why don't I have a look?" She parted the boy's hair. In less than five seconds, Carla counted a dozen little buggers, and a thriving crop of shiny, teardrop shaped eggs. It was Times Square in there. No wonder the kid was itchy. Carla parted another section. Along with mobs of lice, she found infected scratch divots. The boy had been clawing at himself. *For how long?* she wondered.

Meanwhile, the mother warily watched Carla. In equal parts, the look said, "Please let him be okay," "Don't blame me," and "How much is this going to cost?" Carla stepped away, removed her gloves and put them in the medical waste can. If the mother thought she was saving herself time by postponing the doctor's appointment, she was in for a shock when she found out what was in store for her now: washing all the bedding in hot water; vacuuming all the carpets, upholstery, and furniture twice; putting all stuffed animals and pillows in garbage bags for two weeks washing all of Jamal's clothing, coats, hats, backpacks; replacing all brushes; to say nothing of the hours she'd have to spend picking through his hair with a fine-toothed steel lice comb.

"At the start of the school year, we see a lot of lice. You should report his condition to his teachers so his classmates can be checked," said Carla. "We have a fact sheet with instructions."

"Okay," said the mother, impatient or . . . what? Resentful. Blaming the messenger.

"The eggs or nits are tough to get rid of. But if you don't, he'll suffer a reinfestation. Also, Jamal's scalp is infected from scratching and he'll need a prescription antibiotic."

"How much is that?" asked the woman.

Carla said, "That depends on your plan." Judging the look on the woman's face, she didn't have health insurance. In New York, lower-income families qualified for the affordable state plan called Child Health Plus. The paperwork was a bit challenging. A lot of overworked parents didn't have the time or wherewithal to sort through it.

Carla said to the mother, "I should take a look at your scalp, too."

"Me? I'm fine."

The woman had an elaborate woven hairdo that would have to be unraveled. It probably costs quite a bit at the beauty shop. More than the antibiotics her son needed.

"The exam shouldn't take more than a minute," said Carla, giving it another try.

"I said I'm fine."

Carla sighed, and made eye contact with Tina. She had her witness that Ms.—she checked Jamal's chart—Ms. Williams refused an examination. But it wasn't enough anymore. She'd have to get it in writing, or Ms. Williams could make a load of trouble later on if she accused Carla of negligence.

"I'm going to have to ask you to sign a piece of paper that states you refused to be examined, all right?"

Ms. Williams rolled her eyes and said, "I'm not signing anything."

Carla, way behind schedule, was not going to argue. "Tina, please give Ms. Williams the fact sheet and instructions. You'll notice that we recommend buying a fine, steel lice comb. The best one is from Germany and costs sixty dollars. It's expensive, but it really works."

"I'll get the lice shampoo for ten bucks at the drug store."

"That won't kill the nits."

"I'll take my chances."

"You'll be right back here in two weeks."

Ms. Williams groaned and asked, "What do you suggest that won't cost me hundreds of dollars?"

Steady, thought Carla. *She doesn't really resent me,* she reminded herself. *It's a tough situation. Empathy. Show empathy.* Carla said, "I know you must feel put out and upset. Getting rid of lice is a job and a half. I'm sorry to have to be the bearer of bad news."

"Yeah," said Ms. Williams, scooting Jamal off the exam table. "Let's get out of here."

"Good luck," said Carla, quickly writing a prescription for antibiotics and forcing it on Ms. Williams before she exited the room. Taking a few deep breaths, Carla tried to find equilibrium, a calm center, the flatland of professional distance. Carla had to get there. And stay there. She had to be perfect, above reproach. Or she'd be hearing from the hospital administrators again.

At the hallway sink between exam rooms, Carla washed her hands several times, and slathered them with antibiotic gel. She pulled the chart off the door of exam room two, and entered.

Another black mother and child. She could count on one hand how many times she'd seen a black walk-in patient with her father. She saw a fair number of white and Hispanic dads. Where were the black fathers?

Her own father, Luther Smith, left when she was three. He was gone, out the door, but just around the corner, in the apartment of another woman whom he quickly impregnated and then abandoned, a cycle he repeated three more times before fleeing Brooklyn for Florida, where he lived now with yet another family. Carla's mother, Gloria, replaced Luther with Jesus Christ.

The upside: Carla was an only child, which was rare in her neighborhood. Gloria divided her time and energy between church and Carla, sheltering her daughter, setting high standards for her academic success.

The downside: Carla was chronically lonely. She was at the top of her class, but she hadn't had a boyfriend until college. Despite spending Sundays in church, Carla never found spiritual comfort there. Carla believed in God and aspired to live by his laws, but she didn't believe he bothered himself with the desires of individual people, or the entire human race. We are ants on a hill, she often thought. God had the universe to worry about.

During med school, Carla was taught day after day about the frailty of the human body, and the tissue-thin protection we had against disease. Doctors repeatedly warned, "The more we know, the less we know we can do." For all the advances of science, healers were still in the Stone Age. To cure cancer, you had to cut out the tumor. To cure a lice infestation, you had to pick nits, one by one.

The girl in exam room two sat on the table. She looked about sixteen, but a glance at her chart put her age at thirteen. The girl looked terrified. Carla assumed the problem was gynecological.

"What can I help you with today"—she glanced at the chart—"Selina?"

The mother said, "Show her."

Reluctantly, Selina removed her shirt. On her shoulders and chest, the girl was covered with fleshy lumps, wartlike, several dozen of them of various sizes, the larger ones like pencil erasers.

The mother asked, "Is it cancer?"

"When did you notice the bumps?" asked Carla, taking a closer look.

"A few months ago," the girl whispered. "Can I put my shirt back on?"

The mother added, "I didn't know anything about them until last night."

Okay, Mom, thought Carla. *No one's accusing you.* "Do they itch?" asked Carla.

"A little," admitted the girl.

Carla gave the girl a brief exam, confirming her immediate diagnosis. "You can put your shirt on." To the mother, she said, "Selina has *molescum contagiosum.* Wartlike legions caused by a virus. She might've caught it anywhere, at school, from a friend who had no obvious symptoms. It's common and *not* life-threatening. There's no way she could have prevented it."

"Why are there so many?" asked the mother.

Carla nodded, good question. "Selina spread the bumps across her chest and shoulders by scratching them, and then touching an un-infected spot." To the girl, she asked gently, "Do you have the lesions anywhere else?"

The horrified look said it all. The girl probably had lesions on her thighs and vulva.

The mother asked, "Is it curable?"

Carla pursed her lips. None of the treatment options were pleas-ant. Surgical removal, or chemically burning off the lesions. And even if every lesion were removed, more would crop up.

"It's not systemic," Carla answered, "so pills or any drug you swallow won't help. You could either wait for the virus to run its course, after which the lesions will fall off on their own."

"How long will that take?"

"Two years," said Carla. "Otherwise, I'm sorry to say that the lesions have to be removed individually."

"Will it hurt?" asked Selina, her eyes big with the beginning of panic.

Why hadn't the girl told her mother about the lesions sooner? No, thought Carla, *don't blame her, she's obviously ashamed and afraid. You can't fix the patient, only treat the disease.* "You'll get topical numbing cream, or a little shot in each lesion before the dermatologist removes them," said Carla.

"The dermatologist? Can't you do it?" asked the mother, eager to get the problem taken care of right here, right now.

It would take at least an hour to excise the scores of lesions, be-sides which, it was hospital policy for the pediatric clinic doc to refer patients to specialists. Carla might take a risk and scrape off a few le-sions, but Selina had too many to count. "I'm so sorry, I can't do that for you," she said. "You want a dermatologist, anyway. Dr. Fein has much more experience with this and he'll do a better job than I could."

"So we have to see another doctor?" asked the mom.

Carla understood her frustration, but she could do nothing to help. This was how the system worked. Tina entered the exam room, giving Carla the "hurry up" look.

"Tina, would you please call Dr. Fein for Selina and her mom and help them get an appointment today?"

Still upset, the mother said, "I can't wait for an hour at another doctor's office *today*. Sometime next week maybe."

Empathy, Carla thought. "I know your time is valuable, and I'm sorry to have kept you waiting."

The woman muttered, "A lot of good that does me."

To Selina, Carla said, "You'll be okay. Don't worry." The girl tried to smile, but she was on the verge of tears. Carla would have loved to give her a reassuring hug, but that was way against hospital policy. No touching for any reason other than the medical exam.

Back at the hallway sink again, Carla again scrubbed her hands. So far, her patients this afternoon were presenting with topical issues. But even surface problems could be painful and upsetting. Carla thought there was a metaphor for life in there somewhere, but she didn't have time to contemplate it.

Her cell phone vibrated in the pocket of her white coat. She checked the caller ID.

"Hey," she said to her husband.

"Glad I caught you," said Claude. "I'm on the Turnpike."

"How'd the meeting go?" she asked. He'd been in Livingston, New Jersey, attempting to sell medical supplies to the buyers at St. Barnabas Hospital.

"Not great," he said dismissively. *Doesn't want to talk about it,* thought Carla. Lately, Claude didn't want to talk about his work—or the boys, or her work. He was having a dry spell, and was frustrated to the point of remoteness. It didn't matter that, due to cutbacks, the entire industry was under water. Claude held himself to a higher standard. If he didn't make a sale, he got mad at himself, and that translated into sulkiness at home. He'd slump on the couch, and leave the cleaning, cooking, and shopping to Carla.

"You there?" asked Claude.

"I'm here," she said. *Still here,* she thought.

He said, "The traffic is murder, and I have to stop at the office to unload supplies."

"You were supposed to pick up the kids after school," she said, looking at her watch. She'd have to run over to Brownstone and bring the boys back here to do their homework in her office. She'd lose half an hour. Her schedule was a train wreck.

"Not going to make it," he said.

"It's my card night," she reminded him. "Will you be home by sevenish to babysit the boys?" Babysit his own sons.

"Card game? Not again," he said. "How much longer are you going to waste time with those women?"

Those *white* women, he meant. Carla asked, "Will you be home or not?"

"I don't get why you're doing this," he said, avoiding the question.

"I'll take the boys with me," she said. Robin would be okay with it. Alicia was bringing Joe, and Bess's daughter, Amy, was also coming to oversee the younger kids. Two more wouldn't be a problem. She'd confirm with Robin, of course.

"They'll wind up watching TV all night," he said. "It's okay at your *friend's* house, but not at home? That's a double standard. They're smart enough to call attention to it."

"I've got to go," Carla said. "Patients."

Patience, she thought. Carla snapped her phone closed. Claude was right. The boys would probably watch TV at Robin's. It was a double standard and—surprising herself—Carla didn't care. She felt a flash of guilt. Was she giving in to temptation? Maybe playing cards *was* slowly eroding her resolve. Claude had criticized her, several times, about drinking on the porch—in full view of all their neighbors. He said that was just as bad as drinking in the house.

He would make her pay for tonight. His weapons of choice would be exaggerated signs of disappointment and stony silences, examples of his passive aggression that had become glaringly, laughably obvious since Robin had pointed them out.

The Black Queen wouldn't feel conflicted about indulging her pleasure. She'd claw and scrape and demand every last drop of what she wanted, when she wanted it.

"Wake up, Mommy," said Tina sharply, standing behind Carla at the sink.

"I'm fine," said Carla, drying her hands, moving toward exam room three.

"You have to *talk* to the mothers," said Tina, blocking her way. "Tell them to bring in the babies at the first sign of trouble. They wait too long! Make them get it. They don't listen to me. I'm just the *nurse*. They need to hear it from the *doctor*."

When Carla was in med school and imagined her professional future, she'd cast herself in the Hollywood role of "family doc." Being personally involved with her patients, serving as their trusted ally, treating them from infancy to young adulthood, being invited to graduation parties, confirmations, even bar and bat mitzvahs. Carla realized her dream of a huge extended family of patients was a response to the loneliness of her own childhood. She also knew it was a fantasy. The reality? In her fifteen years at LICH, Carla had treated thousands of patients, but hadn't felt a close connection to any of them. Her job was to walk on eggshells, live in fear of hospital reprimands, follow the rules, bite her tongue rather than speak critically to a parent who might make a formal complaint. It wasn't worth the risk. She'd diagnose, inform, and treat. The personal touch was against hospital policy.

Tina said, "I feel like I'm doing all the dirty work here."

"It's a dirty job," said Carla.

"We have to start betting," said Alicia later that night in Robin's kitchen. "Hold 'Em is a betting game. Tim and I have been playing at home, and all the fun is in the risk."

"Poker with just two people?" asked Bess, dealing the cards.

Alicia said, "Three. Joe plays with us. I'm proud to say the kid is a genius at poker. He wins more pots. Of M&M's." Seeing Carla's reaction, she added, "You think it's wrong to teach a nine-year-old to gamble?"

Carla shrugged. "I'm not telling anyone how to raise her child."

Robin raised her wineglass. "Drink up, Carla. I'll make a meddlesome yenta out of you yet."

"Do you end up eating all your winnings?" asked Bess.

"What winnings?" asked Alicia. "Every night, I get shellacked."

Robin said, "I hope that's a euphemism for sex."

"Not yet," said Alicia, "but I'm ever hopeful. I do feel like Tim and I are getting closer. Moving in the right direction."

As always, Carla felt uncomfortable when the conversation turned to Alicia's marital woes. Robin could probably make some pronouncement about what her discomfort means, in terms of Carla's own marriage. She hoped to avoid the subject of her own sex life. Although she'd weakened a few weeks ago when the card game was at her own home, and let a sliver of light shine on her problems with Claude, Carla felt uneasy talking behind her husband's back. It violated their privacy, was a betrayal of trust. Whatever her problems were with Claude, they were not for public consumption.

Carla studied her cards. King of hearts, ace of spades. A high percentage hand. If she were playing on the computer, she'd raise. But, at her own insistence, the women didn't bet.

Bess dealt the three flop cards, and said, "Amy came back from London, decked out head to toe in Stella McCartney. She looked incredible. The transformation was complete. She'd gone across the pond a slacker slob and came back a fashionista."

"We're unhappy about this?" asked Robin.

"I've *begged* to take her shopping," said Bess. "I tried to force my Visa card on her, and she refused. But when *Simone* offers, Amy not only agreed, but they have a great time together."

"So your two main problems in life are that your gorgeous husband wants you too much, and that your daughter and mother have a beautiful relationship?" asked Robin.

Bess said, "Yes!"

Alicia and Robin laughed. Carla shook her head. None of them had real problems. They weren't poor or hopeless. Their children weren't sick or hungry. Bess, Alicia, and Robin had no perspective, no idea how blessed and privileged they were. How long could Carla continue to hang out with these people?

Bess dealt the last two cards. Carla won with a pair of kings, but the victory was hollow. No pot to claim. Alicia was right. It wasn't satisfying to play with nothing at stake.

It wasn't satisfying to sit here and listen, if she was putting her problems into the pot, too. Tonight seemed to be about minor gripes. Complaining for the sake of it and expecting others to care seemed outrageously indulgent. Carla was not a decadent person.

But she knew someone who was.

"From now on, while we're playing, I wish to be referred to as the Black Queen," announced Carla.

"Your *nom du poker*?" said Robin. "Love. If you're the Black Queen, Carla, then I must be the Red Queen." She tossed her flaming frizz of hair.

Bess said, "That's good. Call me . . . White Diamond."

Carla couldn't help smiling at how spot-on that description was for beautiful Bess, with her sparkling eyes and blond hair. And Robin was the Red Queen, absolutely.

Alicia, the pint-sized brunette, said, "I guess that leaves me with Wild Heart."

The others nodded admiringly. "Nice," said Robin.

Carla let her back rest against the kitchen table chair, felt herself relax and then her spine lengthen. As the Black Queen, she fisted the deck. With each shuffle, she felt her alter ego gain dominance over her hands, her arms, her chest, and her thoughts.

"We *should* bet," said Carla before she dealt. "But not money. And not M&M's. Something valuable, but noncaloric."

Robin said, "Cigarettes? Like we're in prison?"

Bess said, "I'm never smoking again! That cigarette I had last time gave me a sore throat for a week."

Alicia said, "We should play with poker chips. The woman with the most chips at the end of the night wins things we actually need. Like a night of babysitting." Alicia turned to Carla and added, "Or a house call." To Bess: "Or an outfit to borrow." To Robin: "Or advice."

"I give that away for free!" said Robin.

Bess said, "Anytime anyone wants to borrow clothes or jewelry, all you have to do is ask."

"Same for house calls," said Carla.

Alicia nodded. "And I'd be honored to write pithy slogans to sell your products, whatever they might be. Right. It's a silly idea. Obvi-ously, we'd help each other without needing to win first."

Carla sensed Alicia's embarrassment. She needn't feel it. Her idea had merit. The four of them had gotten to know each other, somewhat. As considerate people, they'd help each other if asked. Theoretically. But if they were betting, and there was a clear winner, they'd be beholden to.

"Not a silly idea," said Carla. "Personally, I have a hard time ask-ing people for help. It's awkward. But if I win the service, I'd use it." She thought of herself hoofing to Brownstone to get the boys that very afternoon, how it'd screwed up her entire schedule, forcing her to rush through patients, rush home to throw dinner together and hurry back to the Heights for cards. Why hadn't she just called Robin or Bess asked them to pick up her boys instead? Both women were available, at school anyway to pick up their own kids, lived close to the hospital. It hadn't occurred to Carla to think of ways to cut herself slack. She was loath to be needy or a bother. However, if she *won* their help, Carla would be able to take it without feeling as if she couldn't handle her own responsibilities.

Robin nodded. "I'm seeing how it might work."

"If I win, I'm going to finally get you guys to plan a Diversity Committee agenda," said Bess.

Robin said, "You know what that means, Alicia? Carla? We cannot let Bess win."

"Just try to stop me," said Bess. "What can we use for poker chips?"

Robin said, "A-ha!" stood up and yelled, "Stephanie!"

A stunning little girl appeared in the hallway and ran toward the kitchen. Carla marveled at Stephanie's long, auburn hair and apple cheeks. She got her coloring from Robin. What had she inherited from her mysterious father?

Stephanie stopped at her mom's chair. "You bellowed?" she asked, which made Carla snort.

"Find Connect Four and the Othello and bring them here."

The girl groaned. "They're buried in the back of my closet."

"You've got three friends and one babysitter back there to help," said Robin. "Go."

Stephanie dramatically rolled her eyes, which made them all smile, but she did as her mother asked. Ten minutes later, each woman had a pile of plastic discs in front of her.

"Where were we?" asked Bess.

Robin said, "The Black Queen was about to deal."

Carla—correction, the Black Queen—felt a tingle of excitement. Once more, she shuffled the cards with as much earnest concentration as administering a vaccine shot to an infant. She felt lucky tonight. Correction. She was Lady Luck herself, and she'd just walked into the joint.

CALL

5

Alicia

"Whoa, Alicia. I didn't know it was you. From behind, you looked like a woman," said Finn Clarke, the hero of Alicia's satisfying yet emotionally hollow fantasy life. He'd just walked into their shared office at Bartlebee, a "boutique" (read: minuscule) "specialty" (read: limited) "agency" of six people, including, along with creatives Alicia and Finn, a CEO, a one-woman art department, and two account managers.

"What, I usually look like a gorilla?" she replied, only half turning around to face him, knowing that her cheeks were pomegranate red.

"It's just that I've never seen your legs before," said Finn, lowering himself into his desk chair and leaning back to appraise her further. "I thought you might be walking around on a pair of Polish sausages."

A plumper woman might've taken offense. But Alicia was, had

always been, slim. Since she hadn't had sex in over two years (and counting), she compensated for the lack of intimacy by working out like a fiend at lunchtime at the Equinox around the corner. Lately, in the mornings, she'd also taken up the routine of masturbating and crying in the shower. These practices had made her as sleek, taut, and high-strung as a whippet.

"If you're so interested in what I've got under my skirt, why don't you take a closer look?" Alicia *thought* to say. But she wouldn't dare. Alicia was not a provocative and flirty type. That would be as odd as, well, wearing a short skirt to the office. And yet, here she was, showing two inches of thigh. And wearing makeup, too.

The outfit was selected by Bess and Robin for Alicia to wear out on a dinner date with Tim. But it would take a keg of dynamite to get Tim to notice her. She'd strutted around their apartment all morning in her sexy costume, and Tim barely glanced at her. Joe, bless his little heart, said, "Mom, why are your eyelids green? Aren't you cold in that skirt?"

Alicia must have been frowning at the memory. Finn said, "Don't be pissed off. You look great. I'm just surprised you've gone female on me."

"The Female," was the nickname they'd given the agency's art director, Sonya, because of her hysterical, insecure overreactions to the slightest criticism. Whenever Sonya burst into tears at a staff meeting, Alicia thanked God for her one-of-the-boys status. It'd be horrible to be thought of as emotionally fragile.

"There's a difference between going female and wearing a skirt," said Alicia. "If you can't handle it, I can put on track pants."

Finn said, "Don't do that! I just need a second to get used to the skin." He gazed at her legs for a count of three. Then he said, "Okay, I'm inured," and turned his attention to the computer to do his morning lap of blogs and email accounts before they got down to the business of the day.

Alicia sat behind her desk and started her own morning lap on the computer, her mind distracted and unsettled. *Finn had been flirting, right?* she asked herself. A fantasy crept up on her, of Finn coming toward her, grabbing her, bending her over her inbox, raising her skirt, and taking her in full view of the entire office.

If such incredible events were to unfold, Alicia would be grateful for it. She would let life happen. She'd welcome the excitement with open legs.

Had there been an exact moment when she decided that having an affair was within her moral capacity? In the last few weeks, her take on infidelity had gone from one extreme (a rot-in-hell sin) to the other (a worthy act of self-preservation). She'd kept her sexlessness a secret for over two years, was rooted in denial about her loneliness. When Alicia revealed the truth at the poker game, her own desperation hit her full force. That brought about a perspective shift. She would not continue to tell herself that (1) Tim's chronic rejection was okay, and (2) she was content with celibacy.

Alicia was in the throes of a reversal of suppression. A 180-degree reversal. Simply put, Alicia had turned into a sex-crazed maniac. If Finn starred in her occasional masturbatory fantasies before, in recent weeks he'd blossomed into a throbbing obsession in Alicia's feverish daydreams.

If only she could have sex with Finn, just once, Alicia believed she'd return to a normal, stable state of mind. Her head would clear and she could accurately assess her life and marriage.

In the meantime, as in, right now, Alicia didn't know which end was up, down, or sideways. If someone put a gun to her head and said, "Do you still love your husband?" Alicia couldn't rightly say. She and Tim were friends and co-parents. Was that love? He seemed content to exist in this half relationship. Indeed, how could he not? His options were limited. Alicia earned the family's income, modest though it might be. If she and Tim split up, what would he live on? Where would he go? How could either of them survive if she was to pay alimony or support Tim in a second apartment? They could barely cover the expenses they had now.

Alicia shook off the image of Tim, destitute, in torn clothes, living under a bridge, cursing her name and shaking his grimy fist at the gods.

It wasn't her fault he couldn't find a job! It wasn't her fault he hadn't had sex with her. If she'd done nothing wrong, why was she being tormented hourly with fantasies of Finn naked with a rock-hard, throbbing, two-foot-long erection?

Alicia put her fingers on her temples and rubbed. These violent swings of emotion were exhausting. This was the unfortunate result of opening up. But she couldn't go back to numb even if she wanted to. An affair would settle her down. If she were held, touched, and treasured by a man for just a little while, she knew she'd feel better about everything. Maybe Tim would instinctively know she'd been made love to, and the heady perfume of sensuality would reignite his passion for her. Alicia was convinced that if she had sex with someone else, Tim would want her again.

She glanced across her desk at Finn. He sensed her eyes were on him, looked up, and smiled at her.

She smiled, too, like a lioness over a flank of raw meat.

"Did you have breakfast?" he asked. "You look hungry."

"We never go out after work," she said brazenly. "I mean just the two of us. We should have a drink."

He squinted at her, trying to figure that out. Finn was too handsome not to register a come-on when he heard one. This one came out of left field, though.

"We totally should," he said, polite and maddeningly neutral. Finn had never shown any particular interest in Alicia's personal life. He knew she was married. Finn had met Tim and Joe a few times. Finn either wrote her off as off-limits or he hadn't thought of his mousy, older (by seven years) office mate in *that way*. But he did like her. They laughed together, inspired each other at work. He respected her.

She said, "How about tonight? Are you free?"

His eyebrows shot up. She was fumbling this. Too aggressive.

"Tonight is the poker game," he said.

"What poker game?" she asked.

"First Tuesday of every month," he said. "Me, Chaundry, Jake, Larry, and a few other guys." He'd rattled off the names of their CEO and account managers.

"Everyone in the agency but me and Sonya?" she asked. "I can see why you didn't ask The Female, but why not me?"

He shrugged. "Do you even know how to play Hold 'Em?"

Alicia suppressed a grin and said, "A little."

"It's a money game," he said. "Big time."

"Really," she said, instantly deflated.

"Yup," he said. "We play for pennies, nickels, and dimes. Think you can handle that kind of action?"

That, and a lot more, she thought. Alicia was struck with an insta-fantasy of Finn losing his shirt to her. And his pants, shoes, and boxers. And then laying down on top of the poker table, ante (way) up.

"I'm in," she said.

●—◆—●

"Raise!" shouted Alicia, tipsy—actually, drunky—as she threw a handful of bottom-of-purse change into the pot.

"Is she talking about the bet or my pants?" asked a friend of Finn's, a chubby leering buffoon who really liked short skirts or flat-chested women. Or both.

"Shut up, McAlvoy," said Finn.

"I can defend myself," said Alicia. "Shut up, McAlvoy."

"Hey, if you want to play with the boys, you've got to be willing to play with the boys," said the idiot, cupping his nuts.

Her boss, Chaundry, said, "I hope you appreciate how respectfully we treat women at Bartlebee."

"You mean compared to this belch?" She jerked her thumb at McAlvoy.

Finn said, "Bet's to you, Larry."

Alicia had a good hand. A very good hand. Two pair after the flop. She'd put two dollars in, raising and reraising with wanton abandon. The guys matched her greed and cockiness. Poker with men was *fun*! It made her women's game seem like a tea party.

The seedy atmosphere fed her newfound adventure-lust. The conference room at night was dimly lit, smelling of open beer bottles and male competition. Alicia sat next to Finn. He rolled up his sleeve and left his bare arm on the back of her chair. Ten times, she'd leaned into it, feeling the heat from his skin all the way through her blouse.

She flashed to what she'd be doing tonight if she hadn't agreed to play poker. Sitting on the couch a good five feet away from ice-cold Tim, laughing half-for-real, half-out-of-habit at his pithy and sarcastic remarks about whatever TV show they were watching. Then purposeful yawning, nocturnal brushing and fussing, winding up with the two of them climbing into bed, aka the loneliest place on the planet, the pit in her stomach growing.

"Oh!" Alicia gasped suddenly, when Finn put his palm flat on her lower back.

"Bet's to you," he said, smiling.

By the river card, everyone had folded, except Finn, McAlvoy, and Alicia. Her hand remained the same, two pair. The five communal cards, a lot of hearts, might mean a flush for the other players.

"Check," she said.

"Check?" asked McAlvoy. "Lost your confidence? I'll raise. Four dollars."

"That's over the limit," said Chaundry, ever the officiator and arbiter (he was a natural diplomat and a good boss). But no one really stuck by the game rules. The bet was to Finn.

He folded. "I'm already down cabfare home."

Alicia eyed McAlvoy. Was the pig bluffing? It was the biggest pot of the night, around twenty bucks. She'd already put in eight dollars. What was another four? She had to see it through, play the hand until the end, regardless of the consequences.

Glancing at Finn, she thought, *If I win this hand, we will have an affair.*

"I'm in," she said, putting her quarters in the pot and her cards on the conference room table.

Two pair, kings and fours.

McAlvoy laughed. "You bitch," he said, and showed his hand. Pair of fours. Nothing.

Alicia screamed and bounced in her chair. She leaned across the table to rake in her winnings, saying, "Mine, all mine! You lose, sucka!"

Finn said to McAlvoy, "You went over the limit on a pair of fours?"

The jerk shrugged. "I didn't think she'd call."

"I called you, all right! In your face!" said Alicia.

"Okay, that's enough," counseled Finn, looking nervously at McAlvoy.

"Oh, come on! He can take a little trash talk," she said.

"Very little," grumbled McAlvoy. "I'd feel better about it if you'd do a victory dance on my lap."

Alicia immediately went for the top button of her blouse. Finn stared, stunned, nearly swallowing his tongue.

She giggled and said, "You really thought I was going to unbutton my shirt?"

Finn dramatically blushed. Fire-engine red. It occurred to Alicia that Finn, for all his serial girlfriends and emotion disinterest at work, might be harboring a little crush on her, too.

She couldn't resist. Alicia reached up to touch Finn's flaming cheek. Instinctively, his hand went up to cover hers and for a nanosecond, they were the only two people in the stuffy, stinky conference room.

Chaundry said to Larry, an account manager, "Do we have a policy on intra-office romance?"

Larry started shuffling. "Fuck if I know."

Alicia dropped her hand and said, "Gimme those cards. It's my deal."

● ◄━━ ●

Hours later, Alicia crept into her Red Hook apartment. It was around midnight. She vaguely remembered swearing she'd be home to tuck in Joe. Oh, well. She'd make it up to him in the morning.

The living room was dark. Tim hadn't waited up, of course.

Alicia crept down the hallway, bumping into the walls only enough to make her giggle. She cracked the door to Joe's room and smiled at her son, visible by lava lamp light, brown hair pressed against his forehead, baby face, sleeping and still.

The pang of regret, a flash of guilt. Just a taste of negative emotions, thankfully mitigated by beer, victory, hot skin, and a purse heavy with quarters.

Alicia closed Joe's door and moved along to her own bedroom. She expected to find her husband asleep is his usual position—curved on his side, facing the wall. Alicia was both relieved and disappointed to find him exactly like that, impenetrable, blocking himself from her, subconsciously or consciously.

She did her bathroom routine, and then returned to the bedroom to undress in the dark. She began with her top blouse button, the one she'd pretended to undo at the game. She smiled at the memory of Finn's reaction. To make a man react! It was almost too arousing—slide-off-the-seat arousing. How had she gone so long without feeling that? Slowly, soundlessly, she shrugged off her shirt and stepped out of her skirt, the garment that started it all, and her underthings.

Once naked, she folded her clothes (needed dry cleaning) and held the pile to her nose. She could still smell Finn on the fabric, the male essence of competition and cologne. She sat at the vanity like that, naked, inhaling the joy of the night, for quite some time, reliving moments, touches, accidental-on-purpose thigh contact under the table, elbows grazing when reaching for cards, his arm on the back of her chair, on the small of her back, her hand on his cheek.

Finn asked her, considering her winnings ($25) and his losses ($15), to share a cab downtown, and drop him first at his place in Battery Park City on her way home to Red Hook. His eyes, the questioning look. She believed he was really asking her to go home with him, or at least make out in the taxi on the way there. She begged off, saying the subway would be faster.

Alicia could rationalize having an affair. But she wasn't quite ready to actually do it.

Besides, the subway might as well have been a magic carpet. At the game, she'd basked in the glory of being a woman—but not a female. She was a cool chick, someone to hang with, but also a turn-on. Her presence had added a sexual tang to the night, and all the players enjoyed the flavor. She smiled at the intoxicating idea that, if even for a fleeting moment, every man there imagined what it would be like to have sex with her.

"What time is it?" warbled Tim from the bed, making Alicia gasp.

"You scared me," she said, clutching her heart. It felt like she'd been caught thinking.

"Midnight," he grumbled, checking his night table clock. "You said you'd be home to put Joe to bed."

"Sorry," she said, finding her contrite voice.

"Good game?" he asked, turning toward her now. "You're sitting in the dark naked?"

"Just finishing up," she said, throwing her blouse into the corner.

"Did you win?" he asked.

"Twenty-five bucks," she said.

She looked at Tim in the bed, now unfolding and opening himself to her. Even in the dim light, she could see the angles of his face, the cheekbones she'd always admired, his long neck. Once, she'd loved to press her mouth against his jugular vein to feel his pulse on her tongue.

Maybe she had one more hand to play tonight.

Standing, she moved toward the bed. Tim watched her coming and shifted a bit under the covers. Maybe her eyes were deceiving her, but Alicia could have sworn she saw something rigid under the moving sheets at hip level. Her heart pounded with surprise and anticipation.

Expect it when you least expect it, she thought. As soon as she was seriously contemplating an affair, her husband returned from the sexually dead.

Alicia slid into the envelope of soft cotton sheets, and stretched, she hoped, seductively, forcing her modest boobs against the covers.

Please, for the love of God, touch me! she screamed at her husband in her mind.

He watched her languid settling in, and said, "Alicia, I've been meaning to talk."

"About?" How much he missed her. How much he wanted her. How much he loved her, didn't want to lose her, deeply regretted hurting her feelings and neglecting her needs. Alicia had never been more eager to have a talk.

He leaned back on the pillows, staring at the ceiling. "Since you started this card game with the mothers, I've felt taken advantage of. And now this new game with the guys at work just makes it worse."

Taken advantage of? "I've been out six nights in the last three months," she defended. "I work hard. I deserve some time to myself." She also thought, but didn't say, "I have friends now—new thing for me—and I need them. Your companionship isn't enough."

"You sound like some nineteen-fifties husband defending his weekend golf game," said Tim. "And I'm like a nagging wifey on pills."

She *was* like a husband, and he the wife, a thought that wasn't flattering to either of them—or sexy.

"Who's stopping you from going out?" She caught herself before saying "after work." Since he refused to discuss his feelings about his chronic unemployment, she'd backed off from asking. But how could he not feel depressed about it? Meanwhile, his criticism wasn't fair. For a "husband," Alicia sure did a lot of wifely chores. They divided duties. She dropped Joe off, Tim picked him up. She shopped, Tim cooked. She did laundry, he vacuumed. She did the dishes, he did the recycling. She wanted more sex, he had a two-year headache.

Tim said, "I've been feeling lately like my life is to make your life possible."

Alicia bundled the comforter tight, her body temperature dropped down to frigid. She shook her head at the ridiculousness of what she'd thought would happen between them tonight. Instead of affection, she got hit with his emasculation. He made her life happen? And all this time, working her ass off, supporting the family, she thought her life was devoted to making *their* lives possible.

"I guess we agree," said Alicia.

"We do?" he said, shocked she'd concede so quickly.

"We're both unhappy. We've been unhappy for a long time," she said.

Tim didn't respond to that. Alicia remembered reading that eighty percent of divorces were instigated by the wife. This last bit, Tim's blaming her for his dissatisfaction, pushed her over the edge. Alicia felt a creeping coldness, not only of body, but of mind. She was starting to hate him.

"Dr. Sacket?" he asked, naming the counselor who steered them through some hard times during the infertility years.

"Do you think that would help?" she questioned.

Tim sighed and said, "When I was twenty years old and I imagined what my life would look like at forty, this wasn't what I pictured."

The choices we made, the long-forgotten decisions, the painfully un-forgettable ones, are the framework of our lives, thought Alicia. All of her choices and decisions had brought her to this moment in bed with Tim. When you looked at life that way, it was hard not to blame yourself for your own unhappiness.

• ⬭ •

"Sex is not the answer," announced Alicia at Bess's brownstone a week later.

"That depends on the question," said Robin, in a silk tunic, patchwork suede maxi skirt, and wool tights. (*Did she* try *to look like an aging anorexic hippie?* wondered Alicia.)

It was the Diversity Committee pre-Thanksgiving gathering. All of the women were under pressure with the holidays approaching. They squeezed in the meeting, though, and Alicia was grateful. Her mood lightened in this circle of friends. She brought Joe with her tonight. Since her talk with Tim, she'd been spending all her free time at home. If she decided to leave him, she wanted to be sure Tim couldn't use nights away from Joe against her in a custody battle. The simple fact that she was having these thoughts shocked and terrified her. This was big. Ending a marriage made celibacy seem a trifle.

Sex was not the answer to her problems. Sexy daydreams about Finn were a pleasant distraction from the potential reality of divorce, poverty, and guilt. But the fantasies kept coming regardless, with furious intensity.

"I take it the wardrobe makeover didn't work?" said Bess, who then coughed and sniffled with gooey gusto. Even with a red nose, the blond host looked lovely in a cashmere sweater and black velour track pants.

Alicia shook her head. "Tim watched me give birth," she said, peeking at a pair of tens in the pocket. "Seeing me in a skirt did not have a dramatic effect."

Carla said, "I'm going to have to insist on gloves, Bess. I can almost see the germs crawling off your hands and all over the cards. I've got twenty people to cook for this weekend, and if I get sick . . ."

"If you get sick, your husband can do the work," said Robin. "It's *his* family, right? You've got just your mother."

Carla warned, "Don't, Robin."

"Don't remind you that Claude makes you do everything and then complains about it?"

Carla shook her head pityingly at Robin. "Always seeing the negative."

"Full house," said Robin. "I mean my cards, not my holiday plans."

Robin gathered her winnings, and stacked the chips before shuffling and dealing the cards. Alicia thought the redhead was being intentionally inflammatory. Robin was definitely testier than usual. For all of Alicia's family troubles, at least she had holiday plans. She wondered if she should invite Robin and her daughter, Stephanie, to her mom's place in New Jersey for Thanksgiving.

Bess must have been thinking the same thing. "Robin, I meant to ask if you and Stephanie would like to come here for Thanksgiving dinner. It's just Borden and me, and the kids. His parents from San Francisco. Maybe my mother if she's in town, which I hope she isn't. And possibly my brother Fred and his family." And then Bess sneezed so hard, she blew her pocket cards across the table. Useless rags, Alicia noted.

"That's it," said Carla. "You're too sick to play. You should've canceled."

Bess said, "We've had the date for weeks. And it was all set up with Amy babysitting, and the kids were all excited to have movie night together . . ."

This was the first time they'd agreed to bringing all the kids over. Bess's house was big enough, for one thing. Carla's sons were thrilled because they were allowed to watch TV and eat junk at *other* people's houses. Robin's Stephanie loved to hang out with the boys. Bess's

Amy got paid by each mother for her babysitting services (*outrageous extortion*, Alicia thought). Joe wasn't so keen on enforced socializing, but Alicia wanted him nearby, and thought the extra time with the other kids would ease his shyness.

"Flush," said Robin, showing her cards, since Bess's were already on the table. "I win. Again." To Bess, Robin added, "You assume I'll be crying in my cocktail on Thanksgiving? Do I look like a pity case to you?"

Bess, who was in mid-noseblow, looked over her tissue at Robin in shock. "I'm so sorry, Robin! I invited you because I'd love your company. The kids would love having Stephanie. I never meant to insult you!"

"I was going to invite you to my mom's in New Jersey," said Alicia to take the heat off of sick Bess. "Is that a tempting offer *or what?*"

Carla said, "I thought about inviting you, too, Robin. But you'd be surrounded by a lot of black people who distrust Jews."

"Hey! I voted for Barack," said Robin.

"I voted for Mike Bloomberg," said Carla. "That doesn't make me Jewish."

"You can say that again," said Robin, laughing. "I appreciate all the invites. And I respectfully decline. Stephanie and I will be passing the holiday at the Atlantis resort on Paradise Island, in a luxury suite with a minibar and dozens of tiny little bottles. The last thing I'd want on Thanksgiving would be to insert myself in other people's obnoxious family dramas."

Alicia said, "Sounds like you should be inviting us to come with you."

Bess said, "Robin, honestly, I didn't mean to offend you."

"I'm not offended," said Robin.

She sure looked offended. Alicia wouldn't have been surprised if Robin's red hair burst into flames.

Bess blew her nose again, her eyes clogging now, too. "Look, I'm sorry, okay? Sorry for trying to be nice. Sorry for not canceling. Sorry for sneezing on the cards. Sorry for anything I've done or ever will do." And then, incredibly, Bess started to cry.

Carla said, "This is what happens when you don't let your body be sick."

"Oh, for God's sake. If I knew you were going to cry, I would have said yes to Thanksgiving with your in-laws," said Robin.

"I'm fine," said Bess, recovering. "I don't get what's the matter with me. I never cry."

"Evidence to the contrary," said Robin.

"Mom?" came a weak voice from the top of the stairs.

Joe. Alicia instinctively sprang to her feet. "Honey? Are you okay?"

She walked up the stairs from the basement to find her son at the top, holding on to the railing, his face streaked with tears. He backed into the parlor room, and Alicia saw his pants were soaked. Her stomach dropped. "Did you have an accident?" she asked.

Joe started crying, hard. He was having difficulty breathing. "No!" he got out. "Charlie squirted me."

"Squirted?"

"He has a Super Soaker. He was squirting everyone. But he did it at me the most. He's a total jerk! Someone should lock him up. I want to get out of here."

"Calm down," she said, alarmed at her son's anger and panic, internalizing his feelings as they crept into her skin and bones.

"Get me out of here! I hate them! We have to leave *now*!" Joe shrieked, his voice cracking and desperate.

The commotion drew the other mothers up the stairs and into the parlor. One look at Joe and Bess said, "What did Charlie do?"

Clutching her like a toddler, Joe cleaved to Alicia's side, grasping at her hips, on the verge of a total meltdown.

Her head spinning with outrage on Joe's behalf, remembered fear from when she was picked on by playground aggressors, embarrassment that her son was a target, shame that she was embarrassed. Rage at her friend's son. A whirlwind of bad feelings.

Bess was already shouting up the stairs for Charlie, a hyperactive mischievous instigator who, at that moment, Alicia would've loved to see boiled in oil.

Charlie trudged down the stairs, followed by Robin's Stephanie and Carla's Zeke. The three of them appeared to be in cahoots, smiling nervously. All the other mothers launched into demands for explanations, what did they do to Joe, did they have any idea the trouble they were in, etc. Meanwhile, Alicia and Joe clung to each other, knowing full well that the other mothers' yelling would only make the other kids pick on Joe with increased vigor at school.

Bess said, "Where is Amy? Amy! Get down here!"

Yes, thought Alicia. *Where is the babysitter I'm paying ten dollars an hour?*

Charlie said, "She's in her room, on the computer."

At the news, Bess trudged up the stairs, presumably to bust her daughter. Spotlight off him, Charlie retreated to his lair. Stephanie and Zeke started to follow him. That brought on a fresh torrent of "Where do you think *you're* going?" and "Hold it right there," from Robin and Carla.

Alicia felt Joe shaking, literally trembling with fear, shame, dread. The physical manifestation of his panic passed through Alicia in waves. She thought she might throw up. She had to get him—and herself—out of there.

"Tell Bess thanks and I'll call her," said Alicia, moving toward the front door.

Robin leaned down, got in Joe's face, and said, "Stephanie is very sorry for whatever she did."

It was the wrong thing to do, wrong thing to say. Carla knew enough to stand back and be quiet. Alicia nodded at Robin and hurried Joe into his coat and out the door.

Alicia was able to hail a cab on Henry Street. She pushed Joe into the taxi and buckled him in. His panic seemed to abate. He was still now, except for intermittent posthysterical rattling breaths. After the panic in the parlor, his sudden stillness seemed sinister and strange.

Alicia had been a socially awkward kid. She'd been a quiet loner. But she didn't remember having episodes like this. For years, she'd assumed Joe had inherited her shyness and would learn to adjust. But now she wasn't so sure that was it. Alicia closed her eyes and let her worst fear come to the surface.

It was possible that something was wrong with her son.

6

Robin

"That bitch," muttered Robin to herself while reading her email at the kitchen table after putting Stephanie to bed.

Alicia had written the subject line: "Don't be mad." In the email, she'd included several links and a list of relevant tidbits. Never in a million years would Robin have asked Alicia to compile the information. Alicia knew as much, hence the subject line. And yet, that hadn't stopped the pocket-sized brunette from doing, as she wrote, "some productive Googling about Mr. Harvey Wilson of Chelsea." Harvey Wilson, Robin's one-night stand, the biological father of her daughter, Stephanie.

Reaching for the phone, Robin dialed Alicia's landline.

Tim, the husband, answered. "It's Robin. Is Alicia there?"

He said, "She has a work thing. You could try her cell, but I tried it an hour ago and it was turned off. It's been off all evening."

"Thanks," she grunted and hung up, leaving Tim, no doubt, holding a dead phone and marveling at the rudeness of his wife's friend. Next, she dialed Carla.

"This is a violation of my privacy!" squawked Robin into the phone.

"Before you start complaining about Alicia, you should know that I encouraged her to do it," said Carla.

Robin said, "What. The. *Hell*, Carla. I count on you to be the repressed one, the one who doesn't believe in prying into others' personal lives."

Carla said, "Whether you like it or not, you have to make contact with this man. Fifty percent of his genes are in your daughter. For her sake, you need Harvey Wilson's family medical history. God forbid Stephanie is at high risk for an inherited but preventable disease."

"Like obesity?" asked Robin, truly and deeply not in the mood to discuss inherited but preventable disease at ten o'clock on a Wednesday night. Maybe with a lit cigarette in one hand and a stiff drink in the other. Speaking of which . . . Robin fished in her purse for her American Spirits Organics. She took a butt out of the pack, opened the kitchen window, and lit up.

"Are you smoking?" asked Carla.

"Was Bess in on your little detective project, too?" Half of Robin's body was leaning out the window, blowing the smoke into the chilly December night.

"You *were* the big winner at the last committee meeting, and that meant the spotlight of our benevolent intervention fell on you," said Carla. "So while you were on the beach at Paradise Island . . ."

"Rained the whole time, meanwhile."

". . . the three of us decided to do your homework for you," said Carla. "Alicia volunteered to deliver the news, which makes her braver than me."

"I'm supposed to just call up this guy, this complete stranger, and tell him that he fathered a child with the three hundred and forty pound woman he screwed one night a million years ago?"

Robin forcibly exhaled a heavy lungful of smoke. It'd been all too easy to ignore the Harvey Wilson situation for a decade. She'd been busy as a new mother. The lifestyle changes of bariatric surgery had been enormous. She'd had a job, the apartment to contend with. Then the distraction of her online dating career. Robin was willing to concede, however, that she wasn't as distracted lately. Nearly ten, Stephanie wasn't such a handful. Robin's weight had been stable for years, and she'd adjusted to her new way of eating. She'd stopped dating since the last Match.com disaster left a sour taste in her mouth. Post-election, her Zogby obligations weren't as urgent.

Until now, as in, this year, this month, this day, Robin simply hadn't been able or willing to contemplate the huge question mark of Harvey Wilson. Maybe that was why she'd opened up to the other moms at the committee meeting about him. She had mental space in her mind. Her subconscious had rushed to fill the vacuum with ghosts from the past, prominently, Harvey Wilson.

"What are you doing?" asked a voice from the kitchen threshold.

Robin's blood flow screeched to a halt. Into the phone, she said, "Gotta go," and clicked the off button.

"Are you . . . *smoking?*" asked Stephanie behind her.

Quickly, Robin crushed out her cigarette on the outer sill, and threw the butt out of the window, shamefully aware that it would land on or close to her building's stoop.

"No!" said Robin, pulling her body into the room and facing her daughter. "I just burned some toast and opened the window to air the room out."

"What toast?" asked Stephanie. The girl crossed her arms over her chest.

"It's gone," said Robin, her brain spinning.

"Where?" asked the girl, walking toward the kitchen garbage.

"I threw it out the window for the birds."

"The birds will eat burnt toast?" asked Stephanie.

"I didn't want it to stink up the room."

"Too late."

Trying to take control of the conversation, Robin demanded, "Why aren't you in bed?"

"I heard you yelling," said Stephanie, moseying toward Robin at the window. To look for the defenestrated toast?

Robin slammed the window shut. "It's cold in here," she said, shivering exaggeratedly.

The girl nodded ambiguously at Robin, still suspicious. The expression on her daughter's face was too reminiscent of Robin's mother's disapproving scowl. Robin felt the same offense ("how dare she not trust me?") all the while smugly aware that she'd been guilty of everything her mother—and daughter—had accused her of, and more.

"Kiss me," said Stephanie, reaching for her mother.

Robin felt the rip in her heart muscle. This was a Catch-22 (Caught-22?). If she kissed Stephanie, the girl would smell her cigarette breath and know Robin had lied (bad). If Robin refused to kiss her daughter, Stephanie's feelings would be hurt and/or the girl would assume Robin refused to kiss her so she wouldn't smell the smoke (worse).

When did kids get so freaking sneaky?

Was ten the new forty?

"Just go to bed," said Robin, turning Stephanie around, and pushing her out of the kitchen and down the hallway toward her bedroom. Along the way, Robin excused herself into the bathroom, and rinsed with mouthwash. When she went into Stephanie's room, the girl held out her arms for a hug and kiss.

Now Robin could give it. She hugged her daughter tight, and kissed her a dozen times all over the girl's face.

"Your hair smells like smoke," said Stephanie.

"Give it a rest," admonished Robin.

"Swear to me you don't smoke. Cigarettes kill people. You should see the pictures of black lungs they showed us at school."

"I swear," said Robin.

"What were you saying when I came into the kitchen?" asked the girl, snuggling into her pillow.

"That I burned the toast."

"On the phone," said Stephanie. "About one night a million years ago."

"Nothing," said Robin. "Grown-up stuff."

One more kiss good night. Then Robin left Stephanie's room, and returned to the kitchen. She put a slice of bread in the toaster and turned it up to Dark.

Ten minutes after *that*, Robin threw a square of charred toast out the kitchen window, just in case Stephanie looked for it in the morning.

●—————●

Harvey Wilson was currently unmarried. He was divorced, no kids. These simple facts pleased Robin as she examined the wealth of information Alicia and Carla had unearthed about her impregnator. She was quite impressed by the Googling, actually. Starting with his name, approximate age, and address, her friends acquired Harvey's phone number. With these few vitals, information about him was as accessible as a hot dog stand. Employment history, announcements (wedding), legal filings (divorce), credit history—and, most interestingly, a year's worth of postings at www.urbanoffroad.com, his blog. Apparently, there was a thriving subculture of New Yorkers who rode bicycles obsessively and exclusively. Harvey was an aficionado of dirt biking on the mean streets. The blog had advertisers, too, for bike shops and gear. According to Alicia's Web research, urbanoffroad. com got 10,000 unique hits *per day*. Surely, a few of those followers weren't bike messengers.

Along with maps, bulletin boards, general biking enthusiast info, and events, Harvey posted photos of himself and his friends on their bikes, in group shots or solo portraits, during the day and at night, rain, shine, fog, in helmets and reflective jackets and heavy chains around their waists. Regardless of the weather conditions, the people in the photos all looked happy and healthy. The profile picture—Harvey in black bike pants (package: impossible to judge) and a red jacket—looked like the same man Robin remembered. He hadn't aged much.

Despite the blog's deadly content (Robin wasn't much of an athlete, and had sworn off bikes for life as an eighty-five-pound first-grader), she made a new habit of reading his archives after putting Stephanie to bed. Occasionally, Harvey veered off track, and wrote a few paragraphs about his personal life, including some broad-stroke comments about a short marriage. Some women's names popped up here and there. Girlfriends? Friends? The names often changed. In his postdivorce dating life, Harvey had been riding the same grueling cycle of anticipation and disappointment that Robin had endured.

Alas, riding his bike and blogging about it did not pay Harvey's bills. He had a peripatetic career history of half a dozen office jobs in the last ten years. From what Alicia and Carla had dug up, he'd worked at a marketing company (the job he'd had when Robin met him), a public relations company, an ad agency (which Alicia had never heard of), a headhunter firm, the headquarters of a clothing retail store. As of two years ago, he'd been a store manager at the Union Square Barnes & Noble. Bikes and books. That was his life. And babes, too, most likely young hard-bodied athletic women.

Robin marveled at how many fans/friends had left comments on his posts. Where had all those buddies been on New Year's Eve at the turn of the century? Hadn't he said he was new to New York? Or had Robin just remembered it that way? Had he acquired pals at his jobs? He'd effortlessly befriended her in three minutes. Perhaps establishing connections was a particular talent of his, one Robin sorely lacked. And what about maintaining contacts? He got divorced after only two years of marriage. What was the story there? He hadn't appeared to have found a replacement for his ex. Perhaps women bonded easily with Harvey as a friend—but only a friend.

It would be ridiculous to think that she would again connect with him romantically, if she could even call their millennial hump romantic. She'd scurried out of his place into the dark night like a fat rat. Did he remember her at all? And there was the little matter of not informing him that he had a daughter. Whenever she thought of Harvey over the years, Robin assumed he'd be grateful for his ignorance. But, having gotten superficially acquainted with the guy online, she suspected he might've enjoyed being a part of Stephanie's life, taught her to ride a bike—which Robin had never done. He'd missed a lot, to be sure. How much more of Stephanie's life would he miss? That was all up to Robin.

Telling no one—not even Alicia, Bess, and Carla, who asked her repeatedly, "Have you read the stuff?" "When are you going to call him?" "What's your plan?"—Robin decided to act. She just had to get a look at him, if for the sole purpose of satisfying her curiosity.

It was mid-December, two weeks before Christmas. Robin took the number four train from Brooklyn Heights to Union Square station in Manhattan. The Barnes & Noble on 17th Street was a downtown oasis. Four floors, miles of aisles of books. Robin had been inside the haven a dozen times during Harvey's tenure as store manager there. She'd never seen him. Or, if she had, she hadn't recognized him. Maybe if she'd crashed into him and landed on top in a straddle, his face would've rung some bells.

She pushed through the doors, her throat dry and cheeks cold (December had turned nasty). She moseyed around the front tables, picking up a book here and there but not really looking at them. Her eyes were up, darting around the store, scanning for people with name tags on their shirts. Pre-Christmas, the store was frustratingly packed with customers, making her mission more difficult. Robin chastised herself for coming at midday, lunchtime. She should have known this was the shopping rush hour.

Milling around the information desk on the first floor, finding no one who resembled Harvey Wilson, in shape and gender, she took the elevator to the second floor. A lap from teen fiction to biographies proved futile. She checked the third floor. Zilch. Not a sign of Harvey at the fourth-floor help desk either.

What now? Her friends' Google reconnaissance had been far more successful than her surveillance. Grumpy and feeling like she'd wasted her time (and let herself get overexcited with the thrill of the hunt), Robin decided to drown her disappointment in espresso. She got on line at the top floor café.

The line was, of course, *endless,* which Robin always took as a personal insult. She eavesdropped on the man and woman in front of her. From the back, he was tall, broad, dark-haired, and annoyingly chatty. The woman was petite, so young she was actually green— a chlorine blonde—and just as loquacious as the guy. They talked at the same time, not listening to each other as their words tumbled forth, making no sense but a lot of noise. When the girl turned profile, Robin noticed her Bluetooth earpiece. The guy also turned to look at the baked goods in the display case, and Robin saw his earpiece. They weren't talking to each other at all, but into their gizmos. This was modern life. Too many people in a too-small space, moving at a crawl toward meaningless short-term gratification, disinterested in those around them. Everyone here, on line, in the store, in this frigging city, was totally oblivious.

Robin exhaled and then thought, "I'm old." When had it happened? She was only thirty-seven, but she was just as haggard, angry, bitter, and bloodthirsty as Madame Defarge.

Would espresso help or hurt the sudden onset of rage? Did she really want it? Just as it was her turn to order, Robin decided to leave, save her dollars and sanity, and get the hell out of there. She turned around, zipped out of the café, and got on the elevator going down. On the next level, a trio of men stood on the metal plate where the elevator ended, literally blocking people as they tried to step off. Yet another example, thought Robin, of the epidemic inconsideration. Nothing pissed her off like idiots selfishly blocking the flow of human traffic. Robin often heard herself mutter "Move it!" to kids at Brownstone who loitered in the middle of a busy stairwell or hovered in doorways, forcing other students to push through the clogged space. It was all about movement, this city, and when morons gummed up the works, Robin's temper sizzled.

"Get out of the fucking way," she seethed at the trio of men as she approached, actually checking one of them in the arm as she nudged her way around them.

He glared at her, his eyes narrow, angry, and Robin enjoyed the reaction. But then it changed. His eyes went wide, surprised, suspicious, doubtful, and then back to good, clean anger.

"Melanie Wilkes," he said to her.

In a flash of recall, Robin remembered that she'd used that name the night she met and bedded Harvey Wilson, the very man fuming at her right now. She hadn't recognized him without his helmet.

"Back from the plantation?" he asked.

The other two men—customers? co-workers?—drifted away. "I'm sorry," said Robin, wondering why and what she was apologizing for.

"You *are* the woman I think you are?" he asked. "New Year's Eve 1999?"

She couldn't help blushing. Harvey was very direct—and confrontational. "Yes, I remember you. I'm a little surprised you recognized me."

A woman with shopping bags stepped off the elevator and said, "Pardon me, you're in the way."

Robin snapped, "Mind your own business."

Harvey frowned, and took Robin by the elbow, leading her three steps away. He said, "You do look different. But I never forget a face."

"My face was a lot rounder then."

"Same face," he said. "The eyes are colder."

Ouch. "It is December," she said.

He would have none of her banter. "Why Melanie Wilkes?" he asked. "Because you were gone with the wind?"

Exactly, Robin thought. Her little joke-to-self. *Heh.* "No one who knew me back then recognizes me now. And we were . . . together . . . only that one night."

"Partial night," he said.

Robin was flummoxed by his bitterness. She'd assumed that, if she found him and he remembered her, he'd be embarrassed by her making contact. Or confused. Or flattered. But angry? She'd done him a favor by sneaking out. Like he'd want to wake up next to the biggest (literally) mistake of his sexual life? "It seemed polite to let myself out," she said. "Really, I'm shocked you remember me."

"You remember me," he said.

Well, he *was* the father of her child. Looking at Harvey Wilson now, she could see the obvious resemblance to Stephanie. He'd given her daughter the full lips, the diamond-shaped face, the inquisitive brow. Stephanie was a beautiful girl, and her father was a handsome man. Solidly built. Good genes. Robin was glad to see this tall healthy male in front of her, knowing instinctually that he was physically sound and healthy with clear skin, bright hazel eyes, thick dark hair. The relief of his strong presence, knowing that Stephanie had inherited it, made Robin's eyes moist. She rubbed them as if adjusting her vision.

She blinked at him a few times, and said, "You look well."

Harvey nodded. "You've lost weight?"

She chuckled at the remark. The gross understatement might've been a dig, but it was too mild to inflict damage. Robin said, "Pound or two," and tried to move the conversation forward. "Tell me about you"—she made a show of reading his name tag—"Harvey. What've you been doing all this time?"

"Working," he said.

"Married?" she asked, even though she knew he wasn't.

"Was," he said, "to another woman who lied."

Oh, Gawd, thought Robin. Stephanie's father was a hostile misogynist. She had to laugh at her ridiculous fantasy that Harvey Wilson would turn out to be kind and gentle and step seamlessly into their lives, filling an assortment of empty holes.

Okay, she thought, *I came to get a good look, and I've done that.* "Nice to see you again, Harvey," she said. "Let's do it again in another decade."

"Just tell me your real name," he said. "I tried to find you, you know. Back then."

"Robin Stern," she replied, not seeing the harm. Her name was common enough—the Jewish equivalent of Jane Smith. He'd never find her, no matter how vigorous his Googling. Besides, why would he come looking? There was nothing here. Robin held out her hand to shake good-bye. It had taken five minutes to satisfy ten-plus years of doubt. She was confident she'd done the right thing, keeping Stephanie to herself.

• — •

"He *what?*" shrieked Robin.

"He's a blogger. He blogs. And you are excellent material," said Alicia, inspecting her cards. They were at Carla's black lacquered table, laden with the same oily supermarket antipasti platter as last time.

"Why didn't you tell me about this the half second after you saw it?"

"Why didn't you tell us you went to see him?" replied Alicia.

"Yes, Robin," said Carla, peeking at her cards. "It's not like you to withhold information. Any information. The details about your last bowel movement, for example."

As if these women had any clue what Robin withheld or divulged. The assumed familiarity at their committee meetings was starting to bug her. "You've all read his post?" she asked. Robin had stopped visiting his blog after their run-in. No point, she figured.

Bess coughed, recovered, and said, "I haven't seen it."

"You're not over that cold yet?" asked Carla, examining Bess across the table, doing the physician once-over twice. "It's been a month."

"This is a new one," said Bess, waving off the concern. "Four kids. It's like this all winter. We take turns being sick."

"I must see what Harvey wrote about me," said Robin, standing. "Take me to the nearest computer, *now*."

"We're in the middle of a hand," said Carla. "And I'm going to win it. So please sit *down*. You can read it later."

"Did you feel attracted to him?" said Alicia, vicarious excitement seeking.

"It's always sex with you. Sex or no sex," said Robin to the celibate brunette, who, now that she considered it, was looking considerably less frumpy tonight. A-line skirt? Clingy silk blouse? High-heeled booties? Alicia was verging on chic. And, dear God, was she wearing blush, too, or was it a natural glow? Perhaps Robin wasn't the only one among them keeping secrets. "How's Tim lately?" she asked. "And that guy in your office. What's his name again? Shark?"

"It's Finn," said Alicia, "and he's fine. Raise five."

"Reraise ten," said Carla.

"Fold," said Robin. "While you guys finish the hand, let me quickly check my email. The computer is . . . ?"

Carla, the evening's host, said, "In my bedroom, and you are not going up there. The boys are doing homework and I don't want them bothered."

Robin longingly gazed at the stairs from her seat at Carla's dining room table. Looking up, she saw the two boys on the landing up top, their heads leaning over the banister to spy on the women. Robin made eye contact with Zeke, her daughter's classmate, and winked. The boy giggled and ducked out of sight.

Bess said, "I fold, too." The blonde reached into her leather purse, rooting around until she found her iPhone. She said, "I've got Internet. Urban off road, right?"

Alicia said, "Do a dramatic reading."

Bess laughed. "I don't want to embarrass Robin," she said, and then sneezed. Even spewing mucus, she was prettily dainty.

"Why the hell not?" asked Carla.

"She said 'hell.' First you let me open a bottle of wine in the house and now you're cursing?" said Robin to her host. "Next thing you know, it's shooting heroin."

"Shhh," said Carla, instinctively leaning forward to peer up the stairs. She caught a glimpse of movement, and a flicker of alarm crossed Carla's strong features. "Boys!" she boomed, loud enough to make Robin flinch. The kids didn't wait for instructions. The sound of scampering feet from the floor above put them in their rooms, doors closed.

Alicia dealt the river card. Carla raised and won the hand with a jack-high flush. The host was on fire tonight. "Another winner for the Black Queen," she said, raking in the chips. To Bess, Carla directed, "Okay, let's hear it. And make it good."

"I would prefer to read it myself, in private," said Robin.

"Too bad," said Carla, and gestured for Bess to go ahead.

The blonde nodded and squinted at the tiny iPhone screen. "I can't see anything anymore." Holding the gadget at arm's reach, she adjusted her vision. "Why are these screens so small?"

"For Christ's sake!" blasted Robin. "Give me that thing!"

Bess held her off, laughing, sneezing.

Alicia, in the scuffle, grabbed the iPhone and said, "I'll read it. *Ahem*. Here we go: urban off-road biker blog, entry dated three days ago. 'I'm sure all of you are dying to hear about the 20K in Central Park last weekend, and I'll get right to it. But first, a brief recount of my dip into the weird this week: a chance run-in with a one-night stand from my past. I was helping some customers at the store and this redhead barrels into me, ranting about blocking the aisle, flying elbows. Subtle? Like a frying pan to the skull. I was reminded of the night I met this woman, how she plowed through a crowd of a hundred thousand in Times Square like it was human butter. So there she was, glaring at me, nostrils flaring. Despite a change in her appearance, I recognized her. She'd lost a lot of weight. Too much. Skinny on her looked old, hard, and bitchy. Last time I'd seen her, she was naked in my bed, soft and sweet, postorgasmic.' "

"Postorgasmic?" shrieked Robin. "That's a lie!"

The women laughed (insensitive wenches!). Bess asked, " 'Postorgasmic' bugs you, but you're okay with 'old, hard, and bitchy'?"

Robin shrugged, "Except for 'old.' "

Alicia continued. " 'We acknowledged our first (and only) meeting, and I asked her how she's been. Then she bit my freaking head off! Like I was the one who sneaked off in the middle of the night without an explanation or apology. I immediately made assumptions about how the last decade had treated her. I know it's wrong to assume. I could have tried to confirm my theories. But it would've been rude to ask her, 'Exactly how long *has* that broom been shoved up your ass?' "

Laughter again from the committee members. Robin said, "It didn't go down like this at all. He's twisting the encounter for comic effect. And he's anally fixated."

Carla said, "Well, you would know."

All four women tittered at that. "Keep reading," said Robin.

Alicia said, "That's pretty much it. Just a parting shot: 'Can't believe I'd pined for this woman for an embarrassingly long time. The book on her? Officially closed.' "

"So he liked me fat," said Robin. "I was always suspicious of the chubby-chasers. I hated being the object of a fetish."

Bess said, "I know what you mean. A lot of men have a thing for blondes."

"Oh, shut up, please," said Robin. "If liking blondes makes you a perv, then every man alive is a fetishist." She took a long draw from her glass.

Alicia said, "Fetishist. Sounds like inferior quality goat cheese."

Carla started shuffling and dealing the cards. "The correct term is 'paraphiliac.' And I think what Harvey wrote was nice."

Robin nearly choked on her wine. "He portrayed me as a raving witch."

"Who rides her broom in a very interesting way," added Alicia.

Bess said, "I agree with Carla. He had a real thing for you. He was hurt when you left in the middle of the night. I don't get chubby-chaser from the way he wrote about you. A man could describe *any* woman as soft and sweet. Soft isn't secret code for fat. The guy recognized you ten years and two hundred pounds later. He liked you, you ditched him, he's still pissed about it."

"Which makes him insane and pathetic," said Robin.

"Is that a step up or down from the guys you're used to dating?" asked Alicia.

The truth was, Robin hadn't been on a date in months. She was simply too angry at the world these days to be open to anyone. She wasn't even interested in anonymous sex with a stranger. "I got an email last night from a guy I dated back in September," she said, looking at her cards. "We had dinner at the Heights Cafe, walked on the Promenade. Talked. It was all very bland and tiring. I said I'd do him anyway. He turned me down—*then*. Four months later, he wants to know if the offer is still good."

Robin shook her head and sighed. When she looked up, she noticed that all three woman's eyes were on her, examining her expression, trying to take her emotional temperature. The sympathy was almost unbearable.

"When you look at me like you feel sorry for me," Robin said to the group, "it only makes me madder."

7

Bess

"What, no stirrups?" asked Bess. She was naked under the paper gown, sliding toward the end of the exam table.

Dr. Able (comforting name for the man holding the speculum), said, "I got new tables two years ago. No stirrups, just the slide out platform for your feet. Women tell me they prefer it."

"I guess it has been a while since I last saw you," she said guiltily. Like most mothers, Bess never missed her kids' annual checkups, and took them to the pediatrician at the slightest sign of trouble. But she'd been hard-pressed to make time for or keep her own annual appointments. Carla insisted Bess get some blood drawn, though, since she'd been sick for so long. She was here, might as well get the royal treatment. Smear, blood, urine. A full body-fluids check.

Scooting to the edge of the table, Bess rested her feet on the slide-out platform, and spread her knees wide, the paper gown stretching and crinkling with each movement. "Oh, yes, this is much more dignified," she said.

Dr. Able said, "Okay, my hands are on your thighs. I'm parting the vaginal lips. I'm inserting the speculum . . ."

She knew the play-by-play was meant to prepare her for his latex touch, but she could have done without it. After four kids, she was practically a gynecologist herself, and had long ago lost any modesty about her vagina. It'd been splayed before dozens of people, had seen a lot of action. It was practically public property.

She felt the cervical scrape, and then the hasty removal of the plastic tool. Dr. Able said, "Most women hold their breath when I do that, followed by the dramatic exhale when it's over."

"I've been telling you for years, Doctor. I'm not like other women," she said.

He prepared the sample for transport, changed his gloves, and then moved to the side of the table. "Slip your arms out of the gown and lower it, please."

Breast exam time. "I should mention that I've had a nagging cold forever," said Bess, lowering the gown. "I made excuses for it, but then I read an article about a woman who ignored chronic headaches, put off going to the doctor, until she dropped dead from a massive brain tumor."

"You suspect a brain tumor?" he asked.

"Sinus infection," she said. "That could creep into my brain and kill me."

Dr. Able laughed. "I can give you antibiotics to treat a sinus infection. I'll take a look. But if you haven't keeled over yet, I'd say you probably just have a persistent cold. Arms over your head, please."

She complied. The doctor reached for her left breast. While he pressed into it, Bess closed her eyes, and relaxed. She tried to remember the last time she'd had a massage. Five years ago? An anniversary gift from Borden that took six months to find its way into her schedule. It'd been a relaxing hour at a spa in the city, but then she'd come home to chaos, the part-time babysitter overwhelmed by the boys' running around, the kitchen a disaster, Amy furious at her for who knows what reason.

Bess tried to remember the last time Amy hadn't been angry or annoyed with her. When she was ten? Eleven? Back then, Amy had been madly in love with Bess. They'd walked down the street holding hands, smiling into each other's faces, going on girls-only shopping trips to the city, and then dinners of French fries and hot chocolate at a diner. Time was, Amy came to Bess to hash over every social squabble ("and *then*, she was like . . ." "and *then*, I was like . . ."). They'd pore over nuance of tone, especially when a boy called Amy ("about homework, yeah, right," said the cynical sixth-grader). Bess believed she could feel any emotion Amy experienced. She felt Amy's joy and pain, had total maternal empathy.

And now? Gone. Bess had no idea what Amy felt or thought about. She tried to understand her daughter, but Amy's black curtain of disdain was impenetrable. Bess longed for the old days, giggling in a booth over milk shakes or hot chocolate. Maybe Amy would agree to a dinner at Teresa's, just the two of them. No pressure, no demands or confrontation. Just some face time. Some eye contact. Exchange of simple words. Hello. How are you? When Amy was home, she holed up in her room. Usually, the teen was out with friends, whoever they were. Bess couldn't help notice—with mixed emotions—that Amy wasn't wearing her Stella McCartney outfits anymore, the ones Simone bought for her in London. A rejection of Simone-style? More likely because, as Bess also couldn't help but notice, Amy had put on some weight lately. At least ten pounds.

Bess's consciousness returned to her boob. Dr. Able seemed riveted by a particular area.

"What?" she asked.

"How long has this been here?" he asked, taking her hand and placing her index finger on the spot.

"I don't feel . . . *oh*," she said, finding what felt like a coffee bean about a half an inch deep under the skin.

Dr. Able felt around her armpit, and her neck, then he said, "Let me check the other breast."

She put her other arm over her head. Finding nothing on the right side, he removed his gloves and asked her to sit up. Taking a seat at the desk, he started typing into his computer.

Bess said, "Well?"

"Five millimeter mass in the upper left quadrant of the left breast," he said. "It's always the left. Someone should do a study."

Bess nodded. Her boob felt tender where they'd been worrying the coffee bean. "Mass, meaning *what* exactly?" she asked.

He said, "Could be anything. I'm writing a referral to the imaging center on Joralemon Street. Go there now. I'll have Belinda call to tell them you're coming."

"I have a Parents Association meeting at the kids' school," she said. "I'm chairwoman of the winter fund-raiser. It's a major planning meeting. I have to go."

Dr. Able frowned. "How long is the meeting?"

"All afternoon," she said, a spark of fear starting to prickle along her spine. But faint. A twinge, sure to worsen by the minute. For a strange illogical moment, Bess felt a wave of fear about how afraid she was going to be in an hour, in two hours, if the bean turned out to be . . . *don't go there yet*, she admonished herself.

"Bess?" he asked. "Are you okay?"

"I can miss the start of the meeting," she said.

"I'm sure they can get along without you," he said.

⬤━━━⬤

I'm sure they can get along without you, thought Bess as she walked to get the mammogram.

I'm sure they can get along without you, she thought as the technician pancaked each of her breasts (both, just to be sure) between the glass plates from multiple angles. The technicians took the pictures, but they wouldn't give her their assessment. Bess would have to wait to hear from Dr. Able, who would be notified as soon as their staff doctor had a chance to examine the film.

Fortunately, the imaging office was in the basement of the medical arts building on Joralemon Street, only a block from the Brownstone Institute. Bess rushed to school, the urgent gathering she'd organized, to plan the all-important winter party/fund-raiser. The Parents Association (aka PA) sponsored a dozen events over the course of the school year, but the winter party was Bess's baby. Even though all decisions were made by the committee, Bess had final say. She'd fought for her smidgeon of power, and aimed to hang on to it, despite some pushing back.

Now her control issues about the party seemed to be the concerns from another dimension. From her parallel universe, Bess could still dredge up the agenda she'd planned, the purpose of this meeting. It was strange, she thought, as she entered the PA's basement office at Brownstone spouting apologies to the gathered moms, that she could be aware of her own denial, and yet continue to enjoy its effects.

The dozen women seated around a rectangular table smiled and welcomed her. She'd known some of them since Amy was in preschool—thirteen years ago; it seemed impossible. Bess was well entrenched in the school's social strata, and this group of women represented the upper echelons. They were uniformly rich, attractive, yoga-hard homemakers. If they'd had careers before kids, their professional ambitions were distant memories. Miraculously, there wasn't a divorcée in the group, although Bess had been propositioned by nearly all of their husbands, in a playfully safe manner, e.g., putting his hand on her ass, and then saying something lame like, "Oops, how did that get there? My bad."

Among Brownstone fathers, the masters of the universe types (severely downgraded these days, of course) seemed committed to the juvenile sexuality of their frat boy pasts. Except Borden. He was a well-mannered grown man. She fleetingly wondered if Borden's hand had ever found its way to any of these women's behinds at a drunken party over the years. No way. Not possible. He loved only her. Her body. But would he feel the same way if she was minus one boob? The left boob. *"It's always the left,"* Dr. Able had said.

"So glad you could make it," said Anita Turnbull, a "my life is my kids" flag-waver—exactly the kind of woman Bess's feminist mother saved her greatest contempt for. "We've made great progress."

Glad you could make it? This was Bess's meeting. "Wonderful," she said, part relieved that she hadn't been asked to explain where she'd been, part resentful that her absence hadn't been a problem. "Bring me up to speed."

"Do you mind if we keep moving forward?" asked Anita. "Hate to break our momentum."

"Just a quick recap," said Bess, settling into her chair. "Did you vote on casino night or an auction? I prefer an auction, myself. The donations are always so cool. Last year, remember that one family donated a weekend in Tuscany? And that father who's a producer on *The View* got a backstage pass . . ."

"We picked casino night," interrupted Anita. "With the recession, we thought an auction wouldn't be as lucrative as in years past. We're up to item eight on the agenda."

The agenda that Bess had spent hours preparing. "Great," she said, feigning enthusiasm. "Casino night, it is. Did you vote on a theme? 'Caribbean' is a nice idea for the middle of the winter . . ."

"We picked 'The Seventies,' " said Anita with a tight grin. "Sorry, I hate to sound impatient. But you were late. We're on a roll. And I've got a two o'clock."

"A two o'clock *what*? Shrink session? What could possibly be so important?" asked Bess, a snide edge in her voice.

The women around the table suddenly perked up, smelling blood. Bess and Anita stared at each other, not bothering to pretend-smile.

Why would Bess feel threatened? It was embarrassing. The PA had elected Bess to be their president. She was the well-liked event chair. Anita, on the other hand, was a self-important Martha Stewart wannabe who spent hours hand-crafting her kids' party invites, baked mountains of brownies, and shlepped her kids to fencing and gymnastics thrice a week. She was a Robo-Mom, a helicopter parent, a manic speck. The woman was already boasting about her ten-year-old's legacy at Harvard. Anita poured every ounce of her hopes and dreams into the flesh buckets of her children. Without them, she didn't exist.

Bess's chest rose and fell, her sudden flare of antipathy shortening her breath. It was not like her to judge so meanly. The coffee bean, poked aggressively by Dr. Able and the mammogram technician, started to throb. Bess tried to get control of herself. Instead, she suffered a rip in her consciousness, an opening of self-awareness that asked, *What makes you better than Anita?* How dare she look down her nose at this woman who showed more creativity and energy as a mother than Bess did? Sure, Bess went through the motions. She baked. She made Valentine's Day cards. Her kids were well dressed and exercised. She packed healthy lunches. She was active in the PA. As the event chair, she should care if the winter fund-raiser was a casino or an auction, Caribbean or Seventies. She should care if her kids went to Harvard.

The opening in her consciousness widened, and Bess realized with a gasp that she *didn't* care—about organizing the fund-raiser, or getting her kids into Harvard, packing healthy lunches, making cutesy party invites. Yes, of course, she loved her children and husband. But did she love *doing* for them? Did she love her day-to-day existence of making other people's lives run smoothly? She was stuck in a loop of 24/7/365 service, errands, and chores. It would be insane for anyone to suggest this was a satisfying, fulfilling existence. And yet, this was the life she chose.

Did Anita truly, deeply, personally *love* this life? Apparently so.

Bess's contempt for her happy homemaker "friend" shifted to jealousy. Anita was happy; Bess was sick of her life. Quite possibly, she was sick from it, too.

If she'd ever wondered what it would take to turn a critical eye on herself, Bess now knew. A five-millimeter mass had done the trick. It was a testament to how crazy-busy Bess had been, that she hadn't had a moment to think about her own dissatisfaction and emptiness. *A mystery mass makes time*, she thought. *It stops time.* But only for an instant. Then the specter of cancer—finally, she used the word in her head—sped everything up.

With the dozen pairs of eyes locked on her face, Bess tried to come up with a single thing she truly, deeply, personally loved doing.

"I love playing cards," she said to herself out loud. "I love it and I'm good at it."

Anita repeated, "Cards."

Bess turned toward the voice and nodded. "Poker. With my friends."

Another mother, Cheryl Baker, said, "I've never played poker with you. Who do you play with?" Over the years, Cheryl had been at Bess's house for dinner parties scores of times. They'd gone on shopping expeditions to Woodbury Commons, their kids had regular playdates. They'd consumed a bathtub of coffee after hundreds of drop-offs. Cheryl had every right to be confused. Wasn't she Bess's friend? A close friend? Each of these women had been her "friend" for years. They were all wondering the same thing, so loud Bess could hear their thoughts: *Who are Bess's card-playing friends, and why hasn't she invited me to play with them?*

It was like junior high redux. Bess, the Ruling Class Queen, breaking popular girl rules by affiliating with the lowly fringe dwellers. Would the other popular girls cast Bess out for socializing below her status? She could admit that she had a card klatch with a trio of undesirables (as these women would see them). Instead, Bess said to Cheryl, and the others, "Old friends. No one you know."

"Should we have poker tables at casino night?" asked Anita, mercifully getting the conversation back on track.

"Yes," said Bess, gratefully. "That's exactly my point. We'll hire dealers, keep the booze flowing, and rake in the bucks. Can you see it? A mirrored ball hanging from the gym ceiling? Disco music? 'Funky Town'?"

A few of the women liked the sound of it. The rest joined in, and the talk resumed a purposeful tone. The women were clearly relieved that Bess had returned to normal. The meeting continued for another hour, the mood light. At two o'clock, they ended it so Anita could rush off to her appointment, which turned out to be a haircut.

No one dared asked Bess about her one-minute mental lapse, although she was sure they'd gossip about it later ("What was *that* about?"). Bess took it upon herself to apologize to Anita for snapping. After all, Anita meant well. She was harmless. Bess was ashamed of herself for thinking critically of her.

When she stepped outside the school, she waited for the others to go their separate ways (in pairs and trios). Then she called Dr. Able's office. The receptionist asked her to hold, and then came back on the line saying Dr. Able was talking to the radiologist right now, and he'd call her back in a few minutes. Not wanting to take that call alone in her empty house, and with an hour to kill before pick-up, Bess went across the street to Traviata, an Italian restaurant. She sat down at the bar, ordered a vodka tonic. Taking her first sip, she thought, *I needed that.*

Dr. Able hadn't called back by the end of the first, or second, cocktail. It was close to 3:00 p.m., pick-up time. Bess got off her chair, felt woozy from the vodka, and put a twenty on the bar. She drew herself up, remembering that she was a lady, and walked as soberly as possible across the street to collect Charlie and Tom, her two younger sons. Amy and eighth-grader Eric had keys and were allowed to find their own way home. It was Eric's first year with key privilege, and he'd been responsible with it, often beating Bess, Charlie, and Tom back to Clinton Street. Amy, however, seemed to enjoy pushing

Bess's anxiety to the limit, not showing up at their townhouse until after six o'clock, the dinner hour, and then refusing to say where she'd been, what she was doing, and with whom.

Bess's cell phone vibrated in her pants pocket. She answered it just as she found Charlie and Tom in the lobby at Brownstone. "Hold on, one second," she said in the phone, and pointed the boys in the direction of home. Charlie tried to say something to her, but she silenced him, saying, "I'm on the phone." The boys shut up, and they walked the three blocks home quietly.

Bess was quiet, too, listening to Dr. Able explain the mammogram findings. In a nutshell (or a coffee bean), the lump in Bess's left breast appeared to be self-contained (good) and dense (also good). But, at this point, it was impossible to tell from imaging alone whether the mass was benign or malignant. The lump would have to come out to be tested.

Bess's mother, Simone Gertrude, had been presented with exactly the same recommendation twenty years ago. Simone's lumpectomy had turned into a radical mastectomy, and another bestseller, *Report from the Front*. The book politicized Simone's cancer experience, criticizing the medical establishment for their love of cutting up women's bodies, the pressure she felt from her male doctors to have a breast reconstructed, and their utter bafflement when she decided not to. She challenged the notions that a woman wasn't complete without cleavage. "Breasts made me a mammal, but not a woman," Simone famously wrote. Her controversial ideas started an antireconstruction movement, short-lived as it was. Simone herself eventually had a reconstruction.

When Bess read *Report*, she'd been impressed by how many slang words her mother knew for breast. Simone used coarse language; she wrote the way men did to describe female objects of lust, envy, and scorn. Simone described her own breast as a sack of fat and tissue, having, apparently, zero emotional attachment to it. Simone hadn't breast-fed Bess and her brothers.

Like many nineties mothers these days, Bess breast-fed all four of her children—for nine months each. She'd been a dedicated dairy bar, in part, because nursing was supposed to prevent breast cancer. She often reflected on specific nursing moments with each of her kids, their infant eyes closed, little lips moving rhythmically, with love and joy. Her breasts had served a purpose, both physical and emotional. Bess had a nostalgic association with her boobs. They'd developed early, at eleven, during the happiest years of her childhood when her father was still alive. As she got older, Bess loved her breasts for how they stopped men in their tracks, filled out a sweater, felt comforting in her own hands. Bess would not politicize her body parts, if those arguments were still being made. If her breast was removed, she'd be devastated. She'd mourn the loss of a part of herself. Simone had been lucky. No recurrence. Bess took heart in that.

If Bess seemed anxious on the short walk from school, Charlie and Tom didn't ask her about it. Once home, the kids were easily diverted by snacks. Bess ushered them into the kitchen, poured milk, and handed over an entire bag of cookies (usually, she plated a few). Then she went up three flights to her private bathroom, locked herself in, and was preparing to cry when her cell vibrated.

"Bess? What's going on?" It was Carla.

"Carla! I was going to call you." She'd thought of calling her doctor buddy, but hadn't had the chance yet.

"Zeke and Manny are waiting for you at Brownstone," said Carla. "You were supposed to pick them up today."

Shit. "I forgot," said Bess. They'd made the arrangement when Carla was the big winner at the last poker night. "I'll go to school right now."

"Thank. You." Then Carla hung up.

Bess would have to postpone her cry. She went back into the kitchen and told her kids that they had to run back to Brownstone and get the Morgans.

Charlie said, "Mom, that's what I was trying to tell you when you told me to shut up."

Bess said, "I did not say 'Shut up.' "

Tom nodded. "You did."

"Let's go," she said. "Manny and Zeke are waiting."

"Can't we wait here by ourselves?" Charlie protested.

"You're too young," she said.

"It's ten minutes," said Tom.

"Fine," said Bess. "Don't eat anything until I get back. If you choke, I won't be here to Heimlich you."

They rolled their eyes. She put her coat back on, and put the bag of cookies in her purse. As if that would stop them from eating anything else in the house.

Bess ran to school, found Carla's Zeke and Manny in the lobby, apologized profusely; the over-the-top groveling made the two boys shrink into each other with embarrassment.

They followed her out of Brownstone, walking a step or two behind her as she stomped back to Clinton Street. Her hands deep in her pockets, Bess visualized the scene of telling Borden about her day, Dr. Able's office, the mammogram, PA meeting, multiple round-trips to Brownstone. She pictured them in their bedroom, after lights out, where and when they always had their talks. Late night was their only opportunity to pay each other undivided attention.

Behind her, she heard Carla's kids giggling. She looked in the direction of their eyes, and saw a couple of teenagers making out on a stoop on Joralemon Street.

Bess's first thought: *They must be freezing.*

Second thought: *I recognize that coat. It's Amy. She's kissing a boy.*

The teens untangled themselves when they realized they'd drawn a crowd. Bess's third thought: *That is not a boy.*

Blinking in confusion, amazement, embarrassment, and several other emotions her mind was too overwhelmed to process, Bess made a small *urp* sound. The Morgan boys, realizing that one of the kissing girls on the stoop was their friends' sister and their own erstwhile babysitter, stepped backward a pace, their eyes huge O's.

Amy, red-faced and puffy (she had gained a lot of weight), shouted to her mother, "What're you looking at?"

Bess said, "Aren't you going to introduce me to your friend?"

Which inspired Amy to grab her girlfriend (?) by the wrist, and scream, "Can't you leave me alone? I hate you! I wish you were dead!"

What could a mother do but start laughing? Her daughter hated her and wished she were dead. This coming only half an hour after Bess had received the news that she might have breast cancer. The irony was too precious.

"And, one day, your wish will be granted," said Bess. "Until then, do you prefer to sit out here in the cold or would you like to come home? Please bring your friend, who must have a name."

Amy was too flooded with adolescent hormones to calm down. Bess watched her daughter's mouth fly as accusations tumbled out— Bess was spying, violating Amy's privacy, not respecting her individuality. Bess wondered, given the fullness of time, if Amy would ever regret this moment. Should Bess's coffee bean turn out to be malignant, should the cancer spread through her body, consume her organs, kill her in her prime, would Amy feel ashamed of ranting at her mother on the street in front of other people?

On one level, Bess understood that Amy was acting like an escaped mental patient because she was in some kind of emotional pain. The glint of maternal empathy was barely detectable. At the moment, Bess felt only her own hurt and anger.

Amy had been handed everything. She'd been loved, placed in the sun, nurtured, tended, and given room to grow. Bess mutely stared at her oldest child's lips twisted in rage, and couldn't understand what she'd done wrong.

Finally, raving monster Amy stopped. The sudden absence of sound was almost louder than the screeching. Then, Amy asked, "Have you heard a single word I said?"

Bess replied, "I left the boys alone at home. I have to go." She turned on her heel, and continued to Clinton Street. Zeke and Manny followed closely. When Bess peeked at them, they seemed astonished. Surely, they didn't see such fireworks in their house. Their family's style was to strike silent blows. She could only imagine what they'd tell Carla about this scene, if they said anything.

They arrived home. Charlie and Tom had not choked on food while she was out. Zeke and Manny ran up to the boys' room, and began doing whatever it was they did. Bess went into her room to lie down. And she didn't get up.

When the boys came into her room looking for dinner, she told them to order a pizza and take the money out of her wallet. When Carla came later to pick up her kids, Bess barely heard the sound of the buzzer, but she did catch the stampede of sneakers down the stairs. She assumed Zeke and Manny let themselves out.

"Are you sick?" Borden asked, upon finding her flat out on the bed, fully dressed at eight o'clock at night.

Sick? She might be *dying*. But, yes, she'd take sick. And tired. Sick and tired of caring for everyone, and no one caring for/about her. For all she'd done for her children, none of them had shown the slightest interest in why their mother was in bed all afternoon and evening.

"They can get along without you," said Dr. Able.

Bess pulled a pillow over her head. Muffled, she asked Borden, "Is Amy home?"

"Don't you know?" he asked in return.

"Just check."

"Okay," he said, and then walked out of their room and down a flight. Bess could hear him knocking loudly on Amy's door.

Murmurs, voices bounced off the hallway, and up the stairs. Amy was home. She'd slipped in at some point. Bess felt her back muscles relax at the knowledge that her entire family was present and accounted for, even if some of its members were ungrateful brats.

They'd be sorry when she was dead. Just to make sure, Bess intended to put that in her will. "To my children," she'd stipulate. "I bequeath all my worldly possessions, and a lifetime of feeling sorry that I'm dead."

When her father died, Bess had felt plenty sorry, for him and herself. Twenty-five years later, she was still sorry. Fifteen-year-old Bess had been just as self-absorbed as Amy. She'd barely gotten to know her father while he was alive. Once he was gone, she got deeply acquainted with missing him. But a parent was never completely gone. His genes were in her; his kindness, consideration, and patience.

Turned out, Bess *had* inherited something from her mother besides feline bone structure and height—the ticking time bomb in her breast. A new wave of resentment for Simone washed over her. Despite the rancor of the moment, it felt good to have a new reason to hate her mother.

Would Amy get breast cancer, too? She would, of course, blame Bess for it.

At what point would it be appropriate, she wondered, to send out invitations to her Pity Party?

Borden reentered their bedroom and closed the door. "Okay, the boys are watching TV, Amy is crying in her bedroom," he said. "I heard you two had a fight?" Borden took off his suit jacket and undid his tie.

"With you, she's Daddy's little girl," said Bess. "I'm the Wicked Witch of the West."

"Just tell me what happened."

"I might have breast cancer. I have a lump that needs to be biopsied," said Bess. "I think that grants me an afternoon in bed."

Borden was on her in a flash. He rolled her onto her back, and started hugging her, petting her hair and kissing her cheeks. He didn't ask any questions, demand an explanation, or act hurt she hadn't called him earlier. His instinctual reaction was to hold and help. Bess had married a good man. She immediately burst into tears.

Once she'd cried herself out, she unraveled the story. Borden said, "So you don't know yet. It could be nothing."

"My mother's breast cancer presented when she was around my age."

"I don't care if you lose a boob. I'll be just as attracted to you as ever. Even more."

"That's simply not true," she said.

"Let's not decide it's cancer," he said, ever the optimist. He stroked her shoulders and arms, his hands wandering to her chest. "Where is it?"

She lifted her shirt and bra and guided him the bean. He said, "I feel it. It's tiny, Bess. Does it hurt?"

"A little, but only since I realized I had it."

"How could I have missed it?" he asked.

"You're not a breast man," she said.

"Who says I'm not?" he replied. "I love your breasts, and I stupidly neglect them. Never again." He proceeded to lavish attention on her breasts—left and right. She felt his erection against her hip.

"A lump turns you on," she said. "Is there anything that turns you off?"

"I told you," he said, between kisses. "I am your slave, your servant. One breast, no breasts. Bald, skinny, I don't care."

Bess and Borden made love that night. Her breath, she knew, was sour from her nap and skipping dinner. But that didn't stop him from kissing her, pecks and deep mouth melds, while he lay on top of her. He was careful, treated her gently, like a precious, fragile doll. When he wasn't kissing her, he was watching her face, promising without words that he'd never look away. The attention Borden paid to Bess's face, to her lips and eyes, was far more erotic and exciting for her than his usual crotchcentric focus. When she came, a slow-creeping orgasm, it was a surprise and a spinesapper. She felt boneless and blissed out after, emptied of her anxiety.

Sadly, the relief was temporary. Her apprehension returned after only a few minutes. She would carry her fear in her chest until it was surgically removed. Perhaps Borden would be ready to go again soon. Bess could easily imagine how a cancer diagnosis might turn someone into a sex maniac.

"I'd want you to marry again," she said to her husband as they lay in each other's arms. "The kids need a mother."

"You're not dying," he said. "Don't you think you'd know if you were? Intuitively?"

"Like how the bullet comes at you in slow motion," she said, "the one with your name on it?"

"Exactly," he said.

Bess searched her intuition for a clue to her fate. Was she dying? Was her lump the slow-motion bullet with her name on it? Only twelve hours since its discovery, her brain was simply not ready to go there. When she closed her eyes and searched her sixth sense, all she saw was the underside of her eyelids.

"Oh, I forgot to tell you," Bess added. "Your daughter is a lesbian."

‹───●══▶━›

Bess showed her full house to the committee members, queens over tens. "I'm a nihilist now," she announced.

"Nice non sequitur," said Robin, folding her cards and taking a single piece of popcorn from the bowl Alicia had put out for her guests. "So you've gone nihilist? Is that like going native?"

Tim said, "How do you make the conversational leap from 'Top Chef' to nihilism?"

Alicia said, "At the end of the day, doesn't it always come around to nihilism?"

"I'd rather it always came around to 'Top Chef,' " said Tim, folding his cards, jumping up from the couch, and jogging a few steps into the kitchen. "Who's ready to try my paella? Saffron imported from Spain."

Carla said, "I wish I lived over Fairway."

Robin said, "I wish I had a husband who cooked. Or just a husband."

Tim clarified, "I don't cook. I chef."

Robin and Bess made eye contact. The redhead mouthed, "Beyond gay."

Alicia whispered, "I saw that."

Robin said, "Tell us, Bess, what brought on your philosophical change?"

"Just thinking about life and death. What really matters," replied Bess.

"Oh, *that*." Robin gathered the cards and started dealing a new hand. "I had a near death experience once."

Alicia said, "When?"

"Back in my fat days," said Robin. "Walking down the steps at the Borough Hall subway station. I stumbled, fell, wound up on all fours, my skirt around my hips, giant granny panties and fish-white thighs exposed for all of Brooklyn to see."

Carla said, "And you nearly died of embarrassment?"

"I *did* die of embarrassment," said Robin. "Saw the light and everything. But I didn't go toward it. It wasn't my time."

Bess listened to the conversation, waiting for it to come back to her. She'd been looking forward to this meeting to tell her three friends (and Tim, a de facto inclusion since it was Alicia's turn to host) about the events of the last two weeks. The discovery of the lump, her renewed responsiveness with Borden (it was like they were newlyweds again), the ongoing frozen silence with Amy, her surgery at Memorial Sloan-Kettering, the week of pain and recovery.

The three days of waiting for a pathology report were the longest of her life—a life that would not be cut short by cancer, at least not yet. Her lump was benign, a calcified duct, left over from her breast-feeding days. Bess decided that the operation was a signpost, marking the end of the first half of her life and the beginning of the rest of it. She'd been afraid to die, but even more afraid that her death wouldn't matter. The world would get along fine without her, whether she died today, next year, or fifty years from now.

When some people had a cancer scare, she knew they rebounded with a commitment to love everything and everyone. Others reacted with anger at fate, God, their genes. Bess hadn't felt bursting with love or anger, but with disillusionment. In the larger scheme of things, there was no larger scheme. There was no smaller scheme, nor a medium-sized one. The fact that she was alive at all? An accident of nature. The point of existence? None to speak of. We were born, after which point we ate, slept, and trudged through time for a while. And then we stopped. If religion and morality were removed from the equation, duty and responsibility were irrelevant. Bess had been a slave to duty. The last two weeks had set her free.

It'd been a bumpy realization, that her children didn't really care what she did for them. She'd reacted against her mother's negligent parenting by devoting herself to her family. But, as it turned out, her kids would rather do more for themselves. During Bess's convalescence, the boys fought over who got to make dinner. Granted, heating up Bagel Bites wasn't on par with the meals she prepared. Again, that *didn't matter*. They been trying to tell her all along, saying, "I can do it myself," and "Let *me*." They'd been chafing for independence. She'd been trying to prolong their dependence. Their need gave her a purpose.

Her youngest, Charlie, in fourth grade, could peanut butter his own sandwich. He could fetch himself a glass of milk. What's more, he could make his own bed, do his own laundry, complete his homework. Tom was in sixth grade; Eric in eighth; Amy in tenth. She did them no favors, as children and future adults, by making their lives easy. Bess finally saw her mother's point. Practically speaking, Simone had helped Bess by leaving her on her own. Simone's emotional neglect was still unforgivable. But forcing Bess to learn coping skills? That wasn't a killing offense. Bess was resolved to take a giant step back, and let her children do more.

During her week in bed, Bess thought about what she'd do to find purpose outside her family. "What do I enjoy *doing?*" she asked herself repeatedly. Bess flashed way back in time, to before she was married, before kids, when she was single and selfish, her first three years in college. Those days were defined by novelty. Meeting new people. Trying new things. She'd had fun, in the collegiate tradition of having a lot of casual sex and experimenting with recreational drugs. Twenty years later, Bess vowed to find that feeling of fun again, but not, obviously, the same way. Borden supported the idea that the kids should do more for themselves and around the house, and that Bess should have "me time." But he didn't like the "nothing matters" rants.

"Your nihilism is bad for the children," he said, which made her laugh.

Bess peeked at her pocket cards. Two of hearts and five of diamonds. A terrible hand. Rags. She should fold.

She said, "Raise five."

Carla said, "Tim, the paella smells amazing."

Alicia said, "I hope it's done soon. I'm dying of hunger."

Robin said, "Is it spicy?"

"You bet," said Tim. He yelled, "Joe! Five minutes' dinner warning!"

"I can't eat it," sighed Robin. "Spicy makes my stomach crazy." She dealt the flop.

Nothing good for Bess. No pairs, nor a possible straight. She said, "Raise twenty."

Carla said, "You're raising twenty, no royals, no straight cards, no flush draws. Either you have a pair of aces, or you're bluffing."

Alicia folded. "All night long, she's had a pair of aces or was bluffing."

Robin folded, too. "A confounding new strategy?"

"It's called having fun," said Bess. "Life is short. I might as well go for it every hand."

Carla folded and said, "You're usually the first to fold."

Robin turned over Bess's pocket cards. "Squat."

"I bluffed," said Bess.

"You don't go from cautious to reckless overnight," said Robin. "*I* do, but you? No."

She thinks she knows me so well, thought Bess, who shrugged and said, "I had a lumpectomy last week."

Stunned silence from the women. Tim in the kitchen froze, mid-pour, and then spilled wine.

Carla said, "You didn't call me?"

"I didn't tell anyone," said Bess. "Except Borden and the kids."

"But I could have helped," said Carla, "or recommended a surgeon at LICH."

"I went to Sloan-Kettering," said Bess. "I had two surgeons in the O.R., actually. The breast surgeon, and a plastic surgeon, in case. If the lump was obviously cancer, they would've done a mastectomy and reconstruction."

"But it wasn't cancer," said Robin.

"Benign."

"Jesus, Bess," said Alicia. "You must have been terrified."

Carla leaned back, scowling. "Why would you choose to go to a hospital in the city, when the hospital two blocks from your house has excellent facilities and surgeons?"

"Sloan-Kettering is the best," said Bess. "Everyone knows that."

"I don't know that," said Carla, clearly offended.

Bess shrugged. "I'm sorry you're insulted, Carla. But your feelings were not a high priority for me last week."

Another silence. Tim coughed and said, "I'll check on Joe."

Robin made slow, steady eye contact with Alicia and Carla. She said, "I'll speak for the group. We're glad you're all right. But we would have loved to help you and support you. We still want to help. What can we do?"

"Nothing," said Bess. "What could you have done for me? You couldn't have the surgery for me. Or taken the pain for me. I didn't want people around. The boys got a crash course in learning how to take care of themselves. It's about time they did. Amy doesn't need me anymore. Borden managed with everything else."

Alicia said, "We could have kept you company. Played Brooklyn Hold 'Em, bedside."

Bess shrugged again. "Doesn't matter."

Robin said, "I think it's weird that you didn't tell us."

"Agreed," said Alicia.

"I wasn't broadcasting the news," said Bess. "It was a private thing. I kept it within the family. And we're not in the habit of doing things for each other, unless it's a consequence of winning at cards. Look, I really like you all. But five months ago, we didn't know each other to say 'Hi.' I wouldn't expect you to rush to my hospital bed or to drop your lives to hold my hand. I didn't want that. I didn't need it. If you're upset, I apologize for not telling you before. I'm telling you now."

"Keeping us abreast," muttered Alicia.

Robin said, "You're acting like this is no big deal."

"It's not!" said Bess. "I had a harmless lump. It's gone. End of story. Nothing to circle the wagons about. And now that that's out of the way, let's eat!" Cupping her hands around her lips, she yelled, "Tim! We're starving out here!"

"If this was no big deal, why the big nihilism announcement? Which, by the way, is making a bit more sense," said Alicia. "But not really. You're acting odd."

"Like they took out the lump, and put in an attitude," said Robin.

Carla said, "No, she's being pragmatic. I respect that." To Bess, she said, "I'm not insulted that you chose Sloan-Kettering over LICH. That's a personal decision that you make with your family. There's no reason any of us should discuss it with each other. Bess's right. We hardly know each other. We play cards once or twice a month. That's all."

"We're spiraling downward," said Robin. "We do better when we talk about men and sex."

Alicia shushed Robin as Tim and Joe came into the living room/ kitchen area.

Tim said, "Are we ready to eat, or do you need a few more minutes?"

Carla said, "We do better when we don't talk at all. Let's just play cards." The Black Queen hugged a pillow to her chest, as if donning a protective shield.

"Don't be so touchy, Carla," said Bess, sounding obnoxious even to her own ears. "You're totally overreacting. I had no idea you were so sensitive."

"Back that up," said Carla. "You can edit that sentence to 'I had no idea,' and leave it at that. She's right. We are a bunch of strangers."

"And diverse!" said Alicia, trying to keep it light. "Maybe this is the night we finally make some plans for the committee. Bess?"

Bess shrugged, her new favorite gesture. "Doesn't matter."

"We're not strangers, Carla," said Robin.

"What are we?" demanded Carla.

None of them knew what to say.

Except Tim. "We're hungry?" he asked.

"That is true," said Alicia.

Carla stared at the wall, or the stack of boxes against it. The woman was clearly uncomfortable, as if she were among enemies, not friends. Bess looked from woman to woman, and saw each as if she'd suddenly removed a mask. The faces seemed off, askew. Who were they, really? A random collection of mothers. She'd told them she had a lumpectomy, inelegantly, perhaps, and how did they react? They were angry at her!

Bess should have known that Alicia, Carla, and Robin would disappoint her. Like Amy, who reacted to the news of the lump by saying, "I don't want to get cancer!" and then, after Borden took her to her room for a chat, she sulked behind her closed door all night long. Simone had been even worse. She didn't return Bess's explicit voicemail—"I might have breast cancer, Mom"—for *three days*. When Simone finally did phone, she spent the first ten minutes of their eleven-minute conversation apologizing for not calling sooner, but she was in Johannesburg attending a conference on women's rights and she couldn't get a signal. "But how *are* you?" asked Simone, finally, the line crackling and patchy. All Bess could think to say was, "I'm fine."

And she was fine. No cancer. Tiny scar on her otherwise enviable breast (for her age and number of children). There was nothing wrong with her, and why should she expect or hope to be treated with special kindness by anyone? None was forthcoming, except from Borden and her boys. Eric, Charlie, and Tom had been sweet, making cards for her, bringing her snacks on the breakfast tray. They wrote and performed a little play for her, pretending to be gods from Mount Olympus, looming from on high, deciding her happy fate. Bess had been treated better by the men in her life than the women.

In Alicia's seedy apartment, the silence grew, as each woman waited for the others to speak. Tim gave Joe a bowl of paella, and the boy knew enough to flee from the toxic air in the main room.

Tim, on the other hand, was not going anywhere in a hurry.

"Here's how we'll do it, women," he said. "We're going to eat, and then we're going to play cards. You don't have to say a single word to each other for the rest of the night. But no one leaves until this horrible tension breaks."

Bowing to the will of the only man in the room, the four women did as they were told.

8

Carla

If Carla needed one word to best define her life, it would be: "Hurry." Constantly behind schedule at the clinic, she hurried through patients. Then she hurried home to make dinner for Zeke and Manny. She was getting sick of hearing herself say, "Let's go," and "Move it or lose it." When her sons dallied, she took it personally. She'd made the necessary concession to let them walk to the clinic after school by themselves. The boys liked being trusted with a taste of independence, if only for the ten minutes it took them to get from Brownstone to LICH. But they resented having to do their homework in her office for two or three hours until she finished for the day. They preferred hanging out at Bess's or Robin's.

Boo-hoo and too bad, thought Carla, washing her hands at the sink for the tenth time that day. Was it wrong to deprive them of Pop-Tarts and YouTube? She liked her children where she could see them.

Bess let her kids run wild. Last week, when Carla arrived to pick up the boys from the Clinton Street townhouse, Bess yelled up the stairs, and the kids came running down. Carla calmly asked Bess what they'd been doing all afternoon, and Bess just shrugged. They could've been watching Internet porn for all Bess knew (or seemed to care).

Robin was hardly more vigilant. The last time Carla picked up her sons there, Robin was making Zogby calls while Zeke, Manny, and Stephanie were in the living room watching an R-rated movie on HBO. Carla walked in on them in time to see a gunman (black, of course) in a speeding taxi shooting bullets at a family of four (white) in a station wagon on the highway. Carla tried to turn off the TV, but there was no switch so she asked authoritatively for the remote. Stephanie, clearly not used to decisive voices, got flustered and couldn't find the box. Carla told her to look harder, and the girl started to cry. Enter Robin, who looked stunned to find her daughter upset, Carla fuming, Manny and Zeke chagrined, and the TV blasting machine gunfire. Robin managed to turn the damn thing off and apologized. But Carla knew: Robin wasn't sorry. She was angry that Carla made her daughter cry. Was Carla the only mother left in the world who tried to shield her children from the garbage that came at them from every direction?

That was the last time Carla had seen or spoken to Robin. Bess was checked out emotionally, mentally, or both. Alicia had been flying under the radar for weeks. Carla's only contact with the other players had been Bess's emails to the entire Brownstone mailing list about the upcoming winter fund-raiser. A Seventies-theme casino night. As the winner of the last poker game, Bess extorted promises from Carla, Robin, and Alicia that they'd all attend. The event wasn't for another couple of weeks (thank God), so Carla wouldn't have to think about it. She hated parent-oriented events at Brownstone. She felt conspicuous, like a raisin in a bowl of oatmeal.

Carla wondered if their most recent, painfully awkward committee meeting was their last. None of the women seemed motivated to set a date, or even discuss what had happened. The game might've run its course. Claude would be delighted to hear it. He'd been hinting that Carla should make new, other (black) friends. He wanted to go on couples dates. The boys were older, he said. They were responsible enough to walk from school to the clinic. Why couldn't they stay alone at home for a few hours, so Carla and Claude could go out by themselves?

"If the Obamas can make time for a weekly date night, so can we," he said one night in bed after they'd made love.

Carla had been thrown by Claude's sudden romanticism. Since the last card night (it annoyed Carla that the others still referred to it as a "committee meeting"), when she'd come home complaining, Claude had been more attentive. He fixed the bathroom door. He brought home eggs. Was Carla's disconnect with Alicia, Bess, and Robin an aphrodisiac for him? He must've felt neglected, or resentful that she'd ventured so far afield. Now she was back, and disheartened. The game had cooled; Claude had heated up. Being pleased with herself for having a happy man at home was nothing to be ashamed of.

"Are you still at the sink?" said Tina, her impatient nurse. "You can't wash the black off, Mommy."

Carla snapped back to the present. Embarrassed, she turned off the water and dried her hands. She'd been zoning out so often lately. Her focus was slipping. Tina was holding out a couple of charts.

"Last two, right?" asked the doctor. She'd already seen thirty patients today.

"And then we're done for the weekend," said Tina. "Exam room one, ear infection. Room two, fungal rash."

"I love to end the workweek with a contagious skin condition," said Carla. "Check in on the boys, would you, please? Make sure they're not on my office computer." The lure of illicit websites was too much for them. At home, she had parental controls on the computer. But not here.

Tina agreed, and literally pushed Carla through the door of exam room one, where a girl and her mother waited.

"Don't I know you?" asked the woman.

Carla lifted her eyes from the girl's chart to take a closer look. Yes, the mother and daughter were familiar to her. The woman was well dressed, a heavyset black woman—Caribbean black, Carla guessed. She was professionally dressed in a black skirt and flat-heeled boots, but the bright red jacket spiced up her look. Carla should try more jackets, not rely so much on scarves and voluminous sweaters to camouflage her thick midsection.

"Carla Morgan," she said, holding out her hand to the woman, a Mrs. Hobart, according to the chart. "I think I've seen you at Brownstone. My sons are in the fourth and seventh grade there."

"Okay, yes, I can place you now," said Mrs. Hobart, smiling faintly. "Shauna is in second grade."

Carla turned to Shauna and asked, "It hurts?" She snapped on some gloves, and unhooked the otoscope from the wall charger. The girl nodded. "Let me take a look."

She examined the child's ears—both of them red, but not full of fluid. "This is your first visit to the clinic?" she asked.

"We usually go to Dr. Stevens's on Remsen Street," said Mrs. Hobart, speaking of a pediatrician in private practice in the Heights. A kind and smart man. When he sent patients to the hospital for testing, Carla often worked with him. "He's out of town this week, and his office referred us here," Mrs. Hobart explained.

Carla nodded. Thank God for Dr. Stevens. A referral from one of his patients meant a $50 co-pay and a nice chunk from private insurance.

"She started complaining about her ear yesterday," said Mrs. Hobart. "I'm embarrassed I waited a whole day to bring her in."

One day? That was lightning speed. Carla said, "Well, from the look of it, Shauna's infection is only just starting. I might not have noticed much evidence of infection yesterday."

"Thanks for saying that," said Mrs. Hobart. "I still feel guilty."

Carla smiled at her patient, and then the mother. "You have nothing to feel guilty about. I'll write you a prescription for antibiotics." Seeing Shauna's reaction, Carla added, "Bubblegum flavor. How's that sound?"

· The girl smiled and said, "Thank you, ma'am."

What a polite, well-behaved child! Carla replied, "You're very welcome."

"We have a church retreat planned for this weekend," said Mrs. Hobart.

"Where to?" asked Carla.

"A mountain lodge in upstate New York."

"Mohonk?" asked Carla. "Our church sponsored a family retreat there last year."

"Same place," said Mrs. Hobart. "So you can understand how much we're looking forward to it."

"I'll give Shauna her first dose now. If you can dose her again at bedtime, she'll feel better in the morning. I see no reason you can't go on the trip. Just bring the medicine with you."

"You are a lifesaver, Dr. Morgan," said Mrs. Hobart, eyes filled with relief and gratitude.

Carla basked in the woman's appreciation and respect. What a refreshing shift, not having to absorb annoyance, anger, and blame for making a diagnosis. "Call me Carla," she said.

"Renee."

The two women smiled at each other, and Carla registered a click-into-place feeling that one gets upon discovering a like-minded soul. While Carla wrote a prescription, she glanced at the contact information sheet in the chart. Renee Hobart had listed her employer as a law firm in the city. Was she married? Carla had to check, out of rank curiosity. Yes. A husband and father in the picture. His contact info had him working at the same firm. A gainfully employed, professional, churchgoing, African-American couple. Exactly what Claude had in mind for couples dates. Come to think of it, why include the husbands at all? Carla and Renee could have a thing. Her poker game seemed to be crumbling. Those friendships hadn't been based on anything concrete, anyway. She and Renee, on paper at least, had so much in common.

She felt the urge to say something, ask her to coffee, but it seemed inappropriate. Maybe she'd email her next week? Did she need an excuse? If so, what would that be?

Incredibly, Renee (a mind-reader?) said, "I know you're very busy—so am I—but I'd love to grab coffee after drop-off some morning."

"Me, too!" blurted Carla, sounding way too eager.

"Great," said Renee. "I'll give you my card."

The women exchanged paper—business card for prescription slip—and an understanding. Carla felt buoyed by the unexpected friendly encounter. She sailed through her next and last exam of the day, a little boy whose feet were crawling with fungus. His openly hostile mother scowled at her child for not knowing exactly when his toes started itching, and at Carla while she explained the lengthy treatment course.

As usual, Tina escorted the patient out, and cleaned up the exam rooms. The janitorial staff would do the hard work later in the evening. Carla left the charts on Tina's desk and washed her hands one more time. Then Carla was free to go.

Still feeling upbeat from meeting Renee and Shauna, Carla floated into her office to grab her coat and bag and tell the boys it was time to leave. She opened the door, and found Zeke and Manny in front of her computer, their faces glowing by its light. They were riveted, and Carla instantly assumed they were watching off-limit videos on You-Tube.

"What are you doing?" boomed Carla at her sons.

"Nothing!" said Manny while fumbling on the keyboard to quit the application.

"Freeze!" she yelled. "Hands up. Back away from the computer."

The boys froze, and Carla then spun the laptop around so she could see what they'd been doing.

On-screen: the green background and 3-D graphics of World Class Poker, a six-player game in progress. The Black Queen was currently table leader with $100,000-plus in chips. She clicked to check the tournament history, and discovered that her boys had been playing Texas Hold 'Em for an hour, surviving four levels, and winning twenty-two percent of the hands they played.

Impressive, she thought. "You're not allowed to play poker! You know I disapprove of gambling!" she bellowed.

"But you play it all the time!" protested Manny.

Tina burst into the room. "What's all the yelling about in here?" she asked.

"The boys were playing poker," said Carla.

"So?" asked Tina. "You play poker every chance you get."

"It's true," said Zeke. "You're amazing, Ma. You've won fourteen tournaments. Your bankroll is ten million dollars!"

It was a vast sum, thought Carla smugly. "I'm an adult," she said. "I can do what I want. You are children, and you shouldn't be playing poker."

"Why?" asked Manny, folding his skinny arms across his chest, looking too much like his father.

"Yeah," said Zeke, imitating his older brother in a way that Carla would have thought precious if it didn't make her mad.

"No big deal, Mommy," said Tina. "It's fun. I've played a few hands myself sometimes."

"You're using my computer?" asked Carla of her nurse.

"Once or twice," said Tina. "It's not real gambling with real money. Better that the boys play cards on the computer than smoking crack in the playground."

"Shut up, Tina," said Carla of her ridiculous overstatement. Then again, where Tina lived, smoking crack in the playground was a reality for some kids. Carla objected to the boys playing poker on-screen because they might want to start a game with their friends. And then start to gamble on a soft scale, for candy or whatever. Computer poker was gateway gambling, like smoking a joint was a few steps away from injecting heroin (although Carla always thought that was bogus, not that she'd say so).

"Okay, I'll forgive you—including you, Tina—for violating my privacy and using my computer without permission. But from now on, you are forbidden from playing poker. Is that understood?"

Zeke and Manny nodded, but Carla caught them sneaking a glance at each other. Tina shrugged and said, "What*ever*, Mommy."

Carla would have to talk to Tina next week about being disrespectful to her in front of her kids. Being disrespectful *at all*.

She packed everyone up and ushered them out the door, undecided if she'd tell Claude what she'd caught them doing.

●—●

Carla and Claude sat at their dining room table, a pile of bills and contracts spread out on the black lacquer surface. How menacing those white sheets looked on the dark surface, thought Carla. The most frightful piece of mail was on top of the pile. Two pieces, actually. The contracts for next year's enrollment at Brownstone. They usually arrived in January, but this year, the agreements were delayed. The board of directors had been engaged in a heated debate about tuition rate increases in a recession.

The Brownstone endowment was small in comparison to other private schools in New York City. The stock market nosedive cut the endowment in half. Without the investment-generated income, the school was near bankrupt. When she first opened the contracts—which she was to sign and return with a deposit to guarantee a spot for next year—she thought the fifteen percent tuition increase (from $28,000 to $32,000 per student) had to be a mistake. Usually, the increases were three to five percent, just keeping up with inflation. In a recession, when people were making less money and couldn't possibly manage to pay more, the powers that be at Brownstone decided to triple the increase. In the enclosed letter, the school president explained that they were raising tuition for those who could afford it, as well as increasing their scholarship and financial aid programs for those who were struggling in this economy. When she first read the letter, Carla nearly swallowed her tongue.

Claude was seeing it for the first time. Aloud, he read the line, " 'Some families should consider applying for financial aid.' " He lowered the letter. "*Some* families. What do you think they mean by that?"

"If only the Brownstone Institute got some of the bailout money."

"Who can afford to pay this?" Claude asked. "You know it's just another way to weed us out. Commitment to diversity. Bull*shit*."

Carla frowned. He hardly ever cursed in the house, especially when the boys were still up. "We should apply for aid," she said softly. They were just getting by at the moment. Not saving anything. They definitely couldn't swing another eight thousand in tuition next year, after taxes. Maybe if Carla went into private practice like Dr. Stevens. But that would take huge start-up expenses. It would take years to establish herself before she'd see a profit.

The clinic at LICH, a public hospital, could afford to pay her only what she was already earning—far less than Dr. Stevens brought in. Cutbacks were always possible. Rumors got louder every day about the city closing hospitals in each borough. LICH was almost always on the Brooklyn short list. Smart people said these dire reports were all about managing expectations. The threat of closing the entire hospital would make the shutting down of certain departments feel like a relief instead of a tragedy. The first department to go? Maternity. Delivering babies and caring for mothers was not profitable for any hospital, public or private. It was a liability, actually. The threat of lawsuits was sky-high. If the economy didn't recover, it was conceivable that uninsured women would have to give birth in their own beds, without a doctor or an anesthesiologist.

Carla drew in a deep breath. This was pessimism at its worst. Or perhaps it was simply the new reality.

Claude said, "We don't qualify for financial aid. I've looked at their program. We make too much money, if you can believe that."

"Even this year?" asked Carla.

This year, Claude would be lucky to bring in a quarter of his usual income. It was an extremely sensitive subject for him. Mentioning it at all was like worrying a bad tooth. Of course, the shortfall wasn't Claude's fault. He worked harder and made less money.

He rubbed his forehead. Carla thought the gesture was to shield his eyes. Claude would not be able to provide this year. The frustration was bitter. And it would make his resentment about Carla's income worse. Even though it made no sense (if she made money, wasn't it good for the whole family?), she understood why Claude struggled with being outearned by his wife. He was a proud man, from the generation of black men who'd made a moral commitment to family life, to be the opposite of their fathers. President Obama was the embodiment of what Claude had set out to be. Carla believed that, as much as Claude idolized Barack, he resented him, too, for making it look easy.

"I know it's hard," said Carla, reaching across the table to touch her husband's arm.

He put his hand over hers, and held it there. "We can't afford this school," said Claude. "I know we agreed to make the boys' education our number one priority. But let's be realistic here. Imagine what our lives would be like if we didn't have these bills to pay? We'd have sixty-four thousand dollars we don't have now."

Carla felt her skin ice over. This was not the answer. "Where would they go?"

"Public school," he replied quickly. "Like we did. And we managed okay."

"I want our sons to do better than okay," said Carla. "You know what the local elementary school is like. Metal detectors for third-graders?"

"It'd be just one more year of elementary in a public school for Zeke," said Claude. "Manny can apply to any middle school in the city. There are charter schools, schools for gifted kids."

"But Manny's not gifted!" said Carla. "He'd never get in. He'd wind up going to some huge school, and then fall off a cliff. He needs the intensity and structure of Brownstone, especially now."

He nodded, agreeing. Not a good sign. Carla knew what Claude would say next. Her worst fear was about to be put on the table. "You're right about that. We could keep Manny at Brownstone," suggested Claude. "We can swing one tuition."

Her turn to nod. He was a hundred percent right. But how on earth could Carla agree to such an experiment? Send one son to private school, and the other to public? She couldn't help wonder if Claude had had this in mind all along. Maybe for years. He was a loving father to both boys, but Carla knew he favored Manny, the first-born son who looked like him and played football. And maybe she'd admit to being a bit extra protective of Zeke, her baby, built small and sensitive.

Zeke needed her to stand up for him now. Carla couldn't deprive him of an equal shot at success in life, and she believed a top-shelf education would give both her boys a tremendous leg up. Unlike most of their classmates at Brownstone—Bess's brood came immediately to mind—Manny and Zeke needed any advantage they could get.

"This is wrong," she said to Claude.

"Zeke can always go back to Brownstone in a few years," he said gently. "The economy will recover. We'll have more money."

"We can take out a second mortgage," she said.

That did it. The man of the house had reached his limit. "No! We're not risking the roof over our heads so Zeke can hang around with a bunch of spoiled white kids. He needs to toughen up. Going to a bigger school will be good for him. I'm done talking about it. Someone has to make the hard decisions around here."

Claude put his hands on the table, and pressed himself into standing. For a passive-aggressive guy, he could show a steely backbone. Claude went into the kitchen and started slamming around in there. He'd surely break something, and then promise to fix it for months before doing anything. If ever.

• ⋯ •

Desperate times called for desperate measures, so Carla decided to take matters into her own large, dexterous hands. Or, more precisely, Carla would use her commanding voice, a mezzo of authority. She knew her tone made people pay attention, or simply do what she said. Often she unleashed her tone to intimidate children, ordering them to sit still for their vaccinations. It'd also worked on select adults.

It occurred to her that she never used "the voice" on her husband. A subconscious decision to keep the peace, or . . . what? Maybe she liked it that he defied her will. A mental movie of Alicia and Tim appeared in her head, of Alicia playfully instructing Tim to do the dishes and then go to bed. He gamely agreed, warning first that he might go write about her in his secret diary. It was funny, made them all laugh. Tim kissed Alicia on the top of her head, not touching his lips to her skin, and left the women alone. Tim was a man who wasn't allowed to be a man. No wonder he'd switched off sexually. Claude, all man, was sexually determined. But he did switch off emotionally, especially when he felt the world pressing against him, despite his best efforts to make a good life for his family. Carla loved her husband, for all he did, and all he wished he could do for her and their children.

"Mrs. Morgan? Come right this way," said Victoria Addams, the chief financial officer at Brownstone.

Carla had been waiting to speak with her for ten minutes, seated comfortably on a couch in Vicki's outer office in the basement level of the school. All of the administration offices were down here, as well as the Parents Association office, the faculty gym, and the band/orchestra/drama rehearsal spaces.

Carla had called in sick. Tina was immediately suspicious. "We have thirty appointments today," said Tina. "It's cold and flu season."

"And I've got a cold," replied Carla. "Reschedule the appointments or get a resident to cover for me."

"Whatever you say," said Tina. "Just so you know, I plan on having a cold next Friday."

Carla stood up, flung her black cashmere shawl over her shoulder, and followed Vicki into her small windowless office. The décor was early WASP, green carpet with a fleur-de-lis pattern, striped wallpaper, large oak desk, too large for the small quarters. Vicki squeezed behind it, and Carla took a seat in one of the chairs opposite.

"How can I help you?" asked Vicki.

Carla smiled at the neat, elderly woman in her gray wool suit and headband. "Preppy" was a word Carla had never spoken aloud. No occasion to. Maybe she'd described Bess as "preppy" to Claude when she'd come home that first poker night. But, in terms of old money 1950s-style, Vicki could be the poster woman. She might've come over on the *Mayflower* herself.

Using "the voice," Carla got right to it. "When we first joined the Brownstone community five years ago, we spoke about the school's commitment to diversity. You had a policy in place to honor that commitment."

"I remember our talk," said Vicki, frowning.

What Vicki had said to Carla and Claude in that meeting, in delicate and careful terms, was that Brownstone was prepared to give them a large break in tuition as a lure. The board of directors had issued a mandate for diversity. They'd actually set percentage goals for nonwhite students. The school needed more black kids, ideally with professional parents who had ties to the community and were out of the running for the few full scholarship slots given to low-income, academic achievers (like Joe Fandine). Competition to get into Brownstone was fierce—something like one acceptance for every hundred applicants. Her sons were no better than many who'd been rejected. Carla was glad that, for once, being black had opened doors. As for a break in tuition, Claude got his pride up, and told Vicki that they didn't need help. Five years ago, he had been right.

That was then.

"Is Brownstone still honoring that commitment?" asked Carla. She gave Vicki a few beats to offer up some "help." She didn't.

"We are still very much committed to diversity," said Vicki, delicate and careful. "And we are prepared for a higher number of families seeking aid this year."

Carla's turn to frown, and to be just as delicate and careful. She would not beg. "I have to assume that many Brownstone families fall somewhere between not being able to afford tuition and not qualifying for aid."

"We're aware of that," said Vicki. "We've changed our aid policy to reflect it."

"So what's the number?" asked Carla. Vicki appeared not to understand. "What's the income threshold to qualify?"

Vicki seemed taken aback by the bluntness. So much for delicacy. "All circumstances are weighed differently," she said, "based on income, net worth, number of children, other factors."

Carla held up her hand. "Vicki? You know my circumstances."

The older woman sighed. Carla felt bad for a second. She didn't want to bully her. Vicki had probably been besieged by strapped parents all week. Carla said, "I'm sorry, Vicki. I'm being rude. My husband and I have been having serious kitchen-table conversations, if you know what I mean."

"Of course I do," said Vicki. Her eyes told Carla she did understand, and she was sympathetic.

"I can't leave any stone unturned," said Carla, picturing Zeke placing his backpack on a conveyor belt to be x-rayed, and then walking through the metal detector on his first day of fifth grade at public school. The image made her throat itch. He wasn't prepared for such a major change. It was criminal to ask that of a little kid.

Vicki said, "Are you all right?"

Carla blinked, got her grip. "I'm fine. I'm afraid for the choices we might have to make. I need to know if we have options."

"Let me check," said Vicki. She started typing something into the desktop computer. Carla was relieved that Vicki seemed to care. Claude was wrong. Brownstone wasn't trying to force out anyone. Times were tough. For people, and institutions, even 150-year-old schools in Brooklyn Heights. Vicki was probably sweating her own job.

The older woman said, "Okay. Again, circumstances are weighed individually, but I can tell you that, for a dual-income family with two students enrolled, partial aid becomes available, on a limited basis, if the gross annual income is one hundred thousand dollars or less."

"For *two* incomes?" asked Carla. It was ridiculously low. Her salary alone was more than that.

"I know it seems low," said Vicki. "A lot of our families, as of this year, have no income at all."

Brooklyn Heights was a bedroom community, historically and practically, for Wall Street investment bankers. A lot of bankers' kids attended Brownstone.

"So the message is, be grateful I still have a job?" snapped Carla. "This is unfair, Vicki. I realize people have been laid off, but they have savings, don't they? Are they living paycheck to paycheck?"

"I can't discuss—"

"I'm not asking about specific cases," said Carla.

"Aid takes net worth into account," said Vicki. "We ask for a full financial profile, including investments. Some of our new aid candidates have lost everything."

Carla had heard rumors—from Robin, of course—about several Brownstone parents, former Lehman Brothers bankers whose entire savings had been in company stock, now worthless. Famously, there were two Brownstone families who'd given their trust and nest eggs to Bernard Madoff. Those families had been destroyed and Carla felt for them. But—they'd lived the high life for years. Carla and Claude had always been frugal and modest. They hadn't lost everything and Carla was grateful for it, but they wouldn't get aid, either.

Her mother would say self-pity was not going to fix Carla's problems.

Sitting in that chair, in the basement office, Carla felt herself and Zeke literally falling through the cracks. She could blame Vicki, but that would be wrong. Vicki didn't make the policy. The board of directors did. It was Vicki's job to deal with angry parents. Carla knew all too well what that was like.

Why was it such a big deal to send her sons to *this* school? Why was the status quo so important to maintain? Brownstone equals safe. The boys' safety had been her only objective since she'd given birth. Now she'd have to compromise for Zeke, her baby. Logically, she knew some of her anxiety was ego related. She felt like a failure on a few counts here.

Maybe public school would toughen Zeke up, in a good way. Carla had to give Claude some credit. He wasn't *always* wrong.

"I'm just . . . trying to figure it all out," said Carla.

"We realize that many of our families need extra time," said Vicki softly. "We've postponed the final deadline for signed contracts."

"June first," said Carla. "I know."

Carla smiled and apologized for any rudeness. Vicki assured her she'd been fine, giving Carla the impression that other parents hadn't refrained from misdirecting their frustration and anger on an innocent bystander. They shook hands, Carla's twice as big, and then she got out of there.

●————●

A diner? Bad idea, Carla thought. There was a chance she'd run into someone from the hospital. Get her nails done? Forget it. She'd bump into a Brownstone mother at a Montague Street salon. Starbucks? Paying four dollars for a cup of coffee had never been acceptable to her, even on an indulgent day of hooky. What Carla really craved, more than food, drink, or pampering, was the peace of her own company. She wanted to be alone.

Easier said than done. Brooklyn Heights was part of a big city, but the neighborhood was a tiny village. Friends, acquaintances, colleagues were on every block. So where might a hearty well-swaddled woman take her solitude on a frigid day in mid-February?

Aha, she thought, and, like a divining rod, pointed herself toward water.

From the steps of Brownstone, it was a short walk—half a mile— to the pedestrian walkway of the Brooklyn Bridge. Carla made the time quickly. Before long, she had climbed the long stairway up to the bridge, and hiked another half mile to the apex, a thin strip of boardwalk between the Brooklyn and Manhattan towers. At this spot, the suspension cables dipped low. The view was unobstructed. Carla could look downtown, and see New York Harbor, the southern tip of Manhattan, the South Street Seaport, the Staten Island ferry landing, the Statue of Liberty, the East and Hudson rivers and New Jersey. She could look uptown, at the Manhattan and Williamsburg bridges, the Empire State Building, the Chrysler Building, the snaking FDR Drive, the curved, notched edges of Brooklyn and Manhattan, jigsaw puzzle pieces that would fit together perfectly.

But Carla's eyes were downcast. She sat on a bench and stared at her feet, throbbing inside her boots. She'd dressed to impress for her meeting with Vicki, and put on her one pair of two-inch-heeled boots. Ordinarily, at the clinic, she wore moccasins or clogs. Her feet were not used to heels. Also, her lungs ached. She needed to catch her breath. She'd walked a mile, and she was practically wheezing for air. As soon as she sat down, sweat streamed down her cheeks from under her hat, and then it chilled on her skin. The wind on the bridge, especially here, the exposed, vulnerable middle section, was whipping.

Despite her physical discomfort, Carla was content to be by herself. She wasn't completely alone. As always, tourists dotted the walkway, posing with cameras. But they were invisible to her. She didn't know them. They didn't know her. They provided human company with no threat of interaction. *We are ants on a hill,* she thought, *at the mercy of forces beyond our control.*

But even as she sat there, not making eye contact, Carla felt pressure to appear a certain way. Dignified, elegant. She kept her back straight and shoulders back. Carla didn't believe she was pretending to be someone she wasn't, or putting on a show. She was a strong, responsible woman. That was how she appeared. And yet, she felt the constant weight of judgment upon her.

Carla suffered an unrelenting conspicuousness, if only in her mind. Black people constantly thought about race, how it underlined everything they saw, heard, said, did. White people? They thought about race only to reassure themselves that they weren't racist.

Carla wondered if Robin felt self-conscious about being Jewish. She'd never ask Robin about it. Identity politics were not Carla's favorite topic of conversation. Robin wouldn't hesitate to ask Carla about hers. The Red Queen let her curiosity roam free, which Carla envied.

Drawing in a few cold deep breaths, Carla peered uptown, at the dark water of the East River. If her sons were comfortable in the white world, they wouldn't feel the pressure, the fear of judgment. For all her misgivings about diversity at Brownstone, even paying lip service was forward thinking. At the school, her sons would learn to be at ease with white people. What a relief and advantage it would be for them, as they grew up and found a place in the world. Like Barack growing up in Hawaii. This was the core benefit of Brownstone to Carla. It was bigger than the quality of education. She wanted her sons—both of them—to be comfortable in their skin wherever life took them.

Carla's problem had an obvious solution. She needed $32,000. But where and how would she get it?

"Carla? Is that you?"

Turning toward the voice, Carla found Bess Steeple standing in front of her, healthy and glowing, panting lightly. The blonde wore tight black workout clothes, sneakers, a skullcap, and gloves. Bess was jogging? In twenty degree weather? This proved she'd completely lost her mind.

"Hello!" said Carla, surprisingly glad to see her.

"What are you doing up here?" asked Bess, stretching her legs, one then the other.

"Just airing myself out," said Carla. "But it's getting too cold to sit."

"Let's walk," said Bess.

"You'll freeze if you stop running."

"I'll be fine."

"Those pants are paper thin."

"Then we'll both run."

Carla laughed heartily at the idea of jogging a yard, much less a mile—in midheel boots, or at all.

The two women started walking back toward Brooklyn.

Walking, not talking.

"How's the nihilism going?" asked Carla finally.

"Very well, thank you," said Bess.

"If nothing matters, why on earth are you *jogging*?" asked Carla.

"I enjoy it," said Bess.

"Hmmm, now I know you've gone over the edge."

Bess laughed. "Will I see you Saturday night?"

"I'm not sure if . . ."

"I won the poker game," said Bess. "And you promised to come to my event as payment. If you don't show up, you're going back on your word."

"Claude thinks it's sending the wrong message. Casino night. A gambling fund-raiser," said Carla. A partial truth. Claude hated the Seventies theme ("Should I dress like Huggy Bear?"), and he absolutely loathed the idea of giving more money to Brownstone beyond tuition. Just to walk in the door of the event, you had to buy tickets at $50 a pop. And then they were expected to buy chips. All cash went into the Parents Association coffers to buy the school extras (the PA had financed the faculty gym, for example).

"I'll have tickets for you and Claude waiting at the door," said Bess. "Also for Alicia and Tim."

The charity cases. "I can afford to pay my way," said Carla, who, like Claude, was too proud to take charity.

"Pay, don't pay, doesn't matter," said Bess. "But you must show up. I need bodies, Carla. The room has to feel crowded. I want lines to get at the gambling tables. People are more likely to buy chips if they see other people doing it. Not that you have to. I'm just saying."

Carla suddenly felt an itch to run. To get away from this conversation, from this woman who had zero clue what other people went through. Not to say Bess's life was perfect. But it was pretty damned close. Emotionally, she was like a child, using the words "need" and "want" only as they pertained to her personal desires. Forty going on sixteen.

"Just come yourself," said Bess. "Please, Carla! I'm sure Claude can survive one night without you."

If Robin had said it, Carla would have laughed. Coming from Bess? The remark sounded like a dig against her husband.

Carla felt a wellspring of dislike, bordering on hate, for Bess. How much of it was resentment about Bess's cushy life? The Steeple family wasn't losing sleep, deciding which of their kids would have to get the short end of the stick. Four kids, all of them with price tags of $32,000 attached. Brownstone would get an incredible $128,000 from the Steeples next school year, and Bess would surely donate more for her fund-raiser to ensure it was a success.

Did Bess give tuition two thoughts? Or did she just agonize about her bratty daughter and selfish mother? Carla reminded herself that Bess had muscled through a cancer scare less than a month ago. She'd thrown herself into a charity event as a distraction. Carla could hardly fault her for that. If only some of the money generated could go directly into Carla's pocket.

Bess said, "I know I wasn't very nice at Alicia's house last time we played. I really am sorry about that. I've apologized already."

By email. Carla said, "Believe it or not, Bess, my mood has nothing to do with you."

"So I'm wrong to feel anger coming off you in waves?"

"My feet are killing me," grumbled Carla.

"Let's go straight to my house. I'll make us lunch!" Sensing Carla's hesitation, Bess added, "To prove to me you're not still angry."

Carla shook her head. "I just don't want to get into it."

"Is it Claude?"

Yes. No. Carla shook her head. Thankfully, they were coming to the end of the bridge. As soon as they reached Cadman Plaza Park in Brooklyn, Carla could make an excuse and escape into the A train subway entrance.

"Is it money?" asked Bess.

"Why do you ask that?" asked Carla.

"If it's not husbands or kids, it's money."

Or all of the above. The two women wound their way around Cadman Plaza Park, an oval of green at the foot of Brooklyn Heights. The subway entrance was just across the street. "I'm going down," said Carla.

"Since there'll be a few poker tables with hired dealers at the event, we could snag one for ourselves, and call it a committee meeting."

"Ourselves."

"You, me, Alicia, and Robin."

"Oh," said Carla. "Sure."

"Do you think Robin will mind waiting for her turn to host?"

Honestly, Carla had already mentally removed herself from the poker game. The last time had been so uncomfortable, Carla wasn't interested in subjecting herself to it again. Bess was clearly trying to make it up to her. She looked so hopeful and innocent with her cap and blue blinking eyes. Why would Bess, the woman who had everything, care about this game so much? Carla's resentment softened a little. Against her will, she felt flattered.

"Why so insistent?" asked Carla. "Since nothing matters."

Under her already red cheeks, Bess blushed. "Some things matter. A lot matters," she said. "That night at Alicia's, I had a moment. Moment over, okay? Back to normal."

"I don't think Robin will mind waiting to host," replied Carla, not sure why she was giving in.

"Great!" said Bess. "I've got to run now or I'll freeze my ass off. See you Saturday night!"

Carla stood there for a minute, and watched Bess lope up the street toward the heart of the Heights.

What ass? thought Carla.

●———●

"Claude, this is Renee Hobart," said Carla, introducing her husband to her new friend. Acquaintance? Person of interest? What should she call Renee?

She'd been dreading Casino Night and the prospect of hours of socializing with Brownstone parents. She was grateful that Claude came along. He looked handsome in his gray suit, and it was easier to navigate with him steering her along. Carla casually mentioned that she might play a hand or two, and he hadn't objected. Given the tension in the house about money, they were both trying to be as nice to each other as possible. Still, Carla felt the strain. When she saw Renee cutting through the crowd like a steamer ship, elegant and large, smiling at her and reaching for her, Carla was awash with relief. A third party. Someone to talk to. Plus, Claude would love her.

"Is your husband here, too?" Claude asked after he and Renee shook hands.

"He couldn't make it," she said.

"Working?" asked Claude.

"I shouldn't complain. At least he has a job," said Renee. "We work at the same firm. Twenty lawyers have been let go in the last few months. The atmosphere is awful, but you have to stay positive."

Renee went on a bit about work, and then the conversation stalled.

"They did up the school nicely," said Carla.

"You should see the gym. It's been discoed," agreed Renee.

The Casino Night activities were spread throughout Brownstone. Gambling in the middle school gym. Dancing in the lower school gym. Drinks and mingling in the main lobby and libraries.

Claude said, "Mirror ball?"

"Several," said Renee. "And some of the parents really dressed the part. Or, I should say, barely dressed."

The three of them were in normal, night-out clothes. Carla wore her regal purple caftan and thought she looked elegant. Renee also had a dramatic presence, in all black with a thick, beaded multicolored necklace. A statement piece. Carla would never wear such a chunky adornment. But with slicked-back hair and high eyebrows, Renee pulled it off beautifully. Instead of feeling jealous, Carla felt a swell of pride in having a handsome companion in Renee.

They agreed to do a lap around the event venues. The threesome headed for the short stairs that led directly to the gym. Carla felt good. Relieved. She hadn't had a chance to call Renee about setting up a coffee, mainly because she didn't want to seem pushy. Seeing her tonight did away with her hesitation. Claude was smiling; he seemed pleased to have an attractive woman on each arm.

Then they were ambushed.

Robin Stern, drink in hand, came up behind them. "Can I steal Carla for a minute?" asked the redhead. "Hello, Claude," she added, leaning in to kiss him. He allowed it. Then Robin introduced herself to Renee. They exchanged vitals—their names, their kids names and grades.

"I like your costume," said Renee.

"My *what?*" asked Robin. She looked down at her peasant shirt and skirt and said, "Not a costume. Believe it or not, I dress like this every day. Stevie Nicks circa nineteen seventy-eight, I know."

"Who?" asked Renee.

Robin burst out laughing. She was drunk. Already. It was only eight o'clock.

The boys were home alone, the first time they'd left the kids without a babysitter. It was Claude's idea, part of his campaign to toughen them up and save a few bucks. His campaign slogan: "They're not babies." He'd said it about a hundred times in the last two weeks. Carla heard the unspoken accusation clearly. When Claude said to her, "They're not babies," he meant, "You baby them." The boys (young men?) echoed Claude every chance they got. "We're not babies, Ma," they said, and the three men in her life would grin sideways at each other. She enjoyed seeing them unified, if only it weren't against her.

"There you are," said Alicia, suddenly squeezing in next to Robin. "Have you seen Tim? He was here a minute ago."

Without preamble, Alicia kissed her way around the circle. She paused at Renee. "I don't know you," she said. "I should know your name before I kiss you, shouldn't I?"

Renee was clearly taken aback by Alicia's forwardness. She was literally in their faces. Carla flashed to the night she met Alicia, that first meeting of the Diversity Committee at Bess's townhouse, when Alicia acted shy and hesitant at first, and then boldly suggested the game of playing for secrets. Alicia pretended to be a mouse—to lull you into a false sense of confidence?—but she was really a mink. Tonight, she wore a tight black dress, showing off her bird-boned and small-breasted body.

Standing next to tiny Alicia and skinny Robin, Carla felt like a rhino. Thank heaven for Renee, who was even more substantial. Compared to the other two women, Carla and Renee had gravity, in more ways than one. Was Renee judging her white friends? Claude seemed annoyed by their presence. He had no love for the poker players, that was well established.

Robin said, "Let's find Bess. I bet she's dressed up like Meryl Streep in *Mamma Mia!*"

Alicia nodded. "What about Tim?"

"Screw him," said Robin.

"Or not," said Alicia.

They giggled.

Carla was mortified. Claude coughed, and nudged his wife. It was her cue to disengage from Alicia and Robin. "We were going to look around. I'll catch up with you guys later," Carla said.

Robin said, "No way! It's meeting time, Carla. A poker table is reserved for the four of us, a hot dealer, drink holders. Game time starts"—she checked her wrist, but wasn't wearing a watch—"in five minutes. Let's go!"

Alicia said, "Bess fronted us a big stack of chips. But"—she leaned forward as if to speak softly—"don't tell anyone!"

Renee asked, "You gamble, Carla?"

Good grief, she thought. Renee *was* judging her. "I play cards," corrected Carla for her churchgoing new friend. "But I never gamble."

Before Carla could explain herself further, Robin and Alicia took her by the arms and pulled her away. She glanced over her shoulder at Claude and Renee. The pair watched with stunned expressions. Then they looked at each other with strained confusion.

Robin said, "He's a big boy, Carla. He can take care of himself for an hour."

More echoes of "they're not babies." How many people were going to accuse her of being overprotective? She realized her muscles had been clenched with tension for hours about leaving the kids home alone, and worrying about Claude having a good time tonight.

Did Claude ever—as in, *ever*—worry about Carla's good time?

Out of the corner of her eye, Carla spotted Tim Fandine, looking incredibly sharp in a brown suit and lavender shirt, holding forth in a tight circle with three rapt women. He was doing just fine away from his wife. Alicia needn't waste a minute worrying about him.

As they pressed through the crowd, Robin said, "Tim's over there."

Alicia, looking straight ahead, said, "I see him."

Okay, maybe Alicia did worry about Tim. Which was worse? Being afraid your husband would have a horrible time and passive-aggressively punish you later, *or* being afraid your husband would have a great time flirting with other woman and ignoring you?

As usual, Robin was particularly observant when drunk. "Sometimes," she said, "I'm glad I'm single."

The three women pushed through the double doors into the middle school gym. Unlike the crowded lobby and the pulsing lower gym disco, this room was relatively quiet. A sudden burst of applause and cheering broke out across the room at what Carla recognized as a craps table. Some small round tables were clustered to the left for blackjack—about a dozen games, six chairs at each, plus standing dealers in puffy shirtsleeves and green vests. They seemed to know what they were doing. Cards and chips moved quickly. Most of the spots were taken by men (dads). A few moms stood behind watching. A few were playing.

To the right, Carla saw larger tables, also filled up with men in casual jackets and slacks. The dealers at these tables seemed to be working at a slower pace. The men seated around were more intense and thoughtful than the impulsive blackjack players. Their eyes were alert, backs straight. Serious men, amber liquids on ice at their elbows. The poker players.

Carla swallowed hard. Her heart started beating chaotically. When she'd fantasized about a real game, she imagined herself inside her CD game, as a 3-D image come to life. But this room, even this cheesy school-gym version of a real casino, had a vibe to it. A smell. The scent of seriousness and deep concentration. Carla inhaled deeply. This was her element. Her frequency.

"There she is," said Robin, waving at Bess, standing in a group with four men, all of them gazing at her blond gloriousness while she seemed oblivious to it. "Holy shit. She looks exactly like Angie Dickinson."

Indeed, their lovely host wore tight white hip-huggers, with huge bell-bottoms, a wide belt with leather fringe, a tight shiny shirt with clownishly wide lapels, and a blond "Police Woman" wig, stiff and sultry. When Bess noticed the three of them, she jumped up and down in her platform boots and clapped her hands together.

Robin said, "If I did that, they'd call for the rubber wagon. She looks like a cheerleader."

Alicia sipped her drink and said, "The definition of 'born with it.'"

Carla said, "Where's Borden?"

"Around here somewhere," said Robin, as they advanced toward Bess.

After the round of kisses and hugs, Bess introduced the men.

Carla was impressed Bess knew all their names, their wives names, and their kids' names.

The dad in a cashmere jacket asked Bess, "This is the poker crew you've been waiting for?"

She nodded proudly at them. Carla would give Bess credit for one thing: She sailed high above appearances. If anything, Robin, Alicia, and Carla were the least polished females in the vast crowded room where Bess was and would always be the shining star. Carla smiled at her host. Bess really was making an effort to put that last poker game behind them.

"Right here, ladies," said Bess, ushering them to the only empty table with a "Reserved" sign on it.

As they sat down, Carla overheard one of the men say, "Salary caps for executives. It's a disgrace. What happened to talent compensation? I don't get out of bed for less than a million."

"That must be some bed," said the balding dad.

"It's a new world out there," grumbled another dad. "The old rules no longer apply."

Was it Carla's imagination or did he shoot a glance her way? To him, she might represent the angry underclass. Five minutes ago, she would've seethed in silence. But now? She was seated and eager to play, to win. The Black Queen asked, "Care to join us, gentlemen?"

Bess pouted, "I thought it was just us."

Cashmere Jacket, a smooth, gray-haired operator with a ready smile and too-white teeth, said, "I'd love to sit in." He pulled the chair next to Bess and sat down, his shoulder brushing hers.

Carla smiled. His concentration wouldn't be worth a dime.

The two other men gamely sat down, too. Robin seemed to zero in on the youngest of the bunch, an overly rumpled alternadad type, midthirties, horn-rimmed glasses, visor haircut, and dark-wash jeans. What was he doing with this bunch of bankers? Carla reminded herself not to make assumptions about someone's financial status or profession based on his or her appearance. For one thing, the best dressed among them might have cracked retirement nest eggs. *And look at Robin,* she thought. *She dressed like a hippie, and could buy and sell half the people in this room.*

The dealer, a young man who'd been shuffling cards patiently, snapped to attention when his table filled up.

The dads emptied their pockets and arranged chips in neat stacks. Bess winked at the dealer, and he proceeded to dispense chips to the women.

Bess said to the women, "I had the dealer hold on to your chips for you."

Robin smiled wryly and took her stack. Alicia quickly snagged her pile and kept a protective hand over it, as if someone would try to take it away. Carla accepted hers, and nodded politely at Bess. There was a thousand dollars in chips here. Had Bess paid for them? The thought made Carla feel sick, but only for a second. She decided to believe Bess had simply arranged for her friends to play for free.

It hardly mattered. No one would walk out of there with money. Winners would "cash in" chips for prize baskets. They were lined up in the back of the room. The descriptions had been emailed to the parents several times this week as an enticement to attend the event. Some of the baskets were made by moms—cookies, little gifts—crap, basically. Some were donated by local businesses. The Trader Joe's basket was full of their signature pastas and Two Buck Chuck wine. Other gift collections were donated by wealthy families. One was for a week vacation in Paris, including a baguette, wheel of Brie, and the keys to the donor's pied-à-terre.

Carla wanted the Orlando package. A four-day vacation for four to Disney World, including plane tickets, park passes, dinner vouchers, and a hotel room. They'd never done the classic Americana trip of going to Orlando. Too much work, not enough money. It'd bothered Carla. When she told Claude the basket was a great prize, a fun treat for the family, he rolled his eyes and said, "Disney World? They're not *babies.*"

The dealer started the game, saying, "Texas Hold 'Em, five and ten dollar blinds." And then they were off.

Carla peeked at her pocket cards. Pre-flop, she raised to $20.

Alternadad said, "So it's going to be like that, is it?"

"Like what?" asked Carla, using the voice.

"Fold," he said. Carla now knew he would only bet if he had face cards, aces, or pairs.

"Don't scare the rabbits, Carla," said Robin, who then folded. "I mean myself."

A few minutes later, Carla won the hand before the river card was dealt. In the pocket, she had a pair of threes. Barely a leg to stand on, and yet she skipped away with the pot.

She suppressed a hoot. That wouldn't be polite. When she won again, and again, her resolve to keep her cool weakened. She was having fun, enjoying the moment. She inhaled the air again, and realized that sweet smell wasn't seriousness and concentration. It was equality. The players might make assumptions—to Carla's advantage, as it turned out—about her abilities. But race, class, social status, none of that mattered at the poker table. And, of course, the cards were color-blind.

Pair of queens, both black, in the pocket. Carla raised pre-flop, $40. Robin, drunker by the minute, sloppily flirting with alternadad despite his wife flitting nearby, folded. Alicia chewed her lip and tugged her earring. She agonized, called, but then seemed to regret it. The banker and the accountant played every hand, losing again and again. Carla assumed they were trying to impress Bess, who gave them no reason to think throwing money around excited her. Bess had been playing well, smartly. She'd had to remove Cashmere Jacket's manicured hands from her shoulder and (Carla suspected) thighs a dozen times.

"I call," said Bess.

The flop: rags and another queen. Carla checked her stack, and saw that, in an hour of play, she was up over a thousand bucks. She'd lure in the remaining players with a small bet, keep the hand alive. "Raise twenty dollars," she said.

A few folds. Bess reraised $100.

Carla called and said, "All for a good cause."

"Paris, here I come," said Bess, winking a false eyelash at Carla.

On the turn, the dealer put down an ace. Suddenly, Carla noticed a lot of red up there. Three of the four common cards were hearts. If Bess had two hearts in the pocket, she'd have an ace-high flush, which beat three of a kind handily. Had she been lured, when she thought she'd set the trap?

Bess smiled sweetly at Carla, waited for the Black Queen to bet. She felt the switch, the Black Queen's ruthlessness clicked into place finally. No more pussyfooting around. Bess—correction, White Diamond—had come to play, too.

"Raise two hundred dollars," said Carla.

"Call," said Bess.

The other players stopped flitting and flirting and drinking, sensing that real poker was being played. As if the signal was sent across the room, a small gathering of people stood around the table, watching.

The river: five of clubs. A rag. No help to either player. If it'd been another queen . . . but no. Carla had to figure out whether Bess was bluffing. Did she have two hearts in the pocket? Two aces in the pocket would also beat her three queens. What were the odds? Would Bess have bet so aggressively on a flush draw?

The dealer said, "Ma'am?"

Carla said, "Raise, three hundred dollars."

Bess hesitated. Behind her blue eyes, she calculated her odds. Carla knew Bess had something. But what?

"Reraise, six hundred."

The crowd murmured. She heard someone say, "Go, Bess!"

"Call," said Carla, dropping her chips into the huge pot.

Bess showed first. In the pocket, she had the ace of clubs, and the three of hearts. Two pair.

A ripple of applause, a few hands patted Bess's shoulders. Carla noticed Borden standing behind his wife, smiling proudly at her gutsy play and solid hand.

Carla turned over her pair.

The dealer said, "Three queens, the winner."

A moment of silence, and then applause from the audience. Clapping louder that anyone, Bess smiled at Carla, radiant, beaming, a bit flushed. She said, "Good hand."

"You, too," replied Carla. Grinning freely, the Black Queen relished the moment, and raked in the pot.

Alicia leaned close to Carla and sniffed. "Funny. You don't smell like you're on fire."

Robin held up her drink. "Cheers!"

Borden kissed Bess's cheek. "Lucky in love," he said to Bess.

It was a cute moment. Carla's heart tweaked. She glanced around, hoping to find Claude among the spectators, to share her excitement with him.

She spotted him in the back of the crowd. His expression would be inscrutable to the casual observer. But Carla read it, as only a wife could. He was embarrassed.

Carla felt a momentary pull to go to him and apologize for whatever she might've done to make him upset. But then the dealer said, "Blinds, please." Coldly, purposefully, Carla returned her complete attention to the game, where it stayed for the rest of the night.

Hours later, Claude and Carla walked to their car, parked two blocks from Brownstone. They each carried two gift baskets, including the Orlando package. Claude rolled his eyes when Carla picked it.

Opening the trunk, Claude said, "They won't all fit."

"Put the YMCA basket in the backseat," she said. A family gym membership, bathrobes, a shower caddy. The Y was only a few blocks from the hospital. She'd work out at lunch, better herself. The boys could take swim lessons.

"Gym membership," he said, shaking his head. "You know you'll never go."

They took their seats, and Claude turned the ignition. Carla was ready, beyond ready, to get home. She was exhausted from three hours of poker. The other players came and went—in Robin's case, to refresh her drink. In Alicia's case, to find Tim, and then leave abruptly (something was going on there, but Carla didn't know what). Bess had PA duties. Carla stayed put. She never left her seat. Bess returned for the entire last half hour, and she and Carla went heads up, just the two of them against each other. Bess went all in with a pair of kings. All night long, Carla had the edge. She finished the night with a pair of aces.

Well, not exactly *finished*. The night was just getting started, in a way. She had Claude and his hurt feelings to contend with. Right now, in the passenger seat, she didn't feel like the night's big winner. She was going home with the booby prize, a prickly husband.

For once, he didn't brood in stormy silence. "You embarrassed yourself tonight," he said, "You were greedy and coarse."

"I didn't embarrass myself," said Carla, suddenly afraid that she had come off as undignified.

"You embarrassed *me*," he said, getting to the point.

"I embarrassed you by winning?" she said. "I outplayed everyone. I was better than everyone. Why aren't you *proud* of me? Why aren't you rooting for me?"

"Why would I be proud to watch you scrape and claw for a place at that table?" asked Claude.

She shook her head. "It always comes back to us against them for you."

Claude said, "You'd go broke sending Zeke to school with white kids before you'd send him to school with black kids for free."

Carla said, "It's not about black and white."

He laughed bitterly, and steered the car out of the parking spot. Then he shifted into static silence, shutting her out. For once, Carla was grateful for it.

She let her head rest against the window, the glass cooling her forehead. At that moment, Carla hated her husband.

Yes, yes, he was an honorable man, a good father. He worked hard and took responsibility. But Claude wasn't kind. He wasn't affectionate. Tonight, they weren't partners on the same team. They were rivals, on opposite sides, fighting for different goals.

RAISE

9

Alicia

"If I choose panties, then this game is over right now," said Finn in his boxers, seated Indian-style on the bed across from Alicia. "If I pick the bra, I'll get to enjoy the view for a while." Between them, fanned out on the bedspread, two hands of five cards. Finn had a pair of eights. Alicia had king high.

She delighted in the insistent tent of his boxers. "What's it going to be?" she asked.

"Bra."

Off with her bra. A 34B, hardly much boob inside it. Alicia often went without bras. As chance would have it, she had been fortunate to wear one today. Strip poker had not been on the agenda when she and Finn suggested they work out of his home office in Battery Park City today. Change location, reset their minds. Alicia was amazed Chaundry, their boss, allowed them to go. They'd had to swear on their jobs that they'd finish a pitch for a prospective new client, Punch Gym.

The New York City chain had a dozen facilities all over Manhattan. Alicia thought their pitch presentation would be a waste of time. Punch could afford to hire a much bigger agency than Bartlebee. They were a boutique agency—as in, writing ads for single-store boutiques, and unglamorous insurance companies—not a megashop for chain stores, car brands, and beer.

"That kind of attitude," said Chaundry to her, "is why you should be glad you have a job at all."

As it turned out, the recession had hit gyms, including Punch, right in the solar plexus. Nonmandatory memberships were at the top of the list of household budget cuts. Punch was bargain hunting for new recruitment-drive ideas. Hence, Bartlebee was asked to prepare a presentation.

They arrived at Finn's apartment at noon. Alicia had been in this building a few times before. She and Tim came to Finn's Christmas party a few years ago. Earlier this year, a Brownstone mom with *way* too much time on her hands (she'd calligraphed the invitations herself) hosted the fourth-grade parents' potluck dinner in her penthouse a dozen flights up. A lot of Brownstone families lived in Battery Park City. It was only a couple subway stops from Brooklyn Heights.

Finn had a modest low-floor studio. It was bachelor-y. Not a lot of food or furniture to distract them, so they got right to work. Within forty-five minutes, they sketched out three print ads and the storyboards for two fifteen-second TV ads. The first was a woman's midsection—six-pack abs, tan and glistening—with two words of copy: "Core Values." The next ad: the back and shoulders of a man while using the lateral press Nautilus machine, his muscles ripped and shining from sweat. The copy, "Strength of Character." The last ad, featuring a pair of gorgeous, shapely female legs in motion on a treadmill with the copy underneath, "Personal Endurance." Their concept was to make staying in shape synonymous with individual integrity. To survive in the new Age of Responsibility, according to their ads, you needed a buff bod. It was simple and serious, which was the advertising zeitgeist of the moment.

After Finn finished the last computer stroke, he leaned toward Alicia and planted a juicy wet kiss right on her lips. It was their first kiss. Months of heavy flirting and back/limb stroking at the guys' poker games had come to this.

She'd spent the last hour fiddling with words about value and character, yet Alicia didn't, not once, hesitate to kiss Finn back. She had proven her values and character, working hard to support her family, making sacrifices for Joe, ignoring her own emotional and physical needs. Alicia's character and values had been tested. She'd endured enough. Finn was offering himself to her. She accepted.

Finn's tongue was soft, warm, and wonderfully alive in her mouth. She kissed him like a drowning woman gulps for air, her hands in his hair, pulling him into her as if her life depended on it. Finn's beautiful long strong fingers—she loved to watch them wrapped around a pencil—were now under her blouse, under her bra. When he cupped her breast, catching her nipple between two fingers, she moaned. Ridiculously loud. It'd escaped from a place so deep in her body, the sound reverberated, nearly shook the apartment windows.

"I've struck gold," he said, laughing.

"Do it again," she gasped.

His glorious hands traveled down her back, across her bottom, pulling a leg up and around him. He pressed himself against her. Even through her skirt and his trousers, she felt the heat coming off his erection. She imagined it a glowing rod of heat and light, pulsing in his pants. Her parts started to pulse in a rhythm, too, getting hot, expanding. She felt slick as an eel, and desperately needed him to touch her and find out exactly how excited she was.

Finn lifted her against him with both hands on her ass. Full frontal contact. He pushed her hair off her shoulder with his nose, and then bit her gently on her shoulder. Alicia had been holding on to his neck with both arms, afraid to let go and fall to the floor. She let one hand trail down his chest and sneak between two buttons of his shirt. Chest hair, dense, coarse, and dark. Finding a soft bump, she squeezed his nipple and he seemed to stiffen. Had she hurt him?

"Now you've done it," he said, his voice hitched.

He unzipped his pants, pushed aside her soaked panties, positioned himself, and then slid into her, tip to nuts.

In those five seconds, Alicia thought she might've seen God. Blinking frantically from the tears that were suddenly streaming out of her eyes, she was overwhelmed by sensation. Finn's hands on her butt, she clutched at his chest and shoulders as his heat drove into her.

Her clit felt big and hot as a lightbulb.

Finn bit her shoulder again, his hands gripping her ass tighter. He lifted her up, tilting her into a more comfortable position, and she let him take her weight. He carried her to his couch, still joined, lowered her onto the cushion, and kneeled in front of her. She could wrap both legs around him now, and lean back to watch his face.

His eyes were wide open, staring back at her. The look on his face, amazement, need, a slight strain from holding back, the O of his mouth as he panted and groaned with each thrust. It was too much, too beautiful and raw. Alicia felt the building pressure, like a balloon filling with liquid gold. Filling and filling, and then bursting, hot gold pumping in and out, up and down her spine. Alicia had never come with her eyes open before. She watched Finn watch her, and it was the biggest turn-on she'd ever experienced.

A second later, he came. His face twisted with relief and joy, his cheeks turned red, his nostrils widened and twitched, his mouth wide open. It was the face of truth and beauty. Absolute perfection.

She'd been wrong. Watching him come was the biggest turn-on she'd ever experienced.

And she wanted to do it again. ASAP.

Finn detached himself, flopped next to her on the couch. They arranged their clothes a bit awkwardly.

"Sorry so short," he said, still breathing heavy.

"Five minutes that changed my life," she said, her tone light.

He was respectfully silent, but then said, "I don't think of you as a cougar or anything."

"A cougar?" He meant much older women who seduced younger men. "I'm only seven years older than you! But thanks for the assurance."

"I liked you from my first day at Bartlebee," he said, turning his head to face her, make sure she knew he meant it.

"Liked me?"

"Thought you were cute," he said. "I remember thinking I was surprised you were older, and had a family. If it weren't for your husband and Joe, I would have gone for it. I had to turn off the switch. Think of you in only one way."

"I did the same thing about you," she said. "Turned off the switch."

"But then you turned it back on," he said, curious. "A few months ago when you joined the poker game."

"You realize, if we'd slept together years ago, we never would have become friends or written all those ads together," she said. "We would've flamed out. We still might. This could destroy a great partnership."

"Partnership," he said, nodding. "Like with your husband?"

She placed a hand on Finn's cheek. "Nothing like that. Believe me. You don't know how not-like-that this is."

"Was it the poker game? Winning seemed to get you going," he said, back to that.

"It was the poker game," she said. But not the one he thought. "I also play with some women every few weeks."

"You told them about me?" he asked, grinning.

"I told them about *me*," she said. She'd opened up at the game, about her sexless marriage. That was the first step that brought her to this blissful moment on Finn's couch.

Finn didn't quite get her point. "Well, whatever you did, keep doing it," he said.

"Let's play now," said Alicia, sitting up, smiling broadly. "Strip poker. It'll be fun."

They played five-card draw, which Alicia hadn't tried before, but got the hang of quickly. Having her mind engaged, hands full, and clothes on—at first—eased the slight weirdness of having just made love to her office mate of five years, cheating on her husband, best friend, and father of her only child. It was a momentous day, for sure! Alicia was basking in the flood of happy hormones coursing through her brain, fully aware that those very chemicals obliterated less joyous thoughts that would surely surface later.

Alicia—no, Wild Heart—lost a hand, and removed her bra. Finn's eyes drank in her small breasts, what Tim called "the fried eggs" (incredibly, it used to sound affectionate).

"You're beautiful," he said.

"You like women with starter boobs?" she asked, instantly regretting how insecure she sounded.

"Not usually," he admitted. "You've seen my ex-girlfriends."

Yes, she couldn't help but notice the parade of curvy half-wits he'd ushered through their shared office. "I'm a departure, you're saying?" she asked.

"More like a late arrival," said Finn.

Too clever, she thought. *Too cute.* What rabbit hole had she fallen into? *No one deserved this kind of happiness,* she thought. *Least of all me.*

"I do have one major complaint about you," he said.

"Just one?"

"You don't know when to stop talking," said Finn.

He moved toward her, pushing her back on the bed, positioning himself on top. In short order, they were completely, rapturously naked, once again fused together.

Afterward, when she returned to earth, Alicia realized that a bunch of cards were stuck to the dewy skin on her back. Finn peeled them off, and showed her each one. Hearts, diamonds. Lots of red.

"You've got a flush," said Finn.

Of course, leaving was agony. Alicia felt like a teenager, her emotions heightened and intense, uncontrollable. She actually cried when Finn kissed her good-bye at his door. He wasn't weirded out, or didn't let on if he was.

But it *was* weird! How would they act tomorrow at the office? Would it happen again? "I will surely die if we don't do this again," she told him at his door.

"Then I guess we'd better!" he said. "I'm free now."

But she had to go immediately or she might never leave Finn's lair. At some point, soon, she and Finn would have to talk. Or maybe not, thought Alicia as she pushed the elevator button. She'd tried to talk to Tim about their marriage, many times—but not for a while, she realized, having given up. Of course, the way the world worked, now that she was moving away from the marriage, Tim would make a push to save it. She laughed to herself, imagining Tim's attempt to romance her, or even (*gasp*) seduce her. The smell of another man on her skin might inflame his proprietary claim on her, if only subconsciously. Tim would never, not in a million years, believe her capable of cheating.

The elevator doors opened.

"Mommy!"

Alicia, standing frozen, registered the shape and face of her son in the elevator. Next to Joe stood her husband, Tim; his jaw dropped to the floor. *Did he look guilty?* she wondered. *Did I?* The doors started to close. A hand shot out between them, and the doors opened again.

"Are you coming in?" asked Tim. "This is a surprise."

Alicia stepped inside the car. "I was at Finn's apartment," she said. "Working."

"I figured," said Tim.

She was about to ask Tim what they were doing there, when Joe grabbed her around the waist, buried his face into her shirt and started crying.

"Oh, my God," she said, hugging him. "What's wrong?"

Tim answered. "We had a playdate at Anita Turnbull's—remember her from the potluck? Joe and Austin didn't get along so well."

"What happened?" she asked her son.

"I hate him," said Joe.

"Why?" she asked.

But her son couldn't or wouldn't say. She looked to Tim for answers. He just shrugged.

"Can we please just go home?" asked Joe. "I never want to come here again." The boy was glaring at his father now. "I *told* you before. I hate Austin. I hate coming here."

"Okay, okay," said Tim. "Message received."

"You come here often?" asked Alicia.

Tim was in charge of after-school activities, including playdates. This was their division of labor. Alicia dropped off, and Tim picked up. The swirl at pick-up was when playdates were arranged. Alicia knew it was better for Joe that Tim served as social director. If that were left up to her, Joe wouldn't have any playdates at all. Except for Bess, Robin, and Carla, Alicia hadn't managed to bond with the other parents in Joe's class, just as she'd predicted and feared.

But charming and available Tim had befriended the one or two other dads at pick-up (Alicia thought of them as "beta husbands"), as well as all the moms. That included, apparently, the pampered and comely Anita Turnbull, the type of woman Alicia found inhumanly intimidating with her polished pilates body with money and supermom cred.

Tim said, "I thought the boys were doing well together."

"I *told* you Austin's a jerk," wailed Joe. "What part of 'I hate him and wish he was dead' don't you understand?"

Alicia laughed despite the tension. The kid was miserable, but he still managed to keep a (dark) sense of humor. *What doesn't kill him would only make him funnier,* she thought. Alicia knew that humor was a defense mechanism. It was her shield of choice, too.

The elevator doors opened into the lobby. The three of them walked in silence toward the subway entrance a few blocks away. According to her watch, it was six o'clock. Tim and Joe had been at Anita's since school ended three hours ago.

Alicia flashed back to that poker night at Bess's, when she'd brought Joe along to hang with the other kids while she played with the moms. She'd been in the game room for two hours before Joe had his meltdown and insisted they leave. If she'd been paying the slightest bit of attention to her son, she would have plucked him out of the difficult situation way before he reached hysteria. Tim yelled at her later that night when she told him what happened, accusing her of not paying enough attention to Joe.

They squeezed into the crowded rush-hour train, bound for Brooklyn. The farther they got from Manhattan, the more Joe seemed to relax. Now that he'd recovered, Joe didn't want her to touch him. She tried to stroke his hair, but he pushed her hand away.

Joe wasn't a baby, true. At ten years old, he was up to her shoulder. In a few years, he'd be a teenager, with a host of complicated emotional, hormonal issues to contend with, on top of his social phobia. The kid was in for a rough ride. No more stalling and hoping the problem would just go away. Whether or not they could afford therapy and medication (if it came to that), Joe needed help now.

Alicia glanced at Tim. His body was there, swaying subtly with the motion of the train. But he was miles away.

"Tell me again," said Alicia later that night, after Joe went to bed. "You and Joe went to Battery Park with Anita and Austin right after school." They sat in the living room, on opposite ends of their lumpy, knotty, ancient couch.

"Everything was fine on the way there," said Tim.

"You got to the apartment, and . . . then what?"

"Anita and I had coffee in the kitchen. The boys went off to play Wii boxing."

"And?"

"When it was time to go, we left," said Tim. "I had no idea Joe had a bad time until he started crying in the elevator."

"I realize Anita's apartment is pretty big, but you must have heard something."

"It sounded like they were having fun."

"What are fun sounds?"

"You know."

"Honestly, I don't."

Tim sighed. "You're being insufferable right now."

"Joe is in pain," she said flatly.

"He's sensitive," said Tim.

Alicia frowned. "I want you to call Anita right now, and tell her to talk to Austin about what happened."

"I can't do that!"

"Then I will."

Tim shrugged (a gesture he was making too often lately; the physical equivalent of "whatever"). It incensed her. Didn't he want to get to the bottom of this? What had that little beast done to Joe to upset him so much?

She got up and rooted around in the kitchen for the Brownstone directory. She picked up the phone, and dialed the number for Anita Turnbull.

The phone pressed to her cheek, Alicia watched Tim's face go from ruddy to pink to pale to chalk white. He said, "You want to make a fool of yourself? Go ahead."

No answer. Voicemail. She hung up. "We are going to get to the bottom of this," Alicia announced. As far as her marriage was concerned, Alicia felt like she'd already reached the bottom.

She dialed another number. "Carla?" asked Alicia. "We're ready for the name of that pediatric psychiatrist."

⁘

A few nights later, the players met at Robin's house. Zeke, Manny, and Amy came with their moms. Alicia didn't dare bring Joe with her this time. Why throw the guppy in with the sharks?

She had taken Joe to see the shrink. He was tested. According to the doctor, Alicia's son fell somewhere on the obsessive-compulsive disorder spectrum, with a touch of anxiety disorder, too. Despite the bad news, Alicia was grateful to have it. OCD-lite didn't seem *that* horrible. And now they knew what they were dealing with, and could proceed with treatment. Dr. Zorn explained their options. Tim was against medication, toeing the "he'll grow out of it" line. Alicia, who remembered her own anxieties and phobias—albeit, not as severe as Joe's—was in favor of giving the kid some relief.

"Close the window, Robin," complained Carla. "It's thirty degrees outside."

"One more drag," said the redhead.

"I don't want Amy to know you smoke," said Bess. Her daughter Amy was babysitting the fourth-grade kids while the women played. Borden was with their three boys at a Knicks game.

"She already knows," said Robin. She took a long drag of her cigarette, stubbed it out on the sill, and then closed her kitchen window. The three other women were shivering around the table. "I'm ready for spring. Beyond ready. Is this the longest March in the history of the world *or what?*"

Bess shuffled the cards and started dealing. "You know how it works," she said. "It's forty one day, and seventy the next. Throw in an April freeze, and by May, we're ready to plant."

Carla peeked at her cards. "Raise five," she said crisply, tossing more chips into the pot.

Alicia didn't like what she saw in her pocket. Rags, a five, and a seven. "Fold."

"I know Anita Turnbull pretty well," said Bess, calling the bet. "She's a flirt. I've had to peel her off Borden a few times at parties. But I don't think she'd jeopardize her marriage by having an affair. Her husband, John, is a nice man."

"Not to mention Midas rich," said Robin.

"That, too," agreed Bess.

Alicia understood the implication. Anita wouldn't risk upturning her gilded apple cart by having a fling with a penniless, if charming and sharp-dressed, man like Tim.

"I confronted the kid," said Alicia. "Austin. I waited at drop-off until Anita left, and told Joe to go return his library books by himself. Then I walked over to Austin in the playground and demanded to know what he did to my son."

Robin laughed and threw her chips into the pot. "Did he piss himself?"

"He ignored me!" said Alicia. "I had to corner him by the swing set before he even looked at me."

"What'd he say?" asked Carla.

"I got a straight answer, I think," said Alicia. "Nothing too dramatic. They played Wii boxing. Austin beat Joe. Then they played Wii tennis. Beat him again. And again in three other Wii games. It could be a straightforward case of Austin being a competitive, gloating shitbag, and Joe feeling beaten down by losing."

"That would have been enough to make me cry," said Robin.

Bess dealt the flop.

Carla checked and said, "You realize you might've made life even harder for Joe by confronting Austin."

"I spoke to the teacher and asked her to keep a close eye on the two of them," said Alicia. "Nothing to report. Yet."

Robin said, "Now that you've warmed up by confronting a spoiled ten-year-old, are you ready to confront Tim?"

"A spoiled forty-year-old?" asked Alicia. She didn't add that she had no right to call out Tim for a dalliance with Anita, or even heavy flirting, when she was in the midst of a full-blown, hot and heavy affair with her co-worker.

None of the committee members knew or suspected. It was way too soon to discuss it openly. But she'd been thinking about it constantly since it happened a few days ago. Wild emotions seesawed back and forth between elation and guilt, gratitude and regret. Although the idea that Tim had touched another woman infuriated Alicia, the reality of it would instantly erase any negative feelings about her affair with Finn. Alicia half-hoped her husband was cheating.

If that wasn't a sign that the marriage was over, what was?

Robin said, "It's against my personal philosophy to defend a man, but you've got to look at it from Tim's perspective. Playdates are horrible! Having to make small talk with mothers, pretending to like the other kid. You can't fault Tim for ignoring the boys and getting an ego boost with Anita."

"If that's all she boosted," said Bess, grinning goofily.

"Listen to you, Pollyanna, with the sexy entendre!" said Robin. "I'm a good influence."

Carla shook her head disapprovingly. "Let's see some cards, Pollyanna."

Bess dealt the turn, a black jack. Carla tossed ten bucks into the pot. Robin folded. Bess scrutinized her cards, looked closely at the four on the table. The tone got serious for a second.

"Call," said Bess.

"Good," said Carla.

Alicia watched, and admired how intense the Black Queen and White Diamond were about the game. They were better players than she and Robin. "Have I told you how impressive you guys were at Casino Night?" she asked. "Beating all those finance pricks at their own game."

Carla deadpanned, "I've got skills."

Robin added, "And you've got a new BFF."

"What?"

"Renee Hobart?" said Robin. "Don't think we didn't notice. You're mighty chummy. Unless I'm mistaken, I saw you two leave school the other morning, and—wait for it—go to *Starbucks* together. The place you've likened to the fourth circle of Hell whenever I suggest going there. Or maybe you're a Starbucks hater only with me."

"Are you stalking me?" asked Carla.

Bess dealt the river. "Oh, that's lovely," she said, reacting to the ten of spades. "All in."

"Fold," said Carla, "even though I'm pretty sure you're bluffing."

Bess raked in the pot. "Pretty sure, but not a hundred percent."

"Nothing in life is a hundred percent," said Robin.

"May I please see your cards?" asked Carla, superpolite.

Bess said, "Of course," and pretended to turn over her pocket cards, only to tuck them into the deck at the last second. "Oops. Sorry, Carla. They slipped."

Alicia smiled at the easy camaraderie. But she disagreed with Robin's comment. Finn was a hundred percent: all man, all sex, all heat, every chance they got. Instead of his usual lap of blog reading at breakfast, Finn devoted that time to her. Laying her down behind their desks, licking her until she was a puddle of satisfaction on the carpet. He'd asked her to wear skirts every day, no underwear. Once she got to the office, her first stop was the ladies room to take off her panties. Even in this last blast of winter chill, she was overheated like a broken furnace. They'd never been known to lock their office door in the mornings, and the change in behavior was surely noticed by the rest of the staff. Chaundry would object, except he was granting them a reprieve. They'd won the Punch Gym account. The contract would keep the agency afloat for another six months, and would probably take Bartlebee to a higher level.

At thirty-six, Alicia had finally discovered true passion, and confidence at work, in the same week. Her office hours were full of kudos and climaxes. Home life? Gray as old mud. She and Tim had been tiptoeing around each other, barely talking, except about Joe.

Robin's turn to shuffle the cards and deal. "I want to know what Renee Hobart has that we don't," she said. "What's the attraction, Carla? It's because she's churchy and black."

"Robin!" said Bess.

Carla laughed hard. Alicia marveled, as usual, at what Robin could get away with.

"Come now, Robin," said Carla. "Don't you ever feel the need for some like-minded company? Don't you have any lushy Jewish friends?"

"Carla!" said Bess.

"No, she's right. I do long for lushy Jewish friends," said Robin, grinning widely. "The problem is, so few of us drink. And look at you, Black Queen, calling me on my shit. I'm a good influence on you, too. Admit it!"

"Being friends with you is what drove me to Renee," said Carla.

That was a brutally honest admission, thought Alicia, not sure how Robin, or any of them, should take it. During the few beats of silence, Alicia checked her hole cards, liking her pair of eights, and throwing a few chips into the pot.

Robin asked, "Diversity is too much of a strain for you?"

"I get what you mean, Carla," said Bess, calling. "You need balance."

"She needs a mirror," said Robin. "Someone you can look at as a reflection of yourself. Too many women use their kids that way. It's healthier to make a friend. And Renee is a great choice, Carla. She's a cool, confident woman. I'm still jealous, though. I demand a coffee date."

"In public?" asked Carla, raising (as usual).

"At *Starbucks*, you bitch. How about *with* Renee?" asked Robin, eyebrows up, folding her hand.

"Boundaries," warned Carla.

Suddenly, Amy appeared in the kitchen doorway; Alicia couldn't help noticing how she'd changed. She'd gained about twenty pounds. Her clothes were grungier, clearly on purpose. Her hair was dirty, and obscuring most of her face. At the beginning of the school year, Amy was teetering on the edge of coltish loveliness. Seven months later, she'd fallen, hard, on the wrong side of the wall that divided pretty and plain, seemingly on purpose.

Bess looked up, smiling sweetly at her seething daughter. "Need something?" asked Bess.

"I'm going to take off now," said Amy, barely audible.

"What was that, honey?" asked Bess.

Amy sighed dramatically, as if repeating herself was beyond human endurance. "It's ten o'clock. Time to go."

Bess said, "We're not quite finished, honey."

Amy threw her hands up and dropped them to slap against her sides, "Stay all night. Has nothing to do with me. I'm just sitting in there watching TV with the kids. They're almost asleep."

Carla said, "That's my cue."

Robin said, "Sit down, Carla. You've got all the chips."

Bess said, "If you can wait ten minutes, Amy, we'll walk home together."

"I'm not *going* home," said Amy. "I'm hooking up with some friends."

"It's a school night," said Bess, her painted-on smile starting to fade.

"So what," said Amy, squaring off her feet (in scary black boots).

Alicia recoiled instinctively. She hadn't been intimidated by a sixteen-year-old girl since she was that age, and every kid in school terrified her.

"We're leaving together in five minutes, and you are coming home with me," said Bess, holding her ground. "It's a school night, and you have to get up early. End of discussion."

Had any conversation really ended with "end of discussion"? It was a launch point, as far as Alicia was concerned. Amy, too.

"You have no right to tell me what to do!" shrieked the ungrateful girl. "If you cared about my homework, you wouldn't have *forced* me to sit in there, bored to *death* for three *freaking* hours already. I need to see my friends. They actually care about me—*me*, who *I* am. I don't give a *shit* about it being a school night or embarrassing you in front of your *friends*." When she said "friends," Amy air quoted.

Alicia, Robin, and Carla eyed each other frantically, unsure what to do or say. Should they step in—Alicia had several choice comebacks knocking around in her head—or let Bess deal with her daughter alone?

Two beats of wired silence. Bess said, "You're only embarrassing yourself."

Pretty lame comeback, thought Alicia, but at least Bess sounded rational.

Robin said to Amy, "I thought you liked babysitting."

"I like getting paid," said Amy.

Robin laughed. "I bet you do." She pushed herself up from the table, found a few bills in her jeans pocket, and handed a twenty and a ten out for Amy. The girl tentatively entered the kitchen, snatched the bills from Robin's hand, and quickly retreated.

Amy looked at Carla and said, "Your kids are here, too."

Carla said, "You won't get a penny from me, young lady. You disrespect your mother and yourself. If you were my child, I'd relax my policy on spanking."

Robin said, "What is your policy on spanking?"

"Not after age seven."

"Lucky seven," said Robin. To Amy, she added, "Carla's right. Gimme my money back."

Amy looked frightened for a second. It was hard to tell, with all that hair in her face. The girl tucked the cash into her pants pocket and ran out of the apartment. The women heard her boots stomping down the hallway.

Bess, meanwhile, had dropped her head in her hands. Alicia reached over to give her a comforting stroke on the back. As soon as her palm touched the pink cashmere of her friend's sweater, Bess started crying, heavy wracking sobs that made her shoulders rattle.

Robin said, "Oh, thank God. I was afraid we'd break tradition and get through a game without someone crying."

"It's always me," said Bess between gulps of air.

"That's true," said Carla. When Alicia and Robin glared at her, she added, "Well, it's never me."

"Black don't crack?" asked Robin.

"You are *bad*," said Carla. "But no, actually, it don't."

Bess recovered enough to speak, "I just don't *get* it. Did I create that monster? I'm not a perfect mother, I realize that. But I'm pretty sure I'm a decent human being. Borden is a wonderful person. How could we have raised a child to turn out . . . like that?"

"Demon seed, you mean?" asked Alicia.

"Yes! Where did she come from?" asked Bess, looking at each woman as if she might have a concrete answer. "Maybe she did come from Hell."

"Amy isn't evil," said Carla. "She's just . . ."

Bess blinked and looked up. "She's what?"

Alicia waited for Carla's answer, too. Perhaps a pediatrician could give a reasonable explanation for why bad children happened to good people.

Robin said, "Well, Doctor?"

Carla sighed. "She's angry and feels misunderstood, we all see that. And resentful, I don't know why. She's hostile, and enjoys test-ing how far she can push you, Bess. She's got a dramatic flair. For example, I wouldn't be surprised if she'd spent the last hour on the couch in the other room mentally composing her little speech."

"So she's creative?" asked Bess, with heartbreaking hope.

Carla smiled balefully. "She's destructive, Bess. The changes she's made in her appearance seem like self-sabotage to me. And her rudeness. She's hurting herself as much as she's hurting you."

"Don't turn her into a depressed mental patient," said Robin. "Amy is just a confused sixteen-year-old with enough intelligence to question authority."

"Like you were?" asked Carla.

"Yes!" agreed Robin. "I mellowed with age."

"Like cheese?" asked Alicia.

Carla said, "You also hated your parents, blew up to over three hundred pounds, had indiscriminate sex with men you barely knew, and the smoking . . ."

Robin shushed her. "Stephanie is in the next room."

Bess said, "Amy didn't ask me once about my lump. Or my sur-gery. She didn't come to the hospital, or to my room during the re-covery. Amy does not care if I live or die. I doubt she cares about anything, except her mysterious friends, a roving pack of teenage les-bians for all I know. She acts like nothing matters!"

"Doesn't care about anything. Nothing matters," said Alicia. "That's sounds familiar, doesn't it? Is she reading Nietzsche, too?"

Bess wiped the tears still streaming down her cheeks. "Maybe I was inspired by *her*," she said. "I used to be able to feel her feelings. Maybe that's where my apathy came from. Amy's attitude infected me. I kept thinking, 'nothing matters.' But what I really felt was, 'nothing *I do* matters.' I can be strict or kind, patient or impatient. It's immaterial. Amy detests me. I have no idea why. I can't make her like me or talk to me. I ask if she's okay. I offer to help. But she screams at me to leave her alone and slams the door. I have to keep trying, though. Which is not easy. Honestly—this is horrible and frightening to say—I kind of hate her right now."

"Me, too," said Robin.

"Same," said Alicia.

Carla said, "We have to remember that her brain isn't fully formed. She looks like an adult—"

"A dirty, scary adult," corrected Bess.

Carla continued, "But she's still a kid. That said, I agree: Amy is not a great advertisement for teenage girls."

"What am I going to do?" asked Bess, crying again, harder. "Have any of you lived with someone who despises you? It's awful."

Alicia looked at her hands. She'd been spared that sorry fate. For all her problems with Tim, the distrust and neglect, her cheating, his suspected flirtations, she didn't actually hate him. He didn't hate her, although he might if he found out about Finn. She dared to look up at the other long faces around the kitchen table. Robin seemed contemplative, for once, short on words. Carla gazed at Bess with professional compassion.

Pricking up her ears, Alicia realized that the house was quiet. Too quiet. The hum of the TV was gone. Little ears had been listening. But for how long?

Alicia said, "I think we have spies."

"Kids!" bellowed Carla. "Get in here!"

Stephanie, Zeke, and Manny waited for a second, and then showed themselves. They'd been listening from right outside the kitchen doorway. They might've heard everything.

"Get your coats, boys," said Carla. "It's time to go home."

The two boys nodded and went to the TV room to get their things. Zipped up, they returned to the kitchen. Carla and Alicia rose, too, readying to depart.

Carla said to Bess, "Call me. I can give you some names, counselors, teen specialists."

Bess nodded, trying to seem happy in front of the children.

Alicia said to Robin, "Thanks for inviting me."

Robin said, "The pleasure is all mine."

They moved to go, but Zeke stepped into the kitchen and went over to Bess. He put his hand on her shoulder and said, "I think you're a very nice person, Mrs. Steeple."

Bess smiled at the ten-year-old and pulled him into a tight hug. She held on to him for a few seconds too long. From the clench, Zeke glanced over at Carla, his mom, as if to ask, "What now?"

Finally, Bess released him. They all left Robin to console Bess further by herself.

Alicia waited until she and the Morgans were on the street, safely out of the building, to say to Zeke, "That was excellent of you to say."

Carla said, "It was very sweet of you, Zeke. But you shouldn't have been eavesdropping. I've half a mind to punish you both."

The boys drooped slightly. Alicia caught Zeke's eye and smiled at him. Carla had to be so proud of these quiet, polite children. The others mocked Carla for her strict rules, but she was doing something right.

Alicia tried to picture Joe making such a kind gesture, being empathically attuned to someone else's sadness or fear. Would he truly feel Bess's pain, or merely witness her having it? The latter, Alicia decided. Her son was stuck in his own head.

Just like Mommy.

10

Robin

"It's too tight," said Stephanie. She and Robin were in a tiny dressing room at the Old Navy at Atlantic Center, near the future location of the long-threatened Atlantic Yards development. If the overlords didn't run out of money, the Nets basketball franchise would soon call this part of Brooklyn their home court. Only two miles from Brooklyn Heights, the proposed development—basketball arena, shops, housing—was causing quite a commotion in Robin's neck of the borough. Residents were concerned with increased traffic, parking problems, human congestion. Robin believed, in her cynical heart, that when Brooklyn Heights people complained about the advancing horde of car and foot traffic, they weren't talking about white people. Black people would come to see the Nets. Black people would occupy the low- and middle-income housing. Black people had already swarmed to Atlantic Center's discount stores, Pathmark, Target, DSW. Robin and Stephanie had been browsing and trying on outfits at Old Navy for an hour already. Not a single white face in sight.

Bess had never been to Atlantic Center. Her brood shopped at Old Navy (these days, even the rich buy cheap), but Bess took them to the store in Manhattan. "The Soho store is much bigger," claimed Bess. Robin didn't think Bess was a racist. More a classist. Bess would buy the same shirt at the same chain store, as long as the store was in a ritzy zip code.

In Brooklyn, you couldn't buy a pair of jeans without it having racial overtones.

"Are you sure?" asked Robin, tugging at Stephanie's waistband. They're a size twelve."

"Mom, that hurts," whined Stephanie. "Can we just go? We'll order online."

"We're here already," growled Robin.

The girl grew out of clothes faster than she could wear them. Robin bought Stephanie six new pairs of pants in September, and now none of them fit. She's apparently blown right through size twelve and needed fourteens. Robin swallowed a gulp of shame. She'd been forcing her kid to walk around in confining size tens for months.

"Wait here," said Robin. "I'll get more stuff to try on."

"Don't leave me here alone," said Stephanie.

Oh, God, the memory of Robin's mother leaving her alone in the communal dressing room at Bloomingdale's hit her like a train. Her worst Mom moment. For a split second, Robin sympathized with her mother. She understood the frustration, the harried annoyance of not being able to throw a wardrobe together for her daughter. At the time, Robin interpreted her mom's behavior as hateful and cruel. But perhaps she'd just been frustrated, like Robin was now.

"I won't leave you alone," said Robin quickly. "I'm sorry I said that. I'm sorry I was impatient."

"Mommy," said Stephanie, starting to show signs of despair. "I feel bad. Nothing fits."

Robin got on her daughter's level. "That's the clothes' fault. Not yours. Okay? You are *fine*."

"Am I fat?" whispered Stephanie, her eyes round and hungry.

Robin's heart broke in half, right there, in the dressing room at Old Navy. How old had Robin been when her fears of being fat kicked in? Younger than ten-year-old Stephanie. Robin's mom put her on a diet at eight. She was in second grade when her mother insisted on Robin's first weigh-in, a weekly event that continued until Robin left for college at eighteen. Several times a day, lest Robin forget, her mother reminded her only daughter that she was "heavy," that "the kitchen is closed," that if Robin served her own portions, or fixed her own lunch, she'd "be big as a house." (As it turned out, ironically, despite—because of?—her mom's efforts, insults, criticisms, enforced diets, and weigh-ins, Robin got bigger than a house. She was a mansion when her mother died.)

Robin's mom couldn't watch her 24/7, of course. During her hours of freedom, Robin ate to her heart's discontent, each bite a rebellious "Fuck you" to her mother for being heartless, and to her father who did nothing to protect her. And to her taunting classmates who called her "beast." Robin had many "Fuck yous" to dispense, many spiteful Twinkies to consume.

To be a mother was to somehow screw up your kids. Robin was certain, as the day was long, that she'd make/had made terrible mistakes raising Stephanie that would damage her in some hideous way in the future. But Robin would not make the same mistake her mother had. She'd *never*—under threat of death—put Stephanie on a diet or make her feel bad about her weight.

"Let's go back out there together and pick some new stuff," suggested Robin.

Stephanie got dressed and they bravely ventured forth. They pulled size fourteen jeans off the shelf. Robin blamed herself for Stephanie's thicker waist this year. She should cook more often. It was torture for Robin to eat vegetables (gastric bypass had ruined her for raw food). But she had to start making salads and veggies for Stephanie. Robin could use her juicer for more than fruity vodka mixers.

Any mother alive would rather her daughter be thin and beautiful, for the kid's sake. Having been a fat pariah for most of her life, Robin knew that being slim was better than being heavy, times a million. Fat-acceptance people were just plain *wrong*. Fat and happy was a pipe dream.

Maybe I'm just too cynical for acceptance, thought Robin.

They grabbed some tops, jackets, and skirts. Their arms full of stuff to try on, the mother and daughter returned to the dressing room. Stephanie sat on the bench inside, and started nibbling on her fingernails. A terrible habit that struck Robin nauseatingly of self-cannibalism. Was it an inherited behavior? Was anyone in Robin's family a nail-biter? She had no clue.

The worst thing that she had ever done to Stephanie, Robin decided while helping her daughter into roomier pants, was depriving her of a family. Robin was the only child of deceased parents. She'd long ago lost contact with her one bitch of an aunt. Her grandparents were long dead. She had no one to offer Stephanie besides herself. They truly were two against the world.

"Those look great," said Robin, bending down to fold up the hem of a pair of black jeans.

"There're too long," said Stephanie.

"We'll have them tailored for a perfect fit, okay?" *The tailoring will cost as much as the jeans*, thought Robin.

"Stacy wears size ten," said Stephanie, speaking of one of her friends from school.

"She's tiny," said Robin. Indeed, Robin feared Stacy was undernourished, that her gymbunny mommy had taken insectlike Stacy off carbs. *That* mother had food issues.

"You're skinny," said Stephanie. "Why am I . . . not?"

"Honey," said Robin, sitting on the bench, pulling Stephanie into her lap. "I'm this way *now* because of that operation I had on my stomach. You know the scar. I was once a size twenty-four—adult size twenty-four. I was . . . I was as big as this whole neighborhood."

"Will I be as big as the neighborhood, too?" asked Stephanie, her eyes tearing.

Oh, God, went down the wrong path again, thought Robin. "No, honey. Look at me. No. You will never be like that. You're a beautiful girl, with a strong healthy body," said Robin.

"But look," said Stephanie, touching a roll of white flesh that puffed over the pants when she sat down.

"I can make that invisible," said Robin, positioning Stephanie in front of the dressing room mirror, and taking a trapeze top with an empire waist from the "try on" pile. She slipped it over Stephanie's head. The bright blue top made the girl's eyes shine, and the swing of the fabric obscured her daughter's midsection. The top fell to her hips, making her legs look long and lean.

Robin watched Stephanie appraise herself. The girl turned to the left and right, did a few model poses, arms akimbo, head tilted just so.

"What do you think?" asked Robin.

"Me likey," said Stephanie, smiling at her own reflection. "Can I wear it out?"

"You bet your sweet ass, you can," said Robin.

They giggled and proceeded to try on a few more pairs of pants, a few skirts, some empire-waist dresses and tops. They had more "no's" than "yeses." But Stephanie's spirits stayed high, thank God. This was a secret of happy shopping, thought Robin. One flattering dress could make you forget the five unflattering ones. Stephanie decided to buy over a dozen articles. They'd come for a new pair of jeans, and were leaving with a trench coat, tops, bottoms, dresses, socks, panties, and belts. It'd be over a couple hundred bucks, figured Robin. She'd pay ten times that much to keep Stephanie's body image in the comfort zone.

The line to pay snaked halfway through the women's department. The recession hadn't kept people from buying shoddy clothes made in China. She glanced at her cell phone to check the time.

"Shit fuck," she said.

"What?" asked Stephanie.

"Fresh Direct in one hour," said Robin, referring to the service that delivered fresh locally grown food, ordered online, in a refrigerated truck. Two guys in gray uniform jumpsuits and leather hernia belts would be arriving at their apartment with their week's groceries in, oops, less than an hour.

"We'll make it," assured Stephanie. "Relax."

They took turns like that, Robin tending to Stephanie's anxieties, and vice versa. Robin didn't want to be Stephanie's friend. Although she was, if she said so herself, very cool, Robin hated the idea of being the Cool Mom, the one who allowed boys to stay over and let her kids smoke and drink in the house. Robin wanted to be Stephanie's uncool mother, issuing demands about grades, steering her away from booze, cigarettes, and drugs. She was a bad example, but Robin was good at keeping her secrets, little lies and huge whoppers alike.

Stephanie would suss out the truth one day. Ideally, she'll be in college and too self-absorbed to care what her mother was up to.

"I just hate feeling anxious about it," said Robin.

"What's the worst that could happen?" asked Stephanie, as the line inched forward. "Fresh Direct will leave a note and come back an hour later."

"They should open another register," said Robin, seeing only two in operation.

"Chill, Mom," said the kid.

She might well have asked Robin to do a back handspring. Not physically possible. Robin watched one salesperson after the other amble by, pause to fold some shirts, and then disappear. Why didn't they get behind a register and start checking people out? It was like they *wanted* to inconvenience customers. Robin felt her blood pressure rise, as it always did on a long line. She seethed, couldn't talk to Stephanie because she had to concentrate on how furious she was about the wait. The cashier at register five was moving in slow motion. Continental drift was faster. Evolution was faster . . .

"Mom?"

"What?"

"Why do Amy and Mrs. Steeple hate each other?"

Groan. "Can we talk about it later? I have to focus on making that cashier's head burst into flames."

"Did you ever talk that way to your mother?"

Stephanie had to be referring to the night a week ago, the poker game when Amy picked a fight with Bess and stormed out of their apartment. "Yes," said Robin. "My mom and I had screaming fights."

"Did you hate her?"

Oh, *yes,* with an epic passion. "Of course not," said Robin.

"Do you think we'll ever have screaming fights?"

Robin sighed loudly. "Amy and Bess don't understand each other, and they lack the tools to get there," she said. Seeing Stephanie's confusion, she added, "It's like they're speaking different languages. Neither one knows how to put herself in the other's shoes. From what I gather, Amy and Bess haven't shared their emotional lives for a long, long time. Bess was just . . . busy, maybe. And Amy kept it all inside on purpose. She was waiting for Bess to open her up. But the wait was so long, Amy sealed shut like a metal can.".

"So they need a can opener," said Stephanie. "That's what you mean by tools."

The woman behind them on line laughed. Robin turned and made eye contact. A friendly smile exchange. Robin felt validation from a stranger that (1) Stephanie was a clever, insightful child, and (2) Robin was a good communicator.

"A can opener would be great," said Robin. "So would a few more open registers."

"You're saying if we always talk about our emotional lives, we'll never have screaming fights?" asked Stephanie.

"Sure," said Robin, checking her cell phone again. Forty-five minutes to Fresh Direct.

"Tell me," said Stephanie.

"Tell you what?"

"About your emotional life," said Stephanie, sounding like a ten-year-old shrink.

The woman behind laughed again.

"Do you even know what an emotional life is?"

The girl nodded seriously. "Thoughts and feelings. Secrets. About boys."

Titter from the woman on line, whose eavesdropping had worn out its welcome.

"I'll tell you when you're older," said Robin.

* ⬤ *

They got back to their apartment with five minutes to spare. Fresh Direct gave a two-hour window, so Robin might've been hurrying up to wait (again).

Weekends were Robin's busiest days. Most people with normal lives and jobs were crazed during the work week, and then relaxed on Saturdays and Sundays. For Robin, it was the opposite. Her workdays were never frantic. She made her calls. Smoked out the window. Ran a few errands. When Stephanie got home from school, they hung out, did homework, watched movies. Weekends, though, were full with tap class, shopping, sleepovers, playdates. Stephanie was a happenin' kid. Tonight, she was off to her friend Stacy's for a sleepover, and Robin was looking forward to having dinner and drinks at the bar at Pete's, her regular place. It was like *Cheers* (everyone knew her name), without the requirement of conversation. She wasn't sure tonight if she felt like talking and drinking, or just drinking.

Just the thought of having a cocktail later made Robin crave a smoke badly. She went to her bedroom, locked the door, and climbed out on the fire escape for a quickie.

Naturally, as soon as she lit her cigarette, she heard the apartment door buzzer.

"Dammit," she muttered. Robin yelled, "Stephanie! Fresh Direct is here! Buzz them in! I'll be right out!"

She heard Stephanie run down the hall and let in the delivery guys. It'd be a minute before they lugged the boxes into the elevator. Robin inhaled the smoke, exhaled, trying to enjoy the sensation, knowing she'd get more of it later after she dropped off Stephanie at her friend's house.

A knock on their apartment door. That was fast. Robin stubbed out her butt and crawled back into the bedroom. She spritzed on her green tea perfume to disguise the smoke smell and proceeded into the hallway to sign for the groceries and tip the delivery guys.

She saw Stephanie holding the apartment door open and talking to someone. *Why weren't the guys bringing in the boxes?* wondered Robin.

"Hello?" she asked, walking up to the open door.

Framed in the threshold stood Harvey Wilson in a puffy vest and jeans, a helmet under his arm, a dirt bike in front of him. The sight was so disorienting, Robin's brain couldn't put it together.

"You work for Fresh Direct?" she asked.

"Pardon?"

"He says he's an old friend of yours," said Stephanie, looking at Robin with curiosity and suspicion. "Do you know him or should I call 911?"

Robin hesitated.

Harvey said, "If you want me to leave, I'll go."

"Okay," said Robin.

But he didn't make a move.

"I'll get the phone," said Stephanie, clearly excited by the idea.

"No, it's all right. I know him. Come in," said Robin, holding the door open for him. "I wasn't expecting to see you. Ever again."

Stephanie glared at him. "Is he from your emotional life?" she asked Robin.

"A past life," answered Harvey.

Robin stepped back, and looked from Harvey to Stephanie and back again. The resemblance was obvious, she realized with a jolt. They had the same eyes, chin, and cheeks. Thank God the nose was all Robin. Harvey's was on the large side. Stephanie had Robin's hair color (the auburn of her youth), but Harvey's luster. Seeing them together like this, how could she be the only one to see the truth written, literally, all over their faces?

"Are you Robin's daughter?" asked Harvey amicably, as she led him to the living room. He'd wheeled his bike inside and leaned it against the wall.

"Obviously," said the little girl.

"How old are you?" he asked.

Stephanie rolled her eyes at the predictable question. "Ten. I'll be eleven in September."

Harvey said slowly, "So you were born in September 2000?"

"September seventh," said Stephanie. "Our school does a September first cut off so I'm one of the oldest kids in my class. Only Milo Abrams is older. His birthday is September fourth."

Harvey appeared lost in thought. Robin's heart skipped a few beats. Horrors, was he doing the math? He studied Stephanie. He looked up at Robin, then down at Stephanie, back at Robin. She started to shake her head. But it was too late.

"Is your daddy home?" asked Harvey to Stephanie, his voice scratchy.

"My daddy was a sperm donor," she announced matter-of-factly.

Harvey stared into the girl's face, and couldn't help but see his own reflected there. "I need to sit," he said suddenly.

He didn't make it to the couch. He fainted, dead away, in the mid-

dle of the living room, a klatch of Barbies arranged in a circle breaking his fall.

"Oh, shit!" said Robin. One of the Barbie's was jabbing him in the
eye. No blood. *Whew!*

Stephanie, hopping up and down, thrilled by the novelty of a
prostrate man on the carpet, said, "Can I call 911, Mommy? Please?
Or I could run across the street and get the firemen?"

"Calm down," said Robin. She bent over, and slapped Harvey's
cheek, repeating his name. Nothing. He was out. "Get me the phone."

The girl pounded into the kitchen and grabbed the handheld.
Robin dialed quickly. When she got an answer, she said, "You've got
to drive over here, now. Emergency! Code red!"

"An emergency is code blue," Carla answered calmly.

"Just hurry. I've got a man down."

Carla was a rock, thought Robin, hanging up. She'd be here in fifteen minutes. Not soon enough. She dialed Bess. "Code red! I mean
blue! Man down!"

"I'm sorry?" said Bess.

"Stop apologizing and get over here! It's an emergency."

"Did you kill someone?" asked Bess, hushed.

Robin pulled the phone away to look at it. Is that what Bess
thought her capable of? Murder on a Saturday afternoon?

"Come over to find out," said Robin, hanging up.

Stephanie peered into Harvey's face, squished as it was on plastic
limbs. "Who is he, Mom? He looks familiar."

"No one! Go to your room," said Robin.

"Like *that's* gonna happen," said Stephanie with a snort.

Robin took a moment to admire her flinty child, and then flew
right back to panic.

The buzzer made Robin's heart jump into her throat. Bess must
have sprinted the two blocks. She buzzed her friend in.

A minute later, two huge men with cardboard boxes arrived in the
hallway.

Stephanie said, "Fresh Direct."

Robin looked up. The delivery guys took in the scene. A mother and daughter poking an unconscious man on the floor.

As if they happened upon men in dubious stages of consciousness every day, one delivery guy said, "Where do you want the boxes?"

Stephanie directed them toward the kitchen, signed the receipt, and had the good sense to go into Robin's purse (thank God the pack of cigarettes was in her bedroom) and find a fiver for a tip.

The guys left, and moments later, Bess appeared in the doorway. The delivery guys must have let her in. They should know not to hold the door open for just anyone. Robin made a mental note to complain, but she was interrupted when Bess gasped and threw herself on the carpet at Harvey's feet.

Bess's blue eyes bugged, and she mouthed, "Harvey Wilson!" She'd read his blog, after all, and looked at his many pictures. "Why is he in your living room?"

"Which room would be better?" ask Robin.

"Did you invite him over?" she whispered. "Oh my God, did you invite him to meet Stephanie?"

"Shut up," whispered Robin, checking to make sure Stephanie was in the kitchen, pawing through the food boxes. "He just showed up. Saw Stephanie, figured it out, and fainted."

"Can't say I blame him," said Bess.

"For being so rude as to pass out on my floor? In front of my kid? I blame him," said Robin.

Stephanie called from the kitchen. "Mommy, can I open the cookies?" Apparently, the kid was already bored by their immobile guest.

"Go ahead!" yelled Robin.

Buzzer. Carla. Robin leapt over the body to let her in.

Carla was huffing when she got to Robin's apartment door. "I broke the speed limit, left my kids at home, and ran from the hospital parking lot," she said. "This had better be serious. I hope you cut off your finger, at least."

Robin brought Carla into the living room and presented the body. *"Ta-da,"* she said. "He fainted. Killed, like, six Barbies."

"Breathing?" asked Carla. "How long has he been out?"

"Since I called," said Robin. "Ten minutes?"

"Did you slap him? Cold water?"

"I did slap, yes," said Robin.

"It's Harvey Wilson," stage-whispered Bess.

Carla got on her knees to check vitals. Robin and Bess joined her on the carpet. The doc rolled him onto his back, freeing the dolls under him. She leaned forward, examining his face.

"What?"

"He sure looks like Stephanie," said Carla.

Robin and Bess, too, came in close to examine his face, the distinct nose, his rounded cheeks and gentle jawline. The dark eyebrows, and the eyes below. Eyes that, suddenly, opened.

The three women screamed and fell backward.

Harvey said, "Where am I?" Leaning left, he pulled a Barbie from underneath his hip, looking at it as if it were a hand grenade.

"He's awake. Not dead, *yay*," said Stephanie at the doorway, munching a cookie.

Carla recovered her breath and said, "Lie down, Mr. Wilson. Let your blood pressure stabilize for a minute."

He looked a tad frightened by the female faces peering down at him. "Look at the bright side," said Bess to him, all smiles. "This'll make a great blog entry."

●━━━●

While Robin unpacked the groceries, Carla gave Harvey a cursory exam. She advised him not to drink tonight. Harvey laughed in her face, but then he politely apologized.

Robin had to take Stephanie to her friend's house for the sleepover. She directed Harvey to Pete's, the bar around the corner, and asked him to wait there for her. It was a good plan. She assumed Harvey wouldn't yell at her or try to kill her in a public place. Also, he'd have twenty minutes or so to calm down before she arrived.

She saw his bike chained up outside Pete's. He'd found it, no problem. Robin walked inside. Harvey was seated on a stool at the bar, a beer in front of him. She took the empty seat to his right, and ordered a vodka tonic.

"I suppose you hate me," she said. "Should I bother explaining myself or is it not worth the breath?"

Harvey said, "Tell me about Stephanie."

Robin painted the thumbnail sketch of her child. The girl's health, her happiness, their dime-sized life together.

"You were selfish," he said. "You kept Stephanie from me because you didn't want to share her. You had her so you wouldn't be alone."

What a great load of "you" sentences. If he knew anything about productive conversation, he would've used "I" sentences, "I think," and "I feel." As in, "*I* think you're selfish, greedy, and lonely."

Robin said, "I understand why you'd jump to those dubious conclusions without knowing the subtle psychological issues."

"Huh?"

"I'm not saying I did the right thing," said Robin. "But I had my reasons. A long list of them. I'm sorry I never got around to telling you about Stephanie. Now you know."

"Never got around to telling me I had a daughter," he said. "Slipped your mind, did it?"

Honestly, it had. For months at a time, Robin didn't have a single thought or pang of guilt about the Big Secret of her life. Who was Harvey Wilson to her? No one. Nothing.

"On some level, I must have known," he said. "Why else would I still think about you and that one night? I have, you know. A lot over the years. After our run-in at Barnes and Noble in December, I felt compelled to find you—which wasn't easy. I had to search property records in Brooklyn. The whole time, I kept asking myself why I cared. You were like a pebble in my shoe. But maybe it wasn't *you*. It was an awareness."

"Oh, for Christ's sake," said Robin. He was a lunatic. But, she would grant him, he had no earthly reason to fixate on her.

Harvey scowled and drank his beer. He seemed young, although he was around her age. "At Barnes and Noble that day, it wasn't a random encounter," she said. "I was looking for you."

"To tell me about Stephanie? But then you lost your nerve?"

She said, "I just wanted to get a look at you, actually. I was curious."

"If I looked like her," he said.

"I was nudged by my friends," she said. "I'd come out to them about the Big Secret. First people I'd ever told. I kept the secret for ten years. And then it just popped out over cards, like it was no big deal. But it is a huge deal." Robin felt her voice shake. She wrestled for control and continued. "I was just ashamed back then. Everything was mortifying," she said. "I was three hundred and forty-two pounds! I felt ashamed walking down the block. Getting knocked up on a one-night stand? That was the mountaintop of shame. I didn't even know I was pregnant for months. My periods were irregular, had been since I was a teenager. I was sick for a while. I thought I had a twenty-four-week stomach bug. When I finally realized I was pregnant, my doctor put me on a strict diet. My weight put the baby and me at high risk of a host of complications. It was a terrifying, horrible mess, the whole pregnancy. And then I had a gastric bypass operation soon after Stephanie was born. I was in transitional mode for years, adjusting to the changes. It's not easy, having a stomach one day, and not the next. Stephanie was a colicky baby, and I had virtually no help with her. Then 9/11. I fell into a depression that I'm still not quite . . . *what*?"

"It's all rationalizations and bullshit," he announced. "It never occurred to you that I might've *helped* you? That I could have lightened the load? No cruel pun intended?"

Robin gulped. What did it say about her that, no, it hadn't occurred to her that Harvey, or anyone, would willingly help her through those years of physical and emotional upheaval? Her parents had always treated her problems like an unwelcome burden, a test on the limits of their patience, another mile in their marathon of parental disappointment. Her friends back then were wrapped up in their own dramas, and drifted away from her at the first sign of trouble. She had no one and nothing. And then she had Stephanie.

"I was selfish," she said. "And greedy and lonely." *Still am*, she thought.

He said, "Well, I'm not. I would have stood by you and helped. If you hadn't run out on me, you might've learned that."

He kept talking as if he would've wanted a relationship with her former gigantic self.

"Are you a chubby-chaser?" Robin couldn't help asking.

Harvey drew back on his stool, incredulous. Considering everything he'd seen and heard today, Robin didn't get why that question would floor him. "I don't know which is worse: How little you think of me, or how little you think of yourself."

"As a narcissist, I'd say how little I think of myself," she answered. "You could use that line, by the way, on your blog. A follow-up to the post you wrote about seeing me in December."

"I won't be blogging about this," he said.

"Bess was right. This is great material!" said Robin. Seeing his face drop, she let it go. "I like your blog, by the way. You write well. I found myself getting involved in your stories, even though I don't care about biking. You should do more with it."

He shrugged. "Do you write?" he asked.

"No discipline," she said, shaking her head.

"I've taken some workshops," he said. "The instructors always talk about the writer's detachment. The writer experiences life, but has to be able to detach from it to look at it objectively. You, Robin, have taken detachment to the extreme."

"Is that a compliment?" Robin had noticed the phenomenon. She often felt like she was a character in her own life, making it up as she went along, without actually living it. The result was that she mistakenly thought her choices were inconsequential.

"No," said Harvey. "It's not a compliment." He drained his glass. "This is overwhelming. I've got to go. I'll be in touch soon. We have to discuss what to do next. Obviously, I want to be a part of Stephanie's life."

They exchanged phone numbers and email addresses. Robin should've felt relieved that the awkward (to say the least) confrontation was over. But, instead, she felt a sense of loss. "Don't go," she said, sounding desperate to her own ears.

Harvey shook his head. "I'm sorry, Robin, I would stay and keep you company. But I simply can't stand to be in your presence for one more minute."

"Oh, well, when you put it like that . . ."

And he was gone. She finished her cocktail in one swallow. At least he hadn't threatened to have his lawyer get in touch, as she feared. He still might. Robin didn't have a clue about the legal ramifications. Stephanie was his genetic offspring, but she was her mother.

Robin closed her eyes and visualized purple smoke swirling out of a shapely bottle. If only she could get the genie back *in*.

The bartender came over, took away her empty. He said, "Need another?"

"Are you kidding?" she asked.

* * *

"You can't cancel," said Robin on the phone to Carla. It was Carla's turn to host the poker game. "I need to see you guys tonight. I'm begging here."

Robin was on her cell, already walking toward Bess's house to catch a ride to Carla's. The babysitter (not Amy) was ensconced at her place with movies, popcorn, and Stephanie. It'd been a week since Harvey Wilson's unexpected appearance, and he still hadn't called to discuss his future as a father. Every day, every hour that went by further convinced Robin that Harvey was making plans to sue her for joint custody. He'd been angry (quiet anger, the scariest kind) and disgusted with her at Pete's. During her hours replaying that conversation, Robin recalled their contentious chat at Barnes & Noble, how he described his ex-wife as "another woman who lied." Lying was a particular sore spot for him, and Robin had done nothing but, as far as he knew.

Harvey's revulsion had to be purged from her thoughts. If Robin couldn't get some love from her friends tonight, she was genuinely afraid for her state of mind. Alicia, Bess, and Carla had received "Harvey watch" updates via daily emails. Caretaker Bess called each morning to check in, and Robin much appreciated the dutiful attention. But Robin needed face time. She needed Carla to screw her head on straight. Alicia would make witty little jokes that always took Robin by surprise. And Bess would smile sympathetically; attempt to take Robin's pain onto herself (if only she could).

"I need to see you," said Robin, her voice devoid of irony.

Carla sighed into the phone. "I know you do. But it's not a good time. Claude is home. We're in the middle of a discussion."

"A fight," said Robin.

"His company went under," said Carla. "A week ago. And he only just told me."

"Shit," said Robin, getting a flash of dread on Carla's behalf. "Interesting. Your bad news made me forget my own problems—but just for a second. What else you got?"

Carla laughed. "My roof is leaking. Does that help?"

"Thank you, Carla. You're a good friend."

"I was able to reach Alicia, but Bess's home phone has been busy for an hour and her cell is off."

"I'll tell her," said Robin.

"Good. I've really got to go," said Carla. She hung up.

Robin flipped her phone closed just as she reached Bess's town-house door. Maybe Alicia would come *here,* thought Robin. Bess loved to host. Robin buzzed and waited on the stoop. The night air was finally warm enough for just a jacket. Spring was close, hovering on the brink, in need of one good push over the edge. Like an orgasm, just one stroke away.

I must be horny, thought Robin. She should be. It'd been an incredible eight months since she'd been naked with a man. This card game had, strangely, replaced her sex life, such as it was. Was that a good thing? A bad thing? Probably both, she decided.

Bess appeared in the vestibule between the two front doors. Her yellow hair shone under chandelier light. She was luminous, really. *And I don't hate her for being beautiful,* thought Robin. How could that *be?* It must be real friendship, the kind that transcended petty jealousy.

But her beautiful friend didn't look happy. Opening the street door, Bess frowned at Robin, stress lines on her forehead.

"I should have called you," said Bess. "Borden's father had a massive heart attack. He's on life support in San Francisco. We're packing to leave tomorrow morning with the kids. His mother is freaking out. Borden is a wreck."

"Poor guy," said Robin. "How old is his dad?"

"Seventy-two," said Bess. "But he was in excellent shape. No one saw this coming."

Robin felt an urge to hug her friend, to show her support. But before she could get in there, Bess dangled her car keys. "Take the car to Carla's. It's in the garage on State Street. I called to tell them you might be coming. Just park it back there when you're done. In fact, use the car whenever you want. I'm not sure when we'll be back. Not until after the weekend."

"Okay," said Robin, taking the keys. "Do you need me to help you pack? Maybe Borden would like to get his mind off it. Play a few hands of poker?"

"That's totally sweet of you to offer," said Bess. "But I'm pretty sure he wants to be alone. I mean, just family."

"Say no more," said Robin. "Give him my best."

They said their good-byes. Now what? Alicia would be home tonight, thought Robin. She'd take Bess's car and drive to Red Hook. Tim and Joe loved poker. They could fill in for Carla and Bess. It would be swell. Tim could whip up some pasta or a frittata—soft yummy stuff that Robin could stomach. They'd let Joe win, have a few laughs. *Game on,* she thought. Spirits rallied, Robin hoofed to the garage.

Robin had never driven a BMW before. As soon as she slipped into the leather seat, she felt like a road-raging asshole—in a good way. She sped down Columbia Street to Red Hook, and parked in the Fairway lot. Despite his sexlessness, Robin liked Tim. He was funny, flirty. A nice night at Alicia's was exactly what she needed.

She buzzed Alicia's apartment. Tim asked, "Hello?"

"It's Robin."

He buzzed her into the building, and then opened the door to their apartment. Natty as usual, Tim wore pressed gray trousers, a lavender shirt, sleeves rolled up to above the elbow to show off his sleek forearms, and black dress shoes. He must've had an interview today, thought Robin. It'd be strange to dress up to watch your kid, she thought.

"'Sup?" asked Robin as she entered the apartment.

"I have no idea," said Tim.

"Where's Alicia?"

"According to her, she's at Carla's house playing poker with you and Bess," said Tim, folding those arms across his slim chest.

Robin gulped, hard. Oh, crap—she'd stepped in it, big time. Maybe she could shovel her way out. "Oops, communication breakdown. I thought I was picking her up on my way over," lied Robin, sounding plausible, she hoped. "Well, I'd better get moving. They probably started without me, impatient bitches."

"Why don't we call Carla, tell them you'll be along in a few minutes?" asked Tim, his expression granite.

"Good idea," she bluffed, taking out her cell phone and starting to pretend dial.

"Allow me," he said, calling her bluff, reaching for a phone on the coffee table.

"Don't bother," said Robin, edging toward the door. "It's only a ten-minute drive."

"You have a car?"

"It's Bes . . . a rental," said Robin. Honestly, if she weren't having such a bad week, she'd be much better at this. She was, after all, a champion fibber. If there were a Liar's Olympics, she'd be a gold medal winner.

"You rented a BMW? To drive the five miles to Windsor Terrace?" he asked, pointing at the key chain in her hand with the brand insignia on it.

While she simmered in a broth of her own lameness, Robin wondered, *Where the hell* was *Alicia?* For her life, Robin couldn't imagine that Alicia's lie didn't involve a man. The hot younger guy from her office? Shark? Guppy? What was his name?

That sneaky mouse weasel, thought Robin. How *dare* Alicia withhold a secret that huge? They'd all had to listen to her whine about not having sex with her husband for months and months. Now that Alicia was getting some on-the-side action, she kept it to herself? As the young folk say, WTF?

Because she's in love, thought Robin.

Meanwhile, Tim was watching Robin too closely. Had her thoughts played out on her face? She'd tried to freeze her facial muscles, but some of them might've twitched.

"Can I get you a drink?" Tim asked suddenly, softening.

If his scheme was to get her drunk so she'd talk, Robin sincerely doubted he had enough alcohol on the premises. "I'm driving, Tim. But just one couldn't hurt," she said. "Joe is?"

From the kitchen, Tim said, "On the computer in his room, playing games. He won't move an inch until I force him to go to bed. Total absorption. The building could be on fire and he wouldn't notice." Tim pulled a bottle of red wine (not her favorite; instant hangover) off a shelf and slowly inserted a corkscrew. "You're sure the other women can wait?"

Robin couldn't help notice the muscles moving in Tim's forearms as he twisted the screw into the cork. She's always found him handsome. Too polished, possibly gay, but still easy on the eyes. She'd had a couple of fantasies about him, Robin had to admit. But she'd also had a few choice daydreams about Borden, too. And one satisfying vision about Claude and his, she imagined, enormous shlong. Didn't all women have little affairs of the mind with their friends' husbands? Robin had fantasized about nearly every man she'd ever met, if only to take two seconds to decide if she'd do him.

Regarding Tim, the answer was yes. In a vacuum, she'd do him. But they weren't in a vacuum, or a bread box, for that matter. Tim was Alicia's husband. Therefore, he was off-limits, no matter how horny, drunk, lost, depressed, amoral, detached, in need of comfort, and desperate for adventure she might be.

And she was.

Very, very much, all of those things. Except drunk. At least, not yet. The night, however, was young.

Tim walked toward her, carrying a full glass of wine. He smiled at her, his cheeks crinkling deliciously. Apart from her encounter with Harvey, this was the most male attention Robin had received in months. It felt good, the simple act of making eye contact with a member of the opposite sex. Robin's blood picked up speed.

"How's the polling biz?" asked Tim.

Robin had made only fifty calls today. Thanks to rising unemployment, a higher percentage of people were home to answer her questions. She couldn't get a dozen respondents off the phone. They were almost tearfully happy someone cared about their feelings.

"Would you like to know the temperature reading of America?" she asked Tim.

"Of course," he said.

"The question of the day: Do you feel like a recovery is close at hand?"

"I'd answer 'No,' " said Tim.

"And I'd answer, 'I don't know,' " said Robin. "Because no one really knows what's going to happen next, with the recession, the country, or our own lives."

"One person's life is a microcosm for the state of the union?"

"Not just one person's," she said. "Every person's. Mine. Yours."

He laughed. "Then let me poll the pollster: Do you feel like *your* recovery is close at hand?" asked Tim.

She grinned and recited, "I. Don't. Know."

"Wait and see," he said, sipping his wine.

"Wait, see—and pray," corrected Robin, "in a godless, secular way."

"A toast to desperate times," he said, raising his glass.

"Cheers," she said, clinking.

They were still standing. Leaning on the kitchen island seemed safer than sitting together on the couch of cold comfort. Alicia had described it to the group as a raft adrift on the turbulent marital ocean. Hard to believe that Robin had never shared a couch with a man, even if it was to sit on opposite ends, not touching. She'd entertained men on her couch. But she hadn't hung out with one just watching TV, reading the paper or a book. She tried to imagine a large hairy being seated in the corner of her sectional. Robin reclined on the chaise part, feet stretched out, resting on the man's lap. Stephanie playing on the floor, organizing a Barbie group therapy session. What a pretty picture.

The man in the picture was Harvey Wilson, unfortunately.

Tim said, "I know you're lying about meeting Alicia at Carla's."

Robin had momentarily forgotten that she was supposed to be rushing off to join his wife at a poker game.

"I'm sure Alicia talks a lot about our marriage," Tim said, barely maintaining a friendly tone.

"Only good things," said Robin, trying to keep it light.

"Bullshit," he said bitterly.

"This is none of my business," she said, finishing her wine, putting the glass on the butcher block island, and backing toward the door.

"There are two sides to the story," he said, moving toward her, in a boldly aggressive manner. "You haven't heard mine."

"Why don't you keep it to yourself?"

"Just listen to me for five fucking minutes."

"Tim, you're too close."

"Whatever she's told you, Alicia has her share of the blame. She's very hard to live with," he said, eyes wide and wild. "First, it was my fault we couldn't get pregnant. Then I couldn't do anything right as a father. Then I was a loser who couldn't keep or get a job. Now I'm her goddamn house slave. Great life, let me tell you. Chores, errands, cleaning, cooking. Shlepping the kid around. It's a real turn-on."

"I should go," Robin said nervously. It made her head hurt, how fast Tim changed from chatty charmer to hostile defender of his own honor.

"I was once a vice president at Macy's, did Alicia bother telling you that? I had a staff. I made six figures. And now I oversee Joe and make dinner. It's like I used to exist, and now I'm nothing," railed Tim. "If a man doesn't make money that makes him a fucking moron?"

"Well, in your case, not a *fucking* moron," she said out loud. Totally by mistake. Slipped out. She felt threatened and instinctively pushed back with her big mouth.

Tim broke the glass in his hand. Wine splattered. Robin's gasped at the sound and sight of it. *Meltdown in progress*, she thought. *Get out now!* Was it safe to leave Joe alone with Tim? Should she grab the kid and run? No, that would make him really lose it.

Better to flee alone. She backed up, toward the door. When she felt it behind her, she managed to get it open and slip through. Running down the stairs (the elevator couldn't come fast enough), Robin flew out of the building and into the parking lot at Fairway, her peasant skirt fluttering.

She fumbled with the fob, but got the BMW door open. Her heart pounding, Robin turned the key in the ignition, stepped on the gas, and drove straight into a pole.

"Shit!" she fumed.

She'd done some damage tonight. No point examining it or worrying about repairs now. She'd deal with it (the car and Alicia) tomorrow. Or the day after.

Throwing the BMW into reverse, she backed up, righted her alignment, and sped out of there.

11

Bess

Charlie, a ten-year-old, knew how to use the computer better than Bess did. It embarrassed her and made her beam with pride at the same time. Bess found herself pretending to understand even less than she actually did. Charlie loved to be the teacher, explaining applications and tricks patiently, as if she were the fourth-grader. Plus, they got to spend time together. It was nice. Charlie was her baby. He'd always love her.

"Do you want to learn video chat?" he asked, sounding so cute with his instructive tone.

"What's that?" she asked.

"Talking to someone else on-screen," he said. "Watch."

Clicking away, Charlie went online, searched through his IM list, instant-messaged his friend Seth, and then they switched to video chat. Suddenly, Seth's freckled face filled the laptop monitor. They began talking in real time. Their other friend Max sent an IM request to join the chat, and then the screen split into a three-way video con-versation.

"This is incredible," said Bess. "It's *The Jetsons*."

"The what?" asked Seth.

"An old cartoon," Bess yelled at the screen.

"You don't have to yell, Mom," said Charlie, rolling his eyes at his friends.

Bess remembered a scene from *The Jetsons*, when Jane (the wife) wore a mask for videophone calls to hide her morning cold-cream face and bed-head hair. Women wore masks to hide the unattractive truth. Even if the mask was an obvious ruse, women were expected to make the effort.

"Is it okay?" asked Charlie, bringing Bess back to reality. The three boys wanted to play a game together online (how they managed that trick could be another tutorial). Bess left Charlie to it.

She wandered down two flights to the kitchen, thinking about her son's future, how he viewed the world in terms of virtual, and actual, limitless possibility. He was smart, confident. A little rough, border-line hyperactive, but those traits could be to his advantage in the fu-ture. Bess felt confident Charlie would be okay. She'd done right by him.

Then again, she'd thought the same about Amy as an adorable ten-year-old. Six years later, her daughter was unrecognizable. No longer adorable. No longer sweet. Girls were harder; everyone knew that. More complicated. More challenging. Her boys, especially Charlie, wouldn't try to think up new ways to hurt her.

Don't be a victim, thought Bess.

At the moment, fiveish on a beautiful Wednesday afternoon, Bess had no bloody idea where Amy was or when she'd come home. Eric and Tom were at soccer until six. They'd come home hungry. Bess got busy making dinner: chopping vegetables, trimming and dressing a whole chicken. Sunlight streamed in through the kitchen window above the sink, and Bess took pleasure in it. The sun was setting later and later these days. In no time, it'd be summer. The boys would go to sleepaway camp in Vermont. Amy would . . . well, that wasn't clear as yet. Bess wanted Amy to get a job locally. Borden was pushing for summer school in the city.

Whatever they figured out, Bess hoped for some time alone with Borden. Even a long weekend. He desperately needed a dose of her undivided love and attention. It'd been a rough year all the way around. Amy, the lumpectomy, the funeral. Borden's father died over a month ago, and Borden was still in the grip of a depression. It could last much longer, years maybe. Major Steeple's heart attack was totally unexpected, a shock. Naturally, Bess thought of her father Fred's car accident twenty-five years ago. Some mornings, even now, Bess woke up and felt the loss like her father had died yesterday.

Borden's dad had never made it out of the hospital. By the time Bess and Borden (and the kids) arrived in San Francisco, Major was gone. He'd died while they were in the air. Borden was devastated. Bess didn't press him, but she assumed he had a few things to say to his dad and now would never get the chance.

He pulled himself together for the funeral. On the flight home, however, Borden's adrenaline wore off and he slumped. For weeks, Bess watched him sink deeper. She figured he used up all his emotional energy getting his job done at Merrill and was exhausted by the end of the day. Borden's sex drive had finally flagged. Bess thought she'd be relieved. She thought wrong. Within days of Borden's turned back in bed, Bess acutely missed his affection. Sometimes she stared at Borden after he'd fallen asleep, noticing new lines around his eyes and lips. On him, wrinkles looked sexy. But his age was catching up. They were getting older. Illness and death would be a constant of their lives from now on. After age forty, life became a process of elimination. Among their family and friends, who would be the next to go? Anyone's guess.

Bess stuffed the bird, and marveled at how quickly her thoughts veered from sex to death. How incongruous it was to think about death at all when the sun was shining, the air perfumed with the just-opened lilacs outside her window. The blooms would last two weeks, at best.

The upside of the funeral week for Bess (if such a thing were possible): getting to know her mother-in-law, Vivian, better. Since Borden's parents lived in California, Bess hadn't spent much time with them. As soon as the kids were old enough, Borden took them to San Francisco by himself once a year for a visit, giving Bess the precious gift of alone time. Of course, she went to the West Coast for Christmas nearly every year (her own mother, Simone, was rarely around), but holiday craziness had always kept Vivian too busy to talk to Bess one-on-one.

At the funeral, Borden and his brothers took over the pragmatic duties: hospital, burial, wake. Bess's sisters-in-law appointed themselves in charge of food and drink. Even Amy was quite helpful and (oddly) cheerful all week. All the practical matters were well attended to. None of the brothers or sisters-in-law were ready, willing, or able to take on Vivian's emotional needs. Bess saw the opening and stepped in.

Vivian had lost her partner of forty-nine years. She managed to keep herself in control when people were around, as long as Bess sat next to her. When Bess left her side, Vivian demanded to know where she was going and when she'd be back. The widow kept hold of her hand as if Bess were tethering her to the earth. Without Bess's grounding presence, Vivian drifted into memories about Major. Three times, Bess found the seventy-year-old woman hiding on the floor of her bedroom closet, attempting to muffle her crying into a dusty felt hat.

Bess had seen a child's pain many times. Broken bones, scraped knees, teeth extractions, etc. When Eric fell off his bike and broke three ribs, Bess felt like she would die from sympathetic agony. She wished she could take his pain. Vivian, also a mother, had no intention of letting anyone suffer for her. Each time Bess found Vivian in hiding, she stepped in (big closet), closed the door, sat down next to her, and cried with her.

Right before they left for the airport to come home, Vivian pulled Bess into the kitchen for a private good-bye. "I'm going to be completely alone," said the widow, "for the first time in my life. I'm terrified."

"You have dear friends who'll take care of you," said Bess. "And we'll come back in August. Just a few months away."

Vivian nodded. "It's not the same."

Not even close to the same, Bess knew. Since they'd been back in Brooklyn, Bess called Vivian every day. She reminded Borden to call. His conversations were awful to listen to. Awkward mutterings, testy questions about practical things ("Did you call the plumber to fix the faucet?"). He loved his mother, but he couldn't talk to her.

Bess's mother, Simone, had sent an enormous arrangement to Vivian's house. It was too big, thought Bess. The two mothers had been cordial, but not friendly. They'd been in the same room only a handful of times. At Bess and Borden's wedding. At the hospital when Amy was born. Vivian attended a San Francisco bookstore reading of Simone's years ago. Apparently, Simone embarrassed Vivian in front of the friends she'd brought along by treating her like any other fan. Vivian felt insulted. Still, Vivian called Simone to thank her for the flowers, leaving a voicemail message.

Simone called Bess two weeks later. "That's life," said Simone. "People drop dead from heart attacks. They get sick. They grow old. They get in accidents. They're killed in war, they starve, they're beaten to death by their husbands."

"Okay, Simone," said Bess, cutting off a speech in the early stage.

"I'm just stating the facts," said her mother.

What an optimistic, pleasant woman, thought Bess. Given the option, Bess would rather dwell on idealism. Her brief foray into nihilism now embarrassed her. She'd much rather look on the bright side of life, even it she burned her eyes out doing so. Bess vowed to herself to stay optimistic, or at least pleasant, until the end. The story of your death, she decided, was the story of your life. Her father had died alone, encapsulated, on a cold dark night. Bess shivered, imagining how trapped—and cold and dark—he must have felt in his marriage.

"About our next brunch date," said Bess, switching the phone to her other ear. "I don't think I can make it. Tom's soccer team has placed in the state tournament and that eats up my Saturdays for the time being."

"I'm sure Amy wouldn't mind coming by herself," said Simone.

Yes, but would Amy be allowed to enter a nice restaurant in her tattered jeans and filthy sneakers? "You haven't seen Amy in a while," said Bess. "She's going through some changes."

"I did see . . . I'd love to see her no matter what she looks like," said Simone.

"Have you two gotten together recently?"

"Why would you ask that? Don't you know what your own daughter is up to?"

Bess told Simone she'd let her know about Amy's availability, and hung up.

Don't you know what your daughter is up to? Ha! As if Simone had any idea what Bess had been up to from age fifteen on. She'd left Bess and her brothers to scratch out a life with their own fingernails. The irony of it: as soon as Simone's first book hit big and money for food flowed in, the refrigerator was perpetually empty. Simone's success equaled less shopping, and then no shopping. When Bess's clothes got tattered and tight, she resorted to wearing her brothers' jeans and shirts. The boys took to wearing their dead father's clothes. Did she tell her mother any of this? Nope. Because she was afraid to? Or was expressing her needs a pointless exercise? Simone was selectively deaf. She heard what she wanted to hear. If pressed, Simone defended her actions by claiming she gave her children the ultimate gift: self-reliance.

The chicken stuffed, seasoned, and in the oven, Bess washed her hands and cleaned the counters. She had an hour to watch the local news on the treadmill. Running had become a daily ritual for Bess since the lumpectomy. She'd been a casual on-off jogger for decades, but she'd shifted into serious speed and was training for a half marathon in August. From whence motivation? The usual of late: health. Regular exercise prevented dozens of types of cancer, heart disease, and other illnesses.

If she wasn't running from death on the treadmill, she was hurtling toward it in an airplane to California.

Bess started slowly, at 5.5 mph, and settled into her rhythm while watching *Live at Five*, the local news hour that seemed to cover every square block of the city, including Brooklyn Heights. She was dismayed by a report—by several, but two in particular—about half a dozen city hospitals on the chopping block, either closing or suffering drastic cuts. Another story confirmed the rumors that the Department of Transportation had finally, after much debate and outcry, suspended service on the bus route that ran up Court Street from Brooklyn Heights into Park Slope. She'd heard Brownstone parents who lived in Carroll Gardens (too close for a school bus; too far to walk) complaining about the possibility of losing their quickest way of getting to and from school. Now they'd have to adjust and figure out a new way of doing things.

Whenever someone she knew suffered a setback, Bess closed her eyes and did a silent prayer for him or her, and another thanking God for his many blessings. She'd been praying more and more. This preoccupation with God, along with her vow to be more optimistic, was her postnihilistic redemption.

The ads between news segments: drugs for arthritis, chronic back pain, asthma, high blood pressure, cholesterol, bowel discomfort, bladder control, followed appropriately by a spot for adult diapers.

She wondered if Carla's hospital would be affected by the closings and cutbacks. Must check later online, she told herself.

Sweating copiously, running at her flat-out fastest pace of seven miles per hour, Bess heard the front door open, and the sound of boys' voices.

"Dinner in half an hour!" she yelled. "Get cleaned up."

Eric and Tom called back, "'Kay," and she heard their cleats clomping up the stairs. Just as they were passing the living room (where she was) on the way upstairs, an image filled the TV screen that was so surprising, Bess broke her rhythm.

"Boys! Get in here," she yelled.

The kids clomped into the living room. Bess pointed at the TV screen, and said, "Look!"

On-screen, a group of older women were standing behind President Obama while he sat at his desk and signed a new bill into law. The bill was a federal guarantee of gender pay equality. When the president finished scribbling on the paper, he stood up and handed the pen to a handsome woman with silver hair in a gray designer suit that probably cost thousands of dollars.

"What?" asked Eric.

"What do you mean *what*?" asked Bess.

"Barack shaking hands with some old lady," he said.

Tom said, jaded, "He shakes hands with old ladies every day."

"You don't recognize her?" Bess asked, slowing down to a walk. The boys shrugged. She said, "That's your grandmother."

"That's not Nana Vivian," said Eric, totally confused.

"It's Simone Gertrude," said Bess. "My mother. Your grandmother."

"Oh," said Eric. "She met Barack. That's cool." The screen changed to drug ads for chronic pain and depression.

"How long has it been since you saw Simone?" Bess asked them.

Eric said, "No clue."

"Go," said Bess, pointing upstairs. "And take off your cleats. You're getting dirt everywhere."

The boys took off their shoes—leaving them right there, on the floor of the living room—and ran off to change. They were good about showering, which Bess dearly appreciated and was grateful for (chalk up another blessing), except they left their mud-caked droppings all over the house.

Her exercise time officially over—there should be a button on the treadmill that said "resume mothering"—she'd done 3.5 miles in half an hour. A decent distance, but too short. She turned off the machine, picked up the cleats, and brought them downstairs to the foyer.

Her sons did not recognize her mother. It shouldn't come as such a surprise to Bess. Simone hardly ever came to Brooklyn. She never invited the boys to brunch, to conferences abroad, or to spend the day in the city. Bess hadn't made a big deal about Simone's rejection of her sons. Today, the dismissal—just because they possessed little penises—enraged Bess. Simone hadn't given them a chance. A flash of memory. Simone celebrated Amy's birth, coming to the hospital, buying extravagant gifts. Two years later, when Bess's second child arrived and turned out (surprise!) to be a boy, Simone took one look at Eric's naked seven-pound body, turned to Vivian and Major Steeple (who'd flown in for the birth), and said, "A boy. You can pay for this one." Then she left the hospital. Simone had never sent a gift or bought Eric—or Tom, or Charlie—baby outfits or birthday presents. Borden deeply resented Simone for the way she ignored her grandsons, but Bess had found ways to forgive her, and to justify it. "She doesn't understand men," she'd say at Christmas when Simone sent two gifts—one for Amy, and another addressed to "The Steeples," usually a cooler of steaks in dry ice.

"Doesn't understand men? Simone was married. She had two sons of her own!" Borden would say.

But Simone hadn't understood her sons. It'd been years since Simone had talked to Simon (who'd been named after her), or Fred (junior, after their dad). Nor had Simone ever understood her husband or her father, mainly because she didn't bother trying. Bess let her get away with it all—Simone's negligence when Bess was a teenager, her rejection of Eric, Tom, and Charlie, how she steamrolled over Bess's authority over Amy, that she'd ignored Bess's pleas for support after the lumpectomy. Maybe Bess was afraid of her mother. Just as, lately, she'd been afraid of her daughter. More accurately, afraid *for* her daughter.

Bess wondered if Amy was Simone's true heir. The evil streak had skipped a generation. Bess wasn't the reason Amy had gone bad, but she might be a carrier of the mean gene. Could she realistically do anything about Amy's personality if her genetic code was programmed for selfishness?

Bess deposited the cleats in the shoe trunk in the foyer, and then went to the kitchen to check on dinner.

The chicken wasn't ready yet. But soon.

●━━━●

"Brutal doesn't begin," said Borden of his workday. It was around midnight. The couple was in bed. He'd come home late, after 10:00. The Wall Street trading day ended at 4:00. He hung around for a while longer, attended to important after-hours and international trading. Lately, there were additional administrative duties to deal with, too, things Borden hadn't been responsible for until this year. Restructuring decisions. Redundancies. Redistribution.

Borden had refused his annual bonus, minuscule as it was in comparison to past years. The bankers who'd accepted bonuses had been pilloried in the press. Some had received death threats. The public perception of bankers hadn't fully penetrated the marble corridors on Wall Street. Borden's bosses believed they'd just been doing business, bundling mortgages, leveraging and buying on margin, selling short. Bess understood that Borden was, according to the rest of America, one of the greedy fat cats who'd destroyed the economy. But to her, he was a kind, loving, generous man.

"Do you want to talk about it?" she asked.

"Talk? God, no," he said. "I'm sick of living it."

"Can I take your mind off your troubles?" she asked, going for comic seduction, including waggling her eyebrows.

Borden smiled politely. He put his arm around her, pulled her in for a hug. But that was it. Bess waited for his hands to start roaming her body, making their usual journey across hill and valley. But tonight, he went nowhere.

And last night. And every night for a couple of weeks. Bess attempted to arouse him, snuggling against his side, pressing her breasts (minus one lump) into him, wriggling.

"I'm sorry, Bess," he said.

"Is it the scar?" she asked.

"You can't possibly think that."

"Your father?" she asked.

He sighed. "I'm just tired."

"And old, don't forget," she added.

"Old, too," he said, smiling weakly. "Old, tired, and at the end of a long day."

Right before her eyes, beautiful Borden had aged ten years. It was like time-lapse photography. His temples grayed, his fine lines deepened, his jaw softened. He'd grown weaker, just as she felt herself gaining emotional and physical strength. A surge of protectiveness overwhelmed her. It wasn't savage maternal protectiveness, however, but a calming call-and-response for support. It was her turn to be the strong one. They'd both worked hard for their family in different ways. Years had blown by. They'd had sex thousands of times. But how often had Bess appreciated or sympathized with the pressure Borden felt to provide, to perform tirelessly? Did he worry she wouldn't love him if he faltered or slowed down?

Although she'd once considered any sign of vulnerability in a man to be a huge turn-off, Bess had never loved Borden with such tenderness as she did at that moment.

"Come here," she said, pulling his head to rest on her shoulder. "Rest now."

"I fell in love with my husband all over again," said Bess to the card-players.

"I fell in love with your husband all over again, too, when he answered the door tonight," said Robin, shuffling.

The game was at Bess's house. Carla was supposed to host, but since Claude was out of work, he'd turned their house upside down fixing all the things he'd neglected for years, including a fresh paint job in their dining room.

Carla said, "I've been feeling good about my marriage, too; there's something inherently sexy about a man in a toolbelt holding a hammer."

Robin said, "What was that *sound?*"

Carla said, "I didn't hear anything."

"I think it was Hell freezing over," said Robin. "You, using the words 'marriage' and 'sexy' in the same sentence."

Alicia asked, "My marriage, meanwhile, still sucks."

The women were seated around the poker table on the garden floor of the townhouse. The doors to the garden were wide open, letting the warm air inside.

Bess said, "I'm sorry, Alicia."

"Don't let my misery stop you from gloating."

"Okay," said Bess, eager to describe her feelings. "We're having this intense, revitalized romance. Kissing, hugging, hand holding, staring into each other's eyes. Meanwhile, we haven't had sex in a month."

Robin signed. "More celibacy? I don't get it with you married people."

Alicia said, "There's some irony for you. Bess stops having sex with her husband. Meanwhile, Tim and I . . ."

"No!" said Bess.

"Really?" asked Robin.

"Please shut up and let Alicia talk," inserted Carla.

Bess, Robin, and Carla's eyes pinned Alicia to her chair. Alicia blinked at them. "I was going to say that, after all this time, Tim and I . . . have decided to put Joe on Zoloft."

That's it? thought Bess.

"Yeah, it was a tough decision, to put your kid on drugs. We did all the testing, consulted with a shrink, and did extensive online research," said Alicia. "Tim and I had many long talks about it, but then we finally agreed to try the drugs, lying in bed . . . *right after we had sex.*"

"You tease." Robin laughed, swatting Alicia's shoulder.

Alicia snorted. "You should have seen your faces when you thought you weren't getting the sex news."

Bess shook her head. "So? How was it?"

"Do tell," said Robin. Even Carla leaned forward.

Alicia asked, "Do you want the full version or the abridged?"

"I'm shocked you have to ask," said Robin. To Carla, she said, "If the details get too disgusting for you, plug your ears."

"I think we should discuss the decision to put Joe on Zoloft," said Carla.

Uh-oh, thought Bess, remembering how angry Carla had been when Bess chose Sloan-Kettering over LICH. Carla had that same look in her eyes now.

Alicia picked up on Carla's sensitivity, too. "Do you think it's the wrong decision?"

"I'm not a psychiatrist," said Carla, clearly miffed.

"I used the shrink you recommended," said Alicia.

Carla leaned back, folded her arms across her chest. "You should have kept me in the loop."

Robin sighed heavily. "Not again. Carla, get over it. Alicia, get on with it."

Alicia said, "Honestly, Carla, I didn't think you wanted to stay involved in the decision."

"Then you aren't paying attention," said Carla. "I want to be included and informed. I want my knowledge and expertise used and appreciated. From now on, if any of you have a health-related issue, I expect to be consulted, from the beginning to the resolution. That's an order."

Bess felt the weight of Carla's authority in her chest. "Yes, ma'am!" she said before she could stop herself.

Robin said, "Actually, I've got a pain. A big pain, in the ass, and it's you, Carla. Can you put your ego in check until after we're heard the salacious details about Alicia's once-in-nearly-three-years boink with Tim?"

"Well, it was incredibly tense, to tell you the truth," said Alicia. "A total surprise, too. I didn't see it coming, as it were."

"Was it the night that we were supposed to play poker at Carla's last month?" asked Robin, looking a mite guilty? Concerned?

"The night you crashed my car?" asked Bess. Robin had repaired the bumper—and had the car inspected and cleaned—before Bess got back from the funeral in San Francisco. That week, a dented bumper had been the least of her worries.

"Let's not talk about that," said Robin, oddly evasive. Why? Had Robin been drinking when she hit—what was it?—a parking meter on Joralemon Street? Bess smiled nervously. Better not press. She just wouldn't lend Robin the car again.

"Funny you should ask," said Alicia. "It was the night after."

"Where were you that night?" asked Robin. "I tried to reach you. I called your cell. And . . . called again."

Bess noticed that Robin looked at her hands when she spoke, and not directly at Alicia. Usually, Robin made eye contact to a fault.

Alicia said, "I was working late. I've been working late a lot. The new account—very consuming. I got home after midnight. Tim was asleep, in his clothes, with an empty bottle of wine next to the bed. His shirt was splattered with dots. I thought it was blood and woke him up in a panic. But he said he spilled wine on himself."

"Butterfingers," said Robin.

"Anyway, the next night, I came home early," continued Alicia. "I was exhausted, and barely had energy to get through dinner and put Joe to bed. I was half asleep when Tim got in bed next to me and started making the moves. It was very strange, kind of desperate. He was grabby and clumsy. No talking, not much foreplay either. It took five minutes before I got over the shock that we were actually doing it."

Bess had to ask, "How did it feel? I mean, after going so long without."

Robin asked, "How long *had* it been?"

Alicia frowned. "You know how long. Almost three years."

"With Tim," said Robin.

This was curious, thought Bess. Alicia and Robin were staring at each other, communicating without words. Bess didn't understand what was going on.

Carla, though, got it loud and clear. "Some things in life are private and needn't be discussed over cards—or ever."

"Said the woman who just demanded to know about every ooze, infection, and cramp," said Robin.

"Leave it alone," warned Carla.

Now Carla and Robin were glaring at each other, and Alicia seemed relieved to have the focus off of her.

"You all make it sound like Alicia's having a secret affair," Bess said. "But that's impossible. She wouldn't do that to her family."

Another touchy silence. What was going on? Bess would have dearly loved to know.

Carla said, "Shuffle and deal, Bess."

She gathered the cards, and started shuffling.

Alicia said, "It was angry sex. Not loving or romantic at all. It was more like an aggressive animal act, which, in a romantic and loving context, can be hot. But, in this context, was soulless and empty. But still physically gratifying. When we finished, Tim said, 'What took you so long?' "

"What did he mean by that?" asked Bess, dealing the pocket car.

"Could be any number of possibilities," said Alicia. "Which I have analyzed to death. One: what took me so long to get home the night before? Two: what took me so long to come? And it did take for*ever*. Three: what took me so long to . . . have an affair? As if he was waiting for me to take action against him, almost as if he wanted me to do it so he could hold it against me. It's totally twisted. A real pretzel of a marriage."

"Wait," said Bess. "You *are* having an affair?"

"Afraid so," said Alicia. "Don't feel bad, Bess. The happily married are always the last to know."

Robin said, "Tim initiated sex to confirm his suspicions."

"Having sex with me would confirm I was sleeping with someone else? How would that work?" asked Alicia.

"For starters, you took 'for*ever*' to come," said Robin. "If I have an afternoon orgasm, it always takes longer to have one at night."

"Who?" asked Bess, trying hard not to sound judgmental.

"Look, Bess, this affair wasn't something I did to my family. I did it for my sanity," said Alicia.

"Are you in love?" asked Bess.

Alicia said, "It's pretty incredible. But I haven't thrown the emotional switch yet that would make love possible."

"Your partner at work, right?" asked Robin. "The younger man?"

The cheater nodded. "Finn. Having sex with Tim did clarify one important issue," said Alicia, peeking at her blind cards. "I'm definitely not in love with him anymore. Maybe that's why I never pressed the point."

"As it were," said Robin.

"And before you ask—Bess—I don't know what's going to happen next," said Alicia. "Except that I'm going to win this hand. Raise."

"Call," said Robin.

"Call," said Bess. "I'm almost too upset about this affair to play."

"Why are you upset?" asked Alicia.

"I feel anxious," she said, not adding, "for Joe's sake."

"I'm nowhere near separation," said Alicia. "I was a lot closer before the affair, paradoxical as that might be."

Robin said, "Flop, please."

Bess liked what she saw, a jack and nine to go with her ten and queen. She had eight "outs" or chances—four eights plus four kings—to make a straight. "Before I forget, I wanted to ask you, Alicia, about summer internships."

"For you?" asked Alicia.

"For Amy," said Bess. "Unless your office is just one big orgy."

They all laughed. *Whew!* Bess was starting to think they viewed her as a paragon of morality. Carla had always taken that role, but not tonight, God (if anyone) knew why.

Alicia said, "I'll see what we can do. Do you think Amy would be a willing coffee lackey?"

"Yes," said Bess. *No,* she thought.

"Amy would be glad to fetch coffee," said Robin, "in Hell."

Bets were called. Alicia dealt the turn. A king. Bess tried not to whoop. Instead, she said, "What's the Harvey Wilson update?"

Robin said, "I've noticed, Bess, that you get awfully chatty when you've got a good hand."

"I'm just asking," said Bess, going for nonchalant.

Robin raised. Carla and Bess called. "Still haven't heard from him since the Barbie massacre. Maybe he's talking to lawyers before he calls me again. He has some rights, as Stephanie's biological father."

Bess nodded. The river card was dealt. Another king. This was her win, for sure. Even if someone held a pocket king, her straight beat three of a kind.

"Raise," said Carla.

Robin snorted. "The Black Queen, on the rampage. Fold."

"Reraise," said Bess. "Carla, I read online that LICH is one of the safe hospitals in Brooklyn."

"That's what they tell us," said Carla, pausing. Looking at her pocket cards. Looking at the community cards. Mulling.

Bess said, "You must be relieved."

Carla said, "All in."

"Call," said Bess in a heartbeat.

Robin said, "Look at Bess. She's salivating."

The blond host triumphantly turned over her cards, one by one. "King high straight," she crowed.

Carla whistled low. "Very nice," she said admiringly.

Bess said, "Thank you. Thank you very much," and started drawing the chips toward her.

"Ahem," said Carla. She turned over one of her pocket cards. A king.

"A straight beats three of a kind," said Bess.

"But not," said Carla, turning over her last card, "four of a kind."

Another king. Bess groaned. Goddamn Carla's luck.

"Will you look at that?" said Robin. "It's no fun to play with you anymore."

Carla laughed wickedly, an outright cackle. "I just love winning!" she said, gathering her chips.

"I'm done," said Alicia. "It's late. For all I know, Tim is waiting for me in bed, naked."

"If you decide to ditch him," said Robin, "send him my way."

Alicia laughed, but Bess didn't think Robin's comment was funny. Bess reminded herself that Robin had had a hard life, much of it spent alone or depressed, and that she used her obnoxious remarks to keep her emotional distance. Given the opportunity, Robin wouldn't, couldn't, seduce one of their husbands.

The thought that *any* of these women would replace her in Borden's heart/arms made her feel nauseated. The whole nonchalant delivery of Alicia's affair, too. The others seemed to think the deterioration of a marriage was a minor concern. Bess alone had filed it under Major Crisis. Then again, perhaps the crisis was the time spent leading up to the decision. It was surely all downhill from there.

"Can I mention the possibility of an internship at the agency to Amy?" Bess asked Alicia as she walked the women out.

"As a possibility. Unpaid," said Alicia.

Kisses all around, and they left. Bess glanced at the clock in the foyer. It was after ten. Borden wasn't home yet.

Her feet dragged as she cleaned up the poker room, shut down the garden-level lights and locks, moved up to the parlor level, the kitchen, checking that the oven was off, then up to the living room level, making sure everything was shut down. Farther up, on the kids' bedroom level, Bess popped her head into the boys' room and told them to get in bed for the night. She paused before Amy's door. The rule was to knock first. If she got no answer from Amy, Bess was to "take the hint" and go away. This vital information was posted on a sign taped to the door, a constant reminder of Amy's insubordination.

Feeling dangerous and armed with the good news of a summer internship at an ad agency, Bess put her hand on the doorknob as if to open it unannounced. Her heart thudded in her chest, more than if she held a pair of aces with a pair on board. She turned the knob exquisitely slowly, silently. Bess wasn't sure why she was creeping into her daughter's "PRIVATE!!!!!" space. Once upon a time, Amy would delight when Bess snuck into her room to deliver a bounty of kisses.

Bess would introduce her presence casually, breezily, as in, "Sorry, forgot to knock."

Just admit you're spying, thought Bess. *You're dying to know what Amy does alone in her room for hours at a time.*

Bess had been curious and concerned. Something was bothering Amy. For the last few weeks, she'd been returning home from school, heading straight up to her room, closing the door, and not appearing again until dinner. She'd collect a plate and take it to her room, eat there, and stay inside for the rest of the night. In the morning, Bess would find Amy's dinner dishes cleaned and left on the side of the sink, as if to send the message, "I'll eat your food, but I won't give you the honor of washing my dishes." Only Amy could turn cleaning up after herself into a hostile "I don't need you" gesture.

Too late, Bess realized she could be barging in to find Amy masturbating. She'd already opened the door wide enough to look inside the room. Exhaling relief, Bess found Amy (not masturbating), seated at her desk, back to the door, laptop open.

On the monitor, Bess saw Simone's face.

A downloaded TV interview?

No, the image wasn't high quality. It was grainy, the movements of her face stuttering like . . . just like the faces of Charlie's friends when he'd showed her video chat.

Bess backed away, closed the door tighter, and put her ear to the crack. She didn't need to see this, but she'd do her best to listen.

Amy whined, "It's been really hard, you know?"

Simone: "I know."

Amy: "She acts like I don't exist."

Bess wondered, *Is she talking about me? I have been giving Amy a lot of room lately. Too much? Her sequestration was a cry for attention, and I blew it.*

Simone: "She's very immature."

Amy: "I feel trapped, but I can't motivate to do anything. It's agony. I hate her! She ruined my life."

Bess frowned. As bad as it was when Amy said, "I hate you!" to her face, it was ten times worse when Amy told Simone.

Amy whined, "But I miss her, too. I really miss her. How could she dump me like that? Tracy already found a new girlfriend. Like, the next day! They probably hooked up while we were together. She might not have really loved me at all!"

Bess's first thought: *Amy and her overpierced girlfriend broke up!* Second thought: *This has nothing to do with me.* Third thought: *Hey, wait a minute, she's confiding in Simone. Not me.*

Her fourth thought: *My baby's hurting. How can I help?*

The right thing to do was to back away from the door. Take some time to think it through. Just as she was stealthily, respectfully shutting the door, she heard Simone say, "What you need is a change of scenery. How would you like to spend part of the summer in East Hampton with me?"

Amy: "Mom would never let me. She wants me to get a job or do a stupid internship."

Simone: "Don't worry about that. I'll take care of *her*."

Bess had heard enough. She crept away from Amy's door and upstairs to her own bedroom, her own sanctuary.

So Simone thought she could pull the strings, and Bess—aka *"her"*—would jerk around accordingly. Granted, Simone had every reason to believe that. She'd been manipulating Bess, uncontested, for forty years. And Bess had just let it happen.

Not this time. Bess lay back on her bed, scheming. She would not let her mother step all over her again.

The chicken was finally done. Red, hot, and ready.

12

Carla

Playing the lottery was for suckers, Carla knew. And yet, she'd started a morning ritual of buying a cup of coffee and a Pick Six ticket at the deli on the way to the clinic each morning. Whenever she tried to stop herself, she thought, *What if this is the morning I would've won?* and then gave in to superstition.

Carla's mother was superstitious. Her fears were wrapped up in her faith. Pagans rubbed a rabbit foot; Gloria Smith compulsively crossed herself, prayed, and spit to ward off the evil eye. She never missed a Sunday in church, believing that, if she dared, she'd bring down the wrath of God on her soul. *What kind of loving God would begrudge an old woman a lazy Sunday morning once in a while?* Carla wanted to know. But she kept her mouth shut. As a girl, she went along with Gloria's religious rituals, and learned to be as afraid of deviation (devotion?) as every other Christian.

She still went to church, and found the community and structure a comfort. But what about the religious aspects? Carla reminded herself that even Mother Teresa had had doubts. After church on Sundays, Carla took the boys to visit her mother at her assisted living facility in Queens. The building was a converted school near a park. Gloria moved herself in, buying a unit with her savings, and using insurance and Social Security payments to cover monthly service costs. To the end—Gloria was an old 79, and arthritic—she would take care of herself.

When Manny and Zeke went outside to roam the grounds with a few other visiting grandchildren, Carla wheeled her mother into the stuffy but sunny common room (formerly, the school cafeteria). She arranged her mom's chair near a window, tried to open it for air and saw that the sill was painted shut.

"How's Claude?" asked Gloria.

"He's great, Ma," said Carla, giving up on breeze, and sitting in a plastic chair next to Gloria.

"Where is he?"

"He's fixing the leak in the roof," said Carla. True.

"Did you go to church this morning?" asked Gloria.

"Yes, Ma."

"Did you pray for guidance about being a good wife? Did you thank God for giving you a reliable, trustworthy man to protect you and provide for you?"

"Yes, Ma."

"God bless that man. Fixing the roof! He's sweating and working on this hot day for you," said Gloria, raising a bent hand to her savior. "Do you understand me, Carla? Thank the Lord for giving you that man. You've been blessed."

"I know," said Carla, impatiently.

Gloria could tell. "I've suffered, and been grateful to God for every day of my life. You've been blessed, and you're bitter. I see the bitterness on your face."

"I'm not bitter," said Carla, *so* beyond tired of this conversation.

She and her mom had been having it for fifteen years, ever since Carla and Claude got married. Should she tell Gloria that Claude wasn't, actually, the best provider? That Carla was the family's sole provider right now? That the sweat of *her* labor kept that leaky roof over their heads, and that Claude had only agreed to climb up the ladder to get out of coming to Queens to visit his God-fearing mother-in-law?

"Look, Ma, we've got to go," said Carla, standing to give Gloria a kiss. "See you next week." A few other Sunday visitors were making their moves, too, so she felt justified in wrapping it up.

Gloria accepted the kiss and said, "Please give Claude my love and tell him I'm sorry he couldn't make it today. Also, tell him I thank God for him."

"What about me?" asked Carla abruptly.

"What *about* you?"

"I'm just wondering if you ever thank God for me."

Gloria gaped, astonished at the question, as if her daughter had just slapped her.

"You do realize, Ma," Carla continued, "that there are two people in a marriage."

"There's only one person who *matters* in a marriage—the person who's willing to walk away and never look back," said Gloria. "That's not you. God will strike you down if you even think of abandoning those boys. But Claude, he could run at any time. You have to take heed, Carla. Give him a hundred reasons to stay."

"Yes, Ma," said Carla, resigned, and then got out of there. As she and the boys drove back to Brooklyn, Carla thought about her mom's two guiding beliefs: (1) thou shall not displease God and (2) thou shall not displease men. According to the Gospel of Gloria, Carla hovered on the edge of the abyss. Only God and Claude could save her.

After drop-off, Carla was to meet Renee at Starbucks. The coffee was twice as expensive as at the deli, so she told herself, "No lottery today."

She arrived a few minutes early and found a seat. But she couldn't wait in peace. The itchy feeling of not buying her Pick Six was all over her skin. Giving in to her superstitions, Carla ran into the pharmacy across the street and bought herself a ticket. Quickly tucking it into her wallet, she rushed back over to find Renee entering the café.

The women greeted each other with a hug and a kiss. Renee was touchy-feely. She took every opportunity to pat Carla's back, rest a hand on her shoulder, press her arm or leg for emphasis when she made her point, in a completely nonthreatening and casual way. Not a casual person, Carla would have rather Renee kept her hands to herself.

"What a weekend!" announced Renee once they got their drinks and were settled on a couch in the rear. "Shauna competed in a chess tournament in Washington, D.C. We drove down, visited all the monuments. We went to the White House. For the first time, I really *felt it*, you know what I'm saying? I felt like a part of America."

Carla, who felt like a part of America every time she paid taxes and voted, said, "We've been meaning to take the kids down."

"You really should," said Renee (knee touch). "Especially now."

Every black American was now honor-bound to make a pilgrimage to Washington. Yes, Carla wanted to go, for herself and her sons. Only, they couldn't afford to leave Brooklyn, much less pay for a hotel room in D.C. The Orlando trip that Carla won at the Brownstone fund-raiser was gone. Before they could make a reservation, Claude's company went bankrupt. He made a convincing argument to sell the vacation package on eBay. They pulled in $3,000. It bought them two weeks of living expenses. Just two weeks. The joy of traveling and the memories would have lasted a lot longer. He'd expected her to be happy about the money. When she said, "I won't see any of it," Claude acted hurt and didn't speak to her for two days.

Carla sipped her coffee. "How'd Shauna do in the tournament?" she asked, even though she didn't care. It was polite to pretend.

"She was brilliant! She beat four kids—white and Asian boys—before she was eliminated," crowed Renee.

"Congratulations," said Carla.

"The Asians are tough to beat," said Renee. "We talked to a Chinese chess coach about Shauna, and he said he demanded a commitment of four hours a week. Shauna is all for it. You can get into Harvard on chess. I worry about pushing her too hard. But then again, God expects us to reach our full potential. We're praying for guidance."

"I'm sure you'll get it," said Carla. Afraid she sounded cynical, she added, "You're a wonderful mom, Renee. I know you'll get the balance right."

Renee smiled and sipped. Putting on her concerned face, she asked (touch elbow), "How's it going at home?"

Cringing inwardly, Carla's instincts told her to lie. Robin or Alicia could have asked her the same question and if Carla didn't want to answer, she'd say, "Shut up and deal." If Bess asked, Carla would've felt obliged to tell the truth. But something about Renee's question raised Carla's walls.

Robin had said that Renee served as Carla's mirror. Yes, they were physically similar. They had culture in common. When Carla looked at Renee, she saw an attractive, well-dressed, responsible, smart, wide-awake woman she couldn't force herself to care about, or even like. She wanted to fall in friend-love with Renee. She'd certainly tried. They'd had weekly coffees for months, even gone on double dates with the husbands. But it just wasn't happening.

Does Renee genuinely like me? Carla wondered. *Does she feel authentic in my presence? What am I to her?* Could be insecurity talking, but Carla thought Renee liked to spend time with her to feel superior. Her life was, by almost any standard Carla could think of, better than hers. Not just financially. Pretty Shauna was an academic superstar. Carla's sons—handsome, hardworking, well behaved, empathetic (Carla would *never* forget her pride when Zeke comforted Bess after Amy had been so horrible)—were average students. Battle of the husbands? Richard Hobart was dashing, extroverted, and, needless to say, employed. Claude? Better looking than Richard, but on their double dates, he'd been garrulous, trying too hard to impress.

"We're doing just fine," said Carla.

"I've been wanting to talk to you about a Parents Association committee I'm forming for the next school year," said Renee. "Mothers of Color. We could organize events and fund-raisers. I thought it'd be fantastic to do a fund-raiser to take Brownstone kids of color to Washington for a weekend. Guess where I got that idea?"

"Like a Diversity Committee," said Carla. "Which already exists."

"It does? Never heard of it. Does the committee *do* anything?" asked Renee.

Carla laughed to herself. The Diversity Committee did *a lot* . . . of eating and drinking and card playing. "I guess it likes to keep a low profile."

"What's the point of that?" asked Renee. Waving away the question, she asked another: "Can I count on you to join *my* committee? No reason Mothers of Color can't put on some big fund-raisers. Maybe even take over the winter event. I'm sure I—*we*—could make a better party than that Casino Night."

"Bess's event was fun," said Carla, remembering her win sweetly (and then bitterly—they shouldn't have sold that trip).

"Oh, I forgot you and Bess Steeple were friends," said Renee.

"I'm sure you'd do a wonderful job," said Carla, feeling in the middle suddenly. How did she get here?

"Casino Night didn't set a good example," said Renee. "I know you enjoy card games. But do we want to condone gambling to our kids? Especially kids of color?"

"Are kids of color prone to gamble?" asked Carla. "More than the colorless kind?"

Renee (hands to herself) frowned. "It's just an idea," she said carefully. "Nothing you need to mention to Bess. I want to be more involved with the school and the Parents Association. But I hate taking orders."

From colorless mothers, thought Carla. "My lips are sealed."

"Good morning, ladies," said a scratchy voice above them.

Carla looked up to find her old friend Dr. Stevens standing in front of their couch with a large cup of coffee. God, he'd aged. Carla had last seen him on the street a year ago? Six months? Out of habit, Carla gave him a visual exam. Skin: dry, pale-greenish tint. Weight: low, possible disease-related anorexia. His slacks were pulled tight by a belt. His shirt was open at the neck—no tie—collarbone sharply defined. *What is that?* she wondered, leaning forward for a closer look. Two black dots on the sides of his neck. She searched his face, finding another pair just behind the gray hairline by his temples. Pencil point tattoos. Radiation treatment guides for the head (brain) and throat. She must've looked concerned. When she met Dr. Stevens's eyes, he nodded ever so slightly. He knew she'd diagnosed him on sight. Any doctor worth her saline could call this one.

Renee said, "Hello, Dr. Stevens! It's wonderful to see you. Shauna and I have missed you."

"I'm back at the office now," he assured her. "If you need to come in, just call my secretary. Enjoy your coffee." He smiled and started to leave out the back door. But then, he turned back around. "Dr. Morgan, do you have a second?"

"Of course," Carla said, standing to walk him to the exit.

He said, "I just wanted to ask you to give me a call later. I have a business proposition for you. You have my number?"

She nodded. "I'll call you this afternoon."

"Good," he said. "Have a beautiful day."

Carla walked back to Renee, deciding to take this break as an opportunity to cut the coffee short. "I've got to run," she said, grabbing her purse.

"He doesn't look too hot, does he?" asked Renee. "He's been disappearing a lot. He was gone when Shauna had her last ear infection this winter. That's how we met, remember?"

It was only a few months ago, thought Carla. *I'm not an idiot.*

Renee continued, "I hope he's all right." She raised her eyebrows at Carla. An open invitation to hazard a guess.

Under no circumstances would Carla speculate with Renee about her colleague's condition. That was gossip at its worst. Wild guessing about someone's health was not conversational sport. An illness was private, and it was up to the individual when and how the information was shared, if at all.

Even as she had these protective thoughts about Dr. Stevens, Carla was aware of the contradiction. She'd insisted at the last poker game that she be kept in the loop about her friends' and their families' medical complaints. Carla thought, thanks to Robin, that her demand had been ego driven. But now she understood it for what it was: a deeper emotional need. She cared about the poker players and their families. She insisted on caring for them.

"I've really got to go," said Carla, and was out the back door before Renee could hug her again.

⚬━━⚬

"Come in, Carla," said the spider to the fly.

Tentatively, Carla entered the office of Dr. James Clifton, the hospital director at LICH, her top boss. The boss of bosses. She'd met with this man and his two associates, both seated at the conference table with him, only a few times before, including the day she was hired fifteen years ago.

Also at the conference room table, her direct boss, Dr. William

Abernathy, the head of LICH outpatient clinic services. She had weekly meetings with him about budget, agenda, staff, budget, services, supplies, budget, special cases, and, just to make sure she absolutely understood the importance of it, budget.

Confronted by four men in suits, Carla felt an immediate self-consciousness that she was fat. Ridiculous, given the context. This meeting was about the health of the hospital. She knew that LICH, like every city hospital, was ailing. Her girth couldn't be less relevant to the dire subject at hand, and yet, Carla felt the fear of being judged by these men on her attractiveness. As she often told her teenage eating-disorder patients (although it rarely penetrated their obsessed minds), anxiety about weight was a convenient distraction for life's real problems. When you were having trouble at school, or at home, or wherever, and couldn't deal with the pressure of the problem, it was a relief for anorexics and bulimics to instead fixate on food. Extra weight was, after all, a "problem" they had some control over.

"Please have a seat, Carla," said the director.

"Thank you, Dr. Clifton," she said, keenly aware of the fact that he called her by her first name while she used his degree and surname. It was a show, on his part, of familiarity. On her part? She would show respect, regardless.

All the men looked worn out. Carla's was one of the last meetings of the day. They'd already seen dozens of staff members. Probably a third had been fired. Carla could smell the lingering stress and sadness in the room.

She sat opposite the men in suits. They smiled at her anxiously. They were not her enemies. They were the bearers of bad news. She tried not to hate them reflectively. "How bad is it?" she asked.

"Twenty percent cuts hospital-wide," said Dr Clifton. "Select departments will have deeper cuts."

"Including the pediatric clinic?" she asked.

He paused, checked his laptop notes.

It's worse than I thought, Carla realized.

"Eighty percent of pediatric clinic patients at city hospitals present with nonemergent health concerns. Many of the illnesses can be cured with a simple prescription. Maintaining the clinic is one of our biggest costs," he read the on-screen missive. "The problem isn't just uninsured patients and expense. The cost is high for parents taking time off work and for kids who have to miss school." He paused, drew breath. "In cooperation with the new Secretary of Health and Human Services, Mayor Bloomberg has decided to try an experimental program in certain parts of New York City to treat nonemergent pediatric concerns. A quarter of funding for city pediatric facilities will be redirected to implement this program."

"The program is?" asked Carla, dying to hear this one.

Dr. Clifton cleared his throat. "If I may continue."

"By all means," she said.

"The program is to have pediatricians hold clinic hours in public school nurses' offices," he said. "Doctors go to the students, instead of the other way around. In counties where this program in under way, minor problems like ear infections, lice infestations, rashes, etc., are caught earlier, before they become severe. Contagions are isolated. Lower incidents of STDs, flu, and a dozen other communicable diseases have been dramatically reduced in the student population. Kids stay in school, parents don't miss work. Hospitals can free up space and money for other departments. Each student's medical insurance information will be logged into the school's records. Those without insurance will be registered, at school, for Child Health Plus. It's a combined effort by the Departments of Education and Health and Human Services. The goal is that, by 2012, every kid enrolled in a public elementary, middle, or high school in New York City will be registered and covered."

Carla nodded. Send the doctor to the kids. It was a brilliant idea that addressed all of her many complaints about the pediatric clinic system. The crowding and long waits. Kids missing a whole day of school just to get an antibiotic prescription. The pissed-off parents who postponed bringing in their child, allowing a minor condition to blow up, for fear of missing work.

"What about the twenty percent of kids who don't have minor complaints?" she asked, picturing the ever-widening crack in the system.

"We'll be redirecting clinic funds for a pediatric specialist in the emergency room," he said. "And more triage nurses for faster intake."

Again, made sense. Often, Carla would take one look at a patient, and have to send him or her out the door to another doctor. She flashed to a few nightmares during her tenure at the hospital, when a child was brought to the emergency room and she had to leave the clinic to tend to that child, creating a huge logjam at the clinic, and insufficient attention to the emergent-care kid. A full-time pediatrician working the emergency room was a great idea.

Send the doctor to the patients. Have schools liaison with insurance providers. It seemed so obvious, a classic case of, "Why hadn't someone thought of this sooner?" The restructuring was outside-the-box thinking—exactly what the nation and the borough of Brooklyn needed desperately. Old think: Wait for things to get better on their own. New think: If a system isn't working, try something completely different.

As the nation goes, so do I, thought Carla. She had no choice but to walk directly into the paradigm shift. It was time for her to try something different, whether she was ready for it or not.

Dr. Clifton cleared his throat. And now, she thought, here comes the big finish. "At LICH, we believe this program represents the future of pediatric health care. We're honored that the mayor has selected our clinic for restructuring." He looked up from his computer screen. "Carla, I'm offering the same choice to all four of our clinic pediatricians. This is a broad-stroke job description, of course. If you are interested in being a rover, you'll be assigned to six public schools in the borough, two elementary, two middle, and two high schools.

Your hours will be determined by need, but you can expect a work-week of around fifty hours. Some doctors keep the school nurse's office open until six o'clock. Your salary would be exactly what you're making now, minus a percentage cut we have yet to vote on. It'll be around ten percent."

More patients, exhaustive travel, longer hours, less money. Carla said, "What are the other options?"

Dr. Clifton clicked them off mechanically, early retirement, part-time this, part-time that, etc., none of them appealing. She must have looked discouraged. He said, "I know it's a lot to think about."

"What about my support staff?" she asked.

"Some will be absorbed by the hospital," he said. "Some will be let go."

"Last question: What about preschool-aged children? Babies and toddlers."

"We're going to combine maternity and early-childhood health care on one floor," he said. "Vern Summers and Kal Vali have already accepted their reassignments."

Meaning, she thought, two of her colleagues grabbed the on-site jobs. And she was left in the cold. Carla knew her reprimands would wind up hurting her, but she had no idea how badly.

"When will you need my decision?" she asked.

"By June fifteenth," he said.

"Why then?"

"On July first, we shut down the clinic."

Tears shot out of Carla's eyes. Literally burst forth, without warning. She'd been in complete control of her emotions until that moment.

Life as she knew it was changing. Although she had "options," she had no choice, really. Carla was forty-five years old. And she would have to start over.

Claude was adamant. "You have to take the rover job," he said. Another "kitchen table" conversation in the freshly painted dining room. "Forget part-time. We can't make it on one and a half salaries."

He'd had some incredible luck this week, accepting an offer to go to work for his former employer's competition—at a twenty percent drop in pay. Unlike Tim Fandine, who hadn't had a job in years, Claude bounced back after six weeks of unemployment. But even with his new job, money was still impossibly tight.

So tight, in fact, that they'd already made the decision about Brownstone. Neither Manny nor Zeke would attend next year. With diminished incomes, they couldn't swing one tuition. Incredibly, they were still earning too much for aid. Carla had already accepted the new reality. She'd fought against it for months, and was now willing to admit defeat—about private school. But Carla still had some fight in her.

Carla said, "The rover job is one option. There is another possibility."

"I'm listening," said Claude.

"Do you remember Dr. Stevens? You met him at a couple hospital benefits. He's a pediatrician in private practice in the Heights."

"Drawing a blank," he said.

"He's a very nice man," she said, trying to warm Claude up to the man, and the plan. "I ran into him a week ago and he asked me to call him to talk about his practice."

"Partnership?" asked Claude, perking up. A partnership in a private practice could mean big money.

She shook her head. "Not exactly."

"What, then?"

"I spent a lunch hour today at his office on Remsen Street. It's the bottom floor of a lovely brownstone building. Very clean, nice, three exam rooms," she said. "His staff seems great. He invited me to shadow him for a while, get a feel for how he runs the place. Then we talked for a few minutes on his stoop."

"Waiting," said Claude, moving her along.

She took a deep breath. "He's dying. Non-Hodgkin's lymphoma. He wants to sell his practice to a doctor he trusts to give his patients a high level of care."

"And he's offered it to you," said Claude. "How much?"

"A pittance, considering," she said.

He laughed. "I know what that means. We can't afford it."

"We could cash out our IRAs and 401Ks, and get a small business loan for the rest."

"Ransack our retirement for a risky business venture, and go in way over our heads in debt? This is the kind of thinking that got us into the recession."

"Don't blame the recession on me," she shouted, getting angry. "This is how people make money, Claude. They take risks. We've been playing it safe our whole lives. Every decision I've made has been about doing the responsible thing, the right thing. Well, look where that's got us."

"You still haven't told me how much," he said.

"It really is hardly anything," she said. "Half a million."

He laughed, holding his stomach, wiping at his eyes. "Oh, Carla. You *are* funny. Take the rover job. We'll get by."

"I'm too old for that job," she said.

"I won't let you put us half a million dollars in debt," he said. "We don't even have the thousands it would take in fees to get a loan. *If* we could get a loan."

That rattle she just heard deep in her chest? It was the last gasp of a dream, of running her own practice and being a family doctor, making an impact on people's health and happiness for their whole lives. She would settle, as Claude wanted her to, for the sake of her own family. Making an impact on her sons' health and happiness would have to be enough.

Claude crossed to her side of the table, and rubbed his wife's broad shoulders. Leaning down, he kissed her sweetly on the neck, and said, "I'm sorry, baby. I know you're upset. But you must have known that buying a private practice was never going to happen."

She let him kiss and comfort her. They made love that night. The unspoken offer had been made and accepted: in exchange for Claude's affection and protection, Carla would comply. As she lay awake, long after Claude fell asleep, she could count backward in time, the generation upon generation of American women—of color, or otherwise—who'd traded their dreams for their family. Carla was sure Bess's mother, Simone Gertrude, the old-school feminist, would have contempt for Carla's acquiescence. What Carla would have preferred, from any woman of any generation, was understanding. Wives and mothers had to make sacrifices. The number one sacrifice on the list? The chance to reach their full potential.

●———●

Last day of school. Why Moving Up Day had to take place at noon on a Wednesday was anyone's guess. Brownstone administrators might've sat around together, asking, "What would be the least convenient time for the parents to drop everything and attend a trumped-up ceremony for ten-year-olds? I've got it! Middle of the day, middle of the week. It's perfect!"

Carla had been invited to Bess's for a party for the kids. The whole poker crew was there, all the kids, along with Tim Fandine and Vivian Steeple, Bess's mother-in-law, the new widow. She'd flown in from California on a moment's notice to watch Charlie's exit from the lower school.

It must be nice to have free time and money to spend, thought Carla. Odd, how she could be envious of a woman who was in obvious pain. Sometimes Carla fantasized about being old, her struggles behind her. Then again, for all Carla knew, when she was old, her struggles could be even worse.

Turn those thoughts around, she instructed herself. It was a beautiful day, and Carla sat on Bess's garden patio, soaking in the June midday sun. On the picnic table nearby, Bess put out four delicious salads from the gourmet deli on Montague Street. The boys were running in and out of the garden, up the stairs, laughing, excited the school year was over. Even Joe Fandine was smiling and engaged with the others. The Zoloft appeared to have helped. Good for him.

Robin tilted her face up to the sun. "Tim looks intense today," she whispered into Carla's ear.

Alicia's husband, standing alone by the grill, beer in hand, eyes narrow and brooding, did look dark and stormy, even in his summer wardrobe of white jeans and a pink shirt.

"We're sure he's not gay," added Robin.

Carla said, "Reasonably."

"Okay, that's one more word out of you," said Robin. "You're up to sixteen today."

Carla shook her head, sipped her Coke. She wasn't in a conversational mood, although she certainly had plenty to say. She still hadn't told the poker players that the Morgan boys would not be attending Brownstone next year or, possibly, ever again. Manny and Zeke knew, of course. She wasn't sure if they'd told the other kids, or if it even mattered to them. When Carla and Claude informed him he'd start at a new school in the fall, Zeke said, "Okay." Manny's response? "Harder or easier?" he asked. Carla replied, "The school might be easier, but I'll be coming down a lot harder on you." That shut him up.

Borden came outside, carrying a platter of uncooked burgers, hot dogs, and chicken wings. Bess followed, carting a basket of buns and condiments, a plate of sliced tomatoes, pickles, and onions on her arm, napkins under her chin. Robin leapt up to help. The three of them started arranging the food on the table and slapping meat on the hot grill. The instant sizzle sound, and seconds later, the smell of barbecue, drove a sigh of pleasure out of Carla's tight lips.

Alicia came through the sliding door. She talked to Tim for a minute, and he went inside, presumably to watch or talk to Joe. Then Alicia took Robin's seat next to Carla at the picnic table.

"Is Claude coming?" she asked, drawing on a beer.

"He's working," Carla answered, as if he'd be here otherwise.

"I've got to hand it to him, finding a job so quickly," said Alicia.

"He was motivated," said Carla.

"To get out of the house, right?" said Alicia.

Probably. "We needed the money," said Carla.

"Who doesn't?" asked Alicia. "God, I wish Tim would just take *any* job. Waiting tables. That'd be the only way I'd get to see the inside of a decent restaurant."

This was proving difficult, having an intimate conversation with Alicia—any of her friends. Carla felt like she was one step out the door, that the connection she'd made with these women would end as soon as they knew her family was done with Brownstone. Their link to the kids' school was really the only thing they had in common. Besides poker.

Bess bubbled over and said, "Hot meat in five."

Borden flipped the burgers, then stepped back inside to call the kids. From outside, the women could hear the sneakered feet stampeding down the stairs, which made them all laugh. *Kids would brave a hurricane for a fresh grilled hamburger,* thought Carla.

As fast as Borden could put the sandwiches together, the kids inhaled them. A sweet moment: Amy, the sullen brat (*forgive me, Bess, but that girl doesn't know how good she has it,* thought Carla), gently helped her grandmother Vivian into an Adirondack chair on the patio, filled a plate for her with salad and a hot dog, and served it to her. Another: Tom (Bess's middle son) accidentally-on-purpose tipping Stephanie Stern's potato salad onto her shorts. An obvious attempt to get the girl's attention. Stephanie said, "If you like me, just tell me! You don't have to ruin my clothes!" Which made Tom turn bright red. Borden saved him by asking him to go upstairs and get more cups. The boy couldn't run away fast enough.

Charlie Steeple, Zeke's best bud, asked Bess, "Mom, can I go to school next year with Zeke?"

Carla froze, fork halfway to her mouth.

Bess said, "I can write an email requesting they put you in some of the same classes, but no guarantees."

"No, Zeke is going to a different school," said Charlie. "And it sounds cool. A hundred more kids, full-sized basketball court outside, McDonald's across the street."

"Oh?" said Bess, smiling at Charlie, and then glancing at Carla.

Here goes everything, thought Carla. She shrugged and said, "Claude and I felt the time was right to make a change."

Silence from the parents. Only the sounds of chewing. The tension was broken (sort of) when Vivian tapped Stephanie on the shoulder and asked, "Where's your daddy today, sweetheart?"

"My biological father was a sperm donor," said Stephanie with comic banality.

"Is that so?" asked Vivian.

"If you think about it," said Stephanie, "all biological fathers are sperm donors. I mean, that's what they contribute to the whole deal. Fathers don't get pregnant or give birth. Mothers do the hard work. In real life, people don't explode fully formed out of Zeus's head."

"Isn't she fascinating?" said Vivian, a bit taken aback by Stephanie's grown-up conversational style—a parroting of things Robin must have told her at some point.

"They had a Greek myths curriculum this year," explained Bess.

As soon as the kids were done eating, they ran back inside, leaving dirty paper plates and edible detritus everywhere. Cue the moms to start cleaning up, and the dads (and grandmother) to find urgent business elsewhere.

Carla was glad the women were alone outside so she could explain herself.

But Robin had some explaining to do, and (not surprisingly) she got there first. "Before anyone asks, I don't want any grief from you all that I haven't told Stephanie about Harvey yet," she said.

Bess dumped some plates into a trash bag. "No lectures for you today, Robin," she said. "On the other hand, *Carla*, I am pissed as hell at you right now."

"Charlie will be fine without Zeke," said Carla.

"I'm sick of you holding out on us," said Bess. "Okay, yes, I held out on you guys about my lump. We've all kept some things private."

Alicia coughed. "Husband within range."

Bess continued. "But this is worse that my lump, Alicia's . . . and Robin's . . . actually, Robin doesn't hold back anything."

"Oh, you have no idea," said Robin. "The drinking, I do."

Carla said, "It's humiliating, okay? I'm supposed to announce to the group that we're broke, that we can't afford Brownstone, that I resent my husband for making me take a job I don't want, that I'm failing my sons and giving up my dreams?"

"Holy smokes," said Robin. "You just quadrupled your word count."

Bess dropped the garbage bag and came at Carla, arms open. Before she could block the contact, Bess got her in a hug. What a funny sight they must have been. A heavyset towering black woman being grappled by a cheerleader blonde. When Bess started rubbing Carla's back, her steel spine softened. She might've choked up a little.

"Let's go inside and sit down at the table," said Bess. "You can tell us what this is about."

Back to where they started, at the poker table Borden never used. Carla shuffled cards for something to do with her hands as she explained the unavoidable and unexpected changes in her life.

Robin, who had managed to keep her mouth shut for fifteen solid minutes, said, "I'll lend you the money to buy the private practice."

"Half a million dollars?" asked Carla.

"Sure," said Robin. "It'd be a business investment. I have a hundred percent faith that you'd make it a huge success."

Carla said, "I can't take your money. But thanks."

"What if Robin and I both lent you some money?" asked Bess.

"Absolutely not," said Carla. "My pride forbids it. I appreciate the offer. But please don't mention it again, really."

Alicia said, "I was prepared to front you a twenty."

"I'd take a twenty," said Carla.

"It's just that we'd love to help," said Bess, shimmering in her radiant loveliness. Carla blinked at her friend, and thought, *This is a good person. They're all good people.*

"But you do help," said Carla, looking at each in turn. "You don't know how much you've helped me get through this year. I know I haven't talked much about what's been going on. It's not my style to complain or overshare. Yes, I mean you, Robin." She paused. Let the truth surface. "It's not that I don't want to express my feelings," said Carla. "I was raised to swallow a lot. My only acceptable emotions growing up were gratitude and humility under God. Expressing any other kind of feeling was selfish, lazy, a sin. Show too much happiness, and you're tempting God to teach you a lesson. Show sadness or fear, and you're asking for more of the same. As a kid, I wanted to sing when I was happy and cry when I was upset, but life was easier for me when I did what I was told—keep it all inside, or else. I had an unsettling realization just last week about how superstitious I've become. It's from the 'or else' part of my childhood. I'm starting to think, though, that I'll never win the lottery. And that if I *don't* take risks, my soul will suffer."

"God helps those who help themselves," said Robin. "And he punishes those who are wimps."

Carla grimaced. "You think I'm a wimp?"

Robin laughed. "You are many things, Carla, but wimpy isn't one of them."

"Playing poker has been a wedge for me," said Carla. "Going for it on a flush or straight draw, and then seeing my card come up on the river? It's a great feeling. And when the card doesn't come up, at least I know I tried. From now on, I want to go for the draw in real life."

Bess clapped her hands together. "Oh God, I just had the most fabulous idea."

"What?"

"Road trip," said Bess. "Atlantic City, tonight. We'll gamble with real money against real poker players. We can sleep over, and drive back early tomorrow morning. Carla, don't even think about the money, not a single penny. This is my end-of-school gift to all of you. A hotel suite, fattening expensive meal, and a nice stack of chips to get started."

"*Our* gift," said Robin. "I'll pay for Carla. You pay for Alicia."

Carla shook her head. "I'm sorry, but—"

"Screw your pride," said Robin. "You can pay me back when you *win*. And you will win. Honestly, Black Queen, do you really think bad luck lasts forever? No, ma'am. It does not. Your karma is already swinging the other way. I can actually see it moving."

"I love this idea," said Alicia. "Speaking for myself, I have zero problem with taking your money."

"What about the boys?" asked Carla. "Clothes?"

Bess jumped and bellowed, "Borden! Honey!"

After a minute, the handsome host descended the staircase to the garden level, revealing himself step by step, as he'd done that first night months ago, taking their breath away.

"The garbage, I know," he said, walking toward the patio.

"Honey," said Bess, stopping him. She put her hands on his shoulders, getting his full attention. "We want to drive down to Atlantic City tonight to play poker and stay at a hotel."

If Carla had spoken that sentence to Claude, he'd have keeled over from shock.

"Sounds fun," said Borden. "And you're hoping I'll watch the kids." Bess smiled and nodded slowly. "Wait, you want me to watch *all* of the kids?"

"Tim will help!" offered Alicia. "I think!"

"And you've got Amy and Vivian," said Bess. "The boys—and

Stephanie—are officially middle-schoolers now. Tom, Eric, and Manny are practically adults. They can take care of themselves. God knows, we have enough sleeping bags. And leftover food."

The decision was made, but Bess gave Borden the courtesy of final approval.

He smiled into his wife's beaming face. How could he, or anyone, deny her? "Go," he said. "I'll keep the kids alive until you get back. But don't expect much more than that."

Bess cutely squealed and hugged Borden, who had to peel her off. The women flew into action, explaining their plan to the children (they all *loved* the idea of a mass sleepover), making the necessary phone calls and arrangements. Vivian's face brightened when she heard the plan. Even Amy seemed to approve of the idea.

Claude was a hundred percent opposed.

"You don't know what the boys will do or watch," he said. "And you're going to gamble? With Robin Stern's money? I can't believe what I'm hearing."

"I'm going," she said succinctly, without regret. "If you want to pick up Zeke and Manny to bring them home, just call first." Then Carla hung up on Claude, something she'd never done before. She might pay for it later. But tonight, she'd speed to the ocean in a BMW with her friends, eat a huge meal, drink as much wine was she wanted, and play poker against real gamblers. The surge of excitement was disorienting. Carla was afraid she might burst out of her skin.

Nine months ago, if someone told her that, come June, she'd abandon her husband and children to play poker in Atlantic City with a bunch of white women, she'd have laughed herself into hyperventilation. She felt eyes, and turned to see that Robin was smirking at her.

"Being bad feels pretty fucking excellent, doesn't it?" asked Robin.

"Please don't curse," said Carla. "And yes. It does."

SHOWDOWN

13

While Carla drove the BMW (Robin was forbidden from getting behind the wheel), Bess worked her iPhone trying to find a hotel room. Spontaneity had its headaches. Most of the big resorts were booked solid. There was crazy talk about turning around, and heading north toward Connecticut's Native American casinos Mohegan Sun and Foxwoods. But that would have added another hour to the trip. On the sixth try, Bess secured a suite for the women at Harrah's, a white elephant of a resort right on the ocean, next to the Trump Marina. None of them had ever been to Harrah's. Only Bess had been to Atlantic City before—with her father when she was a toddler. She didn't remember the trip, but she had a photo of herself, white blond, chubby belly in a green bikini, on Fred's shoulders on the boardwalk. She thought about that photo, and let herself miss her youth and her dad. But only for a second. The women hadn't come for nostalgia. They'd come to play.

The mood in the car started out rowdy, then dialed way down while Bess hunted for a hotel room. With that business concluded, the mood settled into an anticipatory calm. The drive took a while—over two hours. The women talked a bit, but each was in her own head, thinking about what she'd left behind in Brooklyn—unresolved relationships, tough conversations to come, the decisions that had to be made and then lived with. Just as every relationship and decision up to this point had brought them to where they were now—exit 75 on the Garden State Parkway—every future action (or inaction) would carry them to the next phase, what- or wherever that might be. Each woman knew that she was on the brink of ending one part of her life, and beginning another. They were speeding toward the clear dividing moment between "what was" and "what will be." This night would be more than an impromptu road trip for a (diverse) quartet of former strangers, now close friends. Harrah's—or, as they decided to call it, "Hurray's"—seemed as good a place as any to make a change.

A poker player mantra about living in the moment: "The past is history, the future's a mystery." You had to check, fold, call, or raise each hand based on limited information, previous experience, and gut intuition, and accept the consequences of your bet, regardless of the outcome. Play smart and bold, no matter how many chips you hold. Leave nothing on the table.

•───•

They arrived at Hurray's, checked in—no luggage—walked through the clanging, blinking casino floor, and went up to their suite. The consensus about the accommodations? Sopranos Chic. Haute Tacky.

Bess said, "New Jersey Style."

Alicia said, "Now, there's an oxymoron to add to my list. I'll put that between 'military intelligence' and 'compassionate conservatism.' "

They threw open the curtains to let in the last rays of sunlight, showcasing the spotty carpet and faded furniture fabric. Hardly mattered. They hadn't come to sit in a hotel suite. It served a function, and was comfortably enormous. Two bedrooms with twin beds, a large lounge area with a full bar and fridge stocked with fruit, cheese, crackers, candy, cookies, half a dozen chilled bottles. Bess suggested opening some champagne.

Robin said, "We can't drink before we play."

Alicia reeled back in mock shock. "Who are you, and what have you done with Robin Stern?"

"Let's get some food," said Robin, ignoring Alicia. "And then we'll play. I want a full stomach—which should take me two bites—and a clear head."

Carla said, "I noticed a steakhouse in the lobby."

"Fine," said Robin.

"You can eat steak?" asked Bess.

"If I cut a fillet into tiny pieces, I can handle it," said Robin.

The Longhorn Steakhouse was located, to their delight, on the mezzanine level overlooking the poker circle. The women got a table along the balcony and could peer down at some three-dozen tables. The aerial view helped them get the lay of the land. A desk, like a restaurant maître d' stand, blocked the only entrance into the poker circle. The area wasn't a room per se with four walls and a door, but rather an open-air large circle with a hip-high demi-wall looped around it. At the desk, an organizer logged a player's preference into a computer (game type—Hold 'Em, five card draw, etc.—ante maximums, number of players in your party), and then you waited in a cordoned-off outer area for an open seat at an appropriate table. When your name flashed on a digital display over the organizer's desk, you presented yourself to him, and were escorted to your seat by an usher. Only players, dealers, managers, ushers, and servers were allowed inside the circle. Spectators could watch from the other side of the demi-wall. If spectators got too loud, they were asked to leave the area by beefy security guards who patrolled the circle wall.

The action was intense and quiet. Compared to the noisy, blinking, and ka-chinging on the casino floor, the poker circle was a veritable tomb. Huge sums of money were being won and lost down there. And yet, the players acted stoic, unfazed by the dizzying redistribution of chips after each hand. Even though it was nighttime in a windowless casino, half the players wore sunglasses and caps pulled low over their eyes. Some of the players drank cocktails; some had bottles of water. No smoking, which the ladies appreciated (except Robin). And hardly any talking. The tone was serious, somber, and scary as hell.

The Brooklyn women searched the hundreds of players at dozens of tables for others of their kind. But they counted only five women down there. Three cocktail waitresses, one usher, and a manager.

Robin said, "Women don't play poker. They play slots and roulette."

Bess said, "Maybe being female is to our advantage. We might throw the men off their game with our wiles."

Robin said, "You're the only one here with wiles, Bess."

Carla said, "Do the other players look intimidating to you?"

The four women leaned over the mezzanine railing for a closer look at the pockmarked, prison-pallor seedy, shadowed, mysterious, ruthless gamblers below.

Bess shrugged and said, "Men are men."

"They're *terrifying*," said Alicia. "Especially that one." She pointed at a three-hundred-pound man with a full beard, lumberjack shirt, bulging tattooed forearms, black shades, and a trucker hat. "He looks like he escaped from a ZZ Top video, and hasn't left that seat since. We're sure we want to do this?"

"Yes," said Carla. "Let's go now, before any of you chicken out."

They charged the meal to the room, stopped at an ATM for cash (each woman would start with $500), and then approached the poker circle desk.

Robin said, "MILF, party of four."

"Pardon?" asked the organizer, a slicked-back thirty-year-old man in a blazer.

"Texas Hold 'Em, five and ten dollar blinds, four of us," Robin stated.

He tapped into his computer, and said, "I can seat all of you now—if you want to play at separate tables. But if you want to sit together, it'll be a few minutes."

The women huddled.

"If we sit together, we'll be playing for each other's money," said Carla. "Makes no sense."

"I don't want to be alone!" said Alicia.

Bess asked the organizer, "Do you have two seats together?"

"I can put two of you at the same table, and two singles."

"That'll work," said Bess. "I'll sit with Alicia. Robin and Carla, you go alone."

Ushers showed the women to their tables.

●━━━●

Alicia's legs were shaking. Literally knocking between the knees. She loved to play poker back in New York. Her after-work game with the guys was trash talk, under the table groping with Finn, and beer guzzling. The mothers' game was gossip, true confessions, and cocktails. Fun and, ahem, a *game*.

These men weren't playing a friendly game. This wasn't fun. It was work. For some of the players, poker was their livelihood.

Her pal Carla's poker breakthrough had been about the joy of taking risks. Alicia had a poker-related breakthrough, too—about the joy of active escapism. When she was playing cards with her friends and colleagues, Alicia's anxieties, shyness, and nervousness dissolved. She opened up, relaxed. Worry and stress shed off her like a snakeskin. If Alicia hadn't learned to open up while playing poker, Finn wouldn't have seen her as a sexual object. She'd have remained the celibate shrew.

Which was, ironically, exactly what Alicia felt like when she took a seat at the table of men. None of them looked at her. Not even a glance to see who'd come to play. A couple of them noticed Bess, but they'd have to be dead not to. They looked at her blond gorgeousness, and then right back at their cards. No reaction, no masculine posturing. None drew himself up and offered to buy her a drink. In this Twilight Zone, even Bess was invisible.

Alicia felt swallowed up by the disregard. When the dealer asked for her cash to exchange for chips, it took her a second to realize he had spoken to her. She fumbled over her bills, and received a pile of chips. No one else said anything.

And then the dealer started flipping cards around the table. Alicia peeked at her pocket cards and almost gasped. A pair of queens, on the very first hand. She tried to stay calm, not to show her excitement. When the bet came to her, she called.

The flop. Another queen. Alicia had three of a kind. She started sweating profusely and immediately. She wondered if the phrase "flop sweat" had come from poker (never occurred to her before, but it made perfect sense). Bess folded when the guy with a crewcut and Bono shades next to her raised the bet to $50. A few folds, a few calls. Alicia reraised to $100. Crewcut saw her raise.

The turn: a rag. Two of spades. Crewcut bet $200. Alicia called. All the other players folded.

The river: another queen. On her very first hand, Alicia had an all but unbeatable four of a kind. Alicia's stomach had relocated to her knees. Her heart, meanwhile, was threatening to explode out of her chest. Her face? Felt bright red. Her hands? Shaking like mad.

"All in," she squeaked.

Bess gave her a funny look. She mouthed, "Are you sure?"

Alicia ignored her friend. When Crewcut said, "Call," Alicia nearly peed herself. She might've, in fact, lost a few drops. She was going to double her money! In one hand!

Showdown. The dealer invited her to turn over her cards. She showed her pocket pair. The dealer said, "Four of a kind."

A few of the players muttered approvingly.

Crewcut showed his cards. A three and four of spades. Alicia saw the rags and smiled.

The dealer said, "Straight flush wins."

Before Alicia knew what was happening, the dealer moved the pot of chips over to Crewcut. Taking another look, she saw the horrible ugly truth. All of the communal cards were spades, except the queen of hearts, a two, five, and six.

Alicia had been blinded by her four of a kind, and didn't notice all that black on the table.

The dealer called for the big and small blinds, or the five- and ten-dollar table antes. The next hand was already under way. The player to Alicia's right, a fat middle-aged man in a cowboy hat, said, "Bad beat."

The hand had taken ninety seconds to play, about as long as brushing her teeth. In that blink of an eye, Alicia had lost $500 of Bess's money. Her legs wobbling, she managed to pull her chair away from the table, and stand up.

Bess folded her cards, and said to the dealer, "I'll be right back." Then the she got up, and put her arm around Alicia's waist.

Alicia was eternally grateful to her friend for helping her walk. She said, "That proves one thing."

"Bad luck," said Bess. "We'll get you more money."

"No!" said Alicia. "I feel like I'm going to throw up! It's too intense. Whiplash emotions and flooding hormones. I don't have the stomach for it. Go back and play, please. Just let me get out of here."

"What happened to Wild Heart?" asked Bess.

"Wild Heart almost went into cardiac arrest," said Alicia, clutching her chest.

Bess frowned. "What're you going to do?"

"Joan Rivers is performing in the theater later. I'll check her out," said Alicia. "I'll have a couple of drinks—which I desperately need—and play some nickel slots. That's my speed."

"Are you sure?" asked Bess. "You should play at least one more hand."

"One thousand percent sure," said Alicia, feeling her stomach churn at the thought of losing another $500 in ninety seconds.

Bess said, "Charge the Joan Rivers ticket to the room," and returned to the table.

Relieved, Alicia scurried out of the poker circle, and straight to the nearest bar. She downed a vodka tonic, and felt herself begin the journey out of the Twilight Zone, and back to her comfort zone.

Life lesson learned tonight: Alicia loved poker. But gambling? God as her witness, Alicia would Never. Gamble. Again.

●━━━●

And then there were three.

Robin noticed when Alicia fled the poker circle like a terrified bunny. Not too surprising, really. Robin never thought Alicia was a real gambler. Too nervous. Robin felt excited, but not afraid so far. She'd played four hands, and folded all of them. Too impulsive in real life, Robin was determined not to "tilt" or "steam," poker terms for betting by emotion. On the other hand (as it were), she didn't want to be "supertight," or a "nit" either, meaning playing very few hands.

The button had gone all the way around the table before Robin called her first bet. She had two hearts in the pocket. Inspired by Carla's speech earlier that day (was it really the same day?), Robin promised herself to go for it on a flush or straight draw.

The flop: five and ace of hearts. Robin's eyes widened. Only one more heart for an ace high flush. She bet $20, and was reraised another $20. She called, amazed by how quickly a high pile of chips could turn into a short stack.

The turn: ten of clubs. No help. The bet went around the table, and Robin was forced to add another $40 to the pot. At this point, she had nothing. Not even a pair. If the river card wasn't a heart, she'd have to fold—or bluff her way into the pot.

The dealer knocked the table and turned the river card: a freaking diamond. That flash of color made the Red Queen's heart jump, but alas, her flush was not to be.

The bet was to her, another $40. She examined the communal cards. No pairs on board. No straight or flush possibilities. The aggressive bettor—a bald fifty-year-old with thick glasses and a leisure suit, a tourist from Florida?—could have a pocket ace. Robin had junk; anything would beat her.

This was it. To fold or bluff. She decided (impulsively) to go in, over the top. She bet $100.

Incredibly, Florida called. *Shit!* she thought. The dealer asked to see her cards.

"Ace high," he said.

Florida turned over his cards. The dealer said, "Pair of deuces."

In the pocket. He beat her with a pathetic pair of deuces. And now she was down nearly $200.

The men around the table snickered at her. Okay, yes, she was a bad bluffer. She screwed up. The smart play would've been to cut her losses and fold.

Smiling, Robin thought, *Now I've got them just where I want them. They think I'm a bluffer. They'll raise me all night long.*

Several hands later, Robin decided to call on a pocket pair of eights. Those middle pairs were tough. Easy to beat, or a surprise winner. She reminded herself she'd lost already to a pair of deuces. Eights were better than that.

Florida came on strong, betting $60 pre-flop. Clearly, he also had a pair, but of what? Deuces again? Everyone else folded, but the Red Queen smelled a bluff, and decided to call.

The flop: jack of spades, four of hearts, a six of clubs. No help for

Robin. A lowly jack was the high card on the board. Unless he had a higher pair in the pocket, or a jack, she was on top.

The turn: another jack. The pair on the board—the two jacks—was a major danger, even though she had two pair. He could have three of a kind or a better set of two pair.

Robin decided to check, to lull Florida into a false sense of security, only to spring her guns on him when he was already pot committed. He checked, too.

The river: king of spades. No help for the Red Queen. Bet to Florida, he mulled and mulled. Took his sweet mofo time. Every second that ticked by, Robin felt her blood pressure rise. What was he thinking about? Whether she had anything? If he had a king in the pocket, he'd've bet big immediately. If he had a jack, he'd've bet after the turn. So what was the friggin' holdup?

He's got shit, she decided. *He's trying to decide if I've got shit. If he thinks I'm bluffing, he'll bet big to force me to fold because he knows I don't want a showdown with crap again. Act like you've got nothing! Make him come in over the top.*

How exactly did one do that? Robin pretended to be overcome with nerves. She breathed rapidly, and played with her stack.

Florida saw her fidget, and smiled slyly. He said, "One hundred."

"Raise," said Robin way too quickly.

"All in," he said, even faster.

Now Robin wondered if he'd lulled *her* into the pot with a false sense of security. She'd been playing for only a half an hour, and stood to lose all her money on an iffy two pair.

"Fold," she said.

Florida turned over his cards. He had zippo, zilch, a ten and a nine. Her eights beat him by a mile. She'd been bluffed out of half her money by a bald goober.

Robin's stack was down to a dozen chips. Frustrated, she steamed into the pot with a pair of pocket fives, and lost the rest of her money at blinding speed.

When she stood up to leave, none of the men at the table said good-bye. Her chips were gone, therefore, she didn't exist. Poker was dehumanizing. It turned a person into a pile.

She said, "Thank you," to the dealer.

Florida said, "You're welcome," fingering his (formerly her) chips.

Shithead, she thought. Robin fumed out of the poker circle, bound for a casino exit to smoke, or a bar, whichever came first.

Alicia saw Robin coming. The brunette said, "You lasted a lot longer than I did."

"I didn't win a single hand! I was impulsive and emotional," said Robin. "I played like an insecure little girl."

"I played like a jittery mouse," said Alicia.

They sat in silence, both of them ruminating on the "you are how you play" notion.

"Illusions? Officially shattered," said Robin. "To tell you the truth, I'm relieved it's over. I'm completely frazzled."

"Have a drink," said Alicia. "It helps."

⸺

And then there were two.

Carla was in a rhythm. She folded low percentage hands and called all pre-flop pairs, straight draws, flush draws, and face cards with a kicker of ten or higher. After the flop, she folded any hand that didn't have a pair of eights or higher, or twelve "outs" or chances of hitting a straight or flush. She raised after the turn with a high pair, two pairs, three of a kind, or a straight or flush draw with at least eight "outs." She raised or called after the river with three of a kind, pair of kings or aces, a full house, flush, or straight. Otherwise, she folded. These rules had been ground into her head while playing on the computer and with her friends. And she was winning. A lot. Carla's system was a success.

What she came to realize about real poker play: it was a grind. She followed her rules, calculated outs and odds. The universe collapsed into the size of the table. The intensity of studying limited information and projecting a variety of potential outcomes took her back to medical school. The mental process of diagnosing a disease was pretty similar to placing a bet. Going by what you could see, the doctor (or player) then followed the protocol (or rules). Previous research and experience helped improve her cure (or win) percentages. Poker was a system. Carla was a scientist. Her skill at keeping emotions in check made her an excellent diagnostician—and an efficient poker player. Unlike her patients' parents, who expected and wanted Carla to be emotive and sympathetic, the gamblers expected her to be stonefaced as the Sphinx, and ruthless. At the table, Carla was spared the pressure to express herself.

But the play was too mechanical. She felt like a machine. Of course, it was satisfying to win. But beating a table full of strangers—no celebration allowed—was joyless (although preferable, naturally, to losing). She missed the "Come to Mama" moments of exhilaration when playing with her friends. With real money, she took calculated risks, but not wild ones. Real poker wasn't as fun as she thought it would be.

But it was absorbing. Dozens of hands went by in a flash. Players came and went from her table. The dealer changed many times. Alicia and Robin signaled to her from outside the circle to ask if she wanted to take a break and see Joan Rivers's one-woman show. She waved them off. They left. She took a bathroom break or two. Drank a couple of coffees brought to her by servers. Alicia and Robin appeared again. Carla stretched her legs, left her chips on the table, and talked to them outside the circle for five minutes.

"Joan was great," said Alicia.

"She's still got it," said Robin. "But if I hear another joke about geriatric vaginas this year, it'll be too soon. We're going to the casino floor to play the ladylike sucker game of roulette. Wanna come?"

"I'm going to stick around for a few more hands," said Carla.

"It's midnight, you realize," said Robin.

Carla was shocked to hear it. "I've been playing poker for five hours?"

"The chair has formed a permanent impression of your ass," said Robin.

"I lasted less than two minutes," said Alicia.

"Maybe I do need a break," said Carla, rubbing her (now that she thought of it) numb rear end. "Just give me a minute to get my chips."

She returned to the table and said she was done.

"Would you like me to change your chips?" asked the dealer.

"Er, sure," she said, realizing her piles were too high to carry away. She pushed them forward toward her tenth dealer of the night. With dizzying speed, he counted her chips into hundreds. Then thousands. Carla's jaw dropped as the total rose higher and higher.

"Changing five thousand six hundred and forty," the dealer announced. A manager with a computerized clipboard came over to double check the count, and officiate over the transfer to Carla of eleven $500 chips, one $100 chip, and two $20 chips.

Stunned, Carla wandered out of the poker circle like a stupefied zombie, her chips in her cupped hands like eggs.

Robin said, "What's wrong with you?"

"I won five thousand dollars," said Carla, incredulous.

"Holy shit!" her friends squealed, hugging her and dancing around her like little Brooklyn elves.

"Here's your advance," said Carla, flipping Robin a $500 chip.

The redhead caught it. "I told you your luck was changing! Quick, women, to the roulette table." Robin held up the $500 chip, grinning wickedly. "Let's put it all on *black*."

● ━━━ ●

And then there was one.

From the moment she walked into the circle, Bess was blissfully transformed. She loved the instant anonymity and invisibility. In the circle, she was no one's daughter, wife, or mother. She wasn't a blonde. Her tablemates barely looked at her, much less made snap judgments and assumptions about her character, history, personality, or intelligence.

At the poker table, looks, status, and identity meant nothing. The only thing that mattered here was whether you checked, folded, called, raised, or reraised. In the real world, Bess's life burst with responsibilities. Plans to make, things to do, people to see, checks to write, food to cook, dishes to wash, kids to care for. Bess had to keep track of six people's activities, special requirements, and emotional needs. As soon as she settled into the chair's soft leather cushion and pulled herself up to the poker table, Bess's fragmented existence became whole. She transformed into a laser-focused hard (white) diamond of one mind and one purpose: to win hands.

She hadn't entered this state of concentration when she played with the other women in Brooklyn. Those games had too many distractions—the discussion, kids, phones, husbands, food, drinks, and hostessing (a duty that had fallen on Bess more often than the others).

She'd tried to improve her poker play all year. She'd urged the other women to take the rules seriously. But their personal lives always interceded. Rightfully so. Brooklyn Hold 'Em had been made up on the fly, a game of getting-to-know-you. They'd started out as the Diversity Committee. But now they had the same goals and concerns: to help each other. Did friends need to have more in common than involvement in each other's lives? Bess had become deeply involved watching her friends' lives unfold, pulling her in, getting her wrapped up and wanting to know what would happen next. With real friendships, the chapters and stories kept coming, increasing in complexity, until it all ended in death. Of course, Bess had to include death. It was a fact of life.

So there was real friendship. And then there was real poker. This game required no compassion or caring. The story ended after each hand. The only requirement: Bess's undivided attention. She felt her vision tunnel. Extraneous sound and sights dissolved around the edges. A few times, she heard Alicia and Bess try to get her attention and pull her out of the zone. Bess stayed focused. Her absorption seemed superhuman, a power she hadn't known she possessed. It was beyond pleasurable. In fact, it had a sexual reward system. When she won a hand, Bess registered a direct hit on the clitoris. Pulling in one massive pot of over a thousand dollars, Bess thought she might come right there in her chair.

Bess smiled graciously when she won. When she lost a good hand to smart player, she congratulated him—or her (hours into the game, another woman took a chair and did well). Bess's play style was gut-shot *and* mindful. Unlike real life, where Bess craved control, in poker, she loosened up, relinquished mastery of the table action, and mentally opened a window for Lady Luck.

Luck had been floating overhead all night long. Bess had won hands with four of a kind and full houses. One magnificent draw, she pulled the only "out" on the river—the queen of diamonds to make a queen high straight flush (that was her near spontaneous orgasm winner). When she was forced by her bladder to take bathroom breaks, she ran to and from the ladies' room.

At midnight, her friends tried to pull her away. But she begged off. At one o'clock in the morning, she felt as exhilarated and energetic as she had when she first sat down. Her friends were back at the poker circle wall, only a few feet away from where she sat.

"Don't try to talk to her," said Robin. "She's in her happy place."

Carla said, "Look at her piles."

Alicia said, "I'm exhausted. I've got to go upstairs."

"Me, too," said Carla. "After this hand."

Bess was in the middle of a good one. She had a jack and ten of spades in the pocket. On the flop: the eight and king of spades. Flush draw, and a one-way straight draw. The other woman at the table, young and awkward, a college student in an orange T-shirt, had bet aggressively pre-flop. Maybe she had an ace or a king in the pocket. Bess waited to see what she'd do now with a king on the board.

Orange bet big. A thousand dollars. Bess decided Orange had a king in the pocket. Thus far, when the girl bet big, she had the cards to back up her play. Bess hadn't bluffed on many hands. When she did, she had an inner calm about it, intuitive assurance her bluff would fly. This time, she wasn't so sure.

So Bess called. So did Cowboy Hat, an older gentleman who'd been at the table almost as long as Bess. He tended to pick and play hands to the river.

The turn: another spade, a deuce. Bess now had a king high flush. A good hand. A solid winner. Except she had a nagging doubt about Orange's big pre-flop raise. It was just not in character for the girl. Maybe she had a pair of aces in the pocket? Bess's flush beat that.

Bess's turn to act first. She preferred not to lead into the action, so she checked. Orange bet two thousand dollars. Cowboy Hat called. Bess's instinct told her Cowboy Hat was seeing the hand through to the end, as he often did for no good reason. He might have a king, or possibly a flush, too. He'd beat her with the ace of spades in the pocket. Orange could have a flush. But not all three of them. There were only thirteen spades in the deck. The odds of a three-way flush were small, but not impossible. Calling again, Bess moved a high stack into the pot.

The river: deuce of clubs. A pair on the board. No help for Bess's straight flush dreams. But she still felt like she had a very strong hand, a likely winner.

Cowboy Hat checked. He'd been looking to the river for an out— a third ace, if he had two in the pocket?—and, obviously, didn't get it. Orange checked. A sign to Bess that the girl's pre-flop aggressive raise was a ploy to steal the blinds, or overexcitement about a pocket pair. Bess could check, too, and then see their hands and she'd know. But why check when she had a king high flush? This was a betting hand.

She looked over her shoulder at her pals. Carla was whispering to Robin and Alicia, probably explaining to them exactly what Bess was thinking about.

One more review of the hand's history, the pre-flop raise, the calls and checks. Orange's early enthusiasm had cooled considerably. Orange checked after the river. If she had an ace high flush or a full house, she would've raised.

Bess decided to go in over the top. She had a very strong hand. Bess didn't want to risk a showdown if she could intimidate the others into a fold.

"All in," said Bess, pushing her chips into the middle.

The dealer went quickly about the business of tallying her raise. He called out the supervisor, "Eight thousand, two hundred and twenty into the pot."

The manager, a sweet-faced middle-aged woman with a computerized clipboard, came over to the table. She noted the amount.

The dealer said, "To you, sir."

Cowboy Hat folded. *Whew,* thought Bess. One down.

"To you, ma'am," said the dealer to Orange.

"Call," said Orange.

Bess got a sinking feeling. That post-river check had been a lure, and Bess fell for it.

The dealer double-checked Orange's stack.

"The bet is called," said the dealer. A manager came to watch.

The pot was over $20,000. With a nod from the dealer, Bess turned over her cards.

"King high flush," said the dealer.

The eyes of all the players, the dealer, the supervisor, and a large crowd of spectators (they'd flocked when the dealer called out the amount on the table) now turned toward the girl. She revealed her cards.

First card: the king of hearts. Bess wasn't surprised by that. She'd played out the pair of kings in the pocket scenario. So now Orange had two pair, kings and the pair of deuces on the board.

Second card: not a king. Bess sighed with relief. But she realized it was just as bad—a pint-sized coup de grâce, the deuce of hearts.

"Full house, deuces over kings. Winner."

The table and crowd applauded the winner.

Bess joined in. "You raised pre-flop with a king and a *deuce* kicker? And then checked with a full house? You totally played me! Well done," Bess said.

"I can't believe this is happening," the girl said. She was crying with excitement.

Bess felt happy for her, and hoped she'd spend the money wisely. She said, "You should be very proud of yourself." And then stood up to go.

The dealer said, "You're not leaving us."

"My friends are waiting for me," said Bess. "Thank you all so much. I had an excellent time tonight. And what a finish!"

Cowboy Hat said, "You just lost twenty thousand dollars! What're you smiling about?"

"I didn't lose twenty thousand dollars," said Bess. "I lost five hundred dollars—what I had when I first sat down."

"You're crazy," said Cowboy Hat.

Bess shrugged. Frankly, *he* looked a little crazy.

Her friends greeted her with open arms. "Bad beat," said Carla.

"Yeah," said Bess. "But look at the winner! She's ecstatic. Obviously, that girl needs the money more than I do."

"Excuse me," said the manager with her electronic clipboard. She'd followed Bess out of the circle.

Bess smiled at her. "Did I forget something?"

"No," she said, smiling at Bess. "I just wanted to tell you: I've worked the poker circle here for six years. And I have never seen someone lose a big pot as graciously as you just did."

"Did you guys hear that? I'm a good loser!" said Bess, making her friends laugh.

"Are you staying at the hotel?" asked the manager. "May I see your key card for a moment?"

"Sure," said Bess, handing it over.

The woman swiped the card on her computer clipboard, and then typed on the touch screen keypad. Handing the card back to Bess, the woman said, "Graciousness isn't appreciated enough, in my opinion—or rewarded. Please accept a gift on behalf of Harrah's Resort and Casino. Your room and all room charges have been picked up by the hotel."

Robin said, "You can do that?"

"Just did," she said and turned the clipboard around to show them the balance on their room: $0. "I see you're checking out in the morning. Drive home safe, and please come back to Harrah's next time you're in AC," said the woman.

"Hurray's!" said Alicia.

"Is the comp good for the rest of the night?" asked Robin.

"You bet," said the manager, who smiled and then returned to the center of the poker circle.

"You know what this means," said Bess.

Carla said, "That even when you lose, you win? And I do mean *you,* Bess Steeple."

"Well, I had something else in mind," said Bess.

"We're cleaning out the room fridge?" asked Alicia.

"To the last crumb," said Bess.

* ⬥ *

As instructed, the women drove home safely, despite savage hangovers and queasy stomachs. Too much caviar, chocolate, and champagne (or, perhaps, as Robin suggested, "not enough").

"Can we go any faster?" asked Carla from the backseat.

The driver, Alicia, said, "You're in a hurry to get back?"

"I have a meeting at three," said Carla. "With my once and future bosses."

"So you're taking the rover job?" asked Robin, seated in the suicide seat.

Carla exhaled. "When push comes to shove, I'm not such a risk-taker when real money is concerned. I played like a straight arrow last night. It worked for me. So, yes, I'm going to take the job. But I'm using my poker winnings the right way. We *are* going to Disney World."

Bess said, "First class, all the way."

Alicia said, "I have a meeting this afternoon, too. I'll miss the whole workday."

"You deserve it," said Bess. "You're the star of the agency."

"I'm only as good as my last catchy slogan," said Alicia. "My meeting is with a divorce lawyer. Don't tell your kids. Joe doesn't know. Tim doesn't know either."

That quieted the others. Despite their minibreak, real life hadn't stopped.

Robin said, "Are you sure divorce is what you want?"

"If I don't do it, Tim never will," said Alicia. "No more waiting. One of us has to do something now, while we don't hate each other too much."

Bess said, "Next week, I'm supposed to drop off Amy at my mother's apartment. Simone is taking her to East Hampton, where she will do her best to make Amy hate me even more."

Carla, not a hugger, reached across the backseat and gave her friend a squeeze. "Have faith," she said. "Amy will realize all you've done for her."

"But when?" asked Bess.

"Ten years, give or take a month," said Alicia.

"I'd say twenty," said Robin.

Carla said, "Are you all still going to talk to me when I'm not a Brownstone mom?"

"You really are a ridiculous person," said Robin.

"And that really was a stupid question," agreed Alicia.

Carla laughed, booming. Hurt their achy heads.

"Let's agree to a fixed day to play each month at my house," suggested Bess. "All you have to do is be there."

The women made a vow to each other: to be there.

14

Alicia

"Lunch?" asked Finn, stretching at his desk chair, his shirt tightening over his glorious chest. It was Friday afternoon.

For the last six Fridays, they'd taxied downtown to his apartment for "lunch."

"Can't," said Alicia, checking the time, grabbing her purse. "I have an appointment." Her second. The meeting yesterday, right after the AC road trip, had been a $200-per-hour blur. Alicia was so tired and hungover, she'd forgot to ask half of her questions.

"Doctor?" asked Finn, her fabulous, sweetly concerned boyfriend (just the word "boyfriend" was exquisitely sexy). "You're not pregnant, are you?"

That would be a laugh and a half, after her years of infertility, to just drop a bun when she hadn't been watching.

"Lawyer," she said.

"A divorce lawyer?" he asked, attempting to look calm.

Alicia assured him, "Don't worry. I'm not asking you to take me on."

"Maybe I want to take you on," he said. "And Joe."

"Oh, please," said Alicia. "You don't even know what that means."

"Right there," he said, "Great example of the—what word did I use?—the *condescension* I was telling you about."

He had been complaining lately that Alicia didn't take him seriously. Although she regretted insulting him, Alicia couldn't stop herself. The fact was, she was seven years older than Finn. His longest relationship had lasted only six months. At his age, Alicia was already a wife and mother. She'd put in years of emotional agony when she couldn't get pregnant. Finn had no kids, no mortgage, no responsibilities other than to his job.

"I'm sorry," she apologized. "I just feel a responsibility to protect you from what's coming. Divorce isn't pretty or nice. I hope Tim and I can part amicably. But I'm sure we'll wind up fighting over the scraps we've accumulated. And custody."

"Are you divorcing him because you love me?" asked Finn.

"I've told you a dozen times that Tim and I were in trouble long before we started . . . doing what we do."

"But you didn't put the divorce wheels in motion until after we got together," he said, grinning, rising from his chair.

She inhaled the heady whiff of pheromones in the office air. Finn rounded his desk, closed and locked their office door, and gathered Alicia in his arms.

"I like your dress," he said, reaching under it.

"Finn, I pay for the whole hour even if I'm late," she said, but his fingers were doing delicious things inside her panties.

"I'm not letting you go until you tell me the truth," he said, kissing her neck.

Alicia groaned, from pleasure and resignation. "What truth?"

"Am I the reason you want a divorce?"

"Okay, fine. Yes, you are the reason," she said. "I don't have the nerve to sleep with two men at the same time. Lying and cheating makes me extremely anxious. I've wanted to deny it for a long time, but the fact is, I *am* a neurotic mouse. You should have seen me trying to play poker in Atlantic City. It was pathetic! I almost fainted just sitting there. If I don't get myself out of this god-awful situation of loving you and being married to Tim, I'll self-destruct."

"Is it immature of me to feel like the winner here?" asked Finn, nuzzling her shoulder. "The victorious male who gets to claim the prize."

Alicia snorted and pushed him away. "Some prize!" she said, righting her underwear. "A broke soon-to-be single mother with an upcoming avalanche of legal bills."

"You're cute when you're self-destructing," said Finn.

"You're a continuous flow of cute. The Mississippi River of cute," she said, admiring her lover. "Really, Finn. I adore you. You brought me back to life." Then she sank into her chair and commenced to sob. *So* not Alicia's style. She was a quipper, not a crier. Quipping kept her feelings safe and locked up. Crying was for emoters, like Bess.

Finn rubbed her back, lifted her hair from soggy cheeks. "I adore you, too," he whispered. "Your sense of humor, and talent, and face, and especially your very small, microscopic breasts."

"Fuck you," she said, swatting at him. "I'm leaving. You'd better be here when I get back."

"I will," said Finn.

• ——— •

Alicia liked the lawyer, a Brownstone mother she'd met on Parents' Night way back in September. Why she'd thought to ask for the woman's card nine months ago made no sense at the time. That Alicia had kept the card in her wallet through three cleanouts was pretty telling. She knew this day would come, and yet was still amazed that it had finally arrived. She was going to tell Tim that she wanted out.

"You're home early," said Tim, greeting Alicia at their apartment door. She accepted a kiss on the cheek and dropped her purse on one of the boxes they never got around to unpacking. Another clear signal from her (their?) subconscious?

Tim circled around the counter and into the kitchen. "I made a fabulous curry. We're celebrating," he said.

"We are?" she said.

"I got a job offer today," he said.

Thank God, thought Alicia. "Great news, Tim. I'm so happy for you!" Relief flooded over her. This was how she knew for sure the marriage was over: her immediate thought was gratitude to the cosmos for giving Tim something positive in his life to soften the blow she was about to deliver. If she still loved him and wanted to stay together, his new job would've represented a new beginning for them.

"Aren't you going to ask what the job is?"

"Tell me," she said.

"It's a marketing manager job at a start-up men's apparel company," he said excitedly. "It's perfect for me. The money is good. But there is one problem." He paused, making sure Alicia was paying attention. "It's in Los Angeles."

"They don't have marketing managers in California?" she asked. "Why hire someone in New York for a job out west?"

"The designer saw my résumé online at one of those job finder websites I use. I was number three in his top ten matches, based on experience, qualifications, preferences. We did the interview via Skype. He liked me, and offered me the job if I'm willing to relocate."

Alicia was impressed. Tim really had been actively job hunting. She thought he'd been slacking off, had given up. His unemployment had taken a huge toll on his ego. Men without jobs felt emasculated, she knew. Alicia should have been more sensitive to that. Boosting his ego was a wifely duty, and she'd failed there.

"What did you tell him?" she asked.

"I said I had to talk to my wife," said Tim.

She nodded. "Do you want to go?"

He put down the wooden spoon, made eye contact. "Your career has finally taken off and you've made great friends here," he said. "When we moved to Brooklyn, that was the whole idea—that things would fall into place for all three of us. Joe seems to be happy. At the Steeples' sleepover, he really got in the middle of things." Tim resumed stirring the curry, looking into the pot. "So Brooklyn has been great for two out of three of us. Not for me, though, Alicia. Far from it. I've been miserable here. I've lost a year of my life treading water. I want to go to Los Angeles, see if can do better out there."

Alicia bowed her head. *Here it comes,* she thought. *The guilt.* "I should have done more for you," she said. "I was so fixated on my own . . . problems."

"Don't apologize," he said. "Not to seem dismissive, but I don't want to hear it."

Whoa, that had an edge to it. "Tim," said Alicia, suddenly gripped by the urge to confess. "I have to tell you something."

He held up the spoon, stopping her. "You and Joe should stay here," Tim said quickly. "I gave it a lot of thought. It'd be cruel to uproot him again. Three schools in three years? That's just bad parenting. I'll fly back every month to visit. After a year of living apart, we can get a no-contest divorce."

Alicia gasped. Had he seen a lawyer, too? And an icky feeling— was he really going to make it this easy for her? It was wrong. She'd had an affair. She should be held accountable.

"I'll pay for everything," she said. "You don't have to worry about child support or legal bills. It's all on me."

Tim laughed. "That's generous of you to offer, but I won't hold you to it. Right now, you feel guilty. The beauty of a no-contest divorce is how relatively cheap it is. If we stay civil."

"Why wouldn't we stay civil?" she asked, stupidly.

"Well, one possible scenario comes to mind. Say, if I think too much about the last year of my life, realize that I blame you for every horrible thought I've had about myself, and then hate you for it," he said matter-of-factly.

Alicia decided at that moment to willfully put this entire conversation in a box on that very high shelf in her mind. Her habit of compartmentalizing negative emotions hadn't necessarily served her well. It probably was a chief cause for the communication breakdown with Tim. But at least Alicia knew she was purposefully doing it this time, and fully intended to take a closer look at what went wrong. But not for a while.

Her emotions shut down, the pragmatic mind took over. She'd have to hire a babysitter for afternoons. And a housekeeper. Jobs that Tim used to do. No doubt, his unemployment made her life a lot easier.

Alicia realized suddenly that she'd *liked* Tim being readily available, at her mercy, in a financial sense. His dependence, and her rubbing it in—giving him a household allowance, complaining if he hadn't vacuumed, and, yes, disappearing nights for her two poker games—was her revenge against him for making her feel unlovable and unwanted. She thought she'd been heroically tolerant of his chronic unemployment. But, as she realized now, she'd enjoyed watching Tim squirm. Only a horrible, cruel person would be so spiteful.

Goddamn the box! thought Alicia. It wasn't keeping the ugly feelings locked away. At some point over the last few months—due to the free flow of confessions at her ladies poker game?—the box in Alicia's mind had turned into a sieve. She would have to address her worst thoughts, whether she wanted to or not.

Curse those women! she thought. *I'm not ready for emotional maturity!*

"I'm an asshole," said Alicia, welling up. *Oh, God, not again.* She'd have to double up on tissues.

Tim said, "That is true."

"So are you!" she shouted. "You didn't touch me for almost three years! I don't care how emasculated you were about losing your job or feeling like a housewife. Even housewives get horny."

He exhaled a few times. Was Alicia finally going to get an explanation? The reason that Tim turned off?

"I'm sure you felt unloved and unwanted," he said. "Probably because I fell out of love with you, and stopped wanting you. I'm sorry. I know that sounds awful. I'm sure it was tied up with how bad I felt about myself. If it's any consolation, falling out of love was very painful for me. I had, have, a lot of guilt."

So there it was. Her worst fears about Tim's rejection were right on the money.

"You felt nothing for me," she said. "Not even enough to just use each other? For relief?"

He said, "It would have been bad, like the last time." He meant the empty, angry sex they'd had a few weeks ago, which had been soul killing and dehumanizing.

If Tim had told Alicia the sad ugly truth a year ago, she'd have had a complete breakdown. But now? It hurt, to be sure. She'd been insulted and rejected. But Alicia was also free. Tim had completely severed their emotional connection.

"For what it's worth, Tim, I never stopped loving you and wanting you," she said, tears coming against her will. "At least, not until the very end."

He nodded, seemed to tear up a bit. "We'll have to tell Joe," said Tim. "Thank God he's on Zoloft already or we'd have to put him on it."

"Up the dosage," she joked. Not funny. "He's going to miss you badly. You can video chat all the time. And I'll bring him to LA for vacations."

"He's old enough to fly by himself," said Tim.

"Oh no, he's not," said Alicia. And then backpedaling rapidly, she said, "We'll figure it out."

"People do this," he said. "Get divorced."

"We're making a smart fold," said Alicia. "Not to belabor the poker metaphor, but it has been the theme of the year."

Tim said, "We should play tonight. For M&M's."

"Deal," said Alicia.

15

Bess

Bess had always hated waiting for her period, eagerly counted days until it arrived. But for the last few months, she'd dreaded its arrival. Not since *The Shining* or Tim Burton's *Sweeney Todd* had Bess seen so much blood. Convinced she had a gynecological cancer, she paid a visit to Dr. Able. He ordered tests and found nothing amiss, thank God. His theory? Bess, 41, was perimenopausal. Symptoms— heavy periods, light periods, the occasional hot flash, the occasional night sweats—would come and go for the next ten-plus years, until actual menopause.

Bess was supposed to have gotten her period yesterday. Instead, she experienced her first hot flash. The onset was confusing. She was at lunch at the Heights Cafe, with Anita Turnbull, who refused to confirm or deny that she and Tim Fandine had ever done more than flirt (a moot point, but Alicia asked Bess to crack the nut anyway, just out of curiosity). Bess took a bite of salad, and her cheeks felt hot suddenly. Then hotter. Flaming red, out of nowhere. She took off her summer-weight cardigan. Fanned her face with her napkin. Then Bess took an ice cube out of her glass of lemonade, and held it against her cheek. Anita asked if she was all right, fake-concerned. Bess excused herself to the bathroom.

Her whole head felt like it was on fire. She bent over the sink in the bathroom and splashed cold water on her face and chest. The mirror was hung stupidly high, and Bess had to stand on her tippy toes to see how much water splashed on her blouse. Quite a bit. After contemplating the hand dryer, and how she could position herself under it, Bess said, out loud, "Screw it."

Why make herself even hotter for appearance's sake? Why do anything for appearance's sake? Hadn't the time come for Bess to get through a day without fear of disapproval, especially from someone she didn't particularly care about? And, if the time hadn't yet come, when would it?

She exited the bathroom and sat back down to lunch. Anita squinted at Bess's wet blouse, but she didn't ask for an explanation, and Bess didn't offer one.

Anita started talking. "I was in the middle of telling you a funny story about something Austin said. He was going through my closet, and found a pair of old Jimmy Choos, which I haven't worn once since I got married. These are serious f-me stilettos, totally impractical for walking, you know what I mean? Anyway, Austin said, 'Are these *shoes*?' So cute, right? I said, 'Mommy hasn't worn those since I was single and had to look good.' He nodded, and that was that. Or so I thought. Later that week, at school, the history teacher was describing how families disintegrated during the Great Depression. So Mr. Unger asked the class to give a reason that so many fathers abandoned their wives and children during the hard times. Austin raised his hand and said, 'The wives stopped wearing Jimmy Choos.' Can you believe it! Isn't that so funny? I nearly died laughing when Mr. Unger told me."

How many stories like this had Bess laughed at over the years? Always delivered to her by other nonworking moms, the stories seemed to reinforce three things: (1) how rich they were, (2) how hot they were, and (3) how witty/smart/sophisticated their kids were. Too many moms (*including me?* wondered Bess) had nothing to offer but "cute" stories about their kids that always reflected favorably on themselves.

Bess said, "That is so funny. My daughter, Amy? She's been a real spitfire this year, too. She gained twenty pounds, started wearing ripped-up clothing, stopped washing her hair, painted her fingernails black—and not Chanel Vamp black, either. She decided she's a lesbian. At sixteen, so precocious. She had a girlfriend and everything. They broke up. But they must've had teenage lesbian sex. Isn't that *so* funny? I almost died laughing when my daughter told me how much she hates me and doesn't respect me. And what's the absolute funniest part? My mother tells me the same *exact* things! They have a lot in common. Except I don't think my mom's a lesbian. She might be. My mom and daughter could go cruising together for dates. Now, that would be *hilarious*."

Bess started breathing rapidly. *Wow, that speech was a lung buster,* she thought.

"Are you okay?" asked Anita, glancing left and right, to make sure Bess's rant hadn't been overheard. *If Anita were so concerned about me,* thought Bess, *wouldn't she be looking at me?*

"I have to go," said Bess. "I don't feel very well."

"What is it?" asked Anita. "Oh, no! Has the cancer come back?"

Christ. "I didn't have cancer," said Bess. "I had a benign cyst."

"That's right," said Anita. "You hear 'lump,' immediately think 'cancer,' and the idea sticks."

"Nope, no cancer," said Bess. "I'll live to be PA president next year. You'll just have to wait awhile longer to take over."

"I didn't mean that!"

"I know. I'm sorry," said Bess. "I used an ironic tone. You didn't hear it because we are not in tune. We have nothing in common be-sides our kids. And, frankly, our kids aren't friends either. We force them together, but they don't really like each other. Neither do we. And I mean that in the nicest way possible."

That hot flash had lit a lightbulb in Bess's brain. It shined on a blinding truth. She did not have time—measured in minutes, hours, or years left on earth—to spend with people she didn't truly love or to do things she didn't enjoy. That included having lunch with Anita Turnbull.

No slam to Anita. The woman was, for the most part, harmless. But harmless just wasn't good enough for Bess. She needed more.

She dropped two twenties on the table, smiled, apologized again to Anita, and left the restaurant.

Bess walked home at a relaxed pace. She was in no hurry. Tomor-row morning, Bess was expected to surrender her daughter to her mother's clutches for a month. Although Amy claimed to "hate the beach," she said she wanted to go to East Hampton. As Simone told Bess, it was two against one.

Despite Amy's repeated whine, "I can't *wait* to get out of here!" Bess had to nag her to pack. Their last night together had been tense and uncomforable. At dinner—the three boys, Amy, Borden, and Bess—conversation focused on sleepaway camp and summer movies. Amy barely spoke, and when they got home, she closed herself in her room as always.

Borden promised Bess that time apart would be good for them. Bess was almost convinced. Around six a.m., she woke up in a puddle of her own sweat, literally dripping wet, the sheets soaked. She'd been having a dream about the East Hampton house's pool. Her mother and daughter were floating in it, and then Bess threw herself in with them.

Bess got out of bed, rinsed off, and emerged pink, clean, and alive with a new sense of purpose. A plan had come to her—in the shower, where so many great ideas were born. She quickly put on shorts and a T-shirt, and started typing on the computer. She had a lot of arrangements to make. By nine o'clock, she's sorted through the logistics. As quietly as she could, she made a few phone calls.

She woke Amy around ten to get ready. They were supposed to arrive at Simone's penthouse on Park Avenue by noon.

Leaving the boys in Borden's care, Bess hustled Amy out of the townhouse and into the BMW. She locked the car doors, and then mother and daughter were off. Bess had been counting on Amy's hostile silence and she wasn't disappointed. Even better, Amy closed her eyes and pretended to be asleep for the drive.

Thirty minutes later, they arrived.

"What the hell?" asked Amy when she opened her eyes and saw where they were.

"Change in plans," said Bess.

"LaGuardia Airport? Am I flying to East Hampton?"

Bess almost spat, "That's just stupid!" but didn't. She parked in the hourly lot, got Amy's duffel bag out of the trunk, and started carrying it toward the terminal.

Amy, confused, curious, ran after her mother, demanding to know what was going on.

Demanding, ha! thought Bess, feeling wonderfully in control. She'd figured it out, thanks to the trip to Atlantic City and her fear-melting hot flash yesterday. If she was okay with losing in exchange for the simple joy of being where the action was, then she could play her hand any damn way she liked. And sometimes, losing wasn't a loss. She could win for losing—a free room, a memorable night with friends, respect, if not from her daughter and mother, for herself.

As Shakespeare wrote (definitely *not* in a poker context): The play's the thing.

Bess made her play: "Your plane leaves in one hour," she said to Amy. "You don't have much time to get through security, so hurry up."

"What plane? What's going on?"

They were inside the JetBlue terminal. Bess was slipping her credit card into the e-ticket kiosk, and getting the boarding pass. She handed it to Amy.

The girl looked at it. "San Francisco?"

"Grandma Vivian needs you," said Bess. "She's very lonely, and she's aged quite a bit since Grandpa died. I'm sure you noticed. You're going to San Francisco to keep her company and help her clean out Major's stuff."

Amy opened her mouth to protest, but nothing came out. Bess stood squarely in front of her, bracing for the onslaught to come. But it didn't.

Bess added, "I thought, maybe you felt like East Hampton was your only option, so you just took it. You haven't spent much time out there, but I can tell you: not a lot to do but go to the beach and seersucker and sundress parties. And correct me if I'm wrong, you hate the beach."

"And sundress parties," said Amy, squinting at Bess from under her hang of hair, unsure what it all meant. But then Amy said, with a micron of excitement, "San Francisco is a cool town."

You can be as gay as you want there, thought Bess.

"You seemed to like the city when we went for the funeral. And Vivian really needs you," said Bess. *Simone, on the other hand, was using you.*

"One-way ticket?" asked Amy.

Bess nodded. "I could be completely wrong. And please tell me if I am. It seemed to me that your plans weren't so much about East Hampton or being with Simone, but just to get away from Brooklyn for a while. It's been a hard year. You're smart, and you knew a change of scenery might help. I totally agree. Nothing like a new place, new walks, new people, to remind you who you are. San Francisco is an amazing city to find yourself in," said Bess. "I didn't want to put a time limit on your experience. I leave it to you to decide when to come home. Vivian is happy to keep you until September."

"Keep me? Am I some kind of human *pet*?" asked Amy. Her words were hostile, but there was little bile behind them. "Are you pawning me off on Grandma?"

"Now you want to stay?"

"No," said Amy.

Bess paused, and then spoke the uncomfortable truth. "I'm not trying to get rid of you," she said, tone measured. "But we can both use a break from each other."

Amy nodded slowly. If Bess's confession hurt her feelings, Amy didn't show it. "Does Simone know about this?"

Not even close, thought Bess, a wicked smile creeping across her lips. "I'll take care of *her*," she loved saying.

"Are you jealous of me spending time with Simone?" asked Amy.

Insightful, thought Bess. But, then again, the tug-of-war over Amy wasn't a state secret. "A little bit, yes," she admitted.

Her daughter laughed, a sound Bess hadn't heard in eons. "That was honest," said Amy. "To be completely honest myself, I was kind of dreading a month with Simone. She talks *way* too much." In a smaller voice, Amy added, "And she never listens."

Bess almost died of happiness to hear it. "I've noticed that, too." The understatement of the year.

"So. I guess I should go," said Amy.

"Yeah," agreed Bess.

Do we hug? wondered Bess. The girl wasn't walking away.

Taking a chance, claiming her right, Bess pulled Amy into a tight squeeze. "No matter how much you hate me," she said, "I'll always love you." Bess held on for only a few seconds, long enough to quell her superstitions about putting her child on an airplane alone, but not too long to embarrass or repulse her daughter.

Amy shouldered her duffel and headed toward the security queue.

Before she left, she raked her hair out of her face—first time in months Bess had seen both of Amy's eyes at the same time—and said, "Thanks, Mom."

A single word of gratitude. It was all Bess had wanted.

Well, not *all* she wanted. Bess also craved satisfaction. And she was going to get it.

She rushed back to the parking lot, and got into the car. Bess had to hurry. Only an hour before she had to be in Manhattan.

•⬛—•

Made it with a few minutes to spare. It'd been a hairy drive from La-Guardia back to Brooklyn Heights, and from there, to the Upper East Side to her mother's apartment on Park and 70th Street.

The doorman alerted Simone to Bess's arrival and let her up in the elevator. The elevator door would open directly into Simone's foyer. The important feminist icon would be waiting there to welcome her grandchild and daughter.

When the elevator doors opened, however, Simone didn't look too happy to see them.

"What's this?" asked Simone, stepping way back to allow Bess—and Eric, Tom, and Charlie, as well as their stuffed duffel bags—into the apartment.

"Change of plans," sang Bess. "I sent Amy to San Francisco to keep Vivian Steeple company. I'm sure you agree, family should care for each other during rough times."

The boys were already "OMG"-ing and "check it out"-ing into Simone's incredible fourteen-foot-high living room ceilings. It was a gilded palace, this place. Old-fashioned and fuddy-duddy Upper East Side décor. Simone sure liked her chintz and chandeliers. A balcony on the second floor overlooked the two-story living room. The boys had found the spiral stairs and were running up and down.

"The boys have two weeks before they go to camp in Vermont," said Bess. "I thought, since Amy is unavailable, and you have an empty house in East Hampton, that you should take the boys to the beach instead."

"The boys . . . *all of them?*" asked Simone, aghast, as if Bess had asked her to entertain a prison colony.

"Believe me, with boys, three is easier than one. They'll entertain each other. Just feed them, show them the pool, and you'll be fine."

"I don't know what to do with them," Simone protested.

"You'll figure it out."

Simone grabbed Bess's upper arm and squeezed. "This isn't what I had in mind when I offered to take Amy."

Offered, ha! thought Bess. She'd demanded the time to nurture and "mold" the troubled adolescent girl whom Simone had decided to anoint as heir apparent. Did Simone care what Amy really needed and wanted, or was she so wrapped up in her own designs?

Bess leaned closer to her mother than she'd been in twenty years, right up in the old woman's face. "I'll tell you what you had in mind: You're grooming Amy to be your replacement. You're afraid to die, and selfish enough to want to live forever through her."

Simone was shocked speechless. Good thing. Bess had more to say. "We saw you on TV, shaking hands with the president," she continued. "Eric and Tom *didn't even recognize you.* That disgusted me. You don't get to pick and choose your family. We certainly wouldn't've chosen each other. But you are stuck with who you're stuck with. You don't have to love us. You don't have to like us. But you have to show respect and put in the time. That is, if you expect me to put in the time for you.

"And your time, Simone, will come," said Bess, getting into it. "And a lot sooner than you think. You're seventy-five years old. When's the last time you spoke to Fred or Simon? I can tell you, my brothers won't lift a finger for you when you're sick, senile, and totally dependent on your family. They'd be happy to lock you in a home, and leave you there to turn to dust. I'm not convinced I should lift a finger for you either."

"Are you threatening me?" asked Simone, absolutely stunned.

"I don't care what you call it," said Bess. "I'm just laying it out as clearly as I can. My cards are faceup on the table. You show me and my children—all of them—the courtesy we deserve, and you can expect the same treatment from us. Otherwise, you can die alone. Your call." Bess smiled sweetly, savagely.

Simone looked like she'd seen a ghost—the ghost of Summer Future? Or herself alone and withered in some nursing home? Bess smiled, tried not to gloat. This was one of the top ten greatest moments of her life. She'd wrestled with her mortality, wondered whether she mattered, if anything mattered. But she had finally figured out everything that mattered: the people she loved. She'd devote herself to them, just as she'd been doing all along. The guilt—about choosing motherhood over a career—was blessedly dissolved. She'd slain the dragon.

If the story of your death was also the story of your life, then caretaker Bess, the gracious host, would die surrounded by family and friends. The thought of it gave her a happy jolt.

She called out, "Boys!"

"Up here!" yelled Eric from the balcony above.

"Come kiss me good-bye. I won't see you for two weeks!"

Her sons stampeded down the spiral staircase, and rushed toward her. They surrounded Bess and shamelessly hugged her the way boys do. She kissed them all, and then waved good-bye to her mother before stepping into the elevator.

●—●

Borden whooped when she told him the story in bed that night. "We should celebrate," he said. "We can do anything. We're completely childless for two weeks. Has this ever happened before?"

"Let's go away," said Bess. "Can you get off work?"

"I can take a long weekend. Where do you want to go?" he asked. "You're going to say Atlantic City."

Bess smiled, and said, "I'll raise that bet."

"Oh?"

"Monte Carlo?" she asked.

Borden laughed. "Just promise you'll spend as much time on the nude beach with me as you will playing poker."

"You want to be seen on a nude beach with a forty-one-year-old, perimenopausal hag with a scar on her breast?" she said.

"A hundred women on the beach, you'll be the only one I see," he said.

And then they made love like they were young.

16

Carla

Hurry up and wait, thought Carla, checking her watch. She'd rushed to get to her appointment with her bosses at LICH. Dr. Clifton, unfortunately, hadn't extended her the same courtesy. Carla had cooled her flats for half an hour outside his office—so far. A dose of her own medicine, sitting outside a doctor's office long past her appointment time. She was guilty of overscheduling, making appointments every fifteen minutes, but what else could she do? Patients needed to be seen.

"Hello, Mommy," said Tina Sanchez, coming around the corner, dressed in a neat little skirt suit. Where had she bought it? In a juniors department somewhere.

"I barely recognized you out of scrubs," said Carla, standing to give her former nurse a hug. Tina had applied for a job in the administrative department of the hospital, attending to the transfer of records from paper to server. Tina hadn't wasted a moment feeling sentimental or nostalgic about the clinic's demise. When Carla asked her about her ennui, Tina replied, "It's business, not personal."

Since Carla's business was to tend to the personal problems of the human body, she had trouble making the distinction. What job was more personal than being a doctor? Carla had learned to keep her emotions out of it, but only to a point. For example: her love-hate relationship with the clinic itself.

"You're here to see Dr. Clifton?" asked Tina.

"He's forty minutes late," said Carla. "I'm going to take the rover job."

Tina looked surprised. "You're going to haul that ass all over Brooklyn for ten hours a day?"

"I don't have a choice," said Carla.

Tina shook her head, clicked her tongue. "There's not another job out there for you? Have you explored your options?"

" 'Explored my options'? Two weeks in a suit and listen to you. We are in a recession, in case you haven't noticed," said Carla, starting to feel defensive. "Jobs aren't falling off cliffs. I mean, trees."

Tina said, "Take it easy, Mommy. You do what you need to do."

After an awkward and quick good-bye, Tina clicked down the hall. Carla stared after her, the *pequeña* dynamo who'd always questioned authority and demanded what she deserved. *Look at her go,* thought Carla, smiling. Life would not dictate to her. Tina would put God on hold.

Another ten minutes of waiting. Carla let her mind drift to dinner, last night, when she told the kids that she planned to take them to Disney World after all. The response had been underwhelming. "You don't seem that excited," she said.

Zeke said, "Let's go to Atlantis in the Bahamas. They've got a shark tank, and water slides. Charlie said it's *awesome.*"

Manny said, "How about Knicks season tickets?"

Claude didn't speak a word. His expression said, "I told you so."

Later on, Carla admitted to Claude that he had been right about

Disney World. The poker money was still hers, though, and she'd decided what to do with it.

"I know what you're going to do with it, so go right ahead," he said.

"That's impressive, since I have no idea," she replied.

He said, "You're going to save it. It's not in your nature to splurge or take risks. Considering how you got the money, if you did anything *but* save it, you'd feel guilty."

"I *earned* this money," she said. "I worked hard to win it." The defense sounded hollow, though. What was worse, Claude had been exactly right. After the Disney bubble was punctured, Carla's first thought was to deposit the money into her savings account until they agreed on a destination. She wasn't sure whom she resented more: Claude for calling her predictable, or herself for being predictable.

The thrill of playing poker with her friends was in taking wild risks. In Atlantic City, she'd been Careful Carla. No risks, only rules. She'd won that way, too. But she'd felt like a cold machine, not a warm-blooded human.

Right now, she just felt tired. If she had to wait one more minute, she might spill right out of this chair and across the hallway floor. They'd have to put her on a stretcher.

A glimpse of her future, the fat woman who'd exhausted herself onto a stretcher due to extreme predictability.

Yesterday, she got a voice message from Dr. Stevens. His practice was still for sale, and he was rooting for her to buy it. She would dearly love to. One problem: she was $495,000 short.

How do you turn $5,000 into $500,000?

She'd asked herself that question a hundred times, and hadn't come up with an answer. Perhaps a magic wand? Genie in a bottle? Bet it all on black, win, and let it ride, doubling her winnings seven times in a row? Buy 5,000 Lotto tickets, and keep her fingers, toes, legs, and arms crossed?

Her cell rang. "Bess," said Carla, answering.

"How was the meeting?" asked her friend.

"How do you turn five thousand dollars into five hundred thousand?" posed Carla, her head fixed on the enigma. "I keep asking myself. But I got nothing. Clearly, I've been asking the wrong person."

Bess said, "Borden might have an idea."

"What's his number?"

"Seriously?"

"Do I sound like I'm kidding?" A few months ago, Carla would never have dared ask Borden Steeple—or anyone—for help. Her pride would have forbidden it. To show any sign of weakness had been anathema to Carla. But, as she'd come to realize, friends (especially a diverse group) were strength. Asking a friend for help was flexing your muscles.

Bess gave Carla Borden's work number, and then asked, "I take it the rover job is not going to happen."

"Over my dead body," said Carla. "And I mean that literally. That job would kill me."

"Carla! Sorry I kept you waiting," said Dr. Clifton, scurrying toward her. "Meetings pile up on the other side of the complex."

Carla said a quick good-bye to Bess, and then stood up to receive a handshake from her once and former boss. "Don't apologize. I want to thank you for being late."

"Thank me."

"It gave me a little more time to think," she said. "I respectfully decline your job offer, sir. I wish you the best of luck with the new program."

Dr. Clifton nodded. "I can't say I blame you, Carla."

"That's Dr. Morgan," she said, and turned and walked out of there, never to return.

─ ◆ ─

The stack of papers rested on the dining room table. Claude and the boys were outside with their neighbors for the annual block party.

She'd sent them out to deliver a platter of hot dogs and buns to the food table. Carla would join the party as soon as possible. Mrs. Browne's famous crab cakes went quickly. They were huge, the size of baseballs. Eating one would be Carla's just reward.

But first, she had some dirty work to do.

Papers arranged to her liking, she went to the front door and opened it. She immediately spotted Claude. Her eye always went right for him. He was laughing, holding a Coke, standing with another father in the middle of a game of running bases. The kids were zipping by on both sides. The two men were officiating in some way. Manny ran up to the base, and then jumped off provocatively. Claude made a move for him and then Manny dashed away with graceful agility. Claude shouted something at Manny, and the boy laughed. Claude's pride in his son shone on his handsome face.

He was a good man. A good father.

She called and waved her arms. Claude noticed, made an apology to the neighbor, and jogged toward Carla on the porch.

"Come into the dining room for a second," said Carla.

Claude followed her in, and saw the stack of papers on the table. "What's all that?"

"I need you to sign some of these documents," said Carla, pushing them forward.

Claude walked over to her, put his sweaty Coke can directly on the table. (Carla flinched, but let it go.) He didn't touch her. He hadn't kissed her or touched her all day. She'd come to realize he only touched her out of bed when he wanted sex that night. Carla wondered if a protocol of hugging or an RDA of casual affection could have prevented this moment. Although Carla had felt sorry for Alicia in a sexless union, at least Tim hadn't deprived his wife of friendly contact, cheek kisses, pats on the back. In a trade—genital-only vs. nongenital-only touching—Carla couldn't honestly say which she'd pick.

"You haven't told me what I'm looking at," he said.

"I've spent the last three days with Borden Steeple, Bess's husband. He works at Merrill Lynch and helped me get the package together." She patted the stack of papers.

"You were at Merrill Lynch? I thought you were doing orientation for the rover job."

"Oh, no, I turned down that job," she said. "I must've forgotten to tell you."

Claude opened his mouth to roar, but quickly realized he was in no position to yell at her about that, having kept losing his previous job a secret for a week. He said, "We agreed that you would try out the rover job for six months."

"No, you told me to do it and I got tired of telling you I didn't want to," she said. "You repeat yourself so many times, you grind me down. Or you refuse to do what I ask so many times that I stop asking. That's how you get your way."

"I *never* get my way," he insisted.

"I believe that you believe that," she said. "Acting put-upon and long-suffering is another way you manipulate me. And I let you do it. I am guilty of that."

The can of Coke was beading, making a puddle on the table. That water mark would be bad, but Carla refused to be distracted. She clicked the ballpoint pen on top of the stack, and pushed the pile toward her husband.

"See the 'sign here' Post-its? There are twelve total," she said. While he flipped through the pages, she explained what they were. "Two sets of documents. The first is an agreement to use our house for collateral against the small business loan for five hundred thousand dollars, along with the paperwork for the loan itself. The second is my contract with Dr. Stevens to purchase his practice, effective as soon as we can transfer the loan money to him. You don't have to sign the purchase contract, but I thought you might want to see it. You do have to sign for the loan, and the collateral agreement."

Carla had used her poker winnings to pay the bank and legal fees to set up the loan and purchase. And that, as Borden showed her, was how to turn $5,000 into $500,000.

"You've lost your mind," said Claude, laughing incredulously. "You want me to sign away my house so you can put us half a million dollars in debt? Why not ask me to burn the house down instead?"

"The practice is highly profitable," she said. "Borden and the Merrill accountants took a close look at Dr. Stevens's books. We'll repay the loan in five years, and still bring in as much income as the rover job would pay."

Claude said, "And what if it doesn't work out? What if all those Brooklyn Heights parents don't want to take their kids to a black doctor? Forget it, Carla. It's too risky."

Carla sighed. She was afraid it would come to this. And yet, now that it had, she was glad.

Taking a deep breath, Carla said, "If you don't sign the documents, I'm leaving you."

Going by his wide eyes and O-shaped lips, Carla felt assured that Claude had not seen that one coming. *Who you calling predictable now?* she thought smugly.

She went on. "We haven't been equal partners in this marriage, Claude. I've made more money, done more of the child care and house care. I make all the appointments, schedule all the activities, pay the bills, cook the food, clean the dishes, shop for clothes. When you have nothing else to do, you do repairs around the house. You deal with the cars, but that's it. Until now, I didn't mind. I was raised to expect nothing from a man, and just be grateful to have one. My father was useless. Your father, too. A whole generation of fathers. I was—am—grateful that you are a responsible dad. The boys love you."

"I do a ton of work," he said, finding his voice again.

"I believe that you believe that," she repeated. "Our marriage isn't a contest of who does more. I'm just saying that I've worked hard all these years doing what you wanted me to. I took the clinic job because you say a black woman couldn't expect better. I grant you, a walk-in clinic might've been the best I could hope for *back then*. But I know I can expect more now. Putting in those fifteen years led me to this amazing opportunity to be a family doctor. To develop lasting relationships with patients, have an impact on people's lives. It's what I dreamed about in med school. I almost let the dream go because I thought it could never happen. Well, it's happening. If you don't sign this loan agreement and let me do this, the love I have for you will turn into hate."

Claude said simply, "You're bluffing."

Carla laughed. "How the fuck would you know?"

She'd cursed in the house. He seemed to be more astonished by her language than her ultimatum.

As a matter of cold, hard fact, Carla wasn't bluffing. She was playing a strong hand, aggressively.

If he refused to sign, she would divorce him. She would not live her life in fear of losing a man.

If he signed, Carla would make a concerted effort to put the resentments of the past behind them and strive for equality in their marriage. She'd be gracious, hardworking, and respectful, as was her natural way. She'd expect him to treat her the same. And maybe, in the not too distant future, their hard times would soften into renewed love.

Carla was absolutely certain—like her mother had faith in God—that she'd be fine. Either way, her life was going to change dramatically, for the better.

⚬━━⚬

Ten minutes later, Carla stood on the sidewalk, chatting with her neighbors on a beautiful June evening in Brooklyn. On her paper plate was one of Mrs. Browne's crab cakes and a wedge of lemon. The kids ran up and down the street, playing running bases. Her mind was spinning with plans, dizzying unknowns, unexplored countries.

In all honesty, Carla was nervous, terrified.

But it was all good.

Claude had signed the papers.

17

Robin

Smoke lingered in the apartment in the humid July air. Robin could throw open every window and run fans, and it wouldn't help. If Robin smoked with her morning coffee, the smell would linger into evening.

Stephanie was at Brownstone. For eight weeks in the summer, the school ran a fairly decent day camp, eight in the morning until three in the afternoon. For Robin, the transition into summer break had been seamless. She and Stephanie kept the same hours during the school year.

Due to the humidity, Robin had to go to the stoop for her cigarette breaks. These time-outs cut into her workday, but she got some exercise going up and down the stairs, and some sun, which gave her vampire skin a rosy glow and fortified her body with vitamin D. That said, Robin didn't like smoking outside, exposing her habit to everyone who entered and left the building, or walked by on the street. She was careful to carry her butts back upstairs and flush them down the toilet.

The last thing she needed was to be accused by her neighbors of littering.

Today, Robin had placed one hundred and ten calls, and conducted seventy-eight interviews. The percentage of calls to interviews was strikingly high. People wanted to talk. Question of the day: "Do you feel hopeful about the future?"

Compared to similar temperature-taking polls she'd conducted in the fall, winter, and spring, the national mood had improved. Unlike the colder months, when the nation's collective mentality was stuck in the snow and mud, the summer poll brought a warm breeze of optimism. Over the years, polls bore out the change in season with a shift in outlook. But this year, according to Robin's sample, the shift had been paradigmatic.

Of the seventy-eight respondents, fifty-seven felt hopeful about the future, or, as many added, unprompted, "Can't get much worse." Only three months ago, that same percentage (roughly, two-thirds) fell into the hopeless category. They were frustrated, in limbo, collectively waiting, praying, for something to happen.

If Robin's data was in sync with pollsters across the nation, TV news correspondents would be fumbling all over themselves tonight to explain what the hell had happened out there to cause such a huge emotional lift. Financial indicators—the Dow, retail sales, unemployment, foreclosures—were slowly, slightly, improving. Nothing seismic. The mood had brightened for no accountable reason.

And yet, Robin, a chronic pessimist, could feel the softening of her own outlook, her muscles unclenching and raw nerves relaxing. Why? That was easy: everyone she loved was doing well.

Stephanie had decided she didn't need Robin to walk her to Brownstone anymore. Robin watched Stephanie ready her backpack (swimsuit, lunch, poncho) and go. Her child was growing up with giddy determination. It was a joy to behold.

Alicia and Tim's split seemed to be progressing amicably. It helped that Tim loved his new job in Los Angeles. The boyfriend,

Guppy (Robin could never remember his name), was backpedaling a bit now that reality had set in. But Alicia seemed okay with it. She told Robin she owed it to Tim and their marriage to sort out what went wrong before getting in over her head with Flipper. Alicia made some quick practical decisions about Joe. First, she put him in Brownstone day camp, where he and Stephanie had become BFFs. That had been a wonderful surprise for the moms. Alicia also hired a woman named Debbie to be Joe's part-time babysitter. (More on Debbie in a moment.)

Bess and Amy couldn't manage a civil word to each other when they were in the same room. But 3,000 miles apart? They couldn't stop talking. Their bicoastal Skype relationship had made Bess a very happy mother. Amy, meanwhile, had blossomed in San Francisco. She was losing weight, and had a short haircut. She'd dyed it blue-black, but at least you could see her face. Amy had a new girlfriend. (Who hadn't seen that one coming?) Apparently, the girlfriend had a problem with her mother, so the two teens spent a lot of time at Vivian's, which helped draw the widow out of her depression. They set her up on Facebook, and Vivian was having a ball reconnecting with old friends.

Carla had successfully moved into Dr. Stevens's practice on Remsen Street, a mere two blocks away. Robin, Bess, and Alicia made a vow to get as many Brownstone families to switch to Carla as possible, to pack that waiting room. Since Carla's office was so close, she came over to Robin's for lunch a couple of times a week.

Last, Robin had a new friend! Debbie, Joe's nanny, often brought the kids home after camp. Robin and Debbie, a Trinidadian native, would chat over iced coffee, or take the kids for ice cream. Debbie was thirty, wise for her years, and deliciously caustic. Robin found it ironic that, this time last year, she had no black friends and reserved her social energies for white men only. Now she spent all of her free time with two black women, and she hadn't been on a date in months.

It all added up to a brightening of the soul. Forward motion, *yay*.

Her friends and family were pointed in the right direction and moving ahead. And yet, she still felt just outside of the paradigm shift. The hateful word Harvey had used was "detached."

As for Harvey, despite the five phone numbers and four email addresses between them, Robin and Harvey had not connected. They'd been trading "call me" messages for two weeks. Robin had placed the last one. It'd been her first call of the day.

It was now 2:00 p.m., and Robin finished logging her data into the Zogby server. She had an hour before Stephanie arrived home. Time for a cigarette break. Grabbing her pack of smokes and ring of keys, Robin took the elevator down to the lobby and out on the stoop.

A man was already sitting in her usual spot on the top step. Muttering, she decided to sit on the next stoop over for privacy. The man turned around when he heard her behind him.

Harvey Wilson.

"Robin!" he said, as if he were shocked to see her on the stoop of her own building.

"I said 'call me,' not 'stalk me,' " she replied.

She sat down next to him and lit a cigarette. In silence, they watched the firemen across the street wash the big red engine inside the station.

He said, "You live across the street from a fire station."

"And three blocks from a hospital. Safety first," she said. "You really didn't have to come out here. You could have called."

"This is bigger than a phone call or an IM. Can we just . . . can we just have a reasonable conversation?"

Clearly, he had no idea who he was dealing with.

She took a drag. "Listening."

He sat there, not talking.

"What exactly do you want?" Robin prompted.

"I don't know," he said, exasperated. "That's why I didn't contact you for a while. I'm still shocked by the fact that I have a daughter. I've been thinking about this constantly, and I still don't have a plan or even a list of requests. I just want to get to know Stephanie. That's the launch point. But beyond that, the details, I'm at a loss. If we set up a visitation schedule, it won't feel natural. It'd ruin any chance of an organic relationship developing between us. It also removes you from the picture entirely."

"Isn't that what you want?" she asked. "Last time I saw you, you said you couldn't stand to be in my presence."

"I was furious when I said that! Give me a break. You dropped a bomb on my life, and I'm not allowed to be angry about it?"

"So Stephanie is a bomb," said Robin. "Well, if that's how you feel . . ."

He groaned. "Can you please stop being defensive for one minute? I don't hate you for keeping her from me—not anymore. I understand why you did what you did. I've been thinking about what you said and putting myself in your place. I get it. I forgive you. Okay? Can we please move forward? I've already lost ten years with Stephanie. I don't want to waste any more time."

He forgives me? she thought. *Not possible.* Robin said, "I still don't see the 'how.' It's very complicated."

"It's simple," he said. "We spend time together." Watching Robin react, Harvey realized, "Stephanie still doesn't know about me?"

Robin took a drag. "I haven't found the right moment."

"Doesn't matter. We can tell her together," said Harvey. "That's what I want. To do things together. The three of us. Take a walk. Have lunch. You and I can spend time together, too."

She laughed. Was he asking her on a *date?* After eleven years and a colossal betrayal? "You can't be serious," she said. "I've read your blog, Harvey. You have friends, adventures. Girlfriends. You're not that desperate."

He said, "Only a desperate man would want to spend time with you? I felt lucky when I first met you. In a crowd of half a million people, we found each other, liked each other, made love, made a baby. I admit, if you told me you were pregnant back then, maybe I would've felt trapped. But you didn't, and here we are. I think it's entirely possible we came back together at exactly the right moment in all of our lives."

He believes in destiny, thought Robin. *What a loon!* "You haven't blogged in a while," she said.

"I haven't been in the mood to write. I've been going to work. Going on long bike rides up the Palisades. Thinking about what you said, about Stephanie," he said. "I only saw her for a few minutes before I, uh, lost consciousness. I wish I had a picture. We could get one taken of the three of us."

Like a family portrait? "I'm sorry, Harvey," she said, his tone and sincerity crumbling her defenses. "I want what you want. I really do. Some version of a normal family. But I can't see it happening. We don't know each other. We didn't back then, and we don't now. My lie might be impossible for you to forgive, no matter how much you want to or think you have. Stephanie is going to hate me for lying to her. She might not forgive me, ever."

"It is within the realm of possibility that she will," he said. "Just concede that some people might not be as determined to stay as angry and resentful as you are."

Robin laughed. "Maybe you do know me a little already."

"Off to a good start," he said, smiling with genuine optimism.

"You look great, by the way," said Robin. "All that bike riding. It shows."

"Thanks," he said. "You look good, too. Maybe gained a pound?"

Robin laughed. "Okay, Harvey. I concede."

"Just like that?"

Why not? thought Robin. Why not go with the idea that, although Robin herself was cynical and pessimistic, other people—Bess, Carla, and Alicia, for examples—were genuinely capable of hoping for the best? Women she knew personally could see the good in others, and had the courage to imagine a happier future for themselves. It *was* within the realm of possibility that Harvey Wilson meant every single word he said. He might very well be a kind, forgiving man who longed for a family. On the other hand, he could turn out to be an asshole piece of shit. Well, Robin was going to find out. She decided—quite suddenly and painlessly—to go for it. No more early folds. Robin would stay in the game until she saw the river.

"Stephanie is coming home soon," said Robin. "I'd rather tell her about you by myself. And then we'll meet you."

"Where?"

"On the Promenade," said Robin. "It's very pretty. You can see the East River, Brooklyn Bridge, Manhattan Bridge. Verrazano Bridge. Statue of Liberty. South Street Seaport. It's landscaped, too, flowers galore. You'll love it."

I sound like the Brooklyn Tourist Bureau, she thought.

"Where is it?"

"Straight that way for three blocks, then make a left. You'll know you're there when you see water."

"And how long will I be waiting?" he asked.

Robin said, "Stephanie gets home at three, and we'll come right to you. I'll tell her while we walk."

"That won't give her much time to prepare," he said.

"You think she'll faint? Like father, like daughter? We're covered. Our pediatrician's office is along the way."

"This is happening," he said. "Today."

Robin felt herself committing to the plan. "Yes."

Harvey smiled and grabbed Robin for an impromptu hug. He squeezed her bones, repeating, "Thank you, thank you, thank you, thank you."

"Okay, okay!" she said, not really wanting the embrace to end. Maybe he'd do it again later. *I want there to be a later,* she realized.

•————•

"You mean that guy who fainted on my Barbies? The guy with the bike?" asked Stephanie as they walked toward the Promenade.

"Right," said Robin.

"So every time I said my father was a sperm donor, I lied."

"Well, I thought of him that way for a long time," she said.

"I have to call everyone I lied to and tell them the truth," said Stephanie, oddly fixating on inadvertently telling a lie instead of the fact that, in five minutes, she was going to meet her father. Maybe that was too big to handle.

"I'll do it," said Robin. "It's my fault."

"What else have you lied about?" asked Stephanie. "Smoking."

Robin admitted, "Okay, yes, I lied about smoking, too."

"If you don't quit, I refuse to meet this man."

The girl stopped in her tracks, folded her arms across her chest, and (yes) tapped her sneaker on the pavement.

"You will meet Harvey," said Robin. "And I promise to stop buying cigarettes. But if, at a party, someone else is smoking, I might want to bum one every now and then. That's my one-hundred-percent-honest answer. If I told you I was never going to smoke another cigarette again as long as I live, I'd be lying to you again."

"None of your friends smoke," said Stephanie.

"So odds are bad for bumming cigarettes at parties," said Robin. "Like I ever go to parties."

"Are you holding right now?" asked Stephanie.

Holding? Where had she heard that? "Maybe," said Robin.

"Mom," said the kid intently, tapping the Converse.

Robin fished her nearly empty pack of American Spirit Organics out of her tote, and handed it to Stephanie. The girl crumpled the cardboard, and then dropped the crushed box into a trash can.

Stephanie smiled and said, "I feel better."

"Me, too," lied Robin.

"You promise to call every person I lied to about the sperm donor thing. Like Charlie's California grandmother."

Jeez. "Yes, I'll call."

"Does Harvey smoke?"

"Only when he's on fire," said Robin.

"Will I like him?" asked Stephanie.

A perfect example of Stephanie's innate confidence. Robin would have asked, "Will he like me?" She could learn a lot from her daughter.

"He's a decent guy," she said.

"Okay," said Stephanie. "Let's go."

The sky was brilliant blue. Her incredible daughter held her hand. And a man was waiting for her. After a long dormancy, Robin felt . . . she *felt*, all over her body, mind, and heart. No longer numb.

They rounded the corner of Hicks onto Remsen Street. Only one block away from the Promenade entrance.

Robin could see the river, shimmering with sunlight. Maybe this time, her card had finally come up.

Epilogue

"First game of the new year!" bubbled Bess, as she took her seat at the poker table, dropping her glass into the cup holder.

"Most people mark the New Year in January," said Robin.

"New *school* year," corrected Bess. "I guess I do think of September as the beginning, instead of close to the end," she said.

Alicia said, "I'll take any opportunity to mark a 'new beginning.' September, January, April eighteenth, which is my birthday, is case you forgot. Please sign up for a reminder on Facebook."

Carla said, "You can call any anniversary a 'new year.' The calendar is full with them."

Bess said, "Today is, actually, an anniversary."

"Of the first meeting?" asked Robin. "Is it really?"

"Let's toast," said Alicia. "To the Brownstone Diversity Committee."

"Who we are, not what we do," said Carla.

"Because the Diversity Committee doesn't do anything," added Robin.

The women clinked their glasses, and drank.

"But this year, we *are* going to plan some events," said Bess. "Right? We can certainly make a wish list of speakers for a lecture series . . ."

"Ever optimistic," said Robin of their host.

"Don't you just love her for it?" asked Alicia.

Carla said, "The committee already realized its goals. Wasn't the point to model tolerance and understanding across racial and religious divides for our kids' sake?"

"What about all the other kids at Brownstone?" asked Bess.

"Who *cares*?" asked Carla. "And I'm not saying that just because my family is out of Brownstone. Abstractly, I care about all children, all over the world. But, from personal and professional experience, I know beyond the shadow of a doubt, you can only influence the kids you come into close contact with. Those are the kids I care about—in an active sense. And I will work my ass off for my children, your children, and my patients. And, considering the size of my ass, that's a lot of work."

"You said 'ass,' " said Robin. "Twice."

Alicia said, "Another toast: To the kids and the moms we care about—in an active sense."

Again, the women drank. And were now in need of refills. Bess went to get more wine from the bar fridge. She returned with the bottle, as well as a robin's-egg blue shopping bag.

"I have gifts!" said Bess.

"World Class Poker, version 2.0?" asked Alicia.

"They don't sell CDs at Tiffany," said Robin, lustfully eyeing the shopping bag.

Bess distributed a small blue box to each woman. She kept one for herself, and watched with giddy excitement as her friends untied the white ribbon and opened their gifts.

"They're charm necklaces," said Bess.

The three other women held up a long silver chain, each with five tiny sterling silver charms. Robin said, "It's gorgeous, Bess!"

"This is too much," said Carla. "Beautiful, but too expensive, Bess."

"How expensive?" asked Alicia.

Robin said, "Chain and five silver charms, from Tiffany. Computer-like brain calculating . . . holy *shit*, Bess! This *is* too much! Not that I'm complaining. Too much is never enough as far as I'm concerned."

Bess said, "You see the charms?"

"A tiny spade, diamond, two hearts, and a club," said Alicia.

Carla, the Black Queen, said, "I take it I'm the spade."

"I'm the diamond," said Bess.

Wild Heart Alicia said, "I'm one of the hearts."

Robin said, "As the Red Queen, I could have been a heart or a diamond. Why heart?"

"I heart hearts," said Bess.

"What about the club?" asked Alicia.

"We are the club," said Bess. "Collectively."

"Oh, Christ," said Robin. "Club, as in club? A poker club? What, are we going to start swapping recipes and reading books now?"

"I hate clubs, too," agreed Alicia. "Except ours."

Robin examined the charms more closely. "I don't think I've seen suit charms in the Tiffany catalog, which I've studied more carefully than I care to admit."

"I had them custom made," said Bess. "These necklaces, ladies, are the only four in existence."

"Four of a kind," said Alicia, smiling at each woman in turn.

Robin reached for the bottle and refilled their glasses. She said, "A toast: To four of a kind!"

Carla clinked and drank to that. "Okay, women. Enough ceremony. Shut up and deal."

Robin held up her glass. "To shutting up and dealing."

"Poker? I Don't Even Know Her!"

Four of a Kind

GAME GUIDE and GLOSSARY

You can laminate this guide, and keep it in the kitchen drawer with your delivery menu collection. That way, the next time you host poker night, the food and rules will be conveniently found in the same place. "What?" you might ask, appalled. "Take-out food? For entertaining?" *Hells, yeah.* Unless you have a houseboy husband or personal chef, do not cook to host a poker game. I don't care if you have a to-die-for new recipe for madras curry. Save it for the knitting club. On poker night, the focus should be on poker. Not pork. Or okra. Fan out your stack of take-out menus like a deck of cards and let your guests pick. When the food arrives, eat Chinese out of the carton with cheap chopsticks or pizza straight from the box. Keep an open trash bag in the kitchen for all garbage. Feel guilty about making so little effort for guests? Save the guilt for when you win big and take their money. *Heh.*

Brooklyn Hold 'Em

Unique to Four of a Kind, Brooklyn Hold 'Em, is as much a card game as a social experiment.

THE OBJECTIVE: To get to know the other players in a hurry.

1. The dealer shuffles, and distributes two facedown "pocket" or "hole" cards to each player.
2. The dealer places five faceup cards in the center of the table. These are the community cards.
3. While the dealer is distributing the pocket and community cards, she is sharing a hidden truth—aka, a "secret"—about herself. It could be a private desire, a long-buried bit of personal history, something interesting that happened earlier in the day, or a matter of the heart she's been bursting to talk about but hasn't, for whatever reason (embarrassment, fear of judgment, etc.)́. When divulging her "secret," the dealer should stop before revealing a crucial final detail or salient piece of information. This will whet the curiosity of the other players.
4. The players examine their cards and try to make the best five-card combination out of the seven available (five community cards + the two pocket cards the players have = seven total cards).
5 The players "showdown," or show their pocket cards.
6 After the player with the best hand is determined (see "What Beats What?" guide below), she is declared the winner and earns the right to ask the dealer one follow-up question about the earlier shared "secret."
7. The dealer answers the follow-up question, and hands the deck to the player on her left (clockwise), who then becomes the dealer herself. Revert to Step One.

BEVERAGE OF CHOICE: Wine. Lots and lots of wine in any hue. For some reason known only to enologists, grown-up grape juice loosens the tongue like no other beverage. When women gather and consume copious amounts of wine, they tell each other deeply personal stuff, and often wake up the next day in dumb amazement and horror at what they'd said. When wine is combined with Brooklyn Hold 'Em, however, women are limited by the game to dole out their secrets slowly, in drips and drabs. They get the pleasure of sharing, but not the head-in-hands shame of having said way too much. Also, by allowing the winner of each hand to ask only one follow-up question, the players' curiosity and attention remains taut and restrained. And since the players have to keep at least a few brain synapses focused on the game, their minds—even wine-soaked—stay somewhat sharp.

Texas Hold 'Em

The classic. The game of choice in the World Series of Poker, and in Casino Royale starring Daniel Craig, the sexiest man on the planet. Ahh, Daniel Craig. Just the fact that he once pretended to play a scripted version of this game in a Hollywood movie should be enough to sell any red-blooded women on its worthiness. The rules aren't that hard. The betting and bluffing parts are where amateurs get into trouble. The one (and only) time I played Texas Hold 'Em in a real casino for real money against real gamblers, I lost $200 in fifteen minutes. And I'd won millions of virtual money on the computer. So be careful out there, peeps! Don't bet your shirt, unless you're playing with Daniel Craig, in which case, bet your shirt, jeans, bra, and panties. Go "all in" with Daniel.

THE OBJECTIVE: Make the best five-card hand out of your two face-down pocket cards, and the five faceup community cards.

1. Before the dealer even hands out any cards, the large and small blinds (the players in the one and two positions to the left of the dealer) put in a forced bet. All the players at the table ante up.
2. The dealer distributes two pocket cards to each player. All players bet, call, or fold their hand based on how much they like their pocket cards. (High cards, same suit, consecutive cards, and pairs are good to go; low- and off-suit cards are "rags" and better off dumped.)
3. The dealer turns over three community cards, called "the flop," followed by another round of betting, calling, checking, and/or folding.
4. The dealer burns a card, and adds card four, "the turn," to the community cards. More betting/folding.
5. The dealer turns "the river," the last of five community cards, followed by the last round of bets and folds by the players.
6. The remaining players "showdown," or reveal their hands.
7. Winner takes the pot. (See the "What Beats What?" below.)

It might seem like all this dealing and rounds of betting takes forever to play a single hand. Not so! Seasoned players' minds are like calculators, making their decisions in nanoseconds. For novices, reasoning through a bet or a hand slows down "the action" or speed of play at the table. For a poker night of novices, it's wise to go slow, get to know the betting style of your opponents, and think for ten seconds or so before you bet or fold.

BEVERAGE OF CHOICE: Cocktails on ice, with sliced fruit and a swizzle stick. My personal favorite is a vodka tonic. The ice is good for contemplative, aggressive chewing during rounds of betting. The swizzle stick gives you something to put your eyes on while bluffing. The alcohol becomes a wild card in and of itself. By round two or three of drinks, the game will get a lot more interesting. Players who can hold their liquor are at a distinct advantage.

Omaha Hold 'Em

Same objective and rules as Texas Hold 'Em, but with four (instead of two) pocket cards per player.

BEVERAGE OF CHOICE: Same as Texas Hold 'Em: cocktails on the rocks with fruit, but with four ice cubes instead of two per glass.

Five Card Draw

The easiest poker game, ergo, a top choice for heavy drinking and clothing removal (see Strip Poker, below).

THE OBJECTIVE: Make the best five-card hand.

1. Each player is dealt five cards facedown. The initial bets are made.
2. Each player can discard zero to three cards, or more, depending on house rules. Another round of betting follows.
3. Showdown. Player with best hand wins the pot.

BEVERAGE OF CHOICE: Beer, like you're back in college at a barley-and-hops-soaked party in a stinky basement. Drink brew straight from the bottle or can, no coasters, or in a plastic cup.

Strip Poker

Same rules as Five Card Draw, but horny. This version can be played "heads up" (with just two players) or in a group. Instead of betting chips or cash between rounds of discarding and dealing, the winner of the showdown takes an item of clothing from his or her opponent(s).

THE OBJECTIVE: To be the last player with any clothes on. Or not.

THE TRUE OBJECTIVE: To get some serious "action" (in the traditional sense). The longer this game lasts, the more sizzling and hot the players will be at its climax (as it were).

BEVERAGE OF CHOICE: Champagne! Or shots of tequila. Or sweet concoctions made with rum and cherries, or Amaretto, or Bailey's Irish Crème, or White Russians of equal parts Kahlua, milk, and vodka.

Seven Card Stud

This game makes my head hurt. It's complicated and annoying and I'm going to breeze through it because no one plays it except for diehards in seedy casinos in Reno.

THE OBJECTIVE: Make the best five card hand out of the seven cards dealt to each player.

1. The dealer distributes two facedown cards and one faceup card to each player.
2. The player with the visible high card is the first to bet. The other players call, raise, or fold.
3. The dealer distributes four rounds of one faceup card to each player, followed by four rounds of betting, calling, or folding.
4. The dealer distributes one more facedown card (making seven for each player still in the game). The visible high hand starts a final round of betting.
5. Showdown.
6. Winner takes the pot.

BEVERAGE OF CHOICE: Cheap whisky in a dirty glass. Use a rusty nail to stir.

"What Beats What?"
Ranking Poker Hands Guide

From best to worst:

ROYAL FLUSH: ten, jack, queen, king, ace of the same suit
(you will never get this, but dare to dream)

STRAIGHT FLUSH: any five cards of the same suit in order
(for instance, all hearts, 6-7-8-9-10)

FOUR OF A KIND: four of the same card
(a hand might look like this: Q-Q-Q-Q-4)

FULL HOUSE: any pair plus any three of a kind (say, 7-7-7-5-5)

FLUSH: any five cards of the same suit

STRAIGHT: five cards in order of any suit

THREE OF A KIND: three of the same card

TWO PAIR: two pairs of any cards

ONE PAIR: you know what this is—two of a kind

HIGH CARD: None of the above? Player with the high card wins.
The ace is the highest card.

If two or more players have a flush, then the "higher flush" wins. To have higher flush, or higher straight, your high card must be better than your opponent. For example, say you have five diamonds (4-6-7-9-J), and your opponent also has five diamonds (2-6-7-9-K). Your opponent wins because she has a king high flush vs. your jack high flush. If you have a straight (8-9-10-J-Q), and your opponent has a straight (7-8-9-10-J), you win with a queen high straight vs. her jack high straight. Same thing with full houses. If you and another player both have a full house, the player with the higher full house wins. Say you have 6-6-6-7-7, and your opponent has 7-7-7-6-6. She wins because her three of a kind is higher than yours.

GLOSSARY

For at-home poker, you can use any damn terms you want. It's your house. Your friends. Your *booze*. Your special brownies. You might not want to say, "I fold." You folded three loads of laundry today already, and don't want the reminder during your fun night of greed and lying. "I call" might remind you that you forgot to return your mother-in-law's five urgent messages. "I check" naturally brings to mind the pile of bills on your desk. Substitute word choice at will. Personally, I prefer to say the noble "acting" to "bluffing." It sounds more creative and artsy.

If you plan a trip to Atlantic City or Las Vegas to play poker against real gamblers with real money, you need to understand and speak the language. Some essential words and phrases:

ACTION: The speed and intensity of play at the table

ANTE: The amount each player adds to the pot at the beginning of each hand

BAD BEAT: Losing with a pretty good hand. If you have an ace high straight, and are beaten by a flush, that's a bad beat.

BET: Putting money in the pot to stay in the hand

BLIND (BIG AND SMALL): The blinds are forced bets that are made before each poker hand. The big blind is made by the player second from the left of the dealer. (In a real casino, there is only the professional dealer, so a dealer "button" moves around the table instead.) The small blind made by the player immediately to the left of the dealer (or dealer button). Typically, a small blind is half the big blind ($3 and $6, for example). As the button moves around the table clockwise, so do the blinds.

BLUFF: Pretending you have a better hand than you really do to make a sucker fold—or, as I like to call it, "acting"

BURN AND TURN: The dealer puts one card to the side before dealing a faceup community card

BUTTON: A plastic button that moves clockwise around the table, denoting the dealer

CALL: Betting the minimum amount to stay in the hand

CHECK: Staying in a hand, but declining to bet. If another player bets, however, you will be forced to call or fold.

CHIP: A troublesome object sometimes found upon one's shoulder, or a yummy morsel of chocolate, or a colored plastic disc used to represent an amount of money

FLOP: The first three community cards in Hold 'Em games

FOLD: What is done with laundry, or dumping a bad hand

HEADS UP: Play between only two players

HOLE (AS IN, "IN THE HOLE"): Facedown private cards

POCKET (AS IN, "IN THE POCKET"): Facedown cards; see "hole"

POT: A metal vessel for cooking which you will not be using tonight, or the big pile of chips in the middle of the table that the winner of the hand will claim while whooping

RAG: A dishtowel you will not be using to clean up with tonight, or a low- or off-suit card that does not help you make a winning hand

RAISE; RERAISE: Adding to the bet another player has made

RIVER: The fifth community card in Hold 'Em games

SHOWDOWN: When players reveal their pocket cards to see who won the hand

STEAM: What happens when a player gets frustrated and starts making emotional, reckless bets

TURN: The fourth community card in Hold 'Em games

WINNER: What you will surely be if you (1) understand the rules, (2) practice your poker face to Lady Gaga-esque perfection, and (3) accept risk as part of poker and life. As winner's say, "Bet big or go home." Since you are, possibly, already home, you've got nothing to lose.

ABOUT THE AUTHOR

VALERIE FRANKEL received critical acclaim for her best-selling memoir, *Thin Is the New Happy*. She was Joan Rivers's co-writer on *Men Are Stupid . . . and They Like Big Boobs* and she collaborated with Nicole "Snooki" Polizzi on the *New York Times* bestselling novel *A Shore Thing*. Val is the author of fifteen novels, including *The Accidental Virgin*, and is a journalist much in demand. Her writing has appeared in *O Magazine*, *Allure*, *Self*, and *The New York Times*, among other publications. Her Q&A Love column in *Mademoiselle* was a popular favorite for many readers. She lives in Brooklyn Heights with her two daughters and husband, opera singer Stephen Quint.

www.valeriefrankel.com.